THE
PLAINSWOMAN

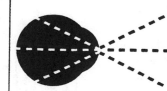

This Large Print Book carries the
Seal of Approval of N.A.V.H.

THE PLAINSWOMAN

Irene Bennett Brown

G.K. Hall & Co.
Thorndike, Maine

Published in 1996 by arrangement with Ballantine Books, a division of Random House, Inc.

G.K. Hall Large Print Western Collection.

The text of this Large Print edition is unabridged. Other aspects of the book may vary from the original edition.

Set in 16 pt. News Plantin by Juanita Macdonald.

Printed in the United States on permanent paper.

Library of Congress Cataloging in Publication Data

Brown, Irene Bennett.
   The plainswoman / Irene Bennett Brown.
     p.   cm.
   ISBN 0-7838-1599-9 (lg. print : hc)
   1. Large type books. I. Title.
  [PS3552.R68559P57   1996]
  813'.54—dc20   95-43260

To Connie
Loving sister, best friend,
enthusiastic fan —
this one's for you.

Prologue

August, 1884 — Kansas

At her employer's push, Amity Whitford rolled from the buggy seat and landed, staggering, in the dusty street before Great Bend's temporarily deserted train depot. Her large satchel followed, striking her just below the knees. She dropped the ticket to Kansas City he'd thrust in her hand.

Chester Fairleigh shook his hat at her. "Go on, now! My wife can't bear the sight of you another minute, nor can I."

"Don't do this, please. I need —"

The Englishman's scowl turned to a look of hatred. "We've no debt to you, after what you've done." He clapped his hat on and took up the reins.

"But I don't know — I don't understand — if you'd just explain." She was dizzy and nauseated from the heat. The temperature had soared well above one hundred at Beaconsfield — *when? for how long?* There was a blank space in her memory, so much confusion. "Wait, Mr. Fairleigh, please." She caught up her satchel and ran after him, but the buggy was rattling away.

7

"You're lucky as it is," he called over his shoulder, whipping the horse. "Jail would be worse!"

"*I have no money, no one —*" Afraid she would vomit, Amity sat on her satchel, head down, waiting for the dizziness to pass. When she looked up again, Mr. Fairleigh had vanished into a cloud of dust. On shaking legs, she walked back to pick up the train ticket.

If she'd not been delivered to hell, then surely this was close, Amity thought the following day in Kansas City. She wasn't sure how far she'd walked from the train depot. She stopped to mop her face with a handkerchief. Heat waves shimmered over the filthy street. The air reeked; dingy laundry flapped from lines overhead. Carts and buggies clattered by. On either side of the street, housewives hung out of open windows and cursed or called to one another in a babel of foreign languages, but nobody seemed to notice Amity as she sagged down to rest on her satchel. Except two ragged boys who stood watching her from a few feet away.

The taller youngster eyed the handsome, dark-haired young woman. "Are you sick, miss?"

The truth was, her head still reeled unnaturally in spite of her comalike sleep on the train; her stomach felt permanently queasy. She ignored his question. "What is that terrible stench?"

He grinned. "The old Missouri, yonder. But mostly the stockyards over thataway, and the rendering plants."

8

A little girl stepped out of a shabby doorway to join the boys. As Amity stared back at the child, a heavy pain filled her chest. She thought of Chester and Leila Fairleigh's youngest child, Nora Ann. . . . What had happened to Nora Ann? If only she could remember.

These urchins couldn't understand what she herself didn't, but Amity told them, "I couldn't have done anything wrong. I shouldn't be here." And with satchel in hand, she moved headlong on down the street.

No stranger among the people she threaded her way through all that day filled her with as much foreboding as the feelings she carried about herself . . . and what the Fairleighs thought she had done. When night came, too weary to run any longer, she crouched among barrels of trash in an alley, and finally slept. Next day, she hurried along the same mean, ugly streets.

The smell of breakfast came from shacks, restaurants, hotels, making her stomach wrench with hunger. Putting aside all thoughts of nicety or pride, twice she asked for work in exchange for a meal and was denied. She hurried by open-air markets that tempted her to steal from burgeoning baskets of peaches, tomatoes, carrots, potatoes.

When Amity could bear her hunger no longer, she followed the example of a street waif and ate her fill from a pile of rotted fruit behind a warehouse.

After days of fruitless searching, unable to find

9

more respectable employment for lack of references, Amity finally took a job in a laundry off Missouri Avenue. But nothing in her life had prepared her for such backbreaking toil. Her boss, Ike Hawes, a sallow man whose moustache diminished what little chin he had, made her uneasy from the first. He plainly enjoyed Amity's discomfort when he stood so close that his trousers brushed her skirts. But she had to survive; the job was better than starving or worrying that her throat would be cut at any time, living on the streets. She had decided to ignore the older laundresses' whispers that Hawes had recently bought into the brothel two doors down.

Her pay was seventy-five cents a day, enough to get her a room, which wasn't quite as dreadful after she'd scrubbed every inch with strong brown soap and gotten rid of the vermin. She could now afford one good meal a day and two cups of tea.

At night, she dreamed of Nora Ann, of holding the still child in her arms and calling her name, but she was unresponsive. Amity would wake to her own pleading cries of "Nora Ann, Nora Ann!"

By morning's light, Amity would reflect that she was not a stupid person, nor careless, nor vindictive and mean — so what could have happened? Had the little girl been lost, ill . . . was she dead? No matter how hard Amity tried to remember, that part of her mind remained a reservoir of sadness and empty shadows. What she remembered clearly was that the Fairleighs blamed her.

For twelve hours a day, perspiration soaking her dress, Amity stood at the ironing table with a hot flatiron like a heavy extension to her arm as she worked quickly to smooth wrinkles from bushel baskets of clothing. The odor of soap hardly competed with the stink of soiled clothing. When the pain in her legs and back grew intense, she wondered if this was her punishment, her lot for the rest of her life. But she reminded herself that it was worse for the older women who tended the washing machines in back. The washerwomen's arms were raw to the elbow from water fouled with soap, bleach, and grease; their backs were permanently bent from lifting heavy loads of wet laundry. Amity's mind rebelled at the fact that most women's work was hardly above that of animals'.

There were few chances for woman-talk, though occasionally a weary woman was heard speaking to another, over the incessant, noisy beaters of the hand-turned washing machines, the thump and slap of the irons.

One day, during the first week she was at the laundry, an old woman commented that Amity must have been hired to replace Lena. "Is she going somewhere? Getting married?" Amity asked, interested. Lena was a thin, nervous girl who scarcely replied when Amity greeted her. Lena's dark, raccoonlike eyes had a haunted look that worsened, Amity had noted sympathetically,

11

when their boss, Ike Hawes, made his inspection tours. The two old women looked at each other but didn't answer, as they took away the shirtwaists Amity had ironed. The following evening, Amity overheard Hawes telling Lena she had to stay late and iron a basket of collars that had been missed.

When the girl didn't appear the next day, Amity asked the other laundresses, "Where's Lena?" As badly as Amity needed work, she didn't want to force Lena out of hers.

A mousy little woman answered in a low voice from where she sorted linens, "Ike Hawes introduced her to his other business last night. But Lena got away, she did. This morning she took herself down to the river, walked in over her head, and drowned." At Amity's gasp, the woman warned, "I'd worry, be watchin' Hawes, myself, miss, if I was a pretty one like you."

The woman was right; she had to get away. But get away where, and how?

Two weeks later, as Amity prepared to depart for the day, Ike Hawes dumped two baskets of freshly ironed linens onto her table. "These weren't ironed proper," he told her, with an oily smile. "You have to stay and do them over."

A quick look showed Amity that the other women were leaving. She did her best to quell her panic, insisting, "I did a proper job on those! It's been a long day and I'm tired."

"Sassy, ain't you?" Hawes laughed, advancing as she moved away. "I'm the boss here, remember? But I could teach you something else 'sides laundry." He grabbed at her, but she leaped away.

His feverish eyes gave Amity little hope that he'd listen to reason, but she tried. "Mr. Hawes, I like my laundry job. I don't mind."

He laughed again and lunged, catching her to him roughly and pushing her backward with him toward a bin of soiled laundry. "Let me treat you to some pleasure," he panted, his smiling mouth closing in on hers as he grabbed at her skirts.

As Amity fought to free herself, she realized they were standing next to the heating plates for the flatirons. Quickly, she clamped a handle on an iron and held the hot appliance between them. "Mr. Hawes, stand away." He shook his head, chuckling. As he reached for her hand holding the iron, she slammed the hot metal against the back of his hairy wrist. He dropped back with a howl, his face distorted with rage. He came at her again. She darted out of reach and threw the iron. It struck him in the chest, and he tipped backward with an explosive grunt, crumpling to his knees. Wheezily, he swore at her, "You're through! Get out, and don't ever come back! I ought to kill you!"

The poster propped in a fly-specked store window offered free land in western Kansas. Amity memorized each word. An impossible goal, she knew, but desperate for refuge — which would have to be of her own making — she set out

13

on foot for the other side of the state.

Pushed by guilt and sorrow, one day after weeks on the road, hungry, tired, footsore, Amity followed a lane off the main road toward a small stone house and outbuildings in a patch of bare trees. They were the only sign of life in a wide expanse of lonely prairie twilight.

Along the way, at an occasional farm, she had been given a meal and a bed for the night. She always hinted that her situation was only temporary, that she wasn't going far. She had chosen a path of silence as much as possible, fearing that she would pour out her frustrated state to strangers; fearing worse, that they would have heard of her. That the Fairleighs would have denounced her: that the news would have spread. Sometimes the food was the family's leavings; with other families it was all they could spare. She cooked for harvest crews, washed dishes, and carried wood in payment. At one house, the elderly grandfather had died, and Amity did the kitchen work to free the women to lay out the body for burial.

Some experiences she wanted to forget. One early dawn, she had stopped two young men on the empty streets of Hutchinson, laborers going to work, to ask if the mills there employed women. They saw in her a lone, threadbare woman and took it as invitation. She'd beaten them with her walking stick, threatening to bash their brains, but even now, remembering, her insides curled.

At the moment, the place ahead looked spooky and deserted, in spite of a drift of smoke from the chimney and a few range cattle. Then a sun-bonneted woman carrying a bucket stepped from the house and headed toward the barn. So Amity followed her, feeling relief.

In the barn, the tall angular woman was pitching hay to a cow in a homemade stanchion. "Mebbe," she answered, when Amity asked for work. "It's 'most more than I kin do to see to my ailin' boy." The woman handed Amity a three-legged milk stool and the pail she'd carried in.

With a sigh, Amity put her satchel on the straw-strewn dirt floor, sat down, took the cow's teats in hand, and squeezed. Nothing happened. She was uncomfortably aware of the woman's flinty glare.

"You ain't never milked!" the woman accused, shoving Amity roughly aside. "Looka here, like this." She snorted, "City girl, useless as teats on a boar." But she let Amity try again.

Amity grimly caught the cow's teats in her two hands and worked them as she'd been shown. She was probably the more surprised when twin streams of milk finally began to *spang* into the tin bucket.

When Amity finally delivered the pail of milk to the house, the hickory-faced woman told her, "You can stay on for now, do the milkin' night and mornin', and help me care for my son till he's better. Pay is half-dollar a day, and you can sleep in the barn unless I need you in the house to see to my son."

Amity agreed, but was sorry when she learned that the ailing son, a bearded giant of a man, lay nearly dead with a gunshot wound in the groin.

Neither the woman, nor her son when he began to recover, asked Amity's name. And they didn't tell her theirs, which fit her own desire to talk little. Odd folks, though, she thought. They gave her no real trouble until she had been with them a month and asked for her pay. The woman slyly told her that she would have to wait until her son was "up earnin' again." When Amity asked about his line of work, she got no answer.

Amity pretended willingness to be their unpaid slave. But two nights later, while the woman was snoring loudly from her cot in a side room and the man was in a deep sleep from an extra dose of laudanum Amity had given him, she got ready to leave them for good. From a full cashbox — it surely held several hundred dollars, maybe a thousand — hidden under the woman's bed, Amity took what was owed her. And from the pantry she filled a tow sack with provisions to last a good while. Then she departed from what she was positive was an outlaw home.

Afraid she would be followed and waylaid on the lonely road, Amity slipped like a ghost through the towns of Stafford, St. John, and on west.

By the end of November, her food and money had again dwindled worrisomely. Her shoes, including an extra pair from her satchel, had worn out and she'd had to buy a pair of sturdy boots in Kinsley. The temperature was near freezing. The going was slow against bitter, dust-laden wind, worse when snow particles seemed to burn her skin.

Around the first week in December, Amity trailed into Dodge City, weak and weary in every limb, half-starved, on the verge of pneumonia. She had hoped, unrealistically, she realized now, to be on her own land before winter set in. But at least she was nearer her destination.

Dodge City's days of trail-town glory had passed. However, Front Street was being rebuilt after a series of fires had destroyed much of the business area the year before. When Amity asked for work as a maid in one of the new hotels going up, she was hired, instead, to make rugs.

With a silent, heartfelt prayer of thanks, she grasped the opportunity. Bed and board came with the job, her pay was one dollar per rug, and she set her own pace, often weaving by lamplight most of the night. Sleep only brought nightmares anyway. Outside, the temperature got down to thirty below zero. But Amity had few reasons to go out, and for the remainder of winter, she was warm, at least, in a clean, cedar-fragrant room of her own, weaving rugs until her fingers bled, healed, and calloused over; thankful to save almost every dollar she earned for her start on the plains.

"This is it?" Amity whispered. The wide rolling

17

land under an immense gray sky was an ocean of *nothing,* save grass riffled by a chilly March wind. She sat on the seat of the loaded, muddy old wagon she'd bought, pulled by a brown horse she called Ben, and stared. So much emptiness was awesome and frightening. Her heart thumped.

The stocky Syracuse land-agent pulled his mount in closer when he noted her hesitation. "You've changed your mind, I reckon? Right smart. A woman ain't got a Chinaman's chance out here, alone. You could sooner pull sunbeams outta cucumbers."

Amity shook her head, smiling stiffly. "I haven't changed my mind. One hundred sixty acres, correct?" She leaped from the wagon. "I am staying!" He had asked her on the way out what she knew of blizzards, breaking sod, rattlesnakes, and loneliness. She had told him that she would learn, couldn't reveal that she had no other choice and would have to exist however she might. She would never forget sweet little Nora Ann, nor her despair at the Fairleighs' accusations, but she had to survive.

Brushing her wind-tossed hair from her eyes, Amity took the mallet the agent handed her, moistened her lips, and drove the first boundary stake deep, then deeper, into the sod.

ON THE HIGH PLAINS

May, 1887

Chapter One

Amity Whitford drove her wagon slowly along the dusty, grass-centered main street of Syracuse, Kansas. What she saw around her held little promise that her trip to town would be worth the effort. She flicked the reins. "C'mon, Ben, we've got no time to fritter." Her bony brown horse continued to plod. The wagon wheels whined for want of grease, their noise embarrassing Amity. She surveyed the drab general store, bank, saloon, and smattering of other businesses squatting like sleepy-eyed toads on either side of the street and sighed heavily. Someone here must give her work. She couldn't give in now.

Because she lived out on the plains and rarely came to town, she knew few of the calicoed town women going about with market baskets on their arms. The old men, watching her from scattered benches, indicated by a smile and nod that they still knew a pretty woman when they saw one. She didn't know their names and she doubted very much that they knew hers, but she smiled back.

Henry Strout, the banker, had told her that among the townsfolk who knew of her, few expected she'd survive the winter. Perhaps the old men thought they were watching a ghost.

Ignoring the despair that threatened to claim her, Amity pulled her wagon in toward the newspaper office. Suddenly, before she could alight, around the corner of a shack came a black-and-white pig squealing sharply, chased by a boy of about eight carrying a switch. The pig went slipping and sliding on dainty feet under her wagon and out on the other side.

"Dammit, Lucille, come back 'ere!" The stout, blond-haired youngster grinned at Amity as he went darting under her horse's nose, causing Ben to rear and plunge, and her wagon to lurch. "Whoa," she said, managing the reins firmly. "Whoa." When Ben had calmed down, she shook a scolding finger at the boy and repressed a smile. Why in heaven wasn't he in school where he belonged? Half the children out here seemed to go to school only at their pleasure, and that too rarely.

Chalk Holden was so taken by the goings-on outside the *Banner*'s dusty front window that he couldn't give a tinker's damn about the complaints of the woman directly in front of him. With half his attention he answered the full-bosomed, thirtyish lady in plum velvet, "Yes, ma'am. Well, sure, ma'am. You're right, Mrs. Strout. More local news. Detailed obits, sure."

Holden had been operating the *Syracuse Banner* a month, but he'd never seen the young woman alighting from the wagon at the hitchrail outside. For damn sure! She was beautiful, seemed curvy

22

in all the right places, too. He all but sighed with regret as she took a blue sunbonnet from the wagon seat and tied it over dark hair. Hell's fire! The pretty heart-shaped face disappeared in the slatted bonnet.

Still, he couldn't take his eyes away. The wind picked up along the main street and the girl was caught in a sudden swirl of dust. The breeze lifted her hem and the triflest bit of slim ankle showed. Then, though he couldn't read her face hidden by the bonnet, something about the girl's movements made her seem desperate, lost even, and for some odd reason his feelings turned protective. His heart gave a happy jolt when she headed straight for the *Banner*'s door.

Amity drew a deep, fortifying breath and yanked open the door of the low sod building housing the local paper. She stood at the threshold, nervous but determined. A brand-new sign in the window read T.S. "CHALK" HOLDEN, EDITOR AND PUBLISHER; a second sign dangled below it: LAW CASES HEARD ON SATURDAYS. The door slipped from her fingers and *thunked* shut, harder than she intended. It was cooler indoors and she drew her shawl close, squinting as she tried to make out the two figures moving slightly in the sudden dimness.

The stringent, musty-clean smell of papers and printer's ink was an odor Amity could appreciate. She tried to relax.

". . . Simply must object to the changes you've

been making, Mr. Holden. Now Mr. Lester's paper was all that anyone could want, truly —"

As she recognized the woman's voice, Amity cringed slightly. Her eyes gradually adjusted to being inside and she saw that the new owner had tacked sale bills, wanted posters, and stories clipped from other papers to his walls. Some of the equipment on the ink-stained plank floor looked new, and the desk up front was unbelievably cluttered. Of course it was Thisba Strout who was complaining to the new editor. An unpleasant woman. Amity was fond of short, owlish Henry Strout, Thisba's husband. The loans he had made her from his bank were all that kept her afloat at the moment, but as much as possible Amity avoided his wife, who reminded her too much of a past she wanted to forget. Of Beaconsfield and the fine Fairleighs.

Disappointed that the newspaperman was busy, Amity still managed a polite, "Beg pardon," as she groped behind her for the door to leave. The editor waved her to stay. Glad not to give up her mission, she nodded and circled the potbellied stove, where coffee perked in an enamel pot. There she could watch the man as his long inky fingers swiftly set type at a waist-high table, while he patiently listened to Thisba Strout's syrupy sweet suggestions for running his paper.

Amity now had a better view of the *Banner*'s new editor and publisher, T. S. "Chalk" Holden, and she doubted she'd seen a more attractive man in her whole life! She couldn't take her eyes from him; an embarrassing warmth spread to her cheeks and a curious weightlessness shoved up against her heart. She opened her drawstring bag and industriously stirred the contents and didn't look up until she was herself again. That was what happened when a person hadn't spent a Saturday in town in a month of Sundays, and loneliness was a big part of her life.

Amity continued to study the man's profile discreetly, guessing that he was three or four years older than her twenty-three. His thick tousled hair and moustache were a rich butternut brown. His rugged, earthy good looks were tamed a tad by wire-rimmed spectacles that made him appear dignified and intelligent at the same time. A wild red tie lay against his rumpled blue-striped shirt. He looked up to find her staring at him and, ignoring Thisba Strout for a second, he asked Amity, "If you're in a hurry, Miss — ?"

"N-n-no." She shook her head, her hand coming to rest over her heart. "Goodness, no. I can wait." She motioned them to take their time, even though she wished Thisba would hurry up so she could state her own case and be done with it; it had been hard enough, making herself come here.

The man turned back to Thisba, his manner so relaxed and casual nobody would think the woman had been giving him hell and what-for about his own paper. "Is it the whole new *Banner* you don't like, Mrs. Strout?" he drawled. "Or just the parts you been mentionin'?" Again from behind his glasses his warm hazel eyes flicked from Thisba to settle on Amity, and he gave her a slow smile.

Thisba Strout looked from one to the other and drew herself up, bidding their attention to herself with a rather fierce frown. She was an attractive woman, who, as one could tell by her smooth, pale rose complexion, spent as little time as possible outside in the hot prairie winds. "Well, there's also the locals column," Mrs. Strout declared, her tone as rigid as her backbone.

Holden's left eyebrow climbed in honest surprise. "I try to get everybody written up as often as I can. Did you have an afternoon tea or make a trip that I missed hearing about, Mrs. Strout?" In spite of appearing sincerely concerned, he took a minute to speed a few pieces of type into place and survey them with a look of satisfaction before he again focused on his critic.

Thisba's well-formed bosom heaved. Her delicate, petal pink skin was darkening above her stylish plum dress, and she made Amity think of a teakettle about to go. A tarnished teakettle, because there was a shady aura about the woman — in spite of her show of breeding and gentility — something Amity couldn't quite decipher from the little she actually knew about Thisba. Anyway, Thisba's name got into the paper far more often than she deserved, Amity thought, even if she was the banker's wife.

The woman's fingers fussed with the saffron ringlets on her forehead. "It — it's the name

26

you've given the locals column, Mr. Holden! It's disgusting. Obscene, actually. My daughter Doridee, for example, is yet a young innocent whom I hate to see exposed to such coarseness. Any sensitive lady in the reading community, and there are many of us —" her look at Amity said she did not consider her one of them "— would be demeaned!"

Amity lowered her eyes and thought, Thank you, too. In some eyes, a single-woman home-steader was considered not much above a dance-hall girl. Of course, the apricot and periwinkle calico print dress she wore was faded; the ruffles and lace at the high neckline and around her wrists were thready. But the frock was clean and starched and the front fit her slim figure like a glove, while the back gathered into a fetching fake bustle. She wore lace gloves to cover her callused hands, a proper head covering, and, though she often went barefoot or wore moccasins on the homestead, today she wore shoes. Scuffed and tight, but real high-topped, pointed-toe shoes. Ah, well —

"I see." Holden answered Thisba while continuing to work.

Thisba went on, pale blue eyes flashing, "Why can't you call the column 'Local Matters'? Something simple and inoffensive. I beg you to drop that awful title 'Buffalo Chips'!"

Amity nearly choked trying not to laugh. It had been a while since she'd seen a copy of the *Syracuse Banner*. Evidently the new publisher had a sense of humor. Good! She would appreciate that quality in an employer — if he should give her work.

"I'll take your suggestions under strong advisement," Chalk Holden said solemnly, the corner of his mouth twitching. Amity had a feeling that the "Buffalo Chips" column would remain "Buffalo Chips." She took a certain vengeful pleasure in the prospect, though none of it was her affair and she had her own business to tend to.

"That's all I had on my mind, then. Henry and Doridee are waiting for their noon meal. Good day." Thisba's strong honeysuckle scent filled the air as she fluffed herself to leave.

"Good day, Mrs. Strout, and thanks for your fine ideas."

"Good day, Thisba," Amity said politely. The woman looked back at her without answering and left.

"Your turn," the newspaper man said gently, squaring to face her. "This is complaint day, so go right ahead."

She moistened her lips. "I'm not here to complain. Not at all —" She paused for a moment, not quite sure how to put it.

"I'm here to ask for a job on the paper," Amity blurted finally. She squeezed her fist to stop its trembling, then forcefully stuck her hand out for him to shake. "My name is Amity Cathlin Whitford and I have a claim eight miles northwest of town. I filed on it two years ago but I'm going to lose it if I don't find an outside job."

She'd promised herself she wouldn't beg in spite of her desperate straits, but she knew she was getting close when she told the editor, "Last winter was terrible for most people in these parts. The blizzard in January killed thousands of head of cattle and the drought the summer before did away with most crops. A lot of my neighbors have already picked up and gone for good. I intend to stay come h— regardless!"

She met his gaze squarely, more troubles having poured out of her than she'd meant to tell. "I borrowed from the bank to buy a milk cow, a few hens, and this spring's seed, but even if we're lucky enough to get rain this summer, I'll need a job to supplement my crop income. There's things I must have to work the ranch and I want to pay off the bank as soon as possible."

She absolutely couldn't lose the homestead, she thought to herself. The improvements she'd made since she filed the claim had already made it more valuable. And John Clyde and she had dug a well that even provided them with fresh, sweet water. She had three years to go 'til she proved up and it all became hers. She just couldn't allow these two years of settling her claim, all her hard work and financial investment, to be in vain. "Sorry, I'm sure you don't need to know my problems. I do need a job, though."

Behind the wire-rimmed spectacles, the frown that had settled on Chalk Holden's forehead as she spoke, deepened. He ruffled his already tousled hair. "Ah —" he murmured.

Amity blushed, realizing she hadn't said one word about her qualifications, only her need. She was no beggar! She rushed on before he could turn her down, "I graduated at the top of my class at Cairo High School —"

He threw his shoulders back in question, "Cairo?"

"Cairo, Illinois, on the Mississippi River. After that, I had a year and a half of art school in St. Louis, where I also studied literature and writing. I enjoy writing and have always kept journals as a matter of habit."

"Quite a background for someone who's trying to homestead in western Kansas." The tone of his voice was gentle but ironic.

She wasn't surprised at his teasing, but she meant to stick with the matter at hand. "I have a typewriter."

"A what?"

"A typing machine to write with. A Remington typewriter made by the folks who make rifles." John Clyde had brought the typewriter with other things, when he had finally found her. "My papa bought it for me as a gift and I'm an excellent typist. It's outside in my wagon. I brought it with me, Mr. Holden, to demonstrate if you've never seen one."

"I've seen 'em." His expression was genuinely regretful as he told her, "But I can't hire you, although I'd give anything if I could. I'm sure with your education you'd make a top-notch reporter and feature writer." He waved his hand nodded as she left. "Thank you again, very much."

Amity sat outside in her wagon, reins in her lap, for several moments. Ben, still hitched, waited patiently, tail switching flies. Tears she refused to give in to ached behind her eyes. Some Arkansas River Valley and high plains folk had given up and gone back to their kin in the east. But if she failed here in Hamilton County, Kansas, she had no where else to go. There was no one left for her in Cairo. Even if there were, she'd never let herself be dependent on others again. *Never*. She'd make her own way, or be damned! Clamping her jaws, Amity lifted the reins, determined to block out the painful memories that threatened.

From his window inside the *Banner* office, Chalk watched the pretty, forlorn figure in the wagon outside as he pretended to study the view — which held only the saloon, the livery stable, and directly across the street in a weedy lot, a tiny vacant shack with a faded sign over the sagging door, MINNIE'S HATS. He sighed. He might hate himself later for what he was about to do, but the raucous rattle of her wagon wheels leaving spun him into action. He rushed to the door and outside onto the dusty plank walk, shouting, "Miss Whitford! Hold up a minute. I might have a suggestion for you." He waved the rolled paper in his hand as he sprinted up and she drew the

to take in the whole room. "You could do lots of other tasks around here, but —" he blew out a long, sorry breath "— I just can't afford you."

Her voice grew small as her hope disappeared. "Oh? I had really hoped —"

"I bought the paper cheap because of bad times hereabouts, but even with that I put everything I had into it. I see little cash from ads or subscriptions; most people pay me with potatoes, onions, eggs, cabbages, venison, or whatever they can spare. One lady does my laundry for her husband's paper. Much as I'd like to, I just don't have the funds to pay you, and you obviously need the money."

Amity persisted, "I saw a sign in your window that you take law cases on Saturday mornings. I thought with that and the paper, too . . ."

He nodded. "That I oughta be a rich man? I practice law. But there aren't that many cases that pay. I also plaster houses now and then, because I'm good at it and if they pay cash it's a big help. I'm sorry, but I have to plow what I earn right back into the business for paper, other supplies, machinery. I just can't take you on right now."

"I-I s-see." She did see. The small amounts of cash she came by went right back into her homestead. Her disappointment was sharp, and the fact that he looked equally regretful didn't help. What was she going to do? The truth was she'd already tried to sell her typewriter for whatever she could get for it, but nobody in Syracuse had need of such a contraption. Henry Strout had allowed her to borrow beyond her limit at the bank; that was as much as the good man could do. There were almost no staples in the cupboards at home. She and John Clyde, her naturally skin-and-bones handyman, had nearly starved last winter, and she'd been able to buy only a few supplies with a bit of the borrowed money this spring to tide them over. She experienced a flash of anger. She had to have a paid job, but for women there were so few opportunities! If a real job were available, it would go to a man.

"Could you take in sewing, miss?" the newspaperman broke into her thoughts to suggest. "Or do some baking?"

She said tightly, "I'm quite confident that fine seamstresses and good cooks abound in Syracuse, Mr. Holden. In any event, either requires buying supplies."

"Any experience teaching?"

An innocent question, but she drew in a shaky breath and nervously fingered the cameo at her throat. *A goose walked on my grave.* She brought her hand down slowly and clenched her fists to still the shaking. She didn't look at him as she replied. "I taught once. I was a governess for — for an English family." She waved a hand, saying, "Look, I'm taking up your time since there's really nothing you can do. So . . ." She had a sudden, splitting headache and she wanted to flee, but couldn't make herself move.

Chapter Two

Chalk Holden's eyes regarded her anxiously, and he reached out as if to touch her hand, but she moved, drawing away. He shook his head. "I'm truly sorry." She needed a job bad to be so upset. For lack of something better to offer, he walked to the overloaded front desk and picked up a fresh copy of the *Syracuse Banner*. "First one of your new subscription to the paper. I'd like your opinion of it."

"Subscription? I can't pay —" The young woman moistened her parched lips. She looked at the paper yearningly a moment and then at the floor. "Some other time, p-perhaps."

"Do you make plum butter?"

"Wild plum butter? Of course." She looked up at him.

"Bring me a couple jars of plum butter this summer and maybe a loaf of bread in payment. How's that?"

The young woman nodded. "I'll pay with fresh fish, too. John Clyde sometimes catches more than we can use." Chalk held the paper out to her and she snatched it greedily. "It's been ages since I've had anything new to read," she said, and

wagon to a halt. Her blue eyes, dark as midnight, were shining with curious expectancy as she looked down at him.

"What is it?" she asked.

"Well, this is not exactly a job. But — where's your paper?"

The young woman flushed as she pulled her newspaper out from under her skirts where she'd been sitting on it for safekeeping.

"Back page." Chalk tapped his finger against the upper right-hand corner of his paper while she unfolded hers with a noisy crackling.

"What? Where?"

"Right up there, election notice."

"Elections?" She frowned at him.

"Just read it."

She read aloud the notice boxed with thick black lines. "Nominations are now being taken for the office of county school superintendent, Hamilton County. *The right man* — needs a background in education and business. His duties will be to oversee school affairs for the twelve Hamilton County schools, their pupils and teachers. In the spring, he will hold normal school for the training of teachers. He will be responsible for the testing and hiring of new teachers. . . ." She shrugged and looked at him. "I don't understand."

Chalk plunged daringly, "Couldn't you do all that? I think you should run for this office."

Amity was thoughtful for a few seconds. "Yes, I could . . . do it. But . . ." Papa had served for years on the Cairo school board and she'd formed strong opinions from his experience, the main one being that browbeating and shaming could kill a budding love of knowledge quicker than anything. She'd loved school herself, had been an excellent student. She frowned at him. "Run for county school superintendent? May I remind you, Mr. Holden, that women don't even have the right to vote! Never mind being considered as officeholders except in rare instances."

He laughed. "You don't have the faintest notion what's been going on in Syracuse, do you, Miss Whitford?"

"Is there something I should know?" she asked briskly.

"Syracuse has an all-woman city council!" Ignoring Amity's gasp of surprise, he went on, "Five of the town's most refined and able matrons took over the town government just last month."

"I don't believe you!"

He nodded. "All the ladies' aid societies banded together and drummed up the votes on a platform of municipal reform. They intend to have a sober sheriff, to get the streets graded, to eventually get a high school established so young people don't have to leave home for more schooling. They'd like to bring in more businesses, see the town thriving and prosperous."

"You're joking! All women? I don't see how —"

"The legislature passed a law in January that Kansas women could vote in city matters and local school affairs, and the ladies of Syracuse were finally able to vote themselves in. They wasted no time after the news came out in March. They had election meetings among themselves and presented a full slate for town government — of women."

"Women actually *voted?*" she exclaimed, but her sudden high excitement deflated swiftly. "Only municipal, then — Kansas women can't vote on other election matters?"

He shrugged. "Not yet."

She answered sarcastically, "Whoop-de-do, giant strides. We women aren't half smart enough to vote in county, state, or federal elections, oh, no!" And then, looking at the announcement again, she shrieked in disbelief, "Really — ?"

"What's the matter?"

"I'd give my soul for this position whatever it paid — but is the salary for county school superintendent really *five hundred dollars a year?*"

"Yeah." Chalk grinned, shifting himself against the wagon. "I thought that would interest you." Counting on his long inky fingers, he said, "You've got the education and refinement, the savvy, you've taught as a governess. You've got plenty of starch, or you wouldn't be homesteading in Kansas. I'd say you're right for the job. Perfect." He nodded, pursing his lips.

"Except —" her shoulders drooped — "They're asking for a he and I'm a she."

"Yeah, I noticed."

Amity went on, reasoning aloud, "Also, it's

a county office. Other women won't be able to vote for me, only men." She read on under her breath, "Be prepared to travel, energy important . . . practical minded . . . be —" her tongue tripped and her voice nearly disappeared, "— be-be of good moral character."

Finally she lifted her head. "It doesn't matter that I'm a woman," she told Chalk Holden. "I have all the other qualifications. If there are women running the government of this town, then it means I have a chance, however slim, in the rest of the county." She folded her paper and tucked it back under her bottom so that it wouldn't blow away in the warm winds tossing her bonnet strings and nipping at her skirts. She stared at him with resolution. "I'm going to run. I've nothing to lose by trying. What do I do next? Shouldn't I file, or something?"

"Yes, over at the county clerk's office."

Amity felt so relieved at this turn of events, this possible answer to her plight, that she was almost giddy. It wouldn't be just a job, either. She could help the children of this strange, lonely land she'd chosen for her own. Some youngsters out here never left their homesteads for even a day's book learning. Not to mention the quality of school life for those who did get some education — that could be improved, too.

Her eyes met the handsome newspaperman's and she leaned forward, smiling, her face inches from his. "The *Banner* would back me, wouldn't it, Mr. Holden?" She'd never ask another thing from him but this, she told herself. The paper's endorsement was essential. "Since it was your suggestion, you'll support my candidacy, won't you?"

Amity waited. Perfectly articulate before, the man seemed to have suddenly lost his tongue. His features grew as red as if he choked on a bucket-sized chunk of limestone. Or had he been snagged sharply on his own hook? she wondered shrewdly. Well, it served him right. She'd just let him dangle. Deliver his soul to hell for making this proposal if he didn't mean it! She pretended to examine a callus on her left thumb, exposed through the torn lace of her glove, glancing at him from time to time as he struggled with her question.

Finally, the man drawled, "I'll announce it in the next issue." He mumbled, unable to keep the dismay from his eyes, "I'll — write an editorial in your support."

Looking back at him, Amity saw that the man was lost in his own thoughts. She spoke loudly, dragging out her paper and waving it at him to wake him up. "Which town holds the county seat just now?"

A ferocious county seat fight had raged the past two years between Hamilton County's three main towns. There had been shootings, men wounded, some killed, over the fierce competition to be the county seat, since only one town in each county out here was likely to truly thrive. She had heard no recent news. "Is the county seat still Syracuse? Or is it Kendall, or Coolidge, Mr. Holden?"

"Syracuse," he said gruffly, clearing his throat. "And, since we're centrally located, and changing county lines have taken Kendall into Kearny County, it'll likely stay Syracuse."

"All right," she said, barely controlling her eagerness, "I might as well file right now."

His face held a strange expression before he finally answered, "Maybe you should think about it awhile. Anyway, the county clerk's office is closed today. Buford stayed home to plant corn."

"No! What a fine how-do-you-do! Is that any way to run the government?"

"That's how it's run around here." He grinned broadly. "But hey, we need to talk more about this." He seemed suddenly revived from his stupor. Behind his glasses, which he thumbed more firmly in place, his eyes gleamed. "Will you stay in town and take supper with me at the hotel? The Dunnington is a fair place to stay. I'll interview you for the editorial. Then you can come back Monday morning to file."

There was no way she could stay in town, for goodness sakes, but she looked at him for a long moment, tempted to her core. The prospect of holding county office was exciting to contemplate. It could change her entire future. She took a breath and decided, "I can come now for coffee, but I have to be home before dark because I've heaps of chores to do." Probably too much work to also fit in the many duties of a school su-

40

perintendent, she thought — in her mind she had the job already. Details would simply have to be worked out. Elections weren't until November. Between now and then she'd have to campaign, do everything she could to win votes, and survive on next to nothing till she won and was earning. She'd worry later.

As if he read her mind, Chalk Holden's soft sandpapery voice grew huskier, and he asked, "Are you sure you want to do this, Miss Whitford? It'd be no bed of roses, you know, and no guarantee you'd win."

She studied him, biting the inside of her cheek to keep from smiling, but feeling stubborn, too. "Having second thoughts, Mr. Holden? You think it's stupid for a woman to try this? You're maybe sorry you even suggested it? Well, don't be, because I thank you from the bottom of my heart. You needn't worry; I'll manage."

His face reddened. "Well, if you're sure." He shook his head, his expression doubtful, as though one of them were leading the other to an uncharted hell.

Giving Amity a strange, tight-lipped smile, with a look in his eyes she couldn't quite decipher, he came around to her side. "Move over, I'll drive us to the Dunnington. They'll give us coffee and pie in the dining room."

"All right." She did as he asked, straightening her skirts and her sunbonnet. "I'm convinced you've saved my life, Mr. Holden, and I want you to know how much I appreciate it." That much was the sincere truth, regardless of what happened.

He climbed up beside her and snapped the reins over Ben's back. She thought he mumbled, "Oh, sweet Jesus," but it hardly mattered and he didn't repeat it. She smiled at him as they squeaked and jangled down the street. "I do hope the Dunnington has rhubarb pie, Mr. Holden. Press on."

Chapter Three

The setting sun cast a reddish gold glow across the wide tableland north of Syracuse, and the earthen lumps that were Amity's house and out-buildings turned soft rose.

Listing sideways to balance a heavy wooden pail of foamy milk, Amity hurried from the low sod barn toward the well a few yards to the left of her house. Zip, John Clyde's mottled blue-and-gray sheepdog, lonely for his master, trotted at her heels. She'd stayed too long in town and now she had to race to complete her chores before the light faded altogether. She wasn't sorry, though. Besides being indebted to Mr. Holden for his suggestion that she run for county school superintendent, she'd found his company an ex-tremely pleasant diversion. In fact, she'd never felt quite as excited as she had today in that man's presence. He'd given her a feeling of giddy hap-piness, of hope, with his welcome ideas and en-couragement. And certainly, the time they'd spent discussing the whys and wherefores of campaign-ing was not a waste.

Though the sun was going down, it was still warm, she realized, wiping her brow with the back of her free arm. She'd meant to plant another quarter acre of potatoes before supper but that would have to wait for daylight. She was without John Clyde's help because he was up north in Colorado, horse hunting for a few days. If he was lucky, he could better their circumstances considerably.

"Shoo!" Amity kicked out, and with an angry *squa-a-w-w-k*, her Rhode Island Red rooster flapped out of her path.

At the well, Amity fastened a rope to the bucket's bail and carefully let the milk down into the coolest place on her farm, to keep it fresh till needed.

Zip and the chickens were fed, Ben was unhitched and grazing in the back pasture — not much else she could do tonight outside except turn Flora, her black-faced, golden Jersey cow, out of the barn to graze with Ben.

After she led the cow out, Amity selected an apron-full of cow chips from the large pile at the west corner of her house, carried them inside, and dropped them into the fuel box by the back door. She brushed her hands off, thinking of the hot fire the chips would make in her cookstove. Then she smiled to herself as she recalled Thisba Strout's fuss with Chalk Holden over the title of the locals column.

That brought to mind her own first meeting in Syracuse with the fancy *Mrs. Strout*. It was on her third trip to town during the first year after she'd come to the plains to homestead —

44

in the two years she'd been there she'd made less than a dozen trips into Syracuse. With very little money, little to trade, and more work than she could handle at home, there was small need to go there. Always present, too, was the fear of crossing paths with someone from Beaconsfield. Someone with knowledge of the Fairleigh affair.

Standing in the drygoods store where she'd gone to buy cheap muslin to line her ceiling, Amity had felt someone staring. When she looked up, she saw a fashionable, fair-haired woman watching from the other side of the store. The woman instantly turned away, as if to flee, and then, slowly, she turned back. Almost in challenge, her manner oddly hostile and defensive, her eyes aglitter with dislike, she stared at Amity. She didn't say anything, but Amity, feeling confused, somewhat fearfully responded, "I beg your pardon?"

The woman advanced on her, asking, "Don't I know you?"

Amity looked at her more closely, suddenly afraid that the woman, who looked faintly familiar, might have known her during that dreadful time in Kansas City, or — "No, I don't believe we've met," Amity began cautiously, and then she went rigid. The thing she had hoped forever to avoid — a chance meeting with someone from Beaconsfield — was at hand. "You're Thisba Marcellus," Amity spoke through a dry throat. "You've changed so much I hardly recognized you —" Thisba had been the Fairleighs' new maid at Beaconsfield, and she had a daughter. At the time, Thisba seemed to feel unnecessary jealousy toward Amity's position with the Fairleighs; in the short while they worked together, it had been impossible to become friends.

Now, the woman's eyes bore into Amity's own, and Amity waited to be accused, to hear what she knew about — Nora Ann, the tragedy. Waited for Thisba to tell one and all what Amity Whitford really was. Finally, the blonde woman's pretty face smoothed out and she smiled. "I'm sorry if I was rude. You look quite different, now, too." She suddenly became effusive. "I do apologize for staring." She held out a gloved hand that tightened in a spasmodic grip around Amity's fingers. "So nice to meet you again. Of course. I'm Mrs. Strout now, Henry Strout's wife. Perhaps you know him? He owns the bank."

Amity had acknowledged with dry humor that she might know him better than anyone, due to their dealings. To her amazement, that had ended the first meeting. Afterward, Amity waited expectantly for something to *happen*. When it didn't, and she could bear the suspense no longer, she sought Thisba Strout out and asked her point-blank about that day at Beaconsfield.

"Oh, my, I wish I could help you," Thisba had said. "I'm afraid I don't know any more than you do, dear. Of course, I heard about the child's death, later. I'm so embarrassed to admit it, but the Fairleighs — wasn't that our employers' name? — let me go just before that terrible oc-

46

currence. Not that I cared to keep such a demeaning job, anyway. I only took it to tide me over 'til something better. So I wasn't there at the time and never knew the particulars. Of course, I heard rumors there was foul play or —" She looked genuinely surprised. "Surely, they didn't suspect *you?*" A frown creased her pretty forehead.

"I'm afraid so. I was also dismissed. But it's so difficult to believe I could have hurt a child — I must have been very ill, because I can recall so little of that day."

"You weren't officially charged then?"

Amity shook her head. "No, I wasn't. Although the punishment I was subjected to could have been worse than any prison." Although he had said otherwise, she thought Mr. Fairleigh had meant it to be worse. "I was lucky to survive." She sighed. "I suppose one day I'll meet someone who does know what took place at Beaconsfield." She didn't admit how much the prospect of what the truth might be frightened her.

"Perhaps." Thisba's supercilious manner had returned. "Perhaps not." The woman's expression was veiled, but Amity sensed that Thisba took malicious pleasure in her misfortune, and she would, if she was anything like the Thisba Amity remembered.

So Amity wasn't surprised on the rare occasions they met after that when Thisba seemed to flaunt her social position over the lowly farmer Amity had become. Amity decided that she was fortunate

47

that Thisba had left Beaconsfield before the tragedy of the child's death. A woman like Thisba, if she knew anything, would want to expose her, not help her to unravel the terrible mystery.

"Oh, a plague on Thisba Strout," she murmured with quiet dismissal after a moment. "She's nothing to me." She pulled her attention back to more pressing concerns, one of which was the hunger gnawing at her thin frame after such a long and eventful day.

After she got a fire going in the cookstove at the kitchen end of her soddy, she cleaned up at the wash bench and got out a fresh apron from a trunk at the foot of her bed. She took pleasure in sniffing the cedar fragrance of the garment before tying it around her small waist.

Stirring a cupful of hominy with a bit of bacon grease in a hot skillet, she looked about her home with immense pleasure and pride. To build it she'd studied a well-used copy of Adam's *Homesteader's Guide* that she had borrowed. The soddy didn't compare to the three-story frame house in Cairo where she'd grown up but it was hers.

Despite sore muscles and huge blisters, she'd built the soddy herself — after staking her claim — while living in a tent on the barren plains for several weeks. During that time, her only company had been a pair of mourning doves residing in the wild plum thicket down by the creek. Though that wild fruit did grow along the banks, she learned that Plumb Creek had been named for a senator, Preston B. Plumb. The resident birds gave her the name for her new home: Dove's Nest.

Amity had to build her "nest" with blocks cut from an acre-and-a-half of sod that sprouted short, wiry buffalo grass. She measured them so they were each four inches thick and twelve inches wide by eighteen inches long. She'd made the walls two sods thick, laying the blocks grass down in staggered rows. The ridge poles supporting the sod roof were cottonwood logs she'd cut, trimmed, and hauled herself from the timber growing along the Arkansas River eight miles distant. An itinerant cowboy had come along in time to help her get the roof logs and upper sods in place. She was very proud of her double mail-order windows at the front of the house, facing south. They'd cost $1.25 each. Her house was cheap, cool in summer and cozy in winter. All year 'round, geraniums bloomed in the window well where she sometimes sat to read or to write in her journal. She felt safe there, because her soddy was also virtually fireproof and windproof; even tornadoes weren't much of a threat against such solid walls.

She had to admit, though, that the soddy could be dark and smoky, and it leaked when it rained. The ceiling was covered with muslin to keep away insects and snakes, and varmints that claimed the place theirs as much as hers. Blankets, rather than a real wall, sectioned off her bedroom from the rest of the house. The first year the two rooms had been barren and ugly, making her feel like an animal living in a hole, but all that changed with John Clyde Rossback's arrival.

As Amity slowly stirred the grits, her thoughts turned to the year she'd lost both of her parents in the terrible Cairo flood of 1882. She had been eighteen and away at art school. A message had come to her at school that the high, filthy waters had killed both of them: Mama died of typhoid she'd caught nursing the sick from the flood; Papa drowned trying to salvage goods from his flooded department store, after losing their home. Suddenly everything wonderful from her childhood, especially their sheltering love, was gone, and she was on her own.

Most of what happened afterward, till she filed for her claim, she kept blocked from her mind, and she pushed it away now. Then just last spring, John Clyde Rossback, a broken-down veteran of the war between the states, had driven into her yard with a wagon load of goods he said was hers. Oh, the treasures! Precious portraits of Mama and Papa, linens, blankets, vases, lamps, carpets, lace curtains. Sheltering a china teapot was the soft gray felt slouch hat that was Papa's favorite, though her mother preferred to see him in his more elegant homburg. Her mother's volumes of Victor Hugo and Charles Dickens. Tables, a brass bed, Mama's diminutive, spindly legged, wheezy melodeon. She sat right down in the grass and cried her heart out when John Clyde told her that Papa had stored these things with a neighbor to be her dowry. But Amity had never returned to Cairo, and the neighbor, who was moving to Oregon, had hired John Clyde to find Amity Cathlin Whitford and give her her things.

Inside, her sod home was now furnished as nicely as the finest homes in Syracuse. When they got down to their last turnip and cup of meal last winter, she'd thought about selling her precious things for food. But John Clyde, bless his dear heart, told her, "You wouldn't get fair exchange if folks did have food to share. Keep your things, Missy. I been a lot hungrier in the war. We're going to be just fine." He went out that same day and with the last of his ammunition, downed an antelope that lasted them for a good while. They did survive the long, cold winter in which January temperatures got down to minus thirty, but many lives were lost all over the plains.

They were lucky; all that was over, and certainly her future looked brighter, more fulfilling, too, now that she was going to run for public office. A political position — and it paid five hundred dollars per year. A two-year term would save her.

Amity sat down to eat, with the precious newspaper Chalk Holden had given her next to her plate. Gentlemen read newspapers, not ladies, and reading at the table definitely wasn't done. She was grateful that living alone lifted barriers she set no store by, anyway.

Not to say she didn't find the first story a touch shocking, though she gobbled it up. One Lillian Harman and E. C. Walker were this spring

51

released from the Oskaloosa jail after sixteen-year-old Lillian's father, Moses Harman, paid court costs for their release. The initial charge against them was for living in sin. The couple had entered into a union the past September without benefit of a traditional wedding ceremony conducted by a clergyman or justice of the peace, but simply sanctioned by the girl's father. They refused accepted marriage rules. Good grief. Lillian's papa, Moses Harman, edited the radical publication, *Lucifer, The Light Bearer*, and liked to trounce in print the institution of marriage, all forms of government, and religion. E. C. Walker, the "groom" was coeditor. Evidently the publication was raising a storm of controversy, not only in Kansas but across the country.

A miller moth fluttered against the lamp in the center of the table, but she ignored it and continued to relish her meal of steaming grits and cornbread with molasses, while she finished the rest of the paper. She read Holden's editorial on better fire protection for Syracuse. "Do it now," he urged. "Let's not wait for the horse to be stolen to lock the barn."

She had hoped there would be an introductory piece about the new publisher so she'd learn more about him, but there was none. Perhaps he'd run that in an earlier paper. Anyway, from their brief meeting, she knew him to be a gentleman, though quite forward, considering how he'd asked her to dinner right away.

She spotted an item about a recent dance where

Miss Doridee Strout, age thirteen, was "the most beautiful young maid present, the most graceful dancer, a treat for all eyes in her white dimity gown trimmed with white ribbons and silk lavender and yellow sweetpeas." That ought to have pleased Thisba a whole bunch. Except that the piece appeared in the column headed "Buffalo Chips," the source of the woman's ill-humor.

In a wedding story, every flower was described; each present listed in detail as to worth. The latter might have pleased Miss Julia Craft, the bride, as it was the custom, but Amity thought that if it were she, she'd not like such private information revealed. Well, she was certainly never getting married, so no matter. Marriage would mean placing her destiny in another's hands and she'd learned her lesson about that when the Fairleighs had left her high and dry to grope like an animal for survival. She'd vowed then to count on no one, to go it alone, or else. Shaking off a feeling of despair as old nightmares began to crowd in, she rattled the newspaper and read on.

Obedience, better known as Beady, Moffat, had given up her intention to go east for a career in order to stay in Syracuse and look after her ailing parents. She was now doing dressmaking from their home.

There was a lengthy column of news from the legislature, which ordinarily she would have skimmed, but she decided to read it carefully since she was about to throw her hat into the ring of politics. Down deep, she distrusted politicians, at least some of them, but she wanted desperately to be the next Hamilton County school superintendent. She would be a good superintendent, she knew she could help.

Among the legislative items she saw that there had been clarification of laws relating to organization of new counties and regulations regarding county-seat elections. They'd also passed a requirement that laborers be paid at regular intervals with lawful money and not any form of scrip or token money, and prohibited pools or price-fixing agreements in grain and livestock. Finally, she found the piece of legislation Chalk Holden had mentioned and she read it with greater interest. Early in the year, the House of Representatives voted for the Woman Suffrage Bill, ninety-one to twenty-two, thus making Kansas the first state to grant municipal suffrage to women. They could now vote in elections for city and school officers and on school bonds, and might hold municipal offices. Nothing was mentioned about county offices, but maybe the tide was turning. Praise God, she had a chance.

Thinking about Monday, when she would return to Syracuse to file, Amity got so excited she found it difficult to concentrate on the rest of the paper. If fortune were on her side, the clerk, Buford Barker, would have his corn in and be in his office. And she would begin her campaign.

As she was folding the newspaper carefully to

54

put it away she read a small headline: "Baby Dies". Details of the sad little story jumped out at her — a Syracuse baby had lost its life to diphtheria. Her stomach clenched and an uncontrollable shivering suddenly possessed her as she struggled to rid her mind of a haunting image of a porch . . . or shelf, and another child so white and still beneath it. She shoved the paper aside. The past was past.

Chapter Four

Amity woke at first light on Sunday, grateful for the slate of a new day. Tossing her quilts aside, she determined to look in but one direction, ahead. As she dressed she remembered there was to be a basket church service at a neighbor's four miles further north on Plumb Creek, but she felt particularly unfit this morning for either church or picnic. She'd plant potatoes, do the washing, and prepare for her trip back to Syracuse Monday morning. She hoped John Clyde would return today. Normally he was away only two or three days, but this time he'd already been gone five days and she was beginning to worry.

Monday morning, she rose early and lost no time getting into town. As she stood before the county clerk, a small dark man in a tight celluloid collar who shuffled papers on his desk pretending efficiency and waiting for her to leave — which she was not about to do without filing — Amity's heart beat fast with trepidation.

"There's no law that says I can't file for county school superintendent, is there, Mr. Barker?" The clerk had been blatantly antagonistic from the moment she expressed her mission, making no move to give her the proper papers to sign.

He surprised her by saying, as tight-jawed as if he cracked black walnuts in his teeth, "Here and there, women have been able to serve in the office of county school superintendent since the seventies." But then he huffed, "That doesn't make it right."

"For ten or fifteen years they could give their time and service but not vote for the office? Don't you see how ridiculous that is? Thank heaven Kansas women now have partial suffrage at least —"

"As far as I'm concerned, the new law is unconstitutional and will perforce be thrown out shortly. I agree with Senator Ingalls. 'A woman is a woman and her place is at home,'" he pontificated. "Now, Miss Whitford, won't you please let me get back to work?"

Amity's face flushed with anger. She smiled down into his vapid blue eyes so long they began to blink. Fury gripped her, as well as stark fear that a chance at the solution to her problems would be denied her after all, and everything would be lost. Unfortunately for him, his distasteful remark only served to fuel her resolve. "Mr. Barker, give me the papers, please." Her tone was soft, even. "Or must I go to a higher authority to make you give them to me? Shall I talk to the county commissioners?"

He looked at her in disdain, and saw that she wasn't going to give an inch. Finally he reached

57

into a drawer and removed a record book in which he wrote a few lines. "Damnable waste of time." He shoved the large book across the desk at her, glowering darkly. "Go ahead and fill it in and sign your name. Doesn't matter if you do file. You haven't got the chance of a blizzard in Hades of winning, Miss Whitford."

The gall of him! "Oh, really?" She snatched the pen from his hand, jabbed it into his inkwell, and wrote quickly, afraid he'd withdraw the book before she had a chance to fill in the lines. "Why don't I have a chance?" she asked as she completed the proper forms. It was more an idle question than anything else. *It was done.* She felt such a tremendous relief as she returned the pen to him, that she knew whatever he said wouldn't bother her.

Yet, he was pleased to spell it out for her. "You're young and pretty, and —" what he clearly considered the most grievous sin "— you're single." He wagged the pen at her. "A older woman, a widow, like those on city council, *might* have a chance; you have none. Anybody but a fool would know that political office is for men, not the weaker sex."

Buffalo-feathers! Weaker sex? *Ha!* Not after homesteading alone out here for two years! And before that — Oh, she could tell him a thing or two! She stiffened in challenge and looked down on him with disdain. "We'll see about that, won't we?"

But as she climbed into her wagon outside

58

Buford's office — a lean-to next to the general store — she worried that if others shared his dim views of her chances, no one would bother to vote for her. As if her gender, youth, and good looks had anything to do with her abilities to run the office! She glared at the shack she'd just left and yanked the reins away from the brake handle. Cussed man!

The irony was that she'd tried hard to make herself look mature and capable today, choosing to wear a sedate pewter taffeta frock trimmed with black grelot, and a matching parasol. The outfit was a holdover from a more prosperous past and one she saved for special occasions. The time she should have spent weeding the turnips this morning, she'd spent on her confounded hair, trying to subdue the dark unruly mass into a smooth chignon. So — was she out of her mind to take precious time to try and win this office? No, she was yet to be convinced of that.

"C'mon, Ben." Amity snapped the reins over his brown back. "There's no time like the present to begin campaigning." She'd spare a precious nickel for lemonade at the Blue Door Café, and if there were willing ears, she'd let it be known of her candidacy for superintendent.

She found the café disappointingly empty. A male cook with damp, thinning gray hair and an enormous belly came from the kitchen to take her order. When he set the tall glass of lemonade in front of her, Amity smiled brightly. "I'd like to introduce myself. I'm Miss Amity Whitford, and I'm running for the office of county school superintendent." She held out her hand.

Watery blue eyes stared blankly as he wiped his stubby, floury fingers on his stained apron. "I've got pies to get into the oven." He ignored her outstretched hand and went back to his kitchen, leaving her embarrassed. *Never mind.* She spent a long time with her drink, choking a bit on the first swallow, then relishing each cold, lemony sip. She kept an eye on the front window from her table, but no one passed and no one entered the café. A decidedly poor start!

She was further convinced of that when she finally decided to leave the restaurant and, on the way back to her wagon, saw Thisba Strout's curvaceous form in rose-pink walking along ahead of her on the board sidewalk, carrying a parasol for shade from the sun. They seemed to have gotten off on the wrong foot from their first meeting long ago, but Amity was eager to share her news. "Mrs. Strout," she called to her. "Do you have a moment?"

The woman turned, her expression wary. They certainly seemed to rub one another the wrong way, Amity thought, but she needed the woman's goodwill if it were at all attainable. "I wanted you to be one of the first to know —" a forced smile fractured Amity's face "— that I'm running for public office. I feel there is a great deal I can do for education in Hamilton County —"

Thisba stared, her face beet red from the heat. "I beg your pardon? If you could hurry, please, with whatever's on your mind?" The back of her hand grazed the moisture on her flushed cheek. She frowned. "I really must get out of this sun."

"Sorry. I'll take only a moment." Amity went on to explain her candidacy and what she felt she could accomplish, saying she hoped that Mrs. Strout would speak of the matter to her friends. Her small speech, instead, seemed to have drawn a cold, glassy curtain down over the other woman's eyes.

"I'm sorry to hear that. I feel it would be a most regretful waste of your time, Miss Whitford, running for public office," Thisba announced, laying her free hand on Amity's arm, tightening it as her voice flattened. "I'm sure you have good intentions, dear, but what you're considering is a lost cause. You may not be aware that county school superintendent is an office of power, best suited to a male. A young woman like yourself should be at home preparing herself for marriage." Amity started to retort but Thisba rushed on, "Take my advice and put your mind to that, my dear. Most young women your age are espoused, with someone to take care of them." She sighed. "We do go begging for marriageable males hereabouts, I suppose." A forefinger pressed a dent into her cheek as she stood there, mouth pursed thoughtfully. "In Oregon and California they're eager for mail-order brides, I hear." She laughed, adding, "Greener grass for a female, you know."

The brass of the woman! Amity held her arms

close to her sides to keep from pushing Thisba aside. Her voice was clipped and full of anger. "Thank you for your concern, but we weren't speaking of my personal affairs. I was talking about the office I'm running for." With supreme effort, Amity kept from exploding, and in the face of the woman's superior smile, persisted with forced calm. "Perhaps I've kept you long enough. It is very warm."

"Indeed."

Amity shook with held in fury as she climbed up to settle herself on the wagon seat. What was wrong with the woman, anyway? Good heavens, they were equals. Thisba ought to want one of her own in the office, not fight it, not freeze her out because of a situation neither of them knew the truth of, or because she felt Amity didn't know her place.

With tenacity of purpose, but still unsettled, Amity guided Ben in the direction of the *Banner* office. The publisher, Mr. Holden, had been very kind to her. Speaking with him again would be comforting.

She climbed down to read the message hanging from the door. In a generous scrawl the notice stated: "Gone to get a story on Duncan Wagner's new bull." It was signed, "Ed."

Sharply disappointed, Amity headed back for the wagon, where she sat for a moment, gaze locked to the scuffed toes of her shoes. She'd hoped to see the photograph that had been taken of her on Saturday. After coffee at the Dunnington, Mr. Holden had insisted she go with him to the drugstore to meet his friend, Noah Porter. The lanky, red-haired, genial Mr. Porter held an astonishing number of positions in town: chemist, merchandiser, postman, and Syracuse's official photographer. He would take her photo for campaign notices. But it was one thing to be admired for her qualifications; another for the two men to insist on a ridiculous number of photos. Smiling, but firm, she'd soon called a halt to the photography session.

Remembering her other reason for coming to the *Banner* office, she opened her drawstring handbag and removed a paper on which she'd written an essay the night before, detailing her campaign promises, which were to appear in the edition following the issue that contained Mr. Holden's endorsement article.

Kneeling, she slid the paper under the door. As she stood up again, she wondered how soon the editor might return to work. There had been little movement along the drab, quiet street since Thisba departed. Amity felt — almost lonely, thinking of Mr. Holden. She admitted that she wanted to *see* him, to be near him, to talk to him. She had felt *different* from the day they'd met. But this schoolgirl whimsy, this yearning for a few words with him, was absurd. "Amity Cathlin Whitford, stop it this minute!" she admonished under her breath.

Before returning home, Amity called on businesses along Syracuse's short main street — the meat market, the general store, the wagonworks — to announce her candidacy to the merchants and ask their support. She skipped the drugstore and Noah Porter because he'd already sworn, with a hand on his heart, to vote for her. She also bypassed the two saloons, since she wouldn't be allowed inside, anyway, but she ventured a surrepetitious peek in the windows, wondering if Chalk Holden might be among the farmers and townsmen cooling their heels at the bar and tables. She didn't spot him in either smoky interior, and she scolded herself for even looking.

All up and down the street, wherever she stopped in to make her announcement, she was met either with apathy, or unabashed amazement, or amusement, and she felt herself getting more angry and determined with each, increasingly negative, encounter. Special tactics were going to be required, then! She'd not be vainglorious but she was determined to be taken seriously, she decided, when she finally gave up for the day. Her penny-poor campaign would take careful planning, but she had filed — she was *in*. When her life depended on it, she could be very resourceful, and this town — the whole county — was about to find that out!

Amity was still smarting as she urged a tired Ben homeward, across the Atchison, Topeka, and Santa Fe tracks and up the sandy north slope of town.

As she drove along, she could hear the hollow

booming noise of a male prairie chicken in court-ship, somewhere ahead. Finally, she spotted him in the deep, waving grasses. He was a big, fat fellow, a foot and a half long. His buff-yellow feathers striped with black were erect, his wings spread and dropped to the ground, as he leaped in a dance to charm his less striking mate. Amity smiled grimly. A lot of western Kansas's wildlife had fled in advance of civilization, like snow before a warm wind, but the prairie chicken seemed there to stay, had even increased with the advent of homesteaders. A good thing, because at times, the game birds were all that kept starvation from the door. The buffalo were all but gone, only about a thousand head left in the whole state. Antelope herds were increasingly rare.

When she reached the high flat tableland, she drew back on the reins. "Whoa!" Ben's shaggy brown hide rippled in the sunlight; he blew through his nose, and shook his head. Noisy insects took to the air around her wagon. Brushing them away from her face, she turned and looked back at the town.

A hawk circled and dipped in the sharp blue sky over the roofs, then lifted away. A few cotton-wood trees grew among the hodgepodge of lead gray shacks, dun soddies, empty lots, and newer frame houses that made up Syracuse. At either end of town stood a windmill to draw water. Below, the Arkansas River, glistening in the afternoon sun, snaked its way across the plains, coming from somewhere up in Colorado and feeding into the big Mississippi 'way south. She sighed, feeling a oneness with the land. Her tension eased. Nothing in her line of vision could be called beautiful, but for her the country held promise of everything she wanted: independence, adventure, and most especially, a new life of her own making.

She drove on, first humming softly, then singing aloud, Whittier's words that she'd learned at school: "Brave brother, true sister, list we call to thee! We'll sing upon the Kansas plains, a song of Liberty." The wind carried her voice out onto the prairie. Ben moved his ears back and forth as they swung along, and Amity laughed. After a while she sobered and stopped singing. The rest of the way home, day passing into evening as her wagon crawled along, she wondered if John Clyde would be there. Hoped he would.

It wasn't only because she desperately needed the money he might make from selling wild horses, or even because he was such a tremendous help around the farm. She just plain missed him. He was the only human company around her little section of the huge flat lands.

When she neared her place, Zip raced barking to meet her, circling her wagon with tail wagging. In the rosy dusk, she saw John Clyde's rangy bay saddle horse, Texas Max, grazing by the sod barn, and she sighed with relief.

She found John Clyde in the barn, his hat crushed against Flora's flank and his sinewy fingers stripping the last of the cow's milk into the wooden bucket held tight between his knees. The three-legged stool he'd been sitting on went tumbling as he stood up. He set the bucket of foamy milk off to the side. A wide grin softened his stubbled, thin, wedge-shaped face, and he whipped off his battered felt hat, a habit he'd had from the first day in her presence. He always called her Missy, too, and treated her like a princess. When the hat came off, a sprig of hair at either side of his head sprang up and he tried to smooth it back as usual, only to have it spring up again. He was so thin he looked half-starved. His clothes were stained with a week's sweat and coated with trail dust, but he'd gone straight to doing her chores before anything else.

"Oh, John Clyde, it's good to have you back. How did everything go? I've been so worried." Relief and happiness that he was home made her want to hug him, but she knew if she put her arms about him he'd die of mortification.

"Good to be back," he said with gruff shyness.

"You've been gone so long. Whatever happened? I've been afraid you'd had an accident or — who knows what?" Anyway, he was here, and her fear that she'd be all alone again could be put to rest. More calmly, she continued, "When I drove in just now, I didn't see any mustangs, just your bay, Texas Max. It doesn't matter, but was your luck so bad?"

"Coulda been better. I'm sorry, Missy." He spat on the straw-littered dirt floor, drew a Bull Durham tobacco sack from an inside pocket, and began to roll a cigarette, his faded blue eyes on her face. "Hate lettin' you down and that's a fact."

"What happened?" she asked quietly, waiting while he touched a match to his cigarette.

He sighed. "Didn't see anything the first day or two up on the range. Then the third mornin' I run onto a band of pretty, white-faced sorrels, ever' one of them fat, glossy, and high-spirited." He settled into the story. "I studied the way they was grazing, see, then easy and gentle-like, I began coaxing them in the direction I wanted 'em to go. Once in a while the whole confounded horse herd'd get turned the wrong way and I'd almost have to kill Texas Max, follerin' at a run. Finally had to concentrate on doggin' just a few of 'em. Wore those four buggers down till they were tame as kittens and ready to be driven off the range."

"But where are they now?"

He took a long pull on his cigarette; he exhaled and the smoke curled up in front of his face. He brushed a fleck of tobacco off his lip with a gnarled hand. "Drove them into Goodland where I sold the four to a banker feller for nineteen dollars each. He'll add some to the price for his profit and resell them to farmers around there. The money's in the house, Missy, hid away for you. I'm sorry as he— heck, I wish it was more."

"It's all right," she told him. "Heaven knows that every little bit helps. Even my butter and egg money adds up. But, John Clyde, you must keep a little of the cash for your own needs. You earned it."

"You damn-sight will take ever' penny and no argument, Missy. I ain't got no need of it, and you do." He wiped the back of his hand across his mouth, thoughtful a moment. "You give me a home when I was the most down-and-out cuss alive. When you put money into improving the claim, it just makes things that much better for me. You hear?"

She heard. "It's only a loan, then, till our situation improves. And I've my own plans for that. Look, we'll be all right." Zip, lying nearby, raised his head as Amity shook off her feeling of desperation, and even managed a laugh. Impulsively, she did a fancy jig around John Clyde, kicking up dust and straw, singing, "I'm so happy to have you back!"

All the excitement scared Flora, who let out a long, low *mooooo*.

"Settle down, girl," John Clyde mumbled.

"Are you talking to me, John Clyde, or to Flora?"

"Both o' you!" Shaking his head and grumbling under his breath, suppressing a grin, he picked up the bucket of milk and started from the barn.

Amity followed, hands clasped tight in front of her, saying to the back of his begrimed shirt, "A lot's happened since you left, John Clyde. I'm going to run for county school superintendent!"

"Goin' to run for county *what*?" he asked from

69

the corner of his mouth.

"I'll explain over supper. It's a near miracle, a grand opportunity. I'm going to need you more than ever. I'll be away a lot." She stopped on the path, declaring suddenly, plaintive, "I don't know what I'd do if you ever left here, John Clyde."

"Never said I was goin' nowhere," he said brusquely without turning.

"I appreciate that." She blinked several times and rubbed a finger under her tingling nose.

Later that night by lamplight, she wrote in her journal:

Dove's Nest, May 5th, 1887. A good day, barring the wind and a few unpleasant exchanges with some locals over my filing for public office. So be it. I have faith in my future and believe everything is going to work out. In fact, I'm as certain of that as I am that Mr. T. S. "Chalk" Holden has golden eyes, which he does.

She re-read the entry, a little surprised at herself for writing about a man she'd barely met. *Merciful heaven!* The man's *eyes?* She had more serious things to think about: bank payments, for instance. She had a next-to-impossible campaign to worry about. With a firm grip on her penholder, she dipped the steel point in the inkpot and drove a thick dark line through the last part of her entry. The image of the man's face particularly his nice, laughing eyes, however, was not as easy to rout from her mind.

Chapter Five

"Now who in the name of wonder is that?" Under a late-day sun, Amity wiped her forehead on the rumpled sleeve of her dress and shaded her eyes with her forearm. With her other dirty fist, she rubbed at the sharp needles of pain in the small of her back. In the distance, a horseman, outlined against the azure sky, churned up a small dust cloud heading toward her homestead. A drifter, maybe, or a peddler with gimcracks to sell from parfleches tied to his saddle. Well, she couldn't stand around gaping. She reached into the heavy canvas bag slung across from her left shoulder for a fistful of kafir corn kernels and dropped four into the impression she had made with her bare foot in the loose dark soil. Not that she wouldn't like a rest, but there was much to be done.

She looked forward to the day when she could afford a real corn planter, but for now she and John Clyde planted their kafir corn the old way. He'd plowed and harrowed the field when the ground thawed in March, before his horse hunt. During the past couple of days, he'd tilled again. Then he'd driven across the rich black field on a four-runner sled pulled by Ben, furrowing the entire field in rows four feet apart. Finally, he'd worked the field crosswise, forming a checkerboard. It was her job today to dig her bare toes into the cool, moist dirt and drop three or four kernels of seed at each intersection. John Clyde followed, tamping each hill in with a light stroke of his hoe.

Amity reached the end of the field, eyed the approaching rider warily, then turned her back and began a new row. She hoped the person coming was not important to her getting the vote for county school superintendent, because today she was anything but presentable. With a quick twist of her grimy toes she made a cup in the soil, dropped four kernels, and moved on. The tilled earth gave under her bare feet with each step.

It had been a week since she'd filed in Syracuse and it fretted her not to be out and about the county campaigning, but before she began she had to take these few days for work at home. If she and John Clyde completed the planting together, then he could handle much of the cultivation of their crops till harvest and she'd be able to campaign in earnest.

It was frustrating, wanting to be two places at once, but she couldn't allow matters to backslide here, either. After two years of endless, grueling toil she finally had forty-five of her one hundred sixty virgin acres under the plow. Down by the creek was a patch of oats she'd broadcast last fall. Near the house a one acre plot was planted with potatoes, turnips, squash, pumpkins, melons, and a few other vegetables she was attempting to grow. She'd learned that not everything that had grown lushly in Illinois could thrive here where it was hot, dry, and windy for weeks on end. Her twelve acres in corn *had* to thrive, as corn was the main staple for herself and her animals. The twenty-five acres north, planted with winter wheat, had recently turned into a lovely sweep of young green and, God and nature on her side, she'd have some to sell in the fall. The seven acres she was planting was for the broomcorn she hoped to sell in Wichita; the remainder of her land she would leave covered in the rich, native buffalo grass for pasture, along with hundreds of acres of unclaimed prairie she could use for free. Her first year, she had built up a decent-sized herd of cattle, started from calves and lame cows Texas drovers had given her as they passed through with their herds. Animals that couldn't possibly keep up on the long trail north to Montana were a nuisance to the cowboys and a bonanza for her. The long drives were all but ended, because much of Kansas had imposed a quarantine against Texas cattle. And last winter's blizzards had nearly wiped out the herd she had built up. She was practically starting over with only eight head. Fortunately, some of them were beginning to calve.

Amity had forgotten the rider until Zip barked sharply and John Clyde shouted, "Afternoon, stranger!"

74

Recognizing Chalk Holden's raspy, deep-timbered, "Afternoon!" Amity turned. Her hand went from her hair to brush madly at her sleeves and her apron-front, to no avail. The neckline of her dress was open at the throat and she quickly buttoned it. She hated being caught looking the way she did. Zip circled the approaching horse with plumed tail waving in friendly greeting, then threw himself to the cool earth and lay there, tongue dripping.

Feeling awkward and sounding more combative than she intended, Amity snapped, "An idle afternoon, Mr. Holden?"

Their visitor sat relaxed on his horse, grinning. Below the wide brim of his flat-crowned gray hat, his eyes held an amused look that ruffled her further. He hadn't worn the wire-rimmed spectacles today — and looked boyish without them. The familiar banner-red tie was in place at his tanned throat, contrasting with his dark suit. Taking off his hat, he said soft and quietly, "Amity, Miss Whitford."

John Clyde joined them, rubbing his long blade of a nose. "John Clyde Rossback," Amity introduced them on a quick breath. "This is the new editor and publisher of the *Syracuse Banner*, Mr. T. S. Holden. Lawyer Holden, too."

"Chalk Holden," he corrected. "The 'Chalk' came from my bad habit as a schoolboy of nibbling on my chalk stick while I was thinking. I guess I had a white line around my mouth much of the time. The other kids gave me the nickname and it stuck. Back home that's all I'm known by."

Holden swung down from the saddle to shake John Clyde's hand. His graceful movements exhibited a tensile strength, and Amity saw that he was a good head taller than John Clyde. He stooped to pat Zip's blue-gray head and the dog's tail thumped the ground joyfully.

Warmth and confusion filled Amity. If the man would just state his business, she might feel less uncomfortable.

"Welcome, Mr. Holden. How can we help you?" She kept her toes tucked under the draggletail hem of her dress. Her hand of its own volition, though, crept up again to tuck a dark brown tangle of hair behind her ear.

"Brought you a copy of this week's *Banner*." He unfastened his saddlebag and took out the newspaper.

"You needn't have! John Clyde or I would have made a trip to town in a few days to pick up our mail, but thank you." She slid the seed bag off her aching shoulder to the ground and took the newspaper. She opened it with a sharp crackle, and beamed when she saw her campaign essay, printed so soon, in the direct center of the front page. The boxed ad filled five column inches. Above the column she read: WHO WILL BE BEST FOR YOUR CHILD? And below: MISS AMITY WHITFORD! CANDIDATE FOR COUNTY SUPERINTENDENT ON THE INDEPENDENT TICKET. It was done. Most everybody in Hamilton County would now know what she was up to.

Perspiration popped out on her forehead. "It's quite . . . quite noticeable, isn't it?" she murmured. There was no way she could read what Chalk Holden had written about her with him looking on, but she spotted the piece in the upper left corner. Good heavens, he'd practically filled the front page with her! She folded the paper quickly and tucked it under her arm. Initially he hadn't seemed eager to back her, but this — "Thank you." His editorial was one thing, but giving such space to an advertisement was something else. "I want to pay you for the ad, Mr. Holden. How much is it?"

"How about supper and we can call it square?" He stroked the handsome moustache that adorned his equally handsome face. "There's matters I'd like to discuss with you, Miss Whitford."

"Oh?" Her bosom rose and fell as anxiety assailed her. "I thought you'd probably come for more than to deliver a paper." Her voice steadied. "It's about the campaign, I suppose? Some folks not taking it well that a young single woman has filed for an important post? Ridiculously, an office we women can't even vote on. Yet."

"I thought you'd want to hear the truth. Your plan to run has set off a hot fuss in town that's likely spreading across the county, the state, maybe. I'd say it's a good thing you're way out here where you can't get singed, till folks start gettin' accustomed to the idea."

"The only reason I haven't been back to town

is that I had some work to finish up here." She wanted him to know definitely, that she was in for the long run. "I'm not afraid of a fight." Once she might have been, but not anymore. Since she'd counted on trouble from the beginning, he hadn't exactly brought news. He obviously had more to tell her; so she invited him to join them. "Please, do stay."

"If we got company for supper, you'll have things to do up at the house, Missy," John Clyde said. "You go on ahead and I'll finish up here."

Chalk nodded at John Clyde. "I'll put my horse in the corral, if you don't mind, and come back and help." Leading his horse, Chalk fell in beside Amity as she strode toward the soddy. "Just thought you ought to know," he said, his voice gravelly yet soft, "your face is as pretty with dirt on it as without."

She turned pink and darted a look at him.

His smiled deepened. "Or maybe even prettier."

"That, Mr. Holden, is a baldfaced lie!" But she laughed as she gathered her skirts and ran to the house.

While she washed up and changed into fresh clothing, regrets chased one after another through Amity's mind. She wished there were time for a real bath, time to wash her hair and fix it properly. She wished now that she or John Clyde had made the planned trip to town to buy supplies. There was hardly enough in the larder to prepare a decent meal for themselves, let alone company.

Still, she'd had beans simmering at the back of the cookstove since noon, and she could roll salt pork in cornmeal to fry it. Then from the meat drippings, a tad of flour, and Flora's milk she could make streaked gravy to serve on hot biscuits. She wished she had fresh garden sass but her vegetable garden was barely coming up, let alone ready.

Amity searched her cupboard shelves, and found a lone can of pears. She'd spoon pears into dessert dishes, add a splash of Flora's cream and a dash of nutmeg. She had the flour, buttermilk, sorghum molasses, and spices to make a somersault pie like Mama used to make in Cairo, but she didn't know if her guest would be staying long enough for pie. She decided to make the pie anyway, and set out the ingredients, taking her rolling pin from the cupboard drawer.

Chalk Holden surely was handsome! Just looking at him made her silly heart race. Since meeting him and being exposed to his warm personality and, yes, his attention, too, she felt as if sunshine had come into her life. But that wasn't what made her want to look better and prepare a nice meal, she thought as she gently cut lard into a crockery bowl of flour for the pie crust. She knew he'd done her an enormous favor by supporting her candidacy in his paper, and by printing such an impressive advertisement for her. Few men would have the courage to support a woman seeking public office! He'd given her a wonderful start on her campaign and she simply owed him in return.

It was dusk and she was just taking the cinnamon-fragrant pie from the oven when the men, finished with planting kafir and choring, came in. John Clyde went directly to the washbench, and with the long-handled granite dipper, splashed water into the basin and began to wash up. Chalk's eyes leisurely took in everything and he sniffed with an appreciative grin on his face. Stroking his moustache, he said, "What a bargain I made!" He followed John Clyde to the basin.

Amity smiled her thanks, and handed him a clean muslin towel. She went back to putting the food on the table, moving the bowl of steaming gravy a trifle to make room for the biscuits. The platter of sizzling pork, she placed next to the beans. Chalk Holden's eyes seemed to follow her every move, bold and thoughtful. Or possibly he was simply hungry, and she was imagining things.

John Clyde looked surprised when he finally noticed the table, embellished with lace tablecloth, Mama's rose china, glassware and silver, and the potted geranium she'd moved from the window well to center the table, but all he said was, "Looks like Missy's put herself out t'night. Got a good appetite, Mr. Holden? Amity's a mighty fine cook." He patted his stringy middle.

"You bet," Chalk Holden answered, seriously, bowing as he pulled out a chair and held it for Amity.

Maybe she'd gone a bit overboard but she'd enjoyed every minute of the preparation; she would enjoy being a hostess more often if she weren't always so busy. Life in Cairo had been very social, and fun. Play parties, church, soliciting Temperance pledges, concerts in the town square, dances, constant visiting back and forth with neighbors and friends. Young men coming to call on the innocent girl she was then. "Please sit, Mr. Holden, and help yourself."

Once they had begun to eat, she asked, "There was something more you wanted to tell me?"

Chalk broke a biscuit and watched the steam rise from it before spreading it with butter. Above the soft clink of silver and clatter of dishes he told her, "Since you're the *Banner*'s favored candidate, I felt it was up to me to give you an idea of what you're up against in the race. Some of it's nonsense, some serious."

"Oh?" Amity said, uneasy again. "What's this all about?"

"*Who* is this all about," he corrected, and explained, "Thisba Strout, to begin with. I've a sneaking suspicion she wouldn't mind being county superintendent, herself, but she doesn't have the nerve — to say nothing of the education — to try for what she feels is properly men's work. Instead, she's chosen to spread the idea around town that you're a 'young bit of fluff' who couldn't begin to handle the responsibilities the right way."

"Really!" *Dear Thisba.* Well, what did she expect? They'd never got along. Amity was miffed, but she maintained her composure. "If that's all, I can —"

81

"There's more. It seems a cousin of hers, a fellow named Seymour Purdue, from Finney County, is planning to run, too. He came in on the train yesterday morning and moved in with the Strouts. I thought you ought to know."

"Doesn't a candidate have to live in the county for at least six months to be eligible for election?" From the corner of her eye she saw John Clyde yawn as she waited for Chalk Holden's answer.

"He's lived here before. Now they're saying he was just visiting in Finney County and Syracuse is his home."

"That's balderdash." She sighed. "There's another man running for the office, too, correct?"

John Clyde scraped his plate loudly, getting a last bit of gravy. Chalk looked at him for a moment, then went on, "Amos Taylor. He is a strong contender with a big following. Amos is a retired judge, a well-respected man who's had the best interests of this part of the country at heart since he came in '73. Of course, he's getting a little long in the tooth. I don't know much about Purdue, Mrs. Strout's cousin, except *what she's trumpeting* to anybody who'll listen."

"Which is?"

"Oh, that he's from a fine Virginia family, his father a Civil War hero on the side of the South. That he was educated at the College of William and Mary and came to Kansas as a surveyor for the railroad a few years ago, then decided to stay. He's had some years teaching, too."

Amity's mouth dried. "Doesn't sound too good for me."

Chalk shook his head. "No, it doesn't, but keep in mind Amos Taylor's age. And from what I saw of Seymour Purdue, he's a wheezy, oversized peacock. The man must weigh three hundred pounds. He has trouble getting around even with use of a cane. My first impression is he's a self-important, empty windbag."

"I hope you're right," she said slowly. His estimation relieved her somewhat. A second thought occurred to her. "Early on, you worried about my running, even though it was originally your suggestion. Do you feel differently, now? Do you feel that I have . . . a chance?"

"I *had* misgivings," he admitted, "but I think you're right for the job. Otherwise, you'd have gotten an inch and a half back by the classifieds instead of the front page of my paper. I got your essay and was mighty impressed. You'll see when you read what I wrote that I used some of your material again in my interview piece. It reads pretty strong. I found it interesting that your father was a schoolboard member for many years in Illinois?" Amity nodded. "And that you plan to implement many of the ideas that proved successful for him in Cairo schools? It'll go down well, since you're a young woman, that you're following an older person's, particularly your father's, precepts."

"True, but I have many ideas of my own, some of which my father wouldn't have agreed with at all," she insisted. "For example, I feel every child needs an education, must have the opportunity to learn. My father felt some 'ornery whippersnappers,' as he called them, were beyond educating — useless flotsam. That principle may be true in a few rare cases, but I think it's accepted more than it should be." She leaned forward. "And I think discipline needs close examination. When I was in school I saw teachers beat students for the least infraction, with the parents' permission because it was the instructor's 'right' and the student 'must have needed' the whipping or wouldn't have gotten it. Often a beating left the child with welts and bruises, and sometimes broken bones." Her manner dared him to contradict her. "Because our future lies in their hands, I'm going to be on the side of the children in a lot of ways. I expect I'll make some enemies."

Chalk whistled softly. "You will. Most parents and teachers feel that sparing the rod spoils the child. Getting the children to come to school won't be easy either. There are a good number who've never attended school a day in their lives and nobody cares, least of all their parents, who make use of their labor at home."

"There'll be changes if I get in! I intend to advocate nonviolent punishment, and I'm for universal education. It's the only answer to civilize this raw country."

"May I quote you?" There was teasing admiration in Chalk Holden's eyes and a soft smile played about his mouth as he took the piece of pie Amity handed him on a delicate china plate. "The two gents have more power behind them, but I want to see you win. It's going to be an interesting brawl," he added, his eyes shining as he leaned back, surveying her. "How soon will you really get into the fray?"

She looked at him for a long time, then stated quietly, "Mr. Holden, how near is the morning?"

"You have a plan?" One eyebrow rose in question as he took a bite of pie. Pleasure wreathed his face when he tasted it. He closed his eyes and chewed slowly. Another, larger forkful quickly followed.

She clasped her hands under her chin, gratified that he enjoyed her cooking. "Of course I have ideas. I think about it all the time. Although there are things I must dig into more deeply." She smiled. "I guess along with everyone else, you'll have to wait to see what my strategy is."

"Up to you," he said, finishing his pie with relish. "Well," he pushed back from the table a few minutes later. "It's time I started for home." He looked around in surprise. "Where's John Clyde? I didn't notice him leave —"

She laughed. "I think he was bored with our talk. He slipped out a while ago for his bunk in the barn."

"Figures, I suppose." He stood up. "Thank you for a fine meal, and a very nice evening, Miss Whitford."

"You may call me Amity. I want to express my appreciation again for all you've done."

He circled behind to pull out her chair for her. "Anything else I can do to help?" He was standing so close behind her that she could smell his spicy shaving soap and feel the warmth of his body. Her blood hummed in her ears, and she stood up from her chair with a jerk. "N-n-n-no, nothing. You've done enough, thank you."

A look of regret shadowed his face, but he told her, "Best of luck, then. You're on the right track!" He lifted her hand, placed it on his palm, and smothered it with the other.

"It's only just begun, Mr. Holden," she answered breathlessly, leaving her hand in the both of his for a second.

"Call me Chalk. Yes, only begun." They were standing very close. His eyes were shiny with emotion. Her eyes fastened on his mouth, the entrancing crease in the center of his full lower lip, as he told her, "You're a beautiful woman, Amity Whitford. If a man asked if he could call on you, what would you say?"

"If a man asked right now, I'd have to say I'm sorry." At his dark, hungry expression she quickly added, "I'm going to be very, very busy, you understand."

"All right." His voice was husky. "But be warned, with so lovely a woman a man might never give up. I'll ask again."

When she heard his horse's hoofbeats leaving the yard, Amity cracked the door and looked out into the moonlit night after him.

Her heart ached as she watched Chalk Holden's broad shoulders moving away into the dark. She pressed her cheek against the doorframe. After a while she got out her journal and wrote, *Dove's Nest, May 12, 1887. Had my life been different, I might allow feelings for a certain gentleman to grow. Alas, I'm afraid he would feel quite differently if he knew all about me. And the life I've planned cannot include another for a long time.* She rested the pen a moment and then took it up again. *What if someone from Beaconsfield should visit Thisba, someone who knows about me? That could ruin everything. I've been lucky to be able to keep to myself for two years, but I can't afford to any longer. If I do, I'll lose all I have from lack of money. A plague on it. I have to take the risk. There's no other choice.*

Chapter Six

"Git!" The blue muzzle of an army revolver was pointed directly at Amity. The angry woman's sharply knuckled hand waved it under Amity's nose.

Her dugout was the first sign of human habitation Amity had come upon after endless hours of driving the lonely sandhills south of Syracuse, almost into the Indian nations. Amity stood rigid, too hot, weary, and scared to move. She'd arrived only moments earlier, asked for, and, kindly enough, been given a drink of water from the well in the dusty yard. The two women had exchanged names. The slat-thin brown mummy of a woman with tangled, graying brown hair was Liddy Dusky. Amity had begun to explain her mission, and she had thought they were getting along just fine when everything suddenly changed. The moment she mentioned school, the gun appeared, glinting in the woman's claw, pulled out from her voluminous calico skirts. Mrs. Dusky's seamed face had turned hard as a hickory nut.

Amity shivered. Surely, the woman wouldn't kill her in cold blood! She had her own pistol, a castoff relic John Clyde insisted she carry everywhere, but it was in the wagon under the edge of the seat. And a thingamajig on her single-action colt revolver was broken; the cylinder had to be turned by hand. She wasn't about to get into a shootout with this woman, anyway.

"Ma'am, I mean you no harm, I only want to talk," Amity tried again, praying Mrs. Dusky's knotty finger wouldn't squeeze the trigger. The woman seemed to be alone at the dugout, but approaching, Amity had seen a half-grown youngster hacking away at weeds in a scraggly patch of corn and another digging a hole for a dog that lay dead at the far edge of the yard. Some distance from the dugout to the west, a thin little girl herded half a dozen lean cows and calves with a stick. The youngsters had only stared when she waved. "Education is particularly needed in rural areas like this. Please let me explain —"

"We ain't got nothing more to say, one to the other," the woman insisted, steadying the pistol near Amity's face.

A chill ran down Amity's spine, but she held her ground. "The children need a school. The nearest is Little Bear School, fifteen miles from here, too far. Your children need a teacher and books. I want to see that you have a school for them and I've come to —"

"Learning is for the lazy and the weak," Mrs. Dusky barked through tight lips. "My children is honest workers and they'll always be. An' besides, her children is all a widder-woman has. Ain't nobody takin' 'em away."

"I — I see, Mrs. Dusky. I understand. You need them. But they could help you so much more, make better lives for all of you, if they only had a few hours of book learning each day. Believe me, please!"

"I want you to go. Now. Git off my land."

Amity took a few steps back from the icy, threatening gleam that glittered in the woman's eyes. "All right. I'm going . . . for now." If she did become school superintendent, it would be her job to do something for these children, and to convince their mother of the necessity of schooling. "I'm sorry if we got off on the wrong foot," Amity called, peeking cautiously over her shoulder as she continued toward her waiting wagon where Ben waited, tossing his head and shaking his tail at flies. "I'd like for us to be friends. I know how it is to be a woman alone, so if you ever need anything at all, Mrs. Dusky, I hope you won't hesitate to ask. My place is on Plumb Creek, northwest of Syracuse about eight miles."

"I didn't ask for nothin'. I only ask you to leave and don't come back."

Amity's shoulders sagged, but she nodded. She climbed into the wagon, shook out the reins, and started off. Her shoulder blades fairly tingled from Mrs. Dusky's steely stare. As she passed the boy digging the hole, she called in soft sympathy, "Dog get sick?"

"Rattlesnake bit 'im." He ducked his dirty, tear-stained face and went back to digging.

Amity started to pull up to help him, but the movement so frightened the boy, she was sure he'd flee, and there was still the mother with a gun leveled at her back. She lifted the reins again and drove on. The soft *shush* of the boy's shovel in the sandy soil echoed in her mind for a long time.

Despite such occasional negative reactions, with every day that she spent meeting them, Amity found her heart growing closer to the people — particularly the children — who struggled to make a home in the godforsaken sandhills south of the Arkansas River and the rest of Hamilton county.

In the weeks following Chalk Holden's visit, she had set out often on horseback or wagon to campaign around the county in an ever-widening circuit. With her own farm as compass point, she began by visiting close neighbors, then further-flung ranches and desolate little homesteads on the prairie north of the Arkansas River, and now south of it.

Standing in their crude kitchens, or forlorn yards — if the people wouldn't allow her inside — she explained her aims for improved schooling for their children and better conditions for their teachers. She asked for their votes. She was treated to the full range of responses; disbelief, disinterest, and open hostility, such as she'd gotten from the widow, Mrs. Dusky, but she had received a lot of kindly interest, too.

Despite everything, the more she talked with

people, the more determined Amity became to do what she could about education for these families. The fact that she'd be earning a salary without which she couldn't survive took on surprisingly small importance in her mind. With every visit, she was all the more convinced she'd found her calling.

One time she helped deliver a new calf in the barn; often, she found herself standing in the field beside a halted team and plow, or by the side of the road next to a buggy or, in a few more fortunate times, seated with the family at their dinner tables, talking hard. Again and again she attempted to wear down tough resistance with quiet, confident argument: A woman, herself in particular, was the best bet for Hamilton County school superintendent and they must vote for her!

Sometimes her sojourns took her miles from home and she was forced to stay the night with whoever would give her a place to sleep. Occasionally she shared a real bed with the women and children of the household. At one stop she was given an extra blanket to add to her own quilt and was shown to the barn to spend the night in a bin of oats! Another time, which she hoped folks would never know about, she'd slept alone under the stars on the open prairie. The most to be said about that bed was that she had plenty of room.

Yesterday, after examining the meagerly furnished Little Bear School, once an abandoned bachelor soddy on Little Bear Creek, she'd spent the night with the teacher's parents. Amity knew that most of the schools would be closed for the season to allow students to help out at home with the coming of summer crops, but she wanted to see the school buildings, such as they were, and to meet the teachers and ask for their support. Lecky Lloyd, sixteen-year-old teacher for Little Bear School, had turned out to be a lively, outgoing country girl just biding her time teaching until she found a husband. But she was friendly and likable. Her parents had not only put Amity up; Lecky's father had good-heartedly promised to vote for her, too.

She felt encouraged that the Lloyds had already read about her in Chalk's paper and she decided to place small political ads in other newspapers around the county, at her own expense. And if those editors would write favorable editorials about her, too, it could only help.

How strange the air feels, Amity thought, traveling on through the miles of wildflower-dotted sandhills. After she had said goodbye to the Lloyds, following a hearty breakfast, she'd stepped outside to find a sweet morning, clear and soft with sparkling dew and the song of many meadowlarks. But then, as the sun mounted toward its zenith, the still air grew insufferably heavy and hot. For hours, there hadn't been a cloud in the sky. No tree or rock to offer shade; only miles and miles of sandhills, divided by dips and draws covered with flowers and grasses, which were being laid flat suddenly by a rising, hungry wind. She welcomed the coolness, though; it was easier to breathe. She bumped along, thinking of the long miles home, wondering what she might encounter on the way. There was nothing to see but cattle grazing, flecks of cinnamon brown in the far distance, and a coyote watching from several yards off the trail.

John Clyde had a fit every time she left home alone, but she felt able to take care of herself. Besides, she needed him to stay and do the work there.

Much later, the skin on the back of Amity's neck began to crawl with a premonition. She looked back over her shoulder and saw a black cloud in the southeast, moving rapidly. She watched it nervously to make sure that it was not funnel-shaped, a tornado. It grew darker, fast. She snapped the reins in an effort to make Ben hurry. All at once a cloud of dust rose up and swirled around them, whipping them, blocking her sight. "Giddyup, Ben!" she shouted and cracked the reins again. She looked for a drainage cut, or draw, to pull into, where she could stop and wait out the storm under her wagon. But there was none, the terrain now abysmally flat.

When the rain came, it came not in drops but in a sudden, blinding, horizontal sheet. She was instantly drenched to the skin. Rain would help their crops, but John Clyde would be frantic about her if the storm was like this at home.

The air grew colder; the rain turned to icy

sleet, then hard, pounding hail. She could feel Ben throw himself into harness, his legs churning into a lurching trot in an effort to escape. Bouncing hard on the wagon seat, she held the reins fast in her chilled fingers as plum-sized hailstones pelted down, stinging and hurting her head, shoulders, and legs in a hundred places. She cowered low, shivering, and peered ahead into the dense, somber storm, praying they wouldn't overturn as they rocked on.

Chapter Seven

Amity stood in the yard and surveyed the damage, feeling mighty cranky from having slept in a sodden bed after she'd arrived home in the middle of the night. At dawn she'd brought out carpets and bedding to dry in the sun, then cleaned up the muddy mess in her house where the sod roof leaked. Her vegetable garden looked chewed up by the storm. Chewed up and spit back at me she thought darkly. No fresh food — starvation again visiting her doorstep! She watched green leaf-bits dance on the soft prairie wind, which ironically, lifted them toward a rainbow in the blue sky. Part of her wheat and all of the broomcorn was beaten flat. Though tears were close, she announced with bitter determination, "We'll try to save what we can and replant the rest, and pray for a long season and later-than-usual frosts."

A few feet away, John Clyde agreed with a deep sigh, scratching a ropey wrist. "Ain't nothin' fer it but to do it all over again."

"We can go further afield to look for wild prairie hay that hasn't been damaged to cut. Mark it as ours by cutting a swathe around it." Neighbors respected such laying claim, as she respected their marked patches. Many of them had been hurt by the hailstorm that had struck the county hit and miss. The bitterest pill was that with all the work at the homestead, her campaign would have to be put off *again*. But, as John Clyde said, they had no choice but to replant. She turned to him with a thin smile. "Let's get to work." She pulled Papa's hat down tighter on her head. When situations looked particularly difficult and she needed to figure things out, or she felt she wanted a man's insight, she would put on Papa's gray, wide-brimmed slouch hat. She considered the hat her good-luck charm, though it had yet to bring her good luck enough to count. Maybe this time . . .

The first planting had used up most of the seed saved from last year's crops, as well as that purchased in town. Still, Amity managed to scrounge a bit from each of the seed kegs in the barn, which were kept tightly closed against invasion by mice. Replanting began. The showing in her fields would be picayune this time compared to earlier expectations, but better that than none, she reflected grimly.

One evening, she wrote in her journal: *I vow to abide these days of toil and tribulation and loneliness . . . or die trying.* But mostly she was too tired to write a thing. The following dawn she was up helping John Clyde to dig an underground silo out behind the small barn. The barn would store only so much feed, beyond John Clyde's

97

quarters and stalls for their horses and Ben. The silo would hold chopped corn stalks and leaves, additional fodder to feed her stock in winter and the driest part of summer. If there *was* a corn crop . . .

The next afternoon, as Amity was filling a basket with wind-dried clothing from the line, Chalk Holden rode into the yard. Her spirits, mostly low of late, took a leap. She carefully folded a flour-sack tea towel, then called out, "Hello! Out and about on business, Mr. Holden?"

"Chalk," he corrected in a friendly growl, "plain Chalk." He leaned forward in the saddle, while his horse shifted beneath him. "On my way home," he told her. "Some folks over west needed my help drawin' up a will. Thought I'd drift out of my way a bit and ask how you're doing with the campaign."

She had about ten seconds worth of news on that score, but she didn't want him to leave so soon. "If you're not in a hurry," she said, ignoring his question, "I can offer you a slice of raisin pie, and coffee."

In the shadows of his hat, Chalk's teeth gleamed in a wide grin. "Nobody but a fool would be in that big of a hurry." He swung down from the saddle.

On the way to the house he asked again how she was doing. "Looks like you've had to do some replanting. Hell of a hailstorm these parts got, wasn't it?"

"Yes," she said, smiling over her shoulder, "it was. But we ranchers have to expect that sort of thing out here, and learn to live with it. I'm managing fine." Of course, her visitor had a lot to do with how bright her day had become, she thought a few minutes later as she set out cups and cut their pie. It got so lonely sometimes. She was more than ready for a long, neighborly chat, about *anything*.

The new green of her plantings had hardly begun to show in the dark earth when the fight against weeds was on, a dawn to dark battle, until she felt the hoe handle was grown to her palm. Fresh blisters turned to hardened calluses as she hacked away under an unmerciful sun. Before her blade the enemy fell: woolly loco. Whitish gray, it was one of the first plants to appear in the spring, and toxic to her animals if left to grow. Thistle, falseboneset, wild buck-wheat, and bundleflower. Creamy poisonvetch, which could cause blind staggers or alkalid disease in her critters if the weed was allowed to stay.

Each morning and evening, framing her day in the fields and in the house, she did her barn chores: letting her hens out of their coop to forage by day, penning them again at night to keep them from marauding coyotes, milking Flora and tending the other cattle, often going out to find them when they strayed. Meals had to be cooked every day, of course. She did the washing every few days or they'd have had nothing to wear. Seen to when she could fit them in were the mending, baking, soap-making. The house was kept tidy by scrubbing tables and cupboards down with dishwater after she'd finished the dishes, and after supper, sweeping out the dust that would only blow in again the next day. Removing the protective fringed shawl, she dusted Mama's small mahogany organ 'til she could see her face in the wood, but had no time to play it.

Two weeks into June her wheat was ripe and had to be cut before there was danger of the grain shattering in the head. There was no way she and John Clyde could cut and thresh the nearly twenty acres that had survived the hail in time. And the wheat looked the most likely to make a cash crop.

A professional threshing crew was the best answer. Grimly, she considered selling off a cow or two to pay a threshing crew but decided in the end that if she wanted to build up her herd after last winter's losses, she couldn't sell any of them off now.

Allowing herself not another minute of debate, Amity packed a trunkful of precious possessions that had been Mama's, mostly silver and china, and drove to the Syracuse bank with them. "These are my collateral for a loan to pay a wheat threshing crew," she told Banker Strout. "I'd like you to hold them, please, till my wheat is in and I've sold what I don't keep for seed. I'll use the profit to pay the loan and reclaim my mother's things."

Nodding, Henry agreed. "M-marvelous ingenuity, ah, um, huum, indeed."

On the way home, with the money in her handbag, she stopped at Joe Samuel's ranch where a vagabond crew was already at work harvesting his wheat. They promised to come to Dove's Nest as soon as they could, but the Bergen place was next. It was the best she could do, and just working out the details gave her intense satisfaction.

Falling into bed bone-weary that night, Amity considered her foolishness in filing for public office. As if there were time for it! But the idea of running for county school superintendent wasn't just a notion; it was something she wanted badly to do. If only a break would come, so she could go out and campaign, talk to folks.

It wasn't until the Fourth of July — her wheat cut, shocked, and threshed, and the bank paid — that the chance finally came.

On the morning of the Fourth, a thin yellow ribbon of daylight showed along the eastern horizon as she made her way through the dark yard to her wagon and briskly climbed up. She settled herself and grasped the lines, thinking ahead to the Syracuse Independence Day celebration. Today was a rare chance to speak with folks by the hundreds. Most of Hamilton County would be there. She couldn't afford to miss it; she could yet regain the time she'd lost. She was eager, too, for a day of relaxation and enjoyment.

"Promise me you'll ride in later?" She looked down at John Clyde, who stowed her picnic basket under the seat behind her. "The heavens won't fall if we leave off work one day to have a good time. Though —" she sighed, "— the potato bugs will likely have a field day in my absence, without me here to pick them off the plants."

He peered up at her, grinning patiently. "I said I'd come in, an' I will, soon's the chores are finished."

"Shouldn't I stay and help?" she asked for the tenth time. "That good-for-nothing red rooster of mine was missing last night when I went to coop the chickens. If he ranges far enough from the house, a coyote is going to get him. I hope you can find him right away. And, John Clyde, let the cream rise on this morning's milking. It's time I made butter; we're nearly out." She felt guilty giving him orders but was anxious to be gone, too. "I could change to my work clothes again." She looked down at her blue French gingham frock trimmed with embroidered batiste, a holdover from lovely picnics in Cairo. She looked back at him. "The two of us together could make short work of what needs doing —"

"Missy, will you please git? You're only holdin' the both of us up. I'll be right along, but you be careful, hear? There'll be a wild bunch in town today for the doins', cuttin' up and bein' crazy. 'Sides that, though they claim the killin' over the county seat is done, I don't put no stock in just say-so. Men, even good men, will ignore the laws and draw blood when they want somethin' bad as that. You take care of yourself till I get there."

She shook a finger but smiled. "Don't start that 'woman alone' talk again. A woman alone is what I happen to be and I know what to do. If I see trouble coming, I'll simply sidestep it as a man of any intelligence would." She understood what he was talking about, though. Two weeks ago, two judges and the clerk of the election in Kendall had been arrested for forging poll books in the previous November's vote. An armed mob had promptly broken them out of jail. Kendall was not accepting new county lines and it appeared the terrible tug-of-war for the county seat would continue.

"Keep your gun handy, anyways," he warned in a low growl, his thin wedge-shaped face solemn. He took a long draw on his cigarette.

Amity laughed. "If it makes you feel better, I will. But there'll be hundreds of decent folk in town today, too, and I'll be fine."

Suddenly, there was a distant *boom* from the direction of Syracuse, and she clapped her hands. "They're firing the Independence Day salute!" As a child on the Fourth of July, she had been the first one out of bed, rushing outside in her nightgown at sunrise to hear the Civil War cannon go off in the Cairo town square. Though in Syracuse it was likely gunpowder being exploded on an anvil. Yes. She listened very carefully and in a moment heard a fainter *boom* coming from the community of Carlisle a few miles east of Syracuse, then another from the west, the community of Lee. "Oh, John Clyde, hurry, it's going to be such fun."

"I'll be there soon's I can," he muttered, getting the last word in as he waved her away and stumped off toward the barn. Zip, tail wagging, trotted at his heels.

Her good spirits held, and after a few miles, passing a neighbor's wagon on the road to town, Amity waved gaily. "Good morning, Mrs. Bergen, Mr. Bergen. Children." They waved back, calling "halloo." Although she rarely saw them, she liked Able and Marta Bergen. A year after her arrival, they had come from Norway to stake a claim four miles northeast of her own. They were good, honest, hard-working folk. She saw with a smile that they continued to multiply; Marta Bergen held a small blanketed bundle in her arms. All sizes of flaxen-haired children sprouted in the back of the wagon among picnic baskets, rolled blankets, and other essentials for a holiday. Able Bergen had fastened little American flags to his driving team's harness.

She had her own extra baggage. A blanket to sit on to watch this evening's fireworks, an extra dress to change into for tonight's dance. It would be a long hot day and the gingham would be soiled by then. She'd known young women to change three or four times at lengthy social affairs.

Big farm wagons filled with laughing, chattering families came off the side roads and the blind lanes onto the main road as Amity drove along. There were buggies driven by sedate older folk or courting couples. Cowboys on horseback tipped their hats to Amity as they trotted by. Most wore guns, but she couldn't see anything unusual in that, doubting anyway that they concerned themselves with political matters. God willing, the county-seat tussle would be set aside at least for today.

When Amity reached town, the procession behind her stretched back for miles. She eyed Chalk's office as she drove by, but like most of the businesses along the windy, dusty street, it was closed. Out front a flag waved in the morning sunshine. Chalk had not been out to the homestead since he'd come by that second time to discuss her campaign. Likely she'd see him today, and they'd get a chance to talk. In fact, if he didn't find her, she'd find him.

Amity drove to the cottonwood grove by the river, where she unhitched the wagon. Sawhorses and lumber were being unloaded from wagons and men were already setting up long tables for the noon feast under the trees. She waved at Arthur Lloyd who was tending a crusty brown side of beef that had been cooking juicily most of the night over a huge bed of coals. Goodness, did that smell good. It was certainly generous of him to donate the beef today, considering last winter's losses. His family had been kind to her, putting her up the night before the hailstorm. His daughter, Lecky, would be one of her teachers if she won the November vote. "I hope you'll be able to join the festivities, Mr. Lloyd," she called out to him. He grinned and waved her on.

She walked the half mile back to town and took a second, light breakfast of jam-biscuits and tea at the Dunnington Hotel, keeping watch on the teeming street from the hotel window. Families were everywhere. A couple of times she started at the explosive crackle of a string of fire-crackers.

In the lobby later she spotted motherly Meda Ginsbach, whom she'd met on her campaign rounds. Meda taught from her ranch kitchen on Shirley Creek. "Nice to see you again, Mrs. Ginsbach."

The woman's round face lit up and her hand affectionately clasped Amity's arm. "So nice to see you, Miss Whitford." She pointed toward a gaunt, bearded man talking with another farmer a few feet away. "I make my Joseph vote for you. I know you'll do us good, be right leader for our schools."

"Thank you, Mrs. Ginsbach! I hope if I win I'll be able to get you a real school built."

"*Ya!*"

After a few minutes of conversation, Amity moved on with a smiling nod and continued to mingle with both the strangers and familiar folk that filled the lobby. Many out-of-towners had chosen to congregate there. She introduced herself to people she'd not met before. In each instance, she took time to visit, talking about the day's festivities to come, the weather, crops, and, whenever the opportunity arose, education and her candidacy. The women were powerless to help her

106

by actually voting, but, like Meda Ginsbach, they could influence the men, and she was not about to ignore the opportunity to sway them if she could.

She was just leaving the hotel when a bubbly voice assailed her. "There you are, my dear!" With a saccharine smile, Thisba Strout in rustling blue silks and heavy honeysuckle scent rushed at her with outstretched arms.

Amity waited. The woman's personality could be so mercurial. "I beg your pardon, Mrs. Strout?" she said cautiously.

"Yes, you, my dear!" She slipped an arm cozily through Amity's. "Some of my lady friends and I would like you to join us today. My," she said, fanning herself with a pretty hand, "it's getting very warm, already." Her face was indeed quite pink and her saffron ringlets were plastered to her perspiring forehead and temples.

"Join you?"

"We have a nice spot picked out to watch the parade together. We can chat, don't you see? We've never really got to know one another, have we?" Thisba nodded to her own question, while Amity listened in amazement as the woman rattled on. "I'm hearing some very nice things about you, Miss Whitford, from every point of the county. It's time you used some of those talents you've kept secret for your community here in Syracuse."

"But I'm —" Amity began, then she said, "I see." Her mail in recent weeks had contained a sudden raft of invitations. Requests for her to join a literary study club, a current-events club, a cemetery association, a world peace group, a quilting bee, and others she couldn't recall in the stupefaction of the moment. She had planned to accept some of the invitations as time allowed in the future. The literary study club particularly interested her. She realized now that Thisba Strout was no doubt behind the missives, but she hadn't the faintest idea what the woman was up to. Unless — in some way Thisba was trying to divert her from her mission of becoming county school superintendent.

She tested Thisba in her sweetest voice, patting the woman's hand on her arm, "Why, thank you! I'd love to join you and your friends. What a nice opportunity to discuss the school superintendency, and ask the women to influence their menfolks to vote for me."

Thisba's face darkened, and she said, "That is one of the things we'd like to speak to you about, Miss Whitford. Women do have their place in creating good for the community, their fellow human family, but I don't think —"

"Really? We belong in chatty little women's clubs, but not in the political arena? Mrs. Strout, I will do whatever good I can, however and anywhere *I* choose." She removed Thisba's hand from her arm, still smiling. How dare the woman treat her like an imbecile. Actually believing she could "show her the right way" by admitting her into her women's groups — behaving as though she were saving Amity from herself! Or vice versa? Protecting the community from Amity? "I'm going to be Hamilton County's next school superintendent, Mrs. Strout. You needn't try to talk me out of it!"

"Well, I never!" Thisba sputtered. "So brazen! You can't possibly win. I'm just trying to save you embarrassment."

Amity bolted into the throngs on the sidewalk, her face flaming, feeling she'd strike the woman if she didn't get away from her. Ahead of her, a huge fat man was shaking the hand of everyone he met as he swayed toward her on the sidewalk, leaning onto his cane. Cousin Seymour Purdue from Finney County, no doubt. Coming abreast, he reached for Amity's hand. His pudgy fingers were sweaty as she gripped them in her own, made strong by two years of farming. She shook his hand so hard his eyebrows tented and he winced. She shouted maliciously, before he could say anything, "I'm Amity Whitford, running for Hamilton County school superintendent and I'll expect your vote, *sir!*" She showed him her teeth in a brittle smile.

She whipped on up the street, but a look over her shoulder seconds later caught Thisba pointing at her and the huge well-dressed man shaking his head.

When she heard the march begin, Amity chose a spot as far from Thisba and her cousin as possible to watch the parade that was just starting up. A winding line of men, women, and children straggled up the dusty street, led by a flag bearer and raucous, off-tune band, playing what she finally recognized as "The Star-Spangled Banner."

She laughed with delight when she saw that John Clyde had arrived. Proudly dressed in his tattered war uniform, he'd joined the band and was playing his kazoo. She shouted and waved at him. He grinned, stepping smartly in time with the drums, the flute, and trumpet, and some makeshift instruments — barn and kitchen tools that served as cymbals, tambourines, kettledrums, and castanets. "Wonderful," she whispered with a smile. "Wonderful."

"Good morning, Amity," a voice rasped deeply in her ear.

She was afraid to turn for fear the joy rising uninvited in her heart would show too well. "Good morning, Mr. Holden."

"Chalk, remember?"

"Chalk."

"Was that you I saw flying up the street like a whirlwind a while ago?" He chuckled. "I was a little afraid for other people on the street."

Her face turned red, and she said defensively, "It wasn't my intention to look ridiculous."

"No, you looked beautiful." His voice rumbled softly.

"Th-thank you. Thisba Strout makes me so angry that I forgot myself, I'm sorry to say."

"Ignore her."

"That's very difficult." She played with the ribbons of her bonnet and looked straight ahead.

"She has clout, but so do you in your own way, Amity."

He sounded so sincere she couldn't help but feel better. For a long time she remained silent, then commented, "It's a very nice parade, isn't it?" Passing them now was a wagon decorated in red, white, and blue bunting, a float carrying as many little girls as there were states, dressed in white with sashes and caps of red, white, and blue, representing each state in the nation. "Aren't they adorable? The Goddess of Liberty is especially beautiful." She nodded at the girl in the front of the wagon, dressed in flowing white and wearing a silver, starry crown on her long saffron hair.

"That's Doridee Strout."

"I know." She considered telling him that she was acquainted with Thisba and her daughter from the past, but that would lead to other things. She bit her tongue and said nothing.

His hand grazed her elbow. "I'd like to sit with you at the noon dinner, Amity."

She hesitated. "People — might think — we're together."

"Is that so terrible?"

"It might be, for my campaign. I don't want tongues wagging. There are very strict rules of propriety for a school leader. If I want to win, I'd need to be a model for my teachers, and my students."

"Maybe people will see me as simply the local newspaper publisher backing my candidate, noth-

111

ing more," Chalk said easily.

"Perhaps," she began, feeling awkward, "but —" She was cut off as Chalk suddenly swung about and caught the arm of a balding, friendly-faced gentleman strolling by. "William Richards, from over at Coolidge, right? Bill, I want you to meet the next Hamilton County school superintendent, Miss Amity Whitford. Keep her in mind come November."

"I doubt that'll be a problem." Smiling, he took in the attractive girl, and shook her hand, then Chalk's. He said to her, "I think you met my twin daughters, Ina and Ona Richards, both teachers in the Coolidge district?"

"Of course! I remember Ina and Ona very well. They told me how miserable they were to be separated, and I promised to put them in a school together. Providing, of course, that I'm elected. They seem to be outstanding teachers, Mr. Richards. You can be proud of them." Pretty young women, the twins more than likely had many suitors, but since they were only sixteen, marriage could be a while in the future. Amity and Chalk talked for a while longer with Mr. Richards and then he moved on.

Chalk leaned to say in her ear, "See what I can do for you? Now, do we sit together at dinner, or not?"

Amity couldn't help laughing. "I think I'd like that as long as . . ."

"I behave? Be a perfect gentleman?"

"I wasn't questioning your behavior."

"Yes you were. But I promise to do nothing to besmirch your good name and reputation." He lowered his voice and added devilishly, "That's only today, of course."

"All right, all right," she agreed with a grin. "I'm not sure I can dissuade you, anyway."

"You can't." Again, he reached out and snagged a passerby from the crowd milling along the sidewalk as they watched the parade. "George, meet Miss Amity Whitford, the next Hamilton County school superintendent."

Amity graciously accepted the farmer's callused hand covering her own. He took off his straw hat, showing a white forehead above his tan, serious face, and they began to talk.

In a very short time, Chalk introduced Amity to more people than she knew she'd ever be able to remember. He hadn't been in Syracuse long, but he seemed to have met most town residents, and many from around the county. When she introduced him to the people she knew, he cleverly brought the conversation around to the November elections, if she didn't.

She hoped they presented a working pair, but the way he kept gazing at her was embarrassing, though somehow it made her feel very alive. It was equally difficult to keep from watching him. He had a charming, courtly way with people. In some wild, inexplicable way, his every movement seemed to thrill her.

"Thanks for all the introductions. I'm beginning to feel really good about my chances. Of

113

course, if you hadn't mentioned the opening to me, I'd likely never have known about it."

"Destiny, wouldn't you say?" An eyebrow cocked at her, and a soft smile played around his mouth.

"Well, yes, destiny, I suppose." She returned his smile. "Certainly my good fortune, if matters turn out as I hope they will."

At the same moment, they noticed that the parade was over and most people were drifting to the meager shade of the cottonwood grove along the river. They walked there together. "Dinner with me, don't forget." Chalk nodded a brief farewell, as he joined a group of men drinking *switchel,* a drink made from cider vinegar, ginger, and fresh spring water that was particularly refreshing on such a hot day.

Amity was sure the temperature had climbed well over the hundred mark, and decided to take Ben to the river for a drink. She washed her hands and splashed water on her face to cool off, and then joined the other women retrieving their food baskets from their wagons.

Thisba Strout and her friends, set off from many of the country women by their nicer clothes and tribunal air, seemed to be in charge of placing the food on the tables. Amity was acutely aware of Thisba's presence and displeasure with her, for as the woman gave orders and made changes along the tables, she frequently sent a disapproving look Amity's way. Finally, watching the array of food being unpacked by others, Amity forgot her. The beef, carved by Mr. Lloyd, was brought to the table on steaming platters by Lecky and her mother. There were also crockery platters of tender, pink sliced hams, fried chicken, fricasseed prairie chicken, browned sausage patties. Bowls of sauerkraut, coleslaw, and butterbeans. Quicker than the eye could follow, elderberry jelly, watermelon pickles, muskmelon preserves, and plum butters, bloomed colorfully on the table.

Amity added her own basket of light bread she'd sliced and buttered at home, a small crock of cider apple butter, a sour cream potato salad, and a kettle of string beans cooked with salt pork. The desserts were already numerous, but she was very proud of her carrot pie, a single crust custard pie made with grated carrots and raisins and baked in a fourteen inch milk pan. Mama's delicious carrot pie had been a popular addition to nearly every Cairo gathering the Whitfords attended.

"My goodness, let me help," Amity said suddenly, seeing Tannis Beneke, the shy young teacher of Sand Creek School, and her small, hunch-shouldered mother in brown calico struggling toward the table carrying a wash boiler filled with hot corn on the cob. Amity swiftly made a place for it, then helped lift it up. Tannis smiled and exchanged friendly comments with Amity while her mother wiped her perspiring forehead on her apron.

"Would you look at all those sweets," Mrs. Beneke said. "Not many of us can afford to buy sugar, so I guess sorghum sweetened most of it. Is that a carrot pie you brought?" Amity nodded and the woman went on, "I love carrot pie. Look, those six pies they're putting down there — they look like apple from the juice poppin' through the crusts, dried apple, likely. Peach pies and raisin pie." She accounted for them with a wide-eyed glance. "Rice pudding, iced doughnuts — Now, would you look at that!"

Thisba Strout was approaching the table bearing an enormous sheet cake iced in waves of creamy white and with an American flag mounted in the middle. "Virginia yam cake," she said proudly to those clustering around as she set it down. Amity watched, too, from a discreet distance. She saw Thisba seem to stumble, then catch herself with her whole hand, which landed in Amity's carrot pie. There was a chorus of gasps. Amity's stomach tightened. She stood frozen.

"Now who put that there, whatever it is. Looks like baby poo." Thisba made a contemptuous face and wiped her hand with her apron. "That spot was saved for the Virginia yam cake. It's the centerpiece!"

Tannis Beneke stared at Thisba Strout, then at Amity. "Miss Whitford," she said in a soft whisper, "she did that on purpose!"

Amity gritted her teeth, then spoke quietly. "I'm sure it was an accident." Thisba watched her for reaction with an expression of triumph. Amity showed nothing and made her voice calm, "With so many desserts, I don't think it'll be

116

missed." She walked unhurriedly to the table and picked up the ruined pie. She gave it to a group of boys playing tag who'd seen the whole thing and were asking for it, making them promise to return the empty pan to her. Tannis Beneke and her mother watched with sympathetic eyes and growing smiles of admiration.

Amity wanted more than sympathy at the moment, however. So as she stepped back from the table, she carefully ground her foot down on Thisba's. Thisba let out a loud squeal and jumped back.

"Oh, my, did I step on your foot?" Amity cried, clutching at her. Thisba, her lips pinched tight with pain and fury, said nothing as she yanked away, but they both knew an eye had just been had for an eye.

Satisfied, Amity hurried off to help a young boy struggling to lift an enormous watermelon onto a bench in the shade a few yards distant. He was a scrawny little thing, dressed in worn hickory overalls and shirt; one of his big toes was darkly scabbed. He looked vaguely familiar. "Did you grow the watermelon?" He nodded, his big brown eyes fastened warily on her face. "It's magnificent," she told him. "These sandhills are known to grow wonderful melons, if enough water can be carried to them." All at once she placed him. He was the boy in the sandhills who was burying his snake-bit dog a few weeks ago; his mother, Mrs. Dusky, had run her off at the point of a gun. She could see from his look that he recognized her as well and, with a quick breath, she smiled encouragingly at him. "What's your name?"

He didn't say anything for a moment. A swallow traveled up and down his thin little neck. Finally he whispered, "Jebby Dusky."

She nodded. "I'm Miss Whitford. Jebby, did you ever go to school?" He shook his head. "Would you like to?" He hesitated then gulped. "Yeah." She put her hand on his shoulder. "All right, Jebby," she said softly, with only a little trepidation, "I'll talk to your mother again."

She moved from group to group, looking everywhere in the next few minutes for the widow, Liddy Dusky. She caught glimpses of her dark, seamed face on the fringes a couple of times, only to have the woman vanish when she reached the spot. We can play hide and seek all summer, Mrs. Dusky, she thought with a wry smile, but one day we will discuss school for your children.

At the noon meal, true to his promise, Chalk encouraged pleasant, offhand conversation chiefly with his friends. Then, a seedy farmer in rustic black from up north, named Ward McChesney, began to complain about a group of German Dunkards who'd recently settled near Coolidge. "Now why they wanta bring their furrin ways to Hamilton County, somebody tell me!"

Of course he didn't want an answer. But Chalk coaxed softly, his eyes glinting, "Now, Ward, if

118

there is anything this county has to offer, it's room — room for everybody. I seriously doubt those Church of the Brethren folks are any threat to you, or me, seein' as how they believe chiefly in peace and the brotherhood of man."

"Brotherhood?" Food bits spewed from McChesney's mouth. "Ya heard 'em talk? Just furrin babble a body can't make head nor tail of. They come here, let 'em talk our way!"

"Give them time," Noah Porter, Chalk's red-haired pharmacist friend, put in. "Who knows what contribution they'll eventually make? My money says it'll be a good one. Aren't you raising Turkey Red wheat?" Porter seemed to be changing the subject. "Heard you got a good crop, Ward."

Chalk was grinning. Ward McChesney frowned hard and dug into his food. For close to fifteen years now, Kansas farmers had benefitted greatly from a strain of winter wheat, Turkey Red, introduced by Russian Mennonite immigrants.

As talk continued around her, and knives and forks clattered against china, Amity was intensely aware of Chalk, the nearness of his body to her, the soft rumble of his voice, the pleasant way he smelled. She could scarcely eat and spoke only when invited to comment, then wondered if she made any sense at all, or if she showed her feelings in her face. She hoped she was only imagining the suspicious gleam in Thisba Strout's eyes, up the table from them. Still, the woman seemed to be watching her every move.

As much as she'd wanted to stay for the whole doings, Amity thought perhaps she should get up and leave right now. If she stayed, could she avoid talk? No doubt Mrs. Strout would use every possible weapon to stop her, if she really didn't want her in office. There was still the musical program, the fireworks this evening, and the dance tonight. What if Chalk Holden asked her to dance? How would it feel, to be held in his arms? No, she couldn't let the woman rule her life. Under a veiled glance, Amity studied Thisba, now serving her cake. Then she looked at Chalk Holden beside her. His head was thrown back in a hearty laugh. A cowman, hand clamped to the newspaperman's shoulder, was regaling him with a story. Her mind was made up. She'd stay, and God help her.

Chapter Eight

"A bachelor doesn't get many opportunities for meals like this," Chalk explained, grinning. Amity picked at her food while Chalk had devoured his and gone back for more. She was amused by his healthy male appetite, as he settled again on the bench beside her.

She asked, "You've never married?" Such a delighted gleam came to his eye that she added with a stiff protest, "I'm not fishing for information; I was just making conversation."

"I'd feel better if you were fishing." As he toyed with his fork, a look of vulnerability and sadness chased across his strong features. "I came close to marrying once, a pretty young Baltimore widow with two children." He put the fork down with a clatter and reared back in his chair. Sunshine glinted off the dark gold of his thick hair and moustache. "I was so sure that Lilly and the kids were going to be mine, that you could have knocked me over with a feather when she told me she was marrying the owner of the Baltimore Stoneware Company." A wry grin tilted the corner of his mouth. "She fell in love with him while choosing the pottery she wanted for the house *we* were supposed to share. At the time, I was trying a long involved case in court and didn't notice what was happening."

Amity decided that Lilly, whoever she was, was stupid. "I'm sorry. Is that why you came here?"

He nodded, "I came to get as far as I could from Baltimore. Decided to become a newspaperman, take only an occasional law case, and dedicate myself to enjoying life more, take each day as it comes along."

"And did you leave family back East?"

"Just my sister, Stella June, and her two youngsters, who are still there in Baltimore. Tried to get her to come out here with me, but she wanted to stay in Baltimore and wait for her good-for-nothing husband, who's likely abandoned her and the kids and will never return." At Amity's raised eyebrows, he went on, "Lorenzo Scarret, her husband, worked as a customs officer at a tobacco warehouse on the Baltimore harbor. He went off to Europe with one of the shipments of tobacco, and she hasn't heard from him since. May even be better off, but things are rough for her and the two kids."

"Good grief! The poor woman . . ."

"She wouldn't be persuaded to leave." He scowled darkly. "Some women are just too damned proud."

Amity bridled. "Pride's not necessarily a bad thing. On occasion that's the only thing a body has left to her. Your sister has a right to follow her heart the same as you have a right to follow yours, Mr. Holden." Then she softened. "I sure hope the course of action you've chosen is the right one for you, this time."

Unexpectedly, his gravelly voice lowered and his eyes twinkling with good humor, he said, "The day I saw you outside my office, I knew I'd made the smartest move of my life!"

"Shhh. Please don't — say such things." Fighting the crazy happiness she felt, her glance darted in Thisba's direction. Fortunately, Mrs. Strout was engaged in an adoring conversation with her cousin, who sat eating from two large plates and taking up at least three spaces on the bench.

Since Thisba Strout seemed to be in charge of the day's affairs, appointed or otherwise, Amity felt no surprise when following more band music and singing, Seymour Purdue appeared as the main speaker on the afternoon program. He spoke in a light Southern drawl, almost a child's voice, of love of country and respect for customs and traditions that continued to make America a great land. When he swung into the subject of devotion to the welfare of one's community, Amity realized that he was using the opportunity to make a pitch for himself for the county school superintendency. He went on with tremulous emotion in a high nasal tone about how he intended to improve Hamilton County's educational state. He ended by paraphrasing the Bible, "The community that begetteth a wise child shall have the joy of him."

"Bravo!" Thisba dabbed at her eyes with a hanky and then, turning this way and that, clapping furiously, prompted the crowd into giving louder applause than they might have otherwise. "Bravo! Bravo!"

Angry as a bear, Amity boldly called out as she strode toward the makeshift stage, "May another candidate speak to you all? I'm also running for Hamilton County school superintendent." There was a rumble of shocked comments and she could feel eyes staring in horror; some folks laughed outright. She recognized the voice of the seedy farmer, Ward McChesney, as he snorted in disgust, "Wimmen is everywhere!" Her step didn't falter.

"That's the end of the program. It's time for the games!" Thisba Strout was emphatic. She muttered orders to first one lady, then another, shoving them into action. "Bring the burlap bags for the sack race. Where are the balls, the bats?"

"We — we want to hear Miss Whitford." Amity recognized the shy, quiet voice of Tannis Beneke from Sand Creek. Tannis was backed by her mother. "Miss Whitford's a candidate the same as the big fellow up there. Give her a chance."

Lecky Lloyd's father, still wearing his juice-stained apron from cooking the beef over the fire-pit, began to clap his hands sharply. He was joined by Meda Ginsbach and her lanky husband; then by William Richards, and the other teachers and their families that Amity had talked with in past weeks. Her Norwegian neighbors, the Bergens, added their support. Able called out, "Miss Vhitford! Ve vant to hear da young lady!"

Amity hesitated, quiet joy in her heart.

John Clyde was shouting with his hands circling his mouth, at those waving her off, "Let 'er talk. Let the gal talk or I'll have ya, by God!"

Finally, a silver-haired, dignified-looking gentleman walked forward stroking his moustache. Fine wrinkles webbed his handsome face. He held his hand up for silence and the crowd quieted. Amos Taylor, the third candidate, bowed to Amity and smiled. "The young lady and I deserve an equal chance to speak. Ladies first."

She flashed a look of thanks and hurried forward, suddenly finding herself being handed up the steps to the stage by a solid, warm grasp on her elbow. Aware that everyone watched, she looked down to see Chalk Holden addressing her with a gentlemanly nod and a smile.

He whispered, "Go to it."

Amity threw her shoulders back, strode to center stage, clasped her hands in front of her, and took a few deep breaths. "I would like to speak more specifically than Mr. Purdue did, about the serious needs of Hamilton County. If elected, I intend to see that each school in the county is well-seated, and with sufficient blackboards, maps, globes, dictionaries, and other necessities." There were hoots and hollers of derision, though others nodded hesitant assent and clapped quietly.

"I knew she'd empty folks' pockets!" someone

125

called out in an indignant yap. Seizing the moment, Seymour Purdue said in his odd light voice, "Those things cost money! Miss Whitford, these folks don't have money to spare for all that folderol." Nearly everyone applauded that, and Thisba nodded triumphantly.

Amity wasn't daunted. "I expect the school board of each district to do their part, to dig a little deeper. Parents, too. There is little so important to the future of this community, to this county, to our whole country, as the education of our young. The future depends on what we do now, to educate them." There were more protests, which she ignored. She took a deep breath, "I will also encourage each school board to clearly lay out a disciplinary system at the beginning of the school year that students can understand, respect, and abide by."

A thread of doubt, of question, rumbled among the listeners. "You'll see," Amity persisted. "What I suggest will work if you give it a chance! I believe every child in Hamilton County deserves the best possible education. I will work with my county neighbors toward that goal, *universal public education*. A good education is not only for the privileged, for those who live in town, it must be there for *your* children, too." There was a frightening silence, then approving shouts and the loudest hand she'd received. Happiness hummed in her ears at the sudden reversal and she finished, "I'm eager to work with you for improvement of classroom instruction. I'll be happy to speak

126

to each of you personally, and answer your questions. My goal is to be of service to the parents, the teachers, and especially, the children, of Hamilton County!"

The crowd clapped their approval, and Amity was helped down from the podium to meet the people who came forward to speak with her and shake her hand. She smiled and answered questions, quietly and thoroughly. A few folks came only to compliment her and wish her well. That they valued what she'd had to say was hosanna to her nervous soul and her confidence soared. Then a woman stated, loud enough for many to hear, "Keeping to yourself the way you do, miss, we don't know a thimbleful about you. You're not of this town; you're practically a stranger to all of us. How do we know we can trust our children's futures to your hands?"

Amity met the glittery black eyes of Abigail Limbaugh, a friend of Thisba's. Grover Limbaugh owned the local livery and wagonworks, and had on one occasion fitted Amity's wagon with a new wheel.

"You can read all about Miss Whitford in the *Banner*," Chalk Holden barked, "so make sure you subscribe!" There was a burst of laughter.

"I'm happy to answer your questions, anything you might want to know that pertains to the job —" Amity tried to make herself heard through the noise. She hoped no one was from out of the county and knew her past.

"Awright, then," a young, straw-haired farmer

127

called out, waving his hat at her, "unless there's something wrong with you, why's a woman who looks like you do not hitched?"

"I'm single because I choose to be." Suddenly, the air felt too thin to breathe; she could feel color flooding her face.

"I still say it looks mighty peculiar for a woman her age and all not to be married," Abigail was saying. "She's hiding something."

But few were listening now. Once again, Amos Taylor came to her rescue, claiming his turn to speak. Amity was flooded with relief when the attention was turned from her to the stately, silver-haired gentleman.

"This isn't an easy task, following you, Miss Whitford," he bowed in her direction, "but I'll do my best." He went on to speak eloquently and with depth on issues she'd brought up, saying many things the way she wished she'd said them. Amity studied the faces around her, saw rapt admiration, and felt less sure of herself. Her heart palpitated. "Don't worry," Chalk said at her elbow, "you did well, Amity Whitford."

"Not well enough, perhaps. Listen to him," she said quietly. "Amos Taylor is more than qualified. These people would be very fortunate if he filled the post."

"The opposition's too tough? Giving up?"

"Of course not." Her chin tilted in defiance. No matter that Seymour Purdue might also pull something out of a hat with Thisba pushing for his election. The truth was the big man'd had

128

a worrisome degree of support today, too, though possibly not to the extent of Amos Taylor's. "Formidable as the battle may turn out to be, I'm staying in, Mr. Holden. I have no choice —"

A sudden deafening explosion shook the earth and jolted Amity against Chalk. Stunned, scarcely aware that Chalk had moved to protect her, Amity saw the woods east of them light up with an eerie light. An ear-rending staccato of crackling and popping noise came from there. Leaves in the trees overhead shuddered, every blade of grass was lit with light. Spangles and driblets of color — green, orange, blue, yellow, red, charcoal, exploded blindly in the trees, upward to the sky, again, and again, and again with each thunderous report. At the same time, a sickening fetor of sulphur and other chemicals spread quickly, bit at Amity's nose. Fear clutched her throat and she gasped, "What on earth — ?"

"My God!" Chalk spoke in her ear just as he let her go. "It's the fireworks wagon — it's gone off! There are kids in that woods!" And he took off running.

Amity clutched her skirts and raced hard on Chalk's heels toward the noisy, fiery scene. She could hear the screaming, sobbing children who began to tumble from the woods, arms and legs flailing, rosettes of blood on cheeks and hands. One small boy, a stick of wood hanging from his side, ran crookedly and dropped to the ground just before Chalk reached him.

A tiny blonde girl in red, sobbing in terror,

spotted Amity and stopped where she was to lift her arms. Amity picked her up. Fighting a tight knot of panic in her stomach, she whispered calmly against the shrieking toddler's soft, tear-wet hair, "It's all right, you'll be fine." Quickly, Amity surveyed the rest of the crying children, but saw no other obvious serious injury; then she placed the child on her hip and motioning, called to the other frightened youngsters, "Come on children, follow me." She fell in behind Chalk who carried the fallen boy, shouldering his way back through the oncoming white-faced crowd.

With the injured boy in his arms, Chalk headed toward the open meadow a few yards distant, shouting over his shoulder at the others, "Make sure all the children got out of the woods! Somebody get Doc and tell him to bring his bag. Bring the worst hurt over here!"

Parents darted about like crazed ants, seeking their own children, calling their names in harsh, panic-stricken voices.

"Take the children to the meadow so we can tend to their hurts," Amity cried above the pandemonium. "Follow Mr. Holden!" She looked over her shoulder, praying all the children were out of danger. The sky above the woods still looked like an ill-timed Aurora Borealis. Trees could go up in flames at any moment. She caught a glimpse of a boy she recognized, alone, plainly confused and in shock. Jebby Dusky, the boy to whom she'd spoken earlier about the watermelon, stumbled along, not crying, but staring at his right hand held before him. Amity looked and saw that the first two fingers were missing, the stubs just starting to ooze blood. Nausea rose in her throat. She struggled against a feeling of dizziness, and turned back to help him, running with the little girl in her arms.

Amity was suddenly blocked by a young woman shrieking in relief, "My baby, Lucy! Oh, Lucy!" The child struggling in Amity's arms, cried out again loudly and reached for her mother. Gratefully, Amity thrust her into the woman's arms. "She's not hurt, just scared." Amity flew to Jebby Dusky. Sitting on the ground, she took his bleeding hand carefully in her own. There wasn't a tear on his face, even as she ripped a piece from her petticoat and tightly bound his hand. "Oh, son, little one —" As she picked him up Jebby fainted, his head lolling onto her shoulder.

Amity struggled through the mad scramble, the boy heavy in her arms, his feet dangling almost to her knees. She spoke to him as he began to stir back to with consciousness. "It's all right, Jebby — you'll be fine, dear." She was relieved to see a bucket brigade forming from the river to the heart of the disaster in the woods. Women were whipping white cloths from their picnic baskets to make bandages if necessary. On the open knoll others were making pallets of blankets; someone was calling for sour milk, and others for clay, to make poultices for the burns.

She saw Chalk, rising from where Doc Gourley, a reedy, stoop-shouldered man in a gray suit, knelt by a boy stretched flat on the ground. She headed that way with her own lad, flinching when she saw a piece of wood with a scarlet tip on the ground near the doctor's knee. Chalk came to help her, but she shook her head and told him, "I'll do this if Doctor Gourley will direct me. Go help the others." Chalk whirled away.

"Got a puncture wound here. What's the matter with that boy?" Doc Gourley barked over his shoulder as Amity eased the child gently to the ground. She crawled a few feet away to retrieve a blanket and make a pallet. She lifted Jebby onto it carefully, as she answered the doctor. "Two fingers blown off. Tell me what to do."

He took a second to soak a cloth with liquid from a brown bottle then passed the wet, bitter-smelling cloth to her. "Clean it up. Make sure there's no dust or chemicals on the stubs."

She swallowed as nausea closed her throat when she unwound the crimson rag from the hand. The boy's big brown eyes stared up at her but he still didn't speak and she was sure he was in shock. The stubs of his fingers must yet be numb of feeling.

"A real task, here," the doctor spoke to her as an equal, "picking debris from this boy's insides. Hmm, looks like the projectile went right between the ribs, internal organs missed or just scraped a bit. Going to keep me busy, though. Can you do what needs to be done with the lad, there? How's it bleeding?"

"Some, not profusely. And y-yes, I'll take care

of it, just tell me what to do."

The doctor's response was a small sound of appreciative satisfaction. "Get the whiskey flask from my bag and get a good, stiff drink down 'im. The nerve endings in those fingers are going to come alive any minute and give him a real fit. The whiskey will take off some of the pain."

Amity held the boy's head in her arm and gave him the drink, as much as he could take. She held him close against her bosom as he coughed and choked, then laid him down again, tenderly smoothing his brow. She asked the doctor working quickly nearby, "What's next?"

The doctor nodded toward a white cloth spread with instruments beside him. "You're going to make a little envelope of flesh over the end of each stub and sew it up. But first grab those little nippers and trim the flesh till it ain't ragged."

Amity's mind reeled. "I don't think I can . . ."

He spoke sternly. "Sure you can. Most ladies sew tidier than the best doctors. Needle and thread in those packets," he nodded matter-of-factly toward the makeshift layout of his tools. "How's the boy doing?"

Jebby's eyes were closed again and he lay very still, breathing deeply. She took his cheek in her palm and wagged his head. "He's either asleep, knocked out from the whiskey, or he's fainted again."

"Good. Makes the whole job easier."

Amity blotted everything from her mind but

the task in front of her. With the inside of her cheek caught between her teeth, scarcely breathing, and fighting to keep her hands steady, she took up a small bloody finger and nipped, tucked, and stitched. Each step went faster than she thought it would and brought a sense of satisfaction. She was at work on the second finger, breathing easier, almost finished, when a shadow halted on the ground beside her and stale essence of honeysuckle drifted the air.

"This is your fault; you know," Thisba Strout accused.

"Not now, Mrs. Strout, we can talk later," Amity begged, her hand holding the needle beginning to shake. Her forehead broke out in cold perspiration. *Good Lord, not now!*

"Listen, you hoyden," Thisba leaned down to hiss. "If you hadn't insisted on making a fool of yourself giving that silly speech, changing *my* schedule, the children would have been playing games in the meadow under their parents' watchful eyes and not fooling around the fireworks wagon."

How could she deny what was true? A cold hand seemed to clutch at Amity's heart. Her flesh prickled. *Please, God, not again!* Around her, everything tilted dizzily and she fought for control, determined to the depth of her being to shut Thisba out and finish with Jebby Dusky. She shook her head to clear it, and in a thin voice she asked Doc Gourley, "What shall I do now? The stitches are in."

She saw that others stood by, watching, and among them was Liddy Dusky, silent, stoic, moist dark eyes on her son's hand. The widow's other two tattered, brown-haired children, a boy and a girl, waited a few steps away, their trust invested in Amity as they looked from their injured brother to her; tears shone on their dirty cheeks. She did her best to smile reassuringly at them, in spite of her own queasy feeling.

Doctor Gourley's voice came through sharply. "Put that ointment on his fingers real thick and then bandage each finger separate and then the whole hand together. Use lots of bandages, for protection while the wounds heal."

Amity did as directed, although her hands were shaking. She wished Thisba Strout would leave, but the woman remained planted, carrying on so everyone could hear, as she surely intended. "That boy will never see his fingers again, thanks to you. You're not fit to have anything to do with children!"

No! Amity cried silently. *Dear God, no — !* Bent over the boy, she weaved under crushing pain of protest. For a moment her mind went blank and she felt the intense heat, as she saw in front of her a child floating away, away from her reach, and then the little girl lay stiff, her flesh icy — Amity blinked hard and the figure lying there was again Jebby Dusky. She bit back tears and shook her head, fighting for control so as not to desert her small charge.

Finally, Doctor Gourley barked, "Mrs. Strout,

we're busy here. You're overwrought and talking nonsense. Go home. Take a sedative and go to bed!"

Go home, go home, go home, echoed in Amity's mind.

"I'll leave when I'm ready, Doctor Gourley! And that won't be until I'm positive that everyone here knows who's at fault for this terrible catastrophe."

Take her away, take her away, take Amity out of sight, to Kansas City, to Topeka — get rid of her! The high, ghostly voice from the past echoed in Amity's mind. She pressed her hand protectively on Jebby's small chest and fought to clear her head. *Hang on!* she admonished herself sharply. This time she must be lucid and know exactly what was happening.

There was a sudden deep growl. "Miss Whitford had nothing to do with this!" How long had Chalk Holden been standing there? How much had he heard?

"She done good by my boy," Liddy Dusky put in, and, moving a paralyzed Amity, now finished, gently aside, she squatted down to scoop Jebby into her arms.

"I'll come to see you," Amity cried, reaching out to touch Jebby's arm, but there was no way he could hear as he was sleeping heavily from the whiskey.

"I thank you, Miss Whitford," his mother said. "You can come to talk, though I can't make no promises about schoolin'." She marched away with her boy in her arms, her other children trotting ahead of her long strides to make ready their wagon.

Thisba opened her mouth to speak again.

"Mrs. Strout, that's enough!" Chalk warned.

As Thisba whirled on him, her tall blonde daughter ran up to stand by her side, eyes flashing with excitement to be part of the goings-on. She slipped her arm loyally through her mother's. Thisba addressed Chalk in tones of ice. "I'd advise you to change your support of this . . . woman for school superintendent, Mr. Holden. Or stand the chance of your paper losing any opportunity to succeed in *this* town!"

Chalk wore a grim smile. His eyes were flinty with barely held anger as he looked from Doridee Strout back to her mother. "Please don't threaten me. Amity's not at fault in this and you've no right to upbraid her the way you were. Woman, what's got into you?"

Thisba began to reply, but Chalk waved for her to shut up. "Wait a minute! The way I hear it, your daughter here, Doridee, and one of her boyfriends told the younger kids where the fireworks wagon was hidden when it was supposed to be kept secret." The smile left the girl's face. Chalk finished, "It didn't take much messing around to set things off. It's damn lucky none of the kids were killed. I think both of you owe Amity an apology."

Amity shook her head. "That isn't necessary. Let's all just drop this, please. It's bad enough the children got hurt."

Doridee protested as she faced her mother. "Mr. Holden's wrong, Mama, I didn't do anything. It's not my fault some of those country bumpkins are so stupid as to fool with the fireworks wagon. We didn't tell them to."

The girl leaned her head to rest on her mother's shoulder and Thisba patted her cheek. "Don't worry, honey, we know what happened."

Amity turned to say, "Doctor, if you don't need me any longer, I'd like to go home." He nodded.

"Amity, wait!" Chalk called as Amity strode off, skirts in hand. He knew nothing about her and if he did — She shook her head and ran, darting around couples moving toward their vehicles for their trip home, children in tow. Little burned arms and faces had been seen to with river clay and sour milk poultices, Doc's ointment supply not being nearly enough. She thought that they looked like small mummies. Only a thin smoke lifted now from the deeper woods, and the voices that carried from there were men staying to keep things in check.

The Fourth of July was over. For her, perhaps much more than that was over. Chalk Holden caught up with her and grabbed her arm just as she reached her own wagon.

"I'm sorry," he said huskily, "for that fool woman's totally unfounded remarks. She just likes to lord it over everybody. Amity, are you all right?"

138

"I'm quite . . . all right," she told him, unable to control the tremor in her voice.

"Amity —" He said her name like a caress, striking warmth in her heart. "Let me drive you home."

"No!" Her hand shook as she swept a strand of hair back from her eyes. "No, thank you, I'm tired — tonight I'd be terrible company. John Clyde is here, anyway."

"Listen, Amity, don't let today bother you. That Strout woman's a fool. I never heard such idiocy."

"She — she didn't b-bother me," she maintained in a staunch lie. "Nothing's the matter."

"Let me hitch up for you, anyway." Amity nodded. She must get away before she broke down. Their hands brushed as he took Ben's halter lead from her. The truth was, though she meant *not* to fall in love, she was losing her heart to Chalk Holden as positively as the sun came up mornings and went down at night. In spite of a life far too complicated already.

A few minutes later, Chalk clasped her waist and lifted her into the wagon. "I couldn't help noticing," his voice deepened with feeling as he went on, "that from the day we met, there has seemed to be more bothering you than you let on. More than the chance of losing your claim, though God knows that's bad enough. What is it, Amity? Tell me." He laid a hand on her arm. "Let's talk, please."

After a moment's hesitation she shook her head.

139

"It's too complicated, Chalk. Maybe we . . . another time." She was glad to see John Clyde approaching, leading Texas Max. As the handyman tied his horse to the back of the wagon, she slid across the wagon seat so he could drive. Seeing Chalk's unhappy expression, Amity said, "I do thank you, Chalk, for today." She did her best to smile, though she wanted nothing so much as to be away from there fast, with time to think.

Chapter Nine

The Santa Fe train rocked across the plains, following the twisting Arkansas River northeast toward central Kansas. Amity was distracted from deep thought only when they approached a town and she sat numbly listening to the train's shrill whistle, and the impatient chuffing as it stopped to load and unload. Sitting on the hard wooden seat, her small satchel at her feet, she only half noticed the dusty hamlets: Garden City, Dodge, Kinsley — pens of restless cattle by the tracks stirring up further dust — Garden City sporting new irrigation canals and plantings of spindly trees along its streets.

She decided fleetingly that Syracuse was no better or worse than the towns she had seen this trip, but she had begun to think of it fondly.

She sagged back against the seat, fanning herself with her small black journal, at the moment giving herself a respite from rereading early entries, putting herself in that time before Beaconsfield.

She sat with her eyes closed, trying to make her mind a blank, but her youthful writings would not leave her head.

March 1, 1882. My heart aches so much. I knew of the flood at home in Cairo, the broken levee, the epidemic diseases and drownings. For weeks I feared for my dear parents, and would have gone home to them if travel would have been allowed. Dear God, it can't be that they are truly gone.

She looked out at miles and miles of rolling land below a dome of blue sky that held not so much as a feather of a cloud. The prairie looked so empty, so lonely. She closed her eyes again. The next day she had written,

It is true. Everything is lost. I am alone, I have no money, I cannot stay at school. My heart grieves so for my dear parents that I cannot think. If only my tears could bring them back. I cannot paint, I don't know what to do. Friends here in St. Louis are comforting. One of the girls, sweet Alice Vaughn, has suggested a possible answer to my situation. I'll think about it tomorrow.

There were no entries for weeks, and then,

I am saved, thanks to Alice V. My trunks are packed and tomorrow I leave for an unusual English barony in Kansas, called Beaconsfield, to be employed as governess by the leader, Chester Fairleigh, and his wife. Alice's parents are acquainted with Mr. Fairleigh through business transactions and they kindly recommended me. I have a description of the family from the Vaughns. Mr. Fairleigh is handsome, I'm told, with very curly hair and moustache. He appears reserved, "well-bred English gentry." Mrs. Fairleigh is fair and delicate, "definitely refined." Their son, Prentiss, is ten years old, and resembles his mother. Dark-haired Colin, whom I'll also teach, is seven. The baby, Nora Ann, is recalled as adorable and, apparently, curly-haired like her father.

Nora Ann, sweet child. Amity touched the journal to her mouth as tears filled her eyes. She would never forget her first sight of her charges, that chilly day in late March. Prentiss, she would learn later, was as mischievous as he was bright; Colin, she would find out, was a love-starved little boy who was often the object of his father's displeasure. Little Nora was a round-faced, well-bundled child all wiggles and smiles, a joy to be near. The children and their handsome parents had met Amity's train from St. Louis, on the very same depot platform in Great Bend where she'd soon be getting off — the same depot where Charles Fairleigh had dumped her. . . .

I wouldn't have hurt you, darling, not for the world. I loved you, Nora Ann.

Amity fanned herself again, feeling suffocated by the sultry, cinder- and sweat-laden heat of the passenger car as well as her memories. She remembered that she had written to Alice Vaughn about six months after filing her claim. The letter came back unopened. Either Alice's family had

143

moved, or Alice believed whatever the Fairleighs had told her. Amity sighed. She'd eaten little of the basket lunch she'd bought from a woman selling them by the tracks in Dodge City. Her eyes burned for want of sleep. Still, she was intensely glad she'd found the courage to make this journey to Beaconsfield. In order for her superintendent campaign to go anywhere she had to put an end to her fear that someone else from Beaconsfield might show up in Syracuse or Hamilton County and reveal a secret she hardly knew the details of herself. She'd have it out with the Fairleighs about that terrible day the baby died. She'd done it, or she hadn't. She was through pushing the tragedy out of her mind, but she must also have help in remembering from others who were there.

She looked out the window and for a flash of an instant saw Chalk Holden's face transposed against the empty prairie, melded to her own actual reflection in the glass. Merciful heaven, couldn't she do anything right? She'd not had a chance to explain anything to him, and she feared that she'd hurt his feelings. He'd been so good to her about the campaign, an enormous help. But the day she'd left town, they had passed on the street and neither of them had done more than nod to the other.

He hadn't bothered to ask why she was leaving town, or where she was going. Of course, she couldn't have told him anyway. Although she hated leaving John Clyde to do the haying alone, she'd told him, without details, that this was an emergency trip to see old acquaintances. "Take your time," John Clyde had urged. "You been looking peaked, Missy, as low as a squirrel 'thout a tree. Don't come back till your up ta it. I can take keer of everything around here." He'd be cutting and stacking wild hay fifteen to twenty hours a day at a killing pace. She should have stayed, dividing the labor by half.

The train whistled suddenly, making Amity start. Great Bend was their next stop. The town was located in the bow of the Arkansas River before it headed south toward Wichita and the Indian nations. She had heard that ten years ago, when it was a railhead on the Chisholm Trail, it'd been a very wild place. That was before state law moved the shipping point thirty miles west of town. Amity looked out the window and saw the huddle of buildings taking shape in the distance.

Clutching her satchel, she moved on wobbly legs from the train, then hesitated a moment by the track to catch her breath in the furnace-like heat. From the station she could see the scattered buildings of town, many of them fine structures, she recalled. The center of town was a good walking distance. She saw the familiar Southern Hotel, and nearer, the farm implement store. Out in front of the store, a farmer was loading a shiny new riding sickle into his wagon, and she experienced a second's envy. Her eyes sought and found the livery. Common sense told her to take a room at the Southern Hotel and set out for Beaconsfield first thing in the morning; it was now late afternoon. But she couldn't wait, even if she'd had the money to pay for a room, which she didn't.

Like Syracuse's, Great Bend's street improvements had far to go, Amity thought as she stumbled along, her feet making tiny dustclouds, her empty stomach churning from nerves. The town seemed oddly quiet; only a few men lounged in front of the storefronts. No women were about, but perhaps that was because they'd be in their kitchens at this hour, preparing supper. For whatever reason, the sparsity of people on the streets made her breathe easier. It was silly to think anyone might recognize her, though, or know anything of her mission. She hardly resembled the innocent young thing she'd been three years earlier.

Even so, at the livery a few moments later, when the freckle-faced stable boy asked in good-humored neighborliness where she was headed off to with the horse and buggy she'd rented, she turned her head and pretended not to hear him. Tossing her satchel into the buggy, she climbed aboard, took up the reins, and set off at a good clip without looking back.

Beaconsfield, as she remembered it, lay north and a little east, hours away. She held the horse to a steady pace the first hour or two, then slowed the animal to a restful walk for a while. Dark would likely find her on the road. But spending

146

the night in Great Bend and waiting 'til morning to start this last leg of her trip hadn't been a possibility. A half hour later, she urged the animal back to a trot. A jackrabbit bounded off on springing legs from the side of the trail. For a long time, with little else to see, she tried to keep her eyes on a hawk making wide circles above the open prairie, but impatience ate at her like a wolf nipping at her heels.

In time, she grew pleasantly drowsy, listening to the evening birds that made their home in the marshlands, which were nearly dry now. The area was fed in good years by both the Arkansas and Walnut rivers. She recognized the clear sweet song of a meadowlark. In the west the sky turned soft pink as the sun went down. A dreadful fatigue settled over her from all the hours of sleep she'd missed, and she fought to stay awake, coming up with a start every while or so. The moon rose, silvering the way.

The rattle of her buggy wheels, the occasional snuffle of the horse, and the plaintive cry of a night bird were the only sounds in the night's stillness and did little to ease her feelings of loneliness, and fear of what lay ahead.

There ought to be more sign of humanity, she thought, even at night. People on the road, horseback riders. But she was very alone in a blue-black sea, with only the moon for company, not even a cabin light anywhere. She should have asked the livery boy to provide her a lantern, but that would simply have led to more questions. Had she gotten off the regular trail, gotten lost? Amity strained to see. Her eyes felt like they had sand in them; she doubted she could keep them open much longer. Finally, fatigued to the bone, and worried about going on, she made a decision. If she was lost, it was best to stop where she was and wait for daylight.

She drew in the reins, pulled off the path, got out, and unhitched and hobbled the animal to graze. Then she curled up on the seat with her satchel for a pillow and fell asleep on the instant.

Warm sun on her eyelids woke Amity next morning. In a flurry of concern, she climbed from the wagon and tried to brush the wrinkles from her clothing. She was a sight for the fine English to see! She made her hair right, drank from her canteen, and washed her face. She got out the food basket she'd paid fifty cents for yesterday in Dodge. There was still some meat, cheese, sliced bread, and a slab of apple pie, all of which she ate greedily.

The horse snuffled and nipped at her shoulder but went back into its traces obediently enough. Then she was on her way, her eyes eager, yet fearful, for the first sign of Beaconsfield.

When it came, a clump of buildings on the horizon, her heart beat so hard she could hardly breathe. She drove on determinedly, eyes fixed on her destination. But the nearer she got, the more confused she felt. There ought to be more movement than a few trees curving before the wind. There was no sign of humanity, of people heading for the fields or out riding. There ought to be glimpses of figures going from shop to shop, or to another's house to visit. Where were their animals, the sheep they kept for wool, the cattle, their riding horses? There ought to be more *color;* the English were so proud of their gardens, sacrificing water to grow flowers for their tables. But the scene ahead was buff and drab and still; *dead.*

The hot winds brushed Amity's cheeks as she stood and surveyed the town. She shouldn't have come to Beaconsfield. The hostler, or anyone in Great Bend, could have told her the village was vacated if she had only mentioned her destination. Her heart twisted with pain. Oh, God, where had they all gone? Taking with them the answers she needed.

The prairie wind whistled around the large, empty hotel that had housed the English the first year, until their own homes could be built, and around the manor house where she'd lived with the Fairleighs for a brief, happy time — until the tragedy. The wind sighed in the few trees that were so much taller now and whimpered, swaying the weeds that choked the polo field, the race track, the tennis courts. She cried out to the wind. What happened here? Why did they leave? How could an empty village provide her with answers?

Amity put the horse to graze and walked slowly

toward the hotel, the first building along the weed-choked street. As she approached the huge postrock building, thirty-one blank windows stared back at her. She hesitated, her heart going still as her glance fastened on the gingerbread-trimmed porch. In all the images that had haunted her, the dead child seemed to be lying under a porch — Her gaze checked every porch in view, all were enclosed down to the ground, unlike that of her nightmare images. She moved swiftly on.

How long had they been gone? Wasn't it enough that whatever happened to her here had nearly destroyed her?

At White Rock Manor, the Fairleighs' home, she looked in the windows. Thick dust coated everything — the wood-paneled walls, the inlaid mirror above the fireplace, the curving banister, the elegantly detailed hanging gaslights. The furniture was gone, the rugs taken up. A rage began to build up as she rattled the door. It was as securely locked as the past she hoped to open. Racing to a window, she banged on the glass with both fists, then she peered inside. Empty. All gone. She turned and sagged against the stone wall, head in her hands.

In a moment she lifted her face and once more peered inside. The earlier splendor came alive in her mind as if it were yesterday. Velvet draperies, polished gracefully curved Queen Anne furniture, richly patterned wallpaper and carpet, paintings in gold frames abounding on the walls; laughter, voices in carefree conversation. Music from the Fairleighs' imported piano played in her mind, a German waltz? No, a quadrille, a dance for couples like the Fairleighs' own old English square dances. Leila Fairleigh, the children's mother, a slender woman of medium height, with masses of white blonde hair caught in an elegant upsweep with trailing curls, and kindly sea-green eyes, floating down the stairs in a taffeta gown the bright yellow of a meadowlark's throat.

One time, Leila had hugged her at the bottom of those very same stairs. "Amity, darling, keep me company in the garden while I gather a bouquet for this afternoon's tea, will you please? Oh, how I miss England's lush sweet roses and carnations. I suppose if we can find enough for a bouquet, pink sweet William and purple iris will do. Leave Prentiss and Colin to do their homework and bring Nora Ann. She can play tag with her puppy on the lawn, and we can talk. If we hurry, we'll have time for a quick game of tennis before tea."

Was it that pleasant and wonderful; was it sweetness and light and happiness and *belonging?* Yes, before baby Nora Ann's fatal accident or illness, the Fairleighs had treated their governess almost as an equal, one of their own. And she had blindly, innocently, believed it would always be so, telling herself she was the most fortunate young woman alive. And then —

Amith whirled and ran down the steps of the porch, feet tapping in echo, wanting to flee and not knowing which way to run. After a few paces she halted, panting, and looked about her. She could hear the pounding of horses' hooves, shouts and laughter, see copper-haired Chester Fairleigh and his friends engaged in a polo game in the field right over there. Could see the sleek, finely muscled horses, racing, turning, chasing, under the hands of their masters attired in pink coats and white breeches.

One day, she had followed him to the stable to tell him that Leila needed him to answer to a bill collector who refused to leave without payment. The money regularly sent from their parents was late in arriving that month. Mr. Fairleigh had teasingly pushed her against the cool stone wall of the stable and tried to kiss her. She had laughed back at him and ducked aside, but her heart had yearned for the kiss and she'd come very close to allowing it.

Amity shuddered now at the memory. She sat down on the ground, knees tucked sideways under her skirts. She snatched at a leaf being tossed in the dry grass by the wind, and tore it to bits. From the first, Mr. Fairleigh had complimented her, and in her own foolish, lonely, girlish way, she had encouraged those compliments. She took special pains with her appearance when he was about. She rushed to fulfill his requests eagerly, whether in tutoring his children or running errands. At night, in her bed down the hall from the master bedroom, she fantasized that she was the wife of Chester Fairleigh, mistress of White Rock Manor of Beaconsfield, Kansas, forever secure, safe, looked after. None of the Fairleigh children, not her good little students, nor tiny Nora, whom she loved to dress and play with, ever entered the fantasies. They were too real, too beloved, to share a dishonest, shameful dream.

Infatuation for her mistress's husband had burned thrillingly in her veins, though she'd tried to keep her feelings carefully concealed. Had Leila guessed? Was that why she had blamed her and shoved her out on her own? If so, she'd been tried and found guilty for feelings only, for a young girl's fanciful dreams. Because she'd never acted on them, had committed no real wrong with the man. Not then, nor later when Chester Fairleigh took her away from Beaconsfield. Then she was sick and confused, and he — so cold and uncommunicative toward her — had put her and her few possessions out on the streets.

Amity got to her feet and wandered through the weed-choked, empty streets of downtown Beaconsfield, past the empty post office, dry goods store, meat market, blacksmith shop, creamery. The ornate restaurant, spartan laundry, lumber yard — all vacant now, abandoned. The elegant English village that had sprouted among the Kansas tumbleweeds was abandoned, after so brief a time, a fact that couldn't be changed.

The desolate Episcopal Church building loomed in her path; the side yard couldn't be avoided. *One single grave.* Was she the cause of it? For a time she looked down into the high-fenced square with its lone tombstone, the monument etched with flowers, the figure of a lamb, and the scrolled words, NORA ANN FAIRLEIGH, AGED 2, WITH HIM IN HEAVEN. Pain was heavy in her heart as she turned away.

Near the village icehouse, she found some blue asters and lacy milkweed, watered in the past from drainage pipes from the icehouse. She stood up, staring at the icehouse as chill bumps raised on her arms, which was ridiculous; the building wouldn't have held ice for a long time. Moving away from the eerie icehouse, across to the empty store, she found a patch of fragrant rose-colored beebalm and she fashioned the flowers into a nose-gay. She tore her long skirt climbing the fence, then knelt by the grave and placed the flowers in front of the small tombstone. With trembling fingers she traced the lamb on the rough stone. "Sweet Nora, can you help me?" she whispered through an emotion-clogged throat.

The wind keened softly in the grasses about her like the sound of a child at play, in a game of tag. She saw Nora running in her ruffled white dress, silky head bobbing with laughter, small arms spread like wings. Nora, sitting in a field of wildflowers of lavender, orange, and blue; herself a small white blossom singing a soft tune.

"Nora Ann? I know that I'm not the kind of person who could've brought you harm. If I was in any way responsible, forgive me —"

"Great stars! Thought I was seeing a ghost!" a voice sang out suddenly behind her, bringing Amity to her feet and making her spin around.

154

And you frightened me! A sun-bonneted woman about her own height of five-and-a-half feet, tall for a woman, tromped the last few paces that separated them, hobnail boots showing beneath the skirts of her filthy, ragged, rose-print dress.

"Land, I'm happy to see that you're real!"

Likewise. She could now see the woman's face, the long perfect nose and wide mouth. Her face, so flushed it seemed to be blooming in the shadows of her bonnet, was framed by russet wisps of hair that'd escaped the ties under her strong chin. Warm brown eyes, full of feeling, surveyed her. Amity guessed the woman's age at something past thirty-five, though considering what the Kansas elements did to one's looks, she could be younger. She was an attractive, lush-looking, robust woman in spite of her crude garb, but her left arm was wrapped in faded calico, the ragged bandage crusted and seeping with putrefaction.

"I was making soap, accidently spilled it on my arm. I can tell a body that hot lye soap will nearly burn your flesh off," the woman explained when she saw Amity's look of concern. "It'll be all right." She stuck out her other hand, brown, callused, dirty. "Chloe Brady. Who might you be, honey?"

She finally found her voice. "Amity Whitford. I-I'm so sorry about your arm." She motioned. "I — I was just placing some flowers on the child's grave." She took a deep breath, peering at the woman through the fence. "Do you know where they went, the people who lived here? What

155

happened?" Was it the death of the leader's child that took them away?

"The English folk took off, oh, maybe two years ago, back to England, every one of 'em, part and parcel. Fancy bloods — they couldn't make it out here. All those folks had on their minds was playing; never did learn to do a good lick of work, any of them. Racing their ponies, drinking and dancing and having tea parties, that's what they were best at. Their folks in Britain got tired of sending them money fast as they went through it, and called them home." She laughed, saying with a wide sweep of her good arm, "This silly place belongs to the coyotes now."

Amity nodded slowly. "The grave — do you know how the child over — over there — died?" Her throat constricted, and her mouth went dry.

"Well, there were rumors aplenty at the time. Mostly it was said that the children's governess went mad because she couldn't have the mistress's husband, the child's father, so she killed the child. But that seems a wild, farfetched claim to me, don't it to you?"

A silent scream of rebuttal echoed in Amity's mind as she stood frozen, unable to speak for several seconds, fighting a wave of nausea. She swallowed hard against it. "I think that story sounds very farfetched," she managed finally. In a thin voice, she asked, "Wasn't there an investigation? Wasn't the truth brought out?"

"All hush-hush. The young woman disappeared

very mysteriously. Don't know what they did with her, maybe she's locked up somewhere if that was the truth they told. Wasn't long after that the town began to fail and the people began to move out and go back home."

"Did you know any of them three years ago, to talk to?"

The woman shook her head. "No, only to howdy. I've got my own place over yonder about five miles and to tell you true, it keeps me busy sunup to sundown and after. I only came by here today because my horse broke loose from my rock sled and run off and I came looking. You didn't happen to see a shaggy, good-for-nothing liver-colored mare running loose by here, did you?"

For a moment, Amity was so preoccupied with her thoughts, the woman's question didn't register. Then she managed a smile as she climbed the fence and dropped down beside Chloe Brady. "I'm sorry, no. I doubt if she went by here. Come get in my rig and we'll go looking."

"Oh, I'm obliged!"

Amity could smell strong sweat and something else from Chloe Brady as they headed for the shade tree where the rented buggy and horse waited. It was the woman's arm she smelled. Chloe requested, "Let's drive back to the rock quarry first. I left Son there alone. That confounded mare could've circled back and be there right now, too, worrying Son about what happened to his mama."

"There's just the two of us," Chloe Brady explained when they were in the wagon and on their way. She motioned the direction she wanted Amity to take.

With effort, Amity pulled her mind away from Beaconsfield and her disappointment at finding everyone gone. She hadn't the means to go to London and question the Fairleighs, even *if* she could find them. . . . "Your husband died?" she asked as they drove along, trying to be at least civil and hold up her end of the conversation.

"Who needs a husband?" The woman on the buggy seat beside her laughed, loudly, musically. "Had me one for less than a year, and that was too long. Don't look so shocked, Amity, girl. Sometimes a woman's freedom is mighty sweet."

So Chloe'd made her own choice; it wasn't necessarily that some cad had gotten her pregnant and then abandoned her. "I've felt that way about independence, myself," Amity asserted. Of course, Chalk Holden came along to confuse matters. "Do you mind, being — alone? All the time? Doesn't it get lonely?"

Chloe said softly, "Yes, a woman gets lonely. But sometimes loneliness is preferable over some other states of affairs. A mean husband is one. A drunken one is another. And I've got a son."

Amity nodded agreement. She studied the woman beside her without actually staring as they bumped along through a stretch of hills and mounds that shimmered gold under the sun.

Beyond the rough edges life had given her,

158

Chloe Brady was a truly beautiful woman. Her kindly manner, pretty face, her comely form, would please a man. At the same time, an aura of independence seemed almost to sizzle from her. Coming to independence out of necessity herself, Amity understood, and felt a closeness to the woman.

In a while, they came to an area where it looked as though a giant claw had ripped the prairie apart. Ravines with outcroppings of layered rock zigzagged off into nowhere. Atop the cliffs, seared grasses clung to thin, rocky topsoil.

"Yonder is the quarry," Chloe said a few minutes later, pointing to a bluff with exposed layers of creamy-buff limestone above and piles of broken stone down below. A liver-colored horse stood switching flies near a stone-boat. Amity pulled the buggy into the shade of the bluff. The noise they made brought a small figure in overalls springing out of a pile of rock to come racing on bare feet toward them, the child clutching an old straw hat with both hands to keep it on.

"Ma, what kept you? Jewell came back, I got her all hitched up again, I was comin' to find you —" He had a very dirty face, and was maybe seven years old; his hair hung almost to his shoulders. He stopped and stared shyly at Amity as she got down and followed his mother.

"Son —" Chloe grasped his thin shoulder affectionately "— say hello to Miss Amity Whitford. You are 'miss,' aren't you?"

"Yes, but call me Amity, please, both of you.

159

It's nice to meet you, Son." She gazed down into his small face, into vivid gray-blue eyes. His features were fine and his expression sweet. His bottom lip had been injured some way and though healed, it had left a protruding lump that changed the perfection of his small handsome face only a little.

"My name's Thaddeus, but you can call me Thad." The lump on his lip traveled with the curve of his shy smile.

"Thank you, Thad." Hearing a moan, she looked away and saw the boy's mother struggling to load a huge block of stone onto her waiting sled. "Chloe, wait, you can't do that with your bad arm. We'll do it!"

Chloe sagged against the mare, her pink face beaded with perspiration. She held her bandaged arm gingerly with her good hand. She smiled in spite of agonizing pain in her brown eyes. "I've — been doing it," she panted. "Though it isn't a job for a weakling, that's certain. Right now, I don't know —"

"We'll finish loading the stone, won't we Thad?" Amity hefted the rock Chloe'd been trying to lift and dropped it with a thud onto the others piled on the sledge. She nodded, "Take the shade while the boy and I handle this." Chloe did as she was told, sinking to the ground with a groan she couldn't hold back. She let her head drop back against the cliffside and closed her eyes.

Amity and the boy worked industriously for a while, until Amity called over her shoulder,

"Don't you think that's enough? I don't believe your horse can pull a bigger load."

Chloe sighed very loudly. "Our Jewell is usually a stout puller, but you're right. That's enough rock." She got to her feet with effort and staggered to Amity, reaching for her hand. "Thank you so much, Amity Whitford. I won't be keeping you any longer. Godspeed, and whatever you were asking for, back there in the graveyard, I hope you find it."

Amity chewed her lip, more worried about the condition of the woman's arm now than Beaconsfield and the mystery that waited there to be solved. "I'm coming with you," she said finally. "I'd like to look at your arm — not that I've done that much doctoring, but maybe I can help."

The other woman blew out a long sigh and finally nodded. "It's hard to change the bandage one-handed, and when the boy tries to do it — well, he gets sick, is what he does. If you'll do that for me, I'd like to give you supper and a bed for the night, if you'd care to stay with us?"

"Thank you. I'll follow in my rig." If there was nothing for her at Beaconsfield, she should get back to her own affairs as soon as possible. But she hadn't yet bought her return train ticket and one meal and a night with the Bradys would certainly help refresh her.

Their home was a cave in the side of a hill, a dugout. The front was built of layers of sod. An adjoining shed contained a couple of storage barrels, a washtub, a pile of sprouting potatoes, a few tools that were old, homemade, and mended. Hens clucked from a coop built to the side of the shed. Staked out and grazing a few yards away was a spavined cow that looked old enough to have been on the Ark. Looking around, Amity thought to herself that the place seemed hardly fit for animals, let alone humans. Chloe explained, with a sigh of pain, "I'm getting the stone to build me and Son the most beautiful house this country ever saw. Trouble is, it takes time to cut, load, and haul stone. Especially with this pesky arm."

Amity smiled in apology for her thoughts. She hardly lived in a palace herself. "Let's see to that arm right away."

Inside, they sat at a crude wooden table. Amity's teeth clenched in determination as she reached for Chloe's arm. Perspiration ran down the sides of her face. Chloe's own face hardened as she braced herself, eyes filled with pain — while Amity unwound the sticky bandage with a careful touch. A putrid odor arose from the arm and Amity's stomach heaved. She peeled back the soiled bandage and saw the decayed flesh clinging to it, Chloe's arm, weeping and gray, red streaks tracing up into healthy flesh. "Oh, Chloe, this has to be attended to by a real doctor! It looks to me like you're on the verge of blood poisoning. You could die!"

"No, Miss Whitford — Amity. You can take care of it. The burn looks a worse mess than it really is." She laughed, "Smells bad, too. *Whew.* I'm sorry. Poor Son. No wonder he has trouble seeing to it for me. Go on, boy." She nodded at the youngster holding his nose. "Bring the saleratus and some water in the washpan."

For a good half hour, Amity worked on the arm, cleaning it thoroughly with the baking soda rinse, then spreading the wound with a thick sour cream the boy brought her next. She wished for a tonic to help kill Chloe's pain, but there was none, not even a drop of whiskey. She found the cleanest cloth available, a scrap of calico from a trunk, and bound the arm again. Afterward, she helped Chloe to lie on the quilt-covered cot in the kitchen, and the woman fell into a deep sleep almost the moment she touched it.

Amity turned to young Thaddeus, who had been watching and waiting, his heart in his small face, the bump on his lip making him appear particularly sad. "She'll be all right," she told him with a forced smile. "Let's see, what shall we fix for supper? Any ideas? I'm a good cook!"

With Thaddeus showing her where to find things, she baked a pan of corn bread, fried slices of salt pork, and boiled a few beet tops from the meager garden outside, for healthy greens.

But Chloe was too tired or too ill to take any of the food. Amity saw that Thaddeus ate, and managed a few bites herself.

When the hour grew late, Amity drew the rocker nearer the woman's bed and spent the dark, lonely hours there wrapped in a quilt. She got up periodically to wipe Chloe's flushed skin with a damp cloth. Come daylight, she decided grimly, truly fearful for the woman's life, she was driving Chloe Brady to Great Bend to see a regular doctor, providing they had one, and if she could keep Chloe alive that long.

Chapter Ten

Gray light filtered through the dugout's one window as Amity slowly lifted her head from the back of the chair and pushed aside the quilt that covered her. She sniffed at the smell of delicious boiling coffee. My goodness, that little Thaddeus was a wonder, waking up before anyone else and making coffee. She stood up, yawning, then saw that the nearby cot was empty. She whirled. Chloe stood at the stove, smiling at Amity over her shoulder. "Mornin'!"

"Chloe! Good heavens, what are you doing up?" Untangling her feet from the quilt, she hurried to put a hand on the sick woman's shoulder. "How do you feel?"

"I'll admit to some pain along about dawn. But 'cry before breakfast, sing before supper.' I'll be fine!" She insisted, "Looks like all I needed was your kindly ministrations to the arm and a good night's rest. I'm fit as a fiddle and soon as we eat, it's back to the quarry. I want a house before winter, a real house."

"Let me see your arm!"

"All right, but I guarantee that it won't make a difference, Miss. I got to work."

Amity undid the bandage daintily, and peeked at the wound that actually did look better this morning; the red threads of infection had faded some, and the flesh didn't feel as hot. "Hmmm, possibly it is improving, but you must keep watch that it doesn't worsen. What had you done for the burn before I came?"

"Put slices of raw potato on it, to take the sting out. I guess that didn't keep it from festering, though, huh?"

"No, I'm afraid it didn't." She held the arm gently, turning it this way and that. "Do you think we might leave it undressed. Maybe drying in the air would help."

Chloe was quick to reply, "There's work to be done. That limey dust would get all over it and it'd have to be chipped off."

"But you do know what the red streaks mean?"

"The poison's spreading. I know that. 'Minds me of that red mercury in a thermometer — rising, then coming back down —"

"And maybe rising higher, next time!"

"I expect I'll just have to take my chances." She winced as Amity swabbed pus from the wound. "There's folks who believe burns can be cured by reburning, did you know that?" she asked through clenched teeth. "When I was a little girl, I heard a girl scream from where she lived away down the road when her father held her hand over the fire to reburn her palm after she'd been scalded with water."

Amity shuddered. "I wish I could convince you to see a real doctor. Please?" She finished rewrapping the arm.

"If one could be found. They come and go in Great Bend. Chances of living are better out here if you can see to your troubles yourself. Folks have died along the way, just trying to get to a doctor." Chloe hadn't combed her hair; it was as wild as a buzzard's nest. She wore the same dirty dress as yesterday. Her hands were probably as clean as she could get them considering the ground-in dirt in the creases and around her fingernails.

Amity sighed and bit her tongue to keep from saying anything. A woman alone with just the small boy's help wouldn't have much time for herself, and maybe, with no one else to see, didn't really care. Still, a little hygiene would help the woman to heal.

"Having you around has been nice, dear," Chloe said as she poured a cup of coffee for Amity. "I suppose you'll need to be leavin' once you've had breakfast?"

Amity hesitated. Chloe was a dear, really, so friendly. A person could hardly ignore the woman's pitiful plight, working to build a stone house with the badly festering arm, on top of her other chores. Never mind that at home John Clyde needed Amity equally as much. The others in the school superintendent race were likely having a field day campaigning in the four days she'd been gone. She managed a reserved smile. "I can

167

give you a few hours help this morning, and then I really must be on my way." The relieved look on Chloe's face told her she'd made the right decision. "But I do insist that if we do this, I take the heavy work and you just supervise, Chloe. And if your arm isn't a great deal better after today, I pray you'll give up on rock gathering till it is."

At that moment, Thaddeus came to the kitchen area, sleepy-eyed, his sweet face breaking into a grin when he saw his mother up and about. Chloe reached out and lovingly smoothed his flowing locks. "I suppose I should cut it. . . ." she told Amity. She looked down at the boy. ". . . But our scissors broke, didn't they? Long time ago and we couldn't fix them." She let her hand rest on his head as she went on, explaining, "I tried to cut it then with a knife. Nearly scared the wits out of him when I'd approach him with that knife in my hand. So I just gave up, decided to leave well enough alone. And Son doesn't mind, do you?"

He shrugged, and Amity guessed he minded, a mite, but not enough to have his hair chopped off with a knife.

"Son, you smell rank as a weed-patch!" Chloe wrinkled her nose at the boy, who was filling his bowl with cornmeal mush from a pot on the stove. "We get our water from a spring," she told Amity, "but this time of year it starts to dry up and we don't get our baths too often."

"Oh." That explained a lot.

"We don't have quarries like this, over west on the high plains where I live." Amity panted as she rested, leaning on the handle of her sledge. "I've heard there's some white magnesian limestone in the bluffs along the Arkansas, though. I wouldn't mind a big stone house someday myself," she admitted, puffing a strand of hair from her eyes. She'd believed herself in good physical condition from work on her own place, but rock cutting was about to cause her to change her mind. In fact, she doubted she'd attempted work so difficult, with fruits of the labor so slow to come. On their arrival, she'd scraped a new area of limestone ledge free of topsoil, while Chloe explained that the deeper the limestone, the softer and easier it was to work with. At first Amity had swung the sledge clumsily, as she tried to break out sections for building blocks from the thick ledge. Chloe teased her, saying that she could do better with just one good arm. Overriding Amity's protests, Chloe would not just sit by but had taken on the job of one-handedly shaping the chunks of soft stone with a chisel, before exposure to the air hardened it.

"More's the pity." Chloe finally replied to Amity's comment about the lack of limestone in Hamilton County, as she hacked away with the chisel gripped in her fist. "Limestone's a boon to those that are able to get it. Once my house is built, I'm building a stone barn and fences, to keep the animals in that I ain't got yet. Right now, the shed's big enough to shelter Jewell, my mare, and my poor old milk cow. I guess if God couldn't give Kansas enough trees, he could at least give us stone, and lots of it. This ledge," she pointed, "goes on for miles." In a moment she asked, "You live with your folks? Your papa a farmer?"

"I have my own place." Amity went on to describe Dove's Nest Ranch, though nothing of how she came to be there. "I want more land, too, when I can afford to run more cattle." There was no way to conceal the pride from her voice. "Any man or woman can file on a claim, but it's the ones who stay who build up a country. I'd like to have my part in that, over west."

"You sound a lot like me," Chloe said, resting a moment, holding her sore arm with her good hand. "Maybe we should join up together and get us a real spread?" They looked one another in the eye a moment, as though considering the proposition, then both shook their heads with the same laughing words: "Too independent — like my own place."

"Well, anyway," Chloe picked up her chisel again, "if we ever did team up, I expect the two of us could move a few mountains!"

"Assuredly so!"

Amity was breathless after a few minutes swinging the sledge. When she rested, Amity explained about her campaign to be Hamilton County school superintendent.

"Why would a woman want to do a thing like

170

that?" Chloe's face was open, honestly curious.

"It's a paying job for me, and I can do a lot of good. I love children."

"That little grave in the Beaconsfield cemetery . . . ?"

"Her name was Nora Ann," Amity whispered. "I especially loved that child." But she said nothing more.

"You don't want to talk about it?"

"I'd rather not."

They worked in silence for a long time, Amity swinging the sledge, breaking out the building blocks, until her shoulder joints, back, and elbows screamed with pain. She wiped the sweat from her forehead on her sleeve, gritting her teeth to keep from groaning aloud, as she looked to Chloe to see how she was making out.

The other woman sat on a pile of stone, knees spread under her long skirts as she hacked away. "It helps," she said, studying Amity, "to look for natural stresses and seams in the rock where it'll break easier."

"Thanks!" Amity said, lifting the five-pound hammer over her head and bringing it down. "I'll remember that!"

They worked on under a sweltering sun. After his mother finished with them, Thaddeus carried those stones he could lift over to the wagon and tumbled them in with a loud thump. The biggest blocks probably weighed at least fifteen pounds each, heavy enough after a while. "Hard work for man or beast," Chloe grunted as she rolled a stone aside for Thaddeus.

"There ought to be an easier way," Amity answered, licking the sweat from her lips and grabbing the place in her back that felt like it was on fire, "beyond pure elbow grease!"

"Maybe a good man to do it for you!" Chloe replied without her usual chuckle. She looked, and sounded, done in, flushed with fever.

Amity looked at the stone pile, and her co-workers, swimming in a sweaty haze. "I don't see any good men." She laughed drily.

"I'm a man!" Thaddeus piped up. "An' I'm helpin'."

"I'm sorry, Thaddeus," Amity said quickly. "You are helping; you're a big help. I don't think a grown man could do your job any better." She felt relieved at his satisfied smile.

"What we all need," Chloe said with a weary sigh, "is to break for lunch."

They sat on rocks under the overhang. The shade made little difference, Amity thought. It was as hot as hades — but would be worse out in the direct sun. The meal was cold patties of fried cornmeal mush and warm water from a canvas-wrapped jug. Amity was starved and ate like a field hand, but again, Chloe hardly ate a thing. "Chloe, are you all right?" she asked. She realized that Chloe was looking different from even an hour ago, more glassy-eyed and feverish, truly unwell.

"I'm just tuckered," Chloe argued. "That's all. This job'll make an old woman of anybody, in no time."

After she'd rushed over to place the back of her hand on Chloe's face, Amity cried, "You're burning up with fever! Good Lord, Chloe —" she knelt in front of her "— I never should've let you come out here today; you should be in bed." Ignoring Chloe's protests, she undid the bandage on her arm, for a look. The red streaks were much plainer this afternoon, reaching almost to Chloe's shoulder. "My God, Chloe!"

Watching them Thaddeus's small face was etched with concern. He laid his last bite of fried mush on the stone beside him, unwanted now.

"Pshaw," Chloe snorted. "If I'd let every little nick and bruise keep me abed, I'd be dead already! I've got the boy to see to here at home. A doctor would likely charge some ungodly amount for treatment —" her voice flattened "— that I can't afford. Take my arm off, maybe, an' who wants that?" She tried to rise, and couldn't. "Now don't get in a froth about this," she commanded, seeing Amity's face. "I'm going to be all right but even if I ain't, I prefer to die in my own bed, thank you."

Few times in life had Amity felt such alarm. "Oh, Chloe. At least let me drive you back to the dugout and put you to bed."

Even with Amity half lifting her, it was difficult for Chloe to get into the wagon. On the way to the dugout she insisted on stopping, pointing to a patch of spindly, topnotched weeds. "Son, you get down and pull up some of that green-thread plant. A tea made of greenthread'll bring

173

this confounded fever down," she told Amity, weaving on the wagon seat.

The tea helped not at all. Nor was the fever phased by the continual succession of wet blankets Amity kept on Chloe's shivering, feverish body.

"Only about another bucketful in the spring," Thaddeus told Amity, his face screwed up with worry, "then it'll be just a seep."

"Bring it, honey."

For hours, she worked over Chloe, frantic to bring her raging temperature down. But as Chloe's condition worsened, Amity knew with almost dead certainty that the poison in the woman's blood was affecting her vital organs, and likely had been for some time, but Chloe had pushed so hard to stay on her feet. *Lord, don't let it be too late.* As Amity exchanged the blanket covering Chloe with one freshly wet, the old one would be hot in her fingers. Desperate, she tried to get Chloe to take more of the greenthread tea, but she couldn't swallow and it spilled down her chin. Chloe coughed and pushed the cup away. "Need to talk," she mumbled, wiping an ugly phlegm from her mouth.

"No, Chloe, please save your strength."

"Too late . . . things got to say —" She panted for breath. "Sorry . . . I got you into . . . this, Amity. Son — ?"

"I gave him his supper some time ago. He went to bed. I'm sure he's asleep." He'd gone so obediently, poor lad, not knowing what else to do.

Chloe was struggling to say more. Amity patted her. "Shh, everything's all right. Don't worry."

But Chloe caught her hand in a blistering hot, feeble squeeze. Her eyes opened and glassy as they were, implored Amity to listen. "I . . . want you to take . . . Son. Please. Raise him as . . . your own. He's smart. Good boy —"

"Oh, plague! Chloe, please don't talk like this. You don't know anything about me. You're going to get better," she lied.

"Know enough," she said in a whispery sigh.

Frantic to try anything, Amity cried, "It might not be too late. Thad can stay with you, I'll ride for the doctor —"

Chloe's breath came in a hissing plea as her head moved slightly on her pillow, "Don't leave us! Listen —"

Amity bit her tongue, and clutched Chloe's hot hand in her own. Chloe's voice came so faint that she had to lean close to hear what she was saying. "Son's quality — like his f-father. Take him — shield —"

Shield him from pain? Shield him from trouble?

What she wanted to do was save his mother from dying, and she couldn't. "I'll see to Thaddy," Amity whispered brokenly in Chloe's ear. "Your boy will be fine. Chloe — ?"

But Chloe was beyond speaking, and in the wee hours of the following night, her tortured breathing stilled for good.

For a while, Amity couldn't believe Chloe was gone. She put her hand in front of her mouth

175

but could feel no breath, touched her temple, laid her hand on her chest.

She went to the door and stepped outside, needing to escape for a few minutes the close confines of the dugout, the smell of sickness and death, to think. She walked into the yard a few paces, hands clasped tightly in front of her, breathing deeply the night air. The last few stars were blinking out; in the east dawn was breaking, the sky a faint pink. Poor, dear Chloe. What was the meaning of everything that had happened the past few days? Was it God's design that she be here for young Thaddeus, when He took Chloe?

She shook her head, brushed at tears, not really sure, but knowing there were very real, sad chores to tend to before the boy awoke. She went back inside. Tenderly, she used the remaining water to wash Chloe's body, dressing the still form in the cleanest garments she could find. She whispered through a painful lump in her throat, "God bless you, Chloe. I thank you from my heart, for honoring me so." Tears blurred as she looked toward Thaddy, curled in a tight ball in his bed in the corner. If only her first responsibility to him didn't have to be to tell him his mother was dead.

"I lost my own mama and papa, Thaddeus. I know how it feels." He let her hold him against her while he sobbed. She explained as best she could Chloe's plans for them. He was very quiet, listening, then he wiped his eyes and nose on her apron, an action that made her heart ache. Her fingers threaded through his long silky hair. "We'll be fine, Thaddeus, just fine."

"I miss Mama," he choked out, "already. It — hurts."

"I know you miss her, honey, and you will for a long time. But you have me, and I'm going to take very good care of you. I think you'll like my home, Dove's Nest, a lot."

The fear and confusion at having lost his mother was still there in his face, though there was some of Chloe's practical stoicism in him, too, as he stopped crying and helped Amity with what had to be done.

It hurt to watch him being so obedient to her every bidding, a seven-year-old child trying to be a man, as they sorted Chloe's things and packed what he needed. There was a small gold pendant watch of Chloe's that he wanted to keep. He flipped the back open to show Amity the inscription inside. *To Chloe from Peter with Love.* "I think my father gave it to her."

"Did you know your father? Can you tell me his name? Where he might be?"

He shook his head. "I think his name was Peter, but I don't know the rest." Matter-of-factly, he added, "Mama said we didn't need my papa."

She questioned him further, in case there were relatives that should be notified. Thaddeus knew of no one. They had lived other places, but he didn't know where. They'd never lived with anyone else; it had always been just the two of them.

Search as she would, Amity found no legal papers signifying any claim of Chloe's to the property, not even that she'd filed for ownership. She could only deduce that Chloe had been a squatter, and perhaps, clear out here, her existence might not have been known to others. At least, not to any who minded.

They buried Chloe on the knoll where she had meant to build her stone house. They chipped her name and the date in a chunk of limestone and placed it at the head of the grave. Amity held the sobbing boy to her for as long as he cried. "Take this," she said, a bit later, and, plucking a stem of purple prairie clover from the bouquet they'd gathered for the grave, she tucked it into his pocket. "It'll dry and be a keepsake of your mama and this place."

For a long time, they stood there, the wind blowing Amity's skirts and trying to lift Thaddy's hat. "All ready?" she asked gently.

Thaddeus, blinking furiously, climbed into the rented buggy beside her. The chickens he'd shooed away, scattering them into the prairie grasses, were returning. "Go away!" he leaned off the side of the buggy to shout at them. "Get on after them damned grasshoppers over there." He pointed. "Damn chickens," he muttered, shaking his head.

He sounded just like Chloe. This once, Amity was going to let him get by with cursing. He deserved to. "How are the cow and Jewell — are they coming right along?" They'd tied the cow and the liver-colored mare to the back of the buggy. Amity would try to sell them in Great Bend; she would need the money to pay for the boy's ticket to Syracuse. While in Great Bend, she would inform the authorities about Chloe's passing.

He looked. "Yep, they're a'comin'."

"Good." Amity placed her hand on his shoulder and repeated, "Good." She still felt the newness of the situation settled on her like a strange mantle. At the same time, she wanted this brave little boy for her own as much as she'd ever wanted anything in her life.

Chapter Eleven

"This is Syracuse," Amity told Thaddeus as they stepped off the train. She felt a rise in emotion as she held his moist, gritty little fingers in one hand, the worn grip of her satchel in the other, and led the way past barrels and boxes waiting to be loaded. It was good to be back, and she nodded and smiled at everyone: acquaintances, townsfolk going about on an assortment of missions, and others there simply to take in the station's goings-on. Most stared at her in return. The train crew were shouting back and forth as they prepared to take on water from the Santa Fe tank and replenish fuel from the coal car. The conductor called for westbound passengers continuing on to Colorado to be ready to leave in fifteen minutes. Thirsty cattle bawled from the stock pens not far from the station.

Thaddeus pressed close to her rustling skirts, head swiveling as he took everything in with wide, slate-blue eyes, his mouth open in curiosity.

Amity took a moment to remove a handkerchief from her drawstring reticule, patting her brow and lips with the square of rough linen. The infernal heat on the ever-blowing wind caused her to pant as she licked her salty lips and told him, "We'll be at Dove's Nest by supper time, but first we have to rent a driver and rig at the livery stable."

"Yes, miss," he answered politely, and she gave his hand a little squeeze of affection.

The dusty, newly graded street to the main part of town lay baking in the sun. Amity reflected that the councilwomen who had taken office this spring were being true to their word; they'd ordered property owners to build new sidewalks before fall, too. It was nice to see the town changing for the better. She smiled to herself as they set off. "Over there's the schoolhouse," she said, pointing out the summer-vacant school to Thaddeus as they passed. Out near the track the few scattered homes were mostly soddies, with a couple of two-story frame houses with porches and picket fences. As they neared the town center, Amity became aware that they were being stared at with far more interest than was usual, even for Syracuse folks. From front porches and doorways, people shaded their eyes and rubbernecked something fierce. But then, she'd hardly broadcast her destination when she left town last week, and here she was returning with a small boy in tow. The short way to the livery stretched like miles with all the busybody eyes.

"Mrs. Bell, good afternoon." Amity smiled and called out to Sheriff Wilf Bell's wife, Miranda, who'd ceased taking her wash from the line to stare, clothespins sticking out of her mouth like cat's whiskers. Amity had met Sheriff Bell on a couple of occasions. He was wiry, tough, basically honest, and he had the handsomest handlebar moustaches she'd ever seen.

"Afternoon, Mrs. Branch." Amity waved at the doughy-faced minister's wife fanning herself on her front porch, and to the woman sitting with her, said, "Abigail." She remembered Abigail Limbaugh's nosy pressure to know all her business and personal history at the time of the speeches on the Fourth of July; the woman's almost uncanny sense that Amity was hiding something. Let her think about *this!*

Abigail and Reverend Branch's wife, Sadie, were close friends of Thisba Strout, Amity reflected. They'd likely give the banker's wife a gossipy report within the hour. The single Miss Whitford coming up suddenly with an unknown child — ? Amity's smile faded. There was something about Mrs. Strout's dislike of her that at times could be as frightening as it was puzzling, though Thisba was hardly a favorite of hers either.

They approached the livery, where a weather vane on the roof whirred in the wind and the sun glinted off twin metal lightning rods. A moment later, Amity led Thaddeus out of the sun's white glare into the cooler, though smelly, shadows of the cavernous barn. Tack hung from every wall, corners were thick with dust-laden cobwebs, horses stood hip-shot in their stalls on the hard-packed, straw-strewn floor. The freckled, red-haired stableboy, whistling softly through his teeth as he worked — she thought he was called Skimmy — was getting her rig ready when the shadow of a rider coming in off the street fell across the dirt floor. Amity's heart leaped as Skimmy greeted the rider, whose form she recognized, "Holden, be right with you."

"Got it taken care of," Chalk replied above the loud banging of hammer on iron from the wagonworks next door. He dismounted with a creak of leather and with a wondering look at Amity and the boy beside her. He nodded and led his horse toward a nearby stall. The horse, clopping along, still dripped water from its muzzle from a stop at the huge trough outside.

Amity held her breath, watching. Doves cooed in the loft above; there was the sound of horses munching, the muted flutter of wings and twittery song of sparrows darting in and out of the barn. She debated only a second longer. Taking Thaddeus by the hand, she led him to where Chalk, muscles rippling under the cloth of his sweat-darkened, blue striped shirt, was lifting the saddle off his horse. She was debating what to say when he turned and took off his hat, a glad look in his eyes.

She returned his smile, dismissing the idea of apologizing for having rushed away at the Fourth of July celebration; it might be best to let the past lie. Nor could she tell him much about where she'd been, and why, as she'd hoped to. She said, "Thaddeus, I'd like you to meet Mr. Holden.

Mr. Holden owns the *Syracuse Banner* newspaper, Thaddy."

Chalk grinned, twirled his moustache, then he squatted and shook the boy's hand, "Nice to meet you, son."

"Hello, Mr. Banner," Thaddeus said gravely.

"Mr. *Holden*, honey; his newspaper's called the *Banner*," Amity corrected, instantly sorry when the boy blushed with embarrassment.

"You can call me Chalk, Thad. I got that name from eatin' chalk instead of writin' with it, when I was about your age."

A slow grin crept over Thaddeus's face.

Chalk couldn't keep his eyes off Amity. "You've been away."

"Yes, it's wonderful to be home again." An image of Beaconsfield, empty, dusty, ghostly, flickered in her mind. "There was something I had to do — that didn't turn out too successfully, I'm afraid." Her heart was thumping furiously from his nearness. She put her arm around Thaddy's shoulder, and said, "If you want to put an item in the paper, Mr. Holden," *to answer all that curiosity out there*, "you may say that Thaddeus is the child of a deceased friend of mine, Chloe Brady. And he's now come to make his home with me."

Thaddeus, in the presence of adults who seemed to have eyes only for each other, had begun to shuffle restlessly, looking toward the wide doors that led to the street. A huge hay wagon pulled up out front.

184

Skimmy, the hostler, called toward the livery office that the hay was there, then led a horse and buggy to where the trio stood. "All ready to go, Miss Whitford."

Before she could move, Chalk stepped forward. "I'd like to drive you out home. We need to talk about your campaign."

Amity drew a long breath in hesitation, her mind battling her heart's insistence. "Th-that's very kind of you, but it's not necessary. I would like to catch up on what's going on in the campaign race, however." She watched Chalk's face light up like a shower of stars on a summer night as she went on, "If you'd like to come out to Dove's Nest, next Sunday, I'd be glad to give you dinner — in exchange for what I need to know."

"I'm much obliged. I'll look forward to it." Grinning, Chalk hefted Thaddeus up and placed him in the middle of the buggy seat. "There you go, boy." He reached down and picked up Thaddy's hat that had fallen off. "A youngster's luck doesn't get much better than being with Miss Amity, as you're gonna find out."

Thaddeus looked shyly from the newspaperman's face to Amity, who stood aside, blushing.

Chalk assisted Amity onto the wagon, letting his hand linger a moment at her waist. She cleared her throat. "Good day, Chalk." She was glad their friendship was on the mend. She signaled to Skimmy that she was ready.

Skimmy gave last directions to an ancient, crippled hostler he was leaving in charge, and leaped into the driver's seat. "Don't try unloading that hay, yourself, Mica," he shouted over his shoulder. "Get Grover, Mr. Limbaugh, from over to the wagonworks to help."

They were driving out of the livery when she heard Chalk calling her name. "Wait," she told Skimmy. He drew up the reins as Chalk strode up to her side of the buggy, a frown creasing his handsome forehead where perspiration formed tiny beads.

"I almost forgot to tell you," he said earnestly. Smoothing back his hair, which was damp and beginning to curl from the heat, he held his hat in his other hand. "I was out by your place day before yesterday and your man, Rossback, was ailin'."

"John Clyde — sick?" Alarm bloomed in the pit of her stomach.

"He said it wasn't much, he'd eaten some spoiled grub, but to be truthful, he was pretty green around the gills. I helped him with the choring and spent the night. He seemed to be gettin' better when I left the next morning."

She thanked him and asked Skimmy to hurry.

"Upset stomach is all!" John Clyde growled, finally convincing her. He responded encouragingly to her ministrations, and doses of sulphur and molasses. After a couple of days, Amity, believing that though he might not be completely well, he was on the mend, faced her other work.

186

"Would you like to help?" she asked Thaddeus. He nodded eagerly and took the bucket she'd filled from the well and followed her to the garden patch west of the house. Zip, John Clyde's dog, loped along at the boy's side; the two of them had become fast friends since the boy's arrival. Thaddy confessed he'd always wanted a dog and it did her heart good to see the boy laughing and looking less sad when he and Zip played. Other times, from the forlorn, faraway look in Thaddeus's eyes, she knew he was mourning his mama.

Her vegetables had come up after replanting but were in desperate need of moisture under this merciless sun, and heaven only knew when, *if* ever, it would rain again. Stooping, she showed Thad how to take the dipper and carefully pour water around each plant. "Potatoes and turnips first," she told him, "then the pumpkins and melons." God help her kafir and the regular corn; there wasn't much she could do about those crops, except pray and water sparingly where she could.

From the first day, Thaddeus was fascinated with her well, loved to let the bucket down and bring it up brimming. But she'd had to warn him that there was a limit; her well could go dry if the heat continued and no rain came. Unboylike, he'd loved his first bath at Dove's Nest. She'd cut his hair so he'd be cooler and discovered what a handsome little rascal he was, when clean and trimmed. Now, as he squatted, taking the dipper from her to water a potato plant, she ventured to brush back the hair at his temple with a tender touch. He grinned at her like a starved puppy. She kissed his cheek, elation warming her that he was taking to her so easily. Maybe not as a substitute for his mother, but he did like her; he needed her. He seemed happy enough to be where he was; only in the evenings did he look sad. It was then he missed his mother most. Amity rose to her feet, looking down at him from under the brim of Papa's old gray hat. No misfortune would ever befall *this* child in her care.

After another day, John Clyde was back on his feet, although Amity meant to see that he didn't overdo. Stopping at the house to fill her water jug, she set out on foot to walk a mile or so north. She shooed her half wild cattle out of the way as she went to join John Clyde. He had driven off to get a load of the hay he'd cut in her absence, which was more than dry enough to store in the barn now. It had been her hope that they'd cut enough extra hay to be able to sell some. But they'd be lucky to get enough put by for their own need. She surveyed the scene as she grew close. John, skinny as a scarecrow, pitched hay into the wagon with their homemade wooden fork. Around him, the area where he'd cut while she was gone was so ragged and uneven, she'd have sworn he'd scythed the patch dead drunk. Normally, John Clyde scythed with a wide, smooth, sweeping arc that cut the grass close and even. Her eyes told her how truly sick he must have been, although he claimed it was just a touch of "whistle-berry poisoning" — tainted beans not setting well on his "pertickaler" stomach — that laid him a bit low.

"How are you, John?" she asked, coming up to touch his arm and hand him the canvas wrapped water jug. He seemed to be improving since her return, subsisting on the soft gruel diet she made him eat for the time being. Believing as her mother did that cleanliness wasn't only godly, but also healthy, she'd turned out his bed from his cubbyhole room in the barn, washed it, and hung it to dry on the line she'd strung from her well posts to the barn.

He let the fork rest in the crook of his arm and took a long draught from the jug. "Right as rain, Missy — or right as rain'd be if the Lord would just give us a few drops."

She shook her head, took off her hat and wiped her face on her sleeve. "We have to have plenty of hay to go along with the grain." She made a face. "My oat yield was positively pitiful." It'd done so poorly she'd been able to cut and bind it herself. She had finished flailing, separating the grain from the straw, late last night. "We must have food for ourselves, but my garden —" she waved her arm "— everything — is slowly drying up. I have the boy watering the garden patch now."

At the mention of Thad, John Clyde's eyes

lit up. He'd never questioned her, had accepted the brief explanation she gave him about Chloe's death, but he seemed to believe she'd gone away to get Thaddeus and bring him here. She saw no harm in keeping to herself her reasons for going to Beaconsfield. "Thaddy's a real worker, and a noble little soul," she answered John Clyde's smile.

"Ain't that the truth. An' he's curious as scat, an' brighter'n a penny." John spat on the ground and smiled. "Makes my bones feel young agin just watchin' him. An' my old lonesome dog acts like a pup around the boy. It's good you brought the young 'un here, Missy, real good." He squinted at her, his pointy face going serious. "An' we're gonna be all right. One way or t'other, we'll figure things out. So don't worry your pretty head about things you can't help, no wise."

She laughed softly at him. "One way I can help is to take better care of you. Except for Thaddy, I'm sorry I went on the trip at a time I'm needed so much here." She strode to where the cradle scythe, taller than she, leaned against the wagon. Pulling her father's hat over her eyes, she took up the scythe with her right hand gripping the short handle and her left holding the long bent wood handle further up. She carried it to where the prairie grass still stood tall and made the first low sweep, the sun glinting off the newly sharpened blade and the golden grass falling before it. Adapting a rhythm, feeling the heavy scythe pull at every muscle in her body, she cut, and cut, and cut, following the path of her swing, tromping over the fallen sheaves of grass. Grasshoppers that couldn't evade her path were crushed under her thin-soled moccasins. Once she might have been squeamish about such, but these years in Kansas had changed that. Sweat got in her eyes, and flies bit at her exposed skin, face, neck, hands. Bees droned up out of the hay when she least expected it and she was constantly dodging and swatting. The sun bore down unbearably hard. She worked on, finding a strength in need. She would feed her people, her animals. She would keep this place. They would survive.

Having the boy made a difference. She hated it, though, that her good fortune came out of Chloe's death. She swung viciously, cropping the grass short in an extra wide swath.

Those carefree days in Cairo, when she was a young, innocent girl, she'd dreamed of having a husband and children, a pretty home. Had written those dreams down at great length in her diary. All that was changed drastically by the events at Beaconsfield. But the boy was with her, and she would honor his mother by giving Thad her utmost love, her attention, her care. In the face of whatever trial might befall her. Whatever enemy — man, woman, weather — might want to do her in, the devil had no chance now. She had her a little boy, and she'd raise him like her own son. The first few days after Chloe's death, Amity had not allowed herself to be happy that she had Thaddeus, but it was getting harder to fight the joy seeping into her soul.

Late one night that week, while Thaddy slept soundly in his corner bed — newly made of cottonwood limbs and a mattress of prairie hay — with Zip at the foot, Amity took time to think about further campaign plans. As she sat rocking in the moonlit kitchen, going over her meager wardrobe, she tried to plot how to look her best. She needed to be well turned out and confident if people were to put their trust in her. She wanted to have a better, more complete answer when people asked, as they were still wont to do, why she, a woman, was running at all. That the woman desperately needed the salary was beside the point. She honestly believed that women understood children better, and therefore dealt with their education with greater wisdom. A woman could be firm, yet gentle at the same time. Men seemed to be not half as patient with children, as a rule. Also, there were more female teachers than male teachers. Who better to deal with the teachers than another woman?

Wishing to catch up on the course of the campaign in her absence, she finally lit the lamp to pore over the papers Chalk had brought out to Dove's Nest while she was away. According to Chalk's accounts, Seymour Purdue, accompanied by his prominent cousin, Mrs. Thisba Strout, was visiting organizations in every town in the county. Speaking to men's clubs, literary societies, Sunday School classes, everything, even sewing bees in bids to get the husbands' votes. Even if he didn't win, Amity thought with amusement, Mr. Purdue was surely enjoying all the free food the ladies would be thrusting upon him. Amos Taylor seemed to be making less fuss, but he didn't need to: Everyone knew him. Amity felt slighted, though she knew there was little to write about her campaign at the moment. Chalk had to be fair to the others, whether he was actually behind them or not.

As she read about county seat fights still raging around the state, she wondered if tensions had waned in Hamilton County. In an editorial, Chalk warned against a repeat of the dispute in Wichita County between rival towns Coronado and Leoti, where the fever got so high the streets were patrolled at night, strangers were not allowed to enter, and where merchants carried guns while waiting on customers. A better way had to be found to settle their own bid for county seat and he begged for lawful order. She scanned the rest of the page: At Arkansas City a pleasure steamer, *Belle of the Walnut*, had been launched. How nice for folks over east, she thought in irony, to be able to play on the water while here in the western region crops and folks were dying for it.

Further down the page, in the "Buffalo Chips" column, she read that Mrs. Thisba Strout had offered her aid and advice in choosing the Syracuse Emporium's next shipment of fabrics. "Mrs. Strout," Chalk had written, "who comes from an Eastern textile mill family, has finally given in to the persuasion of her friends to do this. 'No one in Syracuse has a better eye for fabric or good design,' her friends wholeheartedly claim."

Amity made a small sound of derision. She'd give her soul for one new dress for the campaign. But she couldn't afford to have Beady Moffatt, Syracuse's pretty young dressmaker, make her one, and that was that. She did have to admit that few women dressed better than Mrs. Strout.

Chalk had two law cases she hadn't read about before. The first account concerned a disagreement between two farmers over the ownership of an unbranded calf. The more insistent farmer was ordered to bring in the cow he claimed was the calf's mother; the other farmer was invited to bring his cow. In the street in front of the saloon, the calf settled the matter by going to its own mother. After which, all involved, except the would-be thief and the lady observers, convened for drinks in the saloon.

His other case involved a settler who'd cut timber from someone else's land, that of a speculator who'd got the piece from the railroad. It'd taken the judge and jury, with the aid of the settler's lawyer, T. S. "Chalk" Holden, but a few minutes to find their friend and fellow homesteader innocent. There was an unwritten law that prevailed: timber on land of non-residents should rightfully belong to the homesteaders who were braving dangers and hardships to build up the country — to the profit of speculators. "Yes," Amity whispered aloud to herself. She couldn't agree more with the outcome. Did Chalk Holden receive turnips in payment for the cases, or cash? If the latter, she sorely envied him.

She sighed heavily and leaned back, realizing she ached in every bone from weariness. Eyes closed, her thoughts turned to Mr. T. S. "Chalk" Holden, editor and publisher of the *Banner*. Lawyer, too. A fine friend, too, and so charming . . . Her eyes snapped open. Thinking of him in that way was a pure waste of time! Carefully, she folded the papers to finish another time and pushed back from the table.

Taking a lantern and a dish, she went out to the outhouse. On her way back, she stopped at the well to dip a bit of Flora's cream from the can she drew up. Her habit of spreading thick cream on her face when it was burnt from the sun was all that kept it from looking like brown, fried bacon.

A while later she wrote in her journal: *Dove's Nest, July 16. My homestead is in jeopardy from the accursed sun and drying winds. I must win the superintendency.*

As she crawled into bed, she wondered if she were too far behind to catch up. With Beaconsfield totally abandoned and the English returned home, she determined she would put to rest the worry that someone from there, in addition to Thisba, would show up in Hamilton County and spoil her chances to win the superintendency.

Before the others were up next morning, Amity

195

went over her wardrobe, selecting what might be mended and remodeled, and laying out a bed-spread of her mother's that might be turned into a reasonable garment, possibly a skirt. She yearned again for new dresses and shoes, but the money simply wasn't there. Money was the main problem keeping her from campaigning as she'd like. She briefly considered holding a potluck picnic here at the ranch and inviting those who'd be helpful in getting her elected. She didn't have the means to put on such a party, but neither could she abandon the idea altogether. In the end, she wrote a letter to the new women's council to suggest they sponsor a "Candidates Night" where people might come and meet the candidates and hear from them on a personal level. There had to be some way to remind folks that she was still in the running, too. The councilwomen, she felt, would be interested in bettering education for Syracuse youngsters and all the school-age children of the county. She wished she could attend a council meeting and voice her request in person, but she simply had too much to do. The letter had to suffice.

If it hadn't been for the campaign, she'd have paid her looks no mind, but a thorough study of her reflection in the looking glass by the door made her groan aloud at her hair. She lifted the sun-streaked masses in her hands, felt the dryness. Time was at a premium — there was too much to be done — but she must give a few minutes to concocting Mama's recipe for shampoo from

Cairo days: an approximate ounce each of salts of tartar, powdered borax, and aqua ammonia, added to a quarter of well water. It was good rubbed into the roots of the hair at least once a week, followed by a rinse of sage tea and borax to make the hair soft. A vinegar rinse would give it shine.

"Here, Thaddeus, you take the red and I'll take the black." Across the table, she handed him a paint pot, almost empty, its contents dry and caked. "If we add just the right amount of water we'll have enough to paint with, I think."

On Thad's second evening at Dove's Nest, she'd dug out from a trunk an old paintbox, left-over from her art school days. Partly to distract him from thoughts of his mother's tragic death, and partly to make him feel at home, she had taught him how to use the paints. At first he'd been stiff with awe, but soon he was painting birds, horses, clouds, trees, showing a native talent in the splashes of color.

The paints were out this Sunday, however, to make campaign signs, which she intended to post about the county. Thaddeus knew a few of his letters; Chloe had taught him, but mostly Amity would outline the letters in black and he would fill them in with red.

She'd chosen the line from Chalk's ad as a slogan. Speaking aloud, mostly to herself, she said, "It feels strange writing 'Who will work the hardest for your child? Amity Whitford!' about myself."

"Then sign my name to it!" John Clyde exclaimed from the other end of the table where he sat drinking coffee. "What should be writ, should be writ."

She pulled a long, mocking face at the boy. "Do you agree with that, Sir Thad?"

He giggled and ducked his head. "Yes!"

"Do a good job, then, sweetheart. We'll go to Syracuse where the most people live and post them there first. When we can get away, we'll take them to the smaller communities and fasten them to fence posts."

"And barns and trees," he offered, his tongue circling his mouth as he studiously filled in the color of a large *A*.

"Trees, where we can find them, and barns," she agreed, looking on his work with pride. She loved spending time with the boy, if for nothing more than a laughing game of tag around sundown, or helping him with his numbers, or reading aloud to him by lamplight before bed.

It was quiet in the room as they worked. John Clyde had fallen asleep in his chair. Suddenly, Zip bolted from his place under Thaddy's chair and ripped out the open back door, barking furiously.

"That'll be Mr. Holden," Amity tried to say calmly, "here for Sunday dinner." Her heart set up nearly as much commotion as the dog was making, Lord save her. She refrained from racing to the mirror by the door, and instead, began to gather their materials from the table.

It had been a hot, long, trying week. Working furiously to catch up with haying and other chores, doing her best to see that Thaddeus was adapting to his new home after the tragedy in his life, laying out work for her campaign so that she might at least be in the running with the others, had made it seem absolute ages since she'd last seen Chalk Holden, waving from the door of the Limbaugh Livery.

Chapter Twelve

Amity frowned at the small clutch of delicate, sky blue flowers dwarfed in Chalk's fist. His broad grin making gold wings of his moustache, he held the bouquet of prairie gentians — bluebells — out for her. "They remind me of you. Every other growing thing is withering in these hot August winds, but they stay beautiful." He'd removed his hat, showing a pale line of skin at the top of his forehead, though his face was more deeply bronzed than ever.

"Thank you, that's flattering, but —"

"Congratulations to the next Hamilton County school superintendent!"

Tucking his hat under his arm, he pulled a sheaf of newspaper clippings from inside his vest pocket and crowded them into her hands with the nosegay of wildflowers. "Taking out those ads helped. Because you put money into their pockets, along with sending additional information about yourself, editors all over the county felt obliged to write about you."

"Fairly, I hope?" Amity smiled at him, her spirits climbing. But when she scanned the first papers, her relief and gratitude plunged. "I'd hardly call these endorsements," she said flatly, feeling hollow with disappointment. " '. . . doubtless Miss Whitford is a lady of refinement, culture, and ability, but we must question the propriety of permitting women to become involved in politics . . .'?" She shuffled the clippings. " 'Don't let the beauty of one of the candidates turn your head, gentleman voters . . .'? 'A lady would tire quickly of the difficulties of the office'?" She turned away, fury obliterating everything else. Then she noticed Thaddy and John Clyde standing across the room, all slicked up and hungry for dinner, watching, waiting. Chalk's shadow slanted along the floor from where he filled the doorway, waiting to be asked inside. She stepped back and said, "Please come in."

"I didn't claim the papers backed you a hundred percent," Chalk countered, as he removed his hat and strode into the room, nodding at the boy and her handyman. "But I wouldn't worry. You can open those shortsighted minds and win 'em over."

"Thank you, I intend to try." It helped that he sounded matter-of-fact, but her frustration over stupid attitudes — what women were and weren't fitted for — stayed uppermost in her mind as she set the table for dinner. She slammed the plates down a trifle harder than usual, clattering the utensils down alongside them. It was time for a change, for God's sake. She was eminently equipped for the superintendent's post and she had to have it!

Ignoring her troubled state, the *males* at her table dove into the fricasseed rabbit and dumplings, turnip greens, roasted ears of corn dripping with fresh butter, and corn bread smeared with wild-plum jam. If John Clyde and Thaddy hadn't shot the jackrabbit, which even after stewing all day was still stringy, tough, and tasted strongly of wild sage; if she hadn't babied her corn crop, watering it by hand till her back nearly broke, they would have had little to eat!

How long had Chalk Holden been watching her? Suddenly finding his eyes on her, Amity looked down.

"Amity, are you all right? I'm afraid that you work too hard. Your place, now this campaign . . ."

"Yes, I do work hard, but I have no other choice." She looked up at him then, and she realized that he was feeling guilty about putting an extra burden on her by coming to dinner. "Chalk, please don't think you're an imposition. You're not, honestly. If I gave that impression, please forgive me." Good heavens, he was here at her invitation and she'd been incredibly rude.

He nodded, but he continued to scrutinize her. She was tempted to ask what on earth he was thinking, but she didn't; she'd put her foot in it too deep already.

Two days later Chalk Holden was back. He arrived just as the sun was breaking up the dark eastern sky with ribbons of yellow-rose, and she

202

was coming from the barn with the morning's bucket of milk. He hadn't come alone. Amity set the bucket on the ground, thunderstruck. Chalk headed a parade on his horse. The two older Bergen boys trailed behind on their saddle horses, Mr. Bergen drove his team-drawn riding mower out at the side. There were others on horseback, neighbors she hardly knew except to say hello to. Then Samuel, the elderly bachelor rancher, drove in with a team-drawn rake. "Brought you a hay crew!" Chalk shouted. "Others'll be here shortly. Womenfolk are back there in the dust in their wagons. They'll help you cook dinner; they're bringing fixin's."

"Chalk, I'm used to doing for myself. I don't need —" She wished now she hadn't complained about the difficulty getting hay put up after John Clyde's illness, though it would take a lot of hay to get them through the long cold winter. Help would be a godsend, but — "I have no way to pay them, nothing to trade for their labor. I hate taking them from their own work. God knows we're all fighting the same battle to keep our heads above water, them the same as me."

"Hold up," Chalk said softly, a glint of fire in his eyes. "This is the way of folks out here. You've been working yourself too hard. They're glad to help get the hay in faster for you, and enjoy themselves at the same time. They're being sociable, that's all. Wouldn't hurt you to be, either." With that, he turned on a booted heel to give orders to the new crews coming in. John

Clyde came from the barn, grinning. Chalk clapped a hand on his shoulder, then walked over to Thaddy, who stood shyly just inside the barn door, hanging back. Amity heard Chalk say, as he ruffled the boy's hair, "Ready for a party-day, son?"

"All right," Amity whispered to herself, "if that's how it's to be." She had kept to herself for so long that it had become a way of life. That changed when she asked to lead county education. For better or worse, she was one of these people now. They were here because they liked her. And, like Chalk said, helping neighbors was simply how it was done out here.

It was a relief to joke with the women in the kitchen as they cooked, enjoyable to play a few tunes on the melodeon for them when they asked, to change and cuddle their crying babies, to listen to the women gossip and exchange recipes. When she could take a break from her own duties, Amity helped Thaddeus in his role as waterboy to the workers in the field. Her heart rejoiced for Thaddeus as the day progressed. He, too, had gradually relaxed and romped in games of tag with the younger flaxen-haired Bergen youngsters, and others, around the haystacks building amazingly fast in her barnyard. Zip was a blue-gray streak racing and yipping happily with the children.

The sun was noon-high when the doors of her house and barn were removed temporarily from their hinges and placed across barrels to form tables in the yard. Huge pots of beans, kettles of boiled beef with noodles, sauerkraut with pork, corn pudding, corn dodgers, corn on the cob, corn cake, and hominy, were brought out. Joe Samuel laughingly praised God for corn, then asked His help with this year's doubtful crop. Which prompted one ranch wife to report with a touch of rancor that her collection of recipes using corn numbered thirty-three and her husband to add that he once went a three year stretch with no other bread except corn bread to eat. Many eyes turned to the sky, then, with Mr. Bergen wondering aloud for all of them. "We get all the rain we going to get this summer, I wonder?"

When the sun began to sink in the western sky, her neighbors, with chores of their own awaiting them, departed for home; wagons, horsemen, and equipment silhouetted in a long line against the horizon. Not long after, John Clyde and Thaddeus, tuckered out from pleasure as much as work, went to their beds early.

Chalk stayed behind to hang Amity's doors back in place and help kill the many flies that had taken the opportunity to fill her kitchen. Later, she stepped outside with him to see him on his way. "Everyone was so wonderful today, simply thanking them seemed too little to pay for their kindness and generosity," she lamented.

"You don't have to be such a loner, Amity. Folks won't butt in if they feel they aren't wanted, but they're glad to help if you ask — if you just let them know you need them. Bergen thought you'd probably gotten your hay all in, till I told him, and then he went 'round talking to the others."

"I'd like to reciprocate, if I knew how."

"Make damn sure that you win that office, and then see that their children get a good education. That's something they don't know how to do and it's a hell of a lot more than making hay."

"Thank y—" she started to offer him her appreciation, but suddenly she was in his arms, being pulled close against him.

" 'Scuse me, ma'am," he said huskily, "but I'll take my thanks like this." He kissed her until her head swam. Unable to stop herself, she kissed him back, her arms curling around his neck eagerly. His lips felt wonderful; he tasted of Mrs. Bergen's dried peach pie and of the bottle she'd seen the men passing behind the largest haystack. Then he left her standing alone with her heart pounding. He went to get his horse, saying over his shoulder, so quietly she was less than positive of his words, "See you soon, Amity, darlin'." In the fading light, his sparkling eyes and sensual grin bedeviled her.

Lightheaded, her mouth still tingling from his kiss, she made her way to the house. She kept thinking how much he'd been like a knight in shining armor today: riding in, doing his wonderful deed, riding off again. Still, she dismissed the idea of writing such a silly notion in her journal. Anyway, she thought, sighing and yanking open her back door, not even a real knight in armor could scale the wall that she had to keep between them for now. And a kiss was just a kiss after all.

One thing Chalk had said kept running through her mind the next few days: *Make damn sure you win.* Her woman's heart couldn't stop believing that a new dress would help. She had hay enough for their own use, now, and to spare. She could cut more, if necessary. With prairie hay bringing five dollars a ton, two wagonloads ought to pay for a dress.

She made a trip to town, but wasn't surprised to learn from Skimmy at the livery that Mr. Limbaugh had contracted with someone else for his hay supply and needed no more.

Next, she drove to the Moffats' small frame cottage on a side street up the hill behind town. Beady herself, a pretty, good-natured girl with reddish blonde hair and green eyes that crinkled at the corners with her constant smiles, answered the door.

"My parents are both napping," she said quietly, finger to her lips, leading the way to a cubbyhole sideroom where she did her sewing. The room smelled of dried lavender and roses. She closed the door after them.

"I need a new dress, but we need to talk first about how I might pay," Amity told her, hesitating to take the chair the other girl offered. "I saw that you keep a cow and a horse in a pasture out back, as I drove up. I could exchange two loads of hay for a dress, if that's possible?"

Beady gave it only a second's thought. "Quite possible," she nodded, eyes crinkling. "I get so busy sewing I forget such practical matters as our poor animals' winter feed, I'm afraid. Sometimes till it's almost too late to do anything about it. And of course, Mama and Papa don't consider such matters at all; they count on me." She waved a hand. "Truly, it's settled. I have neighbors in the same boat, if you want me to take orders."

"Well, perhaps I could part with more." Out of principle, she didn't want to sell what her neighbors had been good enough to put by for her, but any she could cut and haul herself, now that Dove's Nest Ranch's demands for hay were met . . .

"I don't make many dresses for country women; they seem to make their own," Beady was saying, "so I don't often get the opportunity for such a profitable exchange."

Amity flushed guiltily. "I should be making the dress myself, except that I have very little time. More than that, I've heard of your reputation with a needle, and this must be a very special frock." She explained about the campaign, Beady smiling and nodding all the while.

As they looked over an assortment of fabrics, the young seamstress chatted with Amity as if they were old friends. "The minute I heard you were running for the office, I said, 'bully for her!' " She chuckled. "I have to admit, some of my customers don't feel the same. Mrs. Strout was positively livid that a woman would 'overstep her bounds.' I declare, I thought she'd go right up in smoke. But I told her that a woman ought to do anything she feels she's capable of, that's what I said. And other folks should support her, not try to tear her down. Here," she said, holding up a bolt of cloth, "this cobalt blue sateen looks fabulous with your beautiful eyes. What do you think?"

Amity pulled her mind away from thoughts of Mrs. Strout. She'd briefly forgotten that Beady Moffat was Thisba's chief dressmaker. But that ought not to matter, she decided. "Sateen would be dressy, but not too dressy?"

"Not if the style is simple, elegant. And there are things we can do to make it serviceable in other seasons. Look in here," Beady pulled an old, well-thumbed copy of *Harper's Bazaar* down from a shelf. She spread the book open on Amity's lap.

Amity's breath caught as she studied the drawings. "You could make these, any of them?"

Beady laughed and answered honestly, "I believe I could, yes."

They decided on a two-piece town dress, to be made of the cobalt blue sateen. The pointed basque waist would have a lace Byron collar and cuffs, and small silver buttons. The collar and cuffs would be detachable, so they could be replaced by the same in velvet for fall and winter. The skirt would be slim in front with a very bouffant draped back. "It's going to be beautiful," Amity said. The last time she'd had a new dress, she'd had Mama's help in making the selection and it hadn't been one dress, but four. "I don't have a hat, but I can dye some old silk flowers to match the dress. I'll attach them to a straw bonnet I have and that will serve."

"There'll be lace scraps to use for part of the bonnet trimming," Beady assured her.

Feeling guilty that she was treating herself to such a wonderful dress, but sure at the same time that it was necessary for campaigning, Amity drove back to the general store and post office where she picked up the mail. The letter on top was from the Syracuse City Council. She tore it open, thrilled to read that "city officials agree wholeheartedly with your suggestion for a Candidates Night and plans are in the making, a date to be set." In her mail, too, was a copy of the *Banner* and her pulse quickened. Reading the articles he wrote from his mind and heart was a way of knowing Chalk Holden without getting into trouble. As she opened the newspaper, a small note fluttered out. She didn't have to see the handwriting to know that it was from Chalk. The small square of folded paper smelled of his soap fragrance. Looking around first to make sure no one in the general store was watching, she held it to her nose for a long moment, remembering his kiss of a few evenings ago. Finally, taking a deep breath, she read the scrawled words *When will you let me court you properly as a gentleman most wants to do?* It was signed *The Hayman.*

She walked out to her waiting wagon with the note. As she climbed up, she saw a small bouquet of blue-and-burgundy bachelor's buttons on the seat. He had to have stolen the flowers from some town wife's carefully tended flower patch or porch box. The fact that he was nowhere in sight when she looked around disappointed her more than was good for her.

She sat reins in her hands, hoping he'd appear, but finally cracked the lines over Ben's back. Then, inhaling the spicy fragrance of the bouquet, she gave Ben his head. The wagon was as far as the edge of town before she decided that if the truth was going to make her free to accept his attentions, then she had to tell Chalk about Beaconsfield. She dreaded the moment as much as death.

One evening a week later, Chalk came driving into her ranch yard in the yellow-wheeled buggy she recognized from Limbaugh's Livery. From the window, she saw that he wore a new doe-colored Stetson. His suit was spotless, and his boots were shining in the soft evening light. He was freshly shaved; his hair tonic smelled wonderful. She hadn't the slightest doubt what he was there for. The one surprise was the large bundle he carried.

"From Obedience Moffat," he said, handing her the package. "She sent it with me as long as I was coming out anyway."

"Oh, my dress!" She nearly yipped with excitement as she motioned for him to come in. She broke the string, opened the package, and a spill of cobalt blue filled her arms: *the dress*. "Oh," she breathed. "It's so lovely!" She held it up to herself, tears of delight stinging her eyes. "Beady's done a magnificent job!"

Chalk stood by quietly, grinning in appreciation of the scene. "It's my campaign dress," she explained, coming back to earth, trying to sound practical and not respond to what she noted in his eyes. "I — I guess part of my thanks for it — should go to you. I bartered two loads of hay for it," she confessed.

"My pleasure. I'll wait while you put it away. Then we're going for a buggy ride. I've a few things to say to you."

She looked at him sharply. "No, I can't go."

He took the dress from her arms, strode to her bedroom, pulled the curtain aside and placed the garment on her quilt-covered bed. "There now. John Clyde and Thad are out at the barn, I saw them. We'll stop to tell them to finish up chorin' without you and get their own supper on, that you're taking an evening ride with me."

His arm was about her waist and he was moving her along with him to the door. "All right," she murmured, ceasing to pull back, straightening her posture, "I'll go." The time had come to tell him the truth about herself. But she was sure that in another hour he would drive away and never want to see her again. Because of all the things a woman might be guilty of, a small child's death had to be the most terrible.

Chapter Thirteen

Chalk drove out two or three miles north along Plumb Creek; Amity's dread grew with every turn of the buggy wheels. Still, when they stopped and she sat with him on the blanket he'd spread in the turkey-foot grass growing on the creek bank, she told him everything, just as she'd planned. Darkness descended around them as she talked about her parents' deaths and feeling so alone; the job she had taken with the Fairleighs to care for and teach their children. Because it was likely the truth, and she wanted nothing left out, she didn't spare herself and related the story she'd been told about Nora Ann's tragic death.

"Evidently, I've blocked most of the details out — from guilt. I remember some sort of porch, and Nora Ann pale and still and so very cold, even though it was summertime." She shivered. "I kept trying to remember more, but I can't. Maybe the exact details don't matter, since Chester and Leila Fairleigh were sure enough that I was responsible for whatever caused little Nora to die. They were understandably distraught and angry. But I was so sick and confused, I hardly knew what was going on, except that Nora was dead and her parents wanted no more to do with me."

Chalk swore under his breath but said nothing, while she waited. Finally, unable to bear his silence any longer, expecting recrimination when he could find the words, Amity said, softly, "I'm sorry I didn't tell you before, and put a stop to — a stop to — us. You may take me home now."

She started to rise. He pulled her back and drew her into his strong arms. She leaned her head against his chest, feeling his heart thump under her ear, relishing the circle of love his arms made for her.

"I don't know what could've happened," he said, holding her tenderly, tilting her chin to look up at him, "this thing you're talkin' about, Amity. But I do know one thing — you did nothing wrong. Nothing. You didn't hurt that little girl except maybe by accident. I've seen you around children, around that boy, Thad. I saw you doing your damnedest to help those children on the Fourth of July. Honey, there's no way on God's green earth you could harm a little one."

Amity felt so exhausted from the strain of the confession, she couldn't move. "I want to believe that, too," she whispered brokenly, "but I — what I did was so awful that Chester Fairleigh drove me to Great Bend and literally dumped me into the street!"

"No," he reassured her, rocking her in his arms, "no. Somebody made a mistake, one godawful mistake. I've never met a sweeter, more loving person than you, sweetheart. You've admitted yourself that you don't really know what happened. I don't know who is guilty, but it wasn't you. I'd bet my life on it — though I don't know why anyone would let you get the blame."

She told him now that she and Thisba had both been employed at Beaconsfield.

"Thisba Strout?" Chalk's eyes narrowed.

"Thisba Marcellus, then. I know what you're thinking, Chalk, but Thisba was relieved of her job before the trouble involving me at Beaconsfield. She had gone, and doesn't know any more than I do."

"You're sure?"

"Absolutely. She wasn't employed there very long. She was a bit snippy — there was a minor squabble or two right off. I wasn't involved, but I gathered that although Thisba was hired to clean, she felt she was above some chores and wouldn't do them. When I got to thinking about it, I remembered a conversation between Mr. and Mrs. Fairleigh to the effect that the new maid wasn't working out and likely they would have to let her go. I'm sure she's not lying; she probably wishes she knew all about the incident, so she could use it against me!" Amity explained to Chalk about her recent trip. "There was nothing else left to do but go back to Beaconsfield to learn the truth. But it was hopeless, Chalk. They'd all gone, the English, back to their homeland. There was no one to tell me what occurred that day."

"Then let's forget it. If you're never going

216

to know, then it doesn't matter. You've got to put the tragedy behind you so you can get on with life. I came tonight to tell you how I feel about you, Amity. And not a word you've said changes my mind a whit. Please, sweetheart, marry me. I'm crazy in love with you. I'm fond of that boy of yours, and I'd like us to have youngsters of our own, someday —"

"Oh, Chalk, please!" She wrested herself out of his arms and got to her feet. "I can't just put a thing like that out of my mind. What if I did it, what if I've been told the truth? Chester Fairleigh liked me, till — that day. He wouldn't have gotten rid of me the way he did unless I'd done something terribly, terribly wrong."

Chalk swore under his breath and stood up. "Maybe there was some kind of accident, something you couldn't prevent." He caught her in his arms again. "People make mistakes, and things happen. Whoever gave you the damned idea that you must be perfect, and anything less makes you unworthy?" He held her tightly so that she couldn't move away. "I know you, Amity. You're kind and loving, the most beautiful woman I've ever seen, and I love you. No, stop," he ordered as she tried to push away. "You know how you feel about me, Amity. Give us a chance, darling, please."

"I — I —" Intoxicated by his nearness, she couldn't think. His lips, sweet and warm, met hers, stilling the protest she tried to make. His arms folded about her tighter, pulling her against his solid body. There was a singing in her blood, in her very soul, as reason fled. She felt weak and wonderful as his mouth found hers again and again with deep, roving hunger. He whispered her name, "Amity. Oh, Amity. I don't care what happened in your past. I know you and I want you."

"I care for you, too, so much I can't think straight. I want — what you want. I want — us, together," she said. "But not until I can learn the truth and the facts show that I'm innocent."

"And if you can't learn that?"

"Then I'm not sure I can m-marry anyone."

He took a few steps away, then he came back to grasp both her arms tightly. He pleaded in a voice heavy with emotion, "Please don't say there's no future for us. Do you want time? I'll wait as long as you need, but I can't give you up, Amity, not now, not ever."

She leaned into him, a bit of her pain easing away. She'd said things tonight she hadn't even allowed herself to *think* until now. It was such a relief that he finally *knew* and he wanted her anyway. With his last words she'd realized, though she maybe knew all along, that she couldn't give him up either, as long as there was the slightest chance to prove she'd done no real wrong at Beaconsfield with the child. "Lately I've been thinking that the postmaster or the Great Bend bank might be able to put me in touch with the Fairleighs in England. I'll write to them and demand an explanation. When they reply, I'll let you judge from their letter how guilty I am. I love you, Chalk," she admitted. "I've loved you from the first second I walked into your newspaper office and saw you."

He pulled her close against him, unable to say anything. Then finally, "Amity, dear love, getting an answer to your letter could take forever. I want to come calling."

"Don't you know that I want that as much as you do? But I want to avoid gossip. I can't jeopardize my chances of winning the superintendency. And it's only a little while to wait. Please?"

He swore under his breath. "Talk about difficult —"

Amity sighed, keeping to herself that the rules requiring teachers to remain single might also apply to the superintendency. If so, she'd simply have to convince county leaders to change the rules and allow her to marry Chalk. She whispered to him, "A few months from now everything could be different, and right."

"I don't know why I'm agreeing to this. It's not what I had in mind at all when I came out here tonight." He caressed her almost roughly. "If this is going to be our last kiss in a while, it's sure as hell's goin' to be one neither one of us will forget!"

He didn't release her for several minutes. When he finally did, her lips burned, the flesh of her breasts and thighs felt engraved by his granite-hard body. He was right. There was no way she could forget.

The remaining harvest chores — picking, preserving, and putting by before winter — consumed Amity's every waking moment for the rest of August. Thaddeus helped her dig potatoes and turnips and gather melons and stow them in the root cellar. All three of them picked what corn had survived the scorching winds, hour after hour tossing it thump-bumping into the wagon to be hauled to the barn for later husking. Leaves and stalks would be turned into silage.

The first Saturday evening in September was chosen for the superintendency candidates' party at the Syracuse schoolhouse. Amity awoke that morning feeling logy and exhausted. For days she'd worked almost the clock around, staying up late at night to go over campaign plans and problems once more.

When John Clyde and Thaddy returned to the field to cut broomcorn after the noon meal, she stayed in the house to bathe and wash her hair. Primping was a luxury she rarely afforded herself. After she slipped on the new cobalt blue gown and fastened the buttons, she felt better; revitalized and ready to show the world that Miss Amity Cathlin Whitford was very much still in the race.

She and Thaddeus drove into town while John Clyde stayed at home, claiming this particular gathering too fancy for him.

As they approached the schoolhouse, Amity was

both surprised and heartened by the sight of at least a hundred rigs belonging to ranchers and farmers from all over the county. Riding horses with oatbags on their muzzles, saddles nearby on the ground, swished their tails and stomped flies in the shed and on the grounds. An excellent turnout! *When Mohammed can't go to the mountain, bring the mountain to Mohammed.* Of course, she'd brought the mountain to her opponents, as well. "Want to play out here with the children?" she asked Thaddeus.

"Yes, ma'am." He nodded, his eyes alight at sight of the other small boys and girls, some at the swing and seesaw, others racing about. "Be a good boy, then." She hesitated a moment with her hand on his shoulder before entering the schoolhouse.

Inside, the place was decorated to a fare-thee-well with red, white, and blue streamers and bunting. The room was full, with the tightest cluster of people at the table of cakes, pies, and cider jugs. It took but a minute to ascertain that Chalk wasn't there yet. Nor could she spot Thisba Strout, who would surely want to be there.

"Miss Whitford! Miss Whitford!" A woman in a forest green dress, brown hair parted severely in the middle and worn in a bun, rushed at her with a welcoming smile and hand outstretched. Amity smiled back, wondering, waiting, as she offered her own hand.

"I recognize you from the Fourth of July speech. You look lovely, dear. Is that a new dress?

I'm Mrs. Roy, Julia Roy, president of the city council. It's a treat to make your acquaintance, dear. I've been admiring you from afar for your courage. I'd like you to meet the other ladies of the council. Do come with me." Pansy blue eyes twinkled in her round face.

"Of course, I want to meet *them!*" As she swept along after Mrs. Roy, Amity was fixed with admiring glances from every corner of the room. She silently thanked Beady Moffat's skill and indulged herself in a few seconds of vanity.

She nodded at people she knew, wondering if Chalk had been outside and she hadn't seen him. Surely he would be covering the event for his paper.

Mrs. Roy made the introductions to the other five councilwomen, and Amity shared a few words with each of them. "You're all doing a wonderful job for Syracuse," she congratulated them.

"Leave it to women," Mrs. Rosalind Spender, a younger council matron with a sadly sweet face, accepted the praise. "Mrs. Bell is bringing Wilford to church every Sunday now. We meant it when we said we wanted an honest, church-goin' sheriff, one we could count on to be sober when we need him."

Mrs. Roy chuckled. "Sheriff Bell knows he can follow our edicts or lose the next election!" She took Amity's hands. "Now, dear, thank you very much for suggesting this worthwhile event. It's time for you to mix and talk with the folks. And don't forget to stop at the refreshment table."

She waved Amity off.

For the next half hour, Amity made her way around the room, greeting and visiting a few minutes with people she was getting to know better and better: Marta and Able Bergen; her bachelor neighbor, Joe Samuel; and coming from farther away, the Ginsbachs, Bill Richards, Mrs. Beneke and her daughter, Tannis, and several other folks Chalk had introduced her to on the Fourth of July.

Suddenly, a loud male voice caught her attention and she turned. It was the cranky farmer, Ward McChesney. His Adam's apple bobbed in his thin throat as he whacked his seedy brown hat against his thigh, complaining as usual to a group of listeners, "We know what works best for us in our little country schools. Why do we need somebody from the outside comin' round to tell us what to do? Ain't nothin' fer a superintendent to do but ride around the country in a buggy, wearin' Sunday clothes, puttin' on airs, an' at our expense, mind you!"

Amity stepped boldly forward. "Excuse me, Mr. McChesney." She nodded at the group as she maneuvered closer to the center. "I believe I can answer your question about why a superintendent is needed."

"Oh," he said, squinting, "it's you. A woman," he told the others, "a woman from back East som'eres thinkin' she can step right in and tell us how to run our affairs."

"She's an official candidate and the reason we're

here tonight so let her speak." Obedience Moffat stepped around a burly farmer blocking her view. She waved and smiled at Amity.

"Thanks, Beady. Now then, folks, Kansas has provided for this office in the state constitution. And that's to your advantage, believe me. It's prudent to have someone see that the state's money is apportioned fairly amongst the district schools and not wasted. And that's only the beginning of a superintendent's duties. It's very important to set standards and encourage education across the county, and if I'm elected, that will be my prime concern." McChesney's scowl said it was time for her to be quiet but she wasn't going to lose the audience gathering to hear her. "I'll do my best to promote harmony within the districts, bring order and some real efficiency to our schools. It's a big job — examining and licensing teachers, visiting schools and making suggestions for improvement.

"I think the present hiring standards for teachers are too casual. It's not enough for a would-be teacher to be able to read a chapter in the Bible, whip the boys, and cipher a few figures! I intend to hold Hamilton County's first teacher training program in the spring, a teachers' institute. Nothing to do, you say? There are so many things I can and will do to improve education in Hamilton County, I can hardly list them all!"

Amity flushed with embarrassment when a few people clapped. She had gone on a bit, but she'd meant every word. McChesney looked like he still wanted to argue, but another farmer had come up to invite him outside for "a snort."

"Two privies for every school, that's what she'll be asking for, wait and see," McChesney grumbled as he headed out, making a hacking motion with his arm. "Tomfool money-stealin' nonsense."

"One privy is more than some Hamilton County schools have!" Amity retorted. She shook her head, half smiling as she watched him go. She suspected his bark was worse than his bite; he was someone who liked to talk. Lord knows, he could get her ire up, though. As she turned abruptly, she ran into a mountain of flesh in a dark suit.

Seymour Purdue leaned down, his puffy, perspiring face almost touching hers. "Ahh, a beautiful gem in our crude country setting. Hel-lo, Miss Whitford! You're here to ascertain the best qualified candidate, Purdue or Taylor, before you drop the race, hmm?" He smiled hugely at his own joke. "Our little Miss Whitford knows she's looking at the best man for the job, correct, dear?" He stuffed an entire doughnut into his mouth, his jaws working like a bull's chewing its cud.

She mustered a faint smile. "Perhaps the best man is a *woman?*" she responded through clenched teeth. "This is your party, too, Mr. Purdue, so I won't keep you."

His smile froze on his fat face. Pulling out a white linen handkerchief, he wiped the crumbs from his face, adding to those that already lay on the vested shelf of his protruding stomach.

Amity shook off her revulsion, and continued her circuit of the room after a pause at the refreshment table for a cup of cider. She stopped every few moments to chat, seeking comfort with familiar faces, but also making a point of talking with people new to her. Pledges to vote for her bolstered her confidence.

Many confessed that they had already made up their minds before they came, but were present for the food and sociability. A lot of the discussion about the upcoming elections focused on the rivalry between Syracuse and Kendall, twelve miles to the east, for the county seat. Patriotism and pride were evoked, since the majority present were positive that Syracuse was by far the best site for the county seat. And more than one conversation Amity walked into, and joined, concerned the end of harvest, and plans for planting winter wheat, culling beef herds, and the like.

"Amity!" Noah Porter, the red-haired pharmacist, Chalk's friend, motioned her to a corner. "Had you heard that Amos Taylor is thinking about dropping out and giving the race to you? I heard the rumor and now I see that he isn't here tonight. I predict you'll win by a landslide."

"You're too generous, Mr. Porter, but even if Taylor quits, there's still Seymour Purdue."

"Purdue," Noah scoffed. "The blowhard sees the superintendency as some kind of political rainbow, I'm afraid. An inside man on county affairs can mingle with county hierarchy, gents who

226

know before anyone else which ranches and farms can be bought for a fraction of their worth and resold for considerable profit. That sort of thing is very attractive to men like Purdue!"

Amity put in very quickly, "You might as well know, Noah, that along with my intention to do all the good I can for Hamilton County education, I also see the superintendent's salary as a lifeline for my ranch."

He shrugged. "I don't begrudge anyone honest pay for honest work. You'll do a good job and deserve every penny, Amity." A grin quirked the corner of his mouth. "Every customer who comes into my pharmacy gets a free speech on your wonderful abilities as I see them, encouraged by my friend, Holden, who, by the way, just walked in." Noah, looking beyond her shoulder, lifted his arm in a wave.

The calm control she'd felt evaporated. Her heart picked up a beat as she turned to watch Chalk's broad-shouldered advance into the room. He was with two other men: leather-faced Sheriff Bell, whose expression was serious as he stroked his long moustache; and silver-haired Amos Taylor. Chalk's eyes traveled the room and stopped when they reached her. His fingers had lifted to remove his hat, but he stopped and stared at her across the room, as he might a beautiful stranger. Amity waited for him to do something.

She'd forgotten Noah Porter beside her until he said close to her ear, "Excuse me, Amity, something seems to be up. I'm going to find out what it is." He threaded his way through the crowd, across the room to where several other men had joined Chalk, Amos, and the sheriff. Weathered faces were grave as they conversed.

Finally, the group broke up, the matter at hand settled for the moment, at least, and the men returned to what they were doing before Chalk, Amos, and the sheriff had arrived.

Chalk turned Amity's way, smiling warmly. She tried to decide whether to wait for him or go across the room to where he stood. She hesitated a second longer as a young woman in traveling dress, a boy and a girl at her side, entered by the main door. The newcomer looked about uncertainly before heading straight for Chalk, a big smile wreathing her attractive face. She moved so fast she was almost running. She must've said Chalk's name. For a second he reacted as if the petite woman was a ghost, before hurtling across the floor to meet her. He grabbed her into his arms and swung her around like a child. While Amity watched, he kneeled and gathered the children, small and delicate like their mother, into one big hug. The youngsters grinned at Chalk, said something back at him. Their mother seemed to be laughing and crying at the same time, talking like a magpie in some kind of explanation. She took off her hat and smoothed her light-brown hair, much lighter than her children's, and then wiped at her eyes with a hanky, still talking to the top of Chalk's handsome head as he knelt with the children. He looked up at her, grinning, nodding. He tugged at the little girl's dark pigtail, and shook the boy's hand before he stood up and pulled the woman into his arms again, holding her like he'd never, ever let her go! Most everyone else in the room, including Amity, gaped at the intimate scene. The woman was laughing, hugging Chalk so tightly in turn that her hat sailed to the floor and her hanky fluttered away like a white dove.

Who was she? Amity had a terrible thought. Could it be Lilly and her children? Had the woman changed her mind about the stoneware manufacturer, or he about her? Amity was seized by a desire to race across the room and tear the woman from Chalk's arms. Send her and her children packing back to Philadelphia — no, Baltimore — wherever they were from! When Chalk saw her watching, his own face took on a strange expression. *Guilt? Concern?* Once again he started toward Amity, but the woman said something and he leaned down to kiss her cheek. Then, his hand cupping her elbow, he led her toward the refreshment table. Others closed in around them now, Chalk laughing and happily introducing the new arrival to his friends. Syracuse women responded by filling plates for the strangers, fussing over the children.

Amity, unable to bear more, bolted for the door.

Outside, she took several deep breaths and leaned against the building for support.

Let him go, let him go, he wasn't yours in the

first place. He asked but you wouldn't say yes. It's too late now. Her mind whirled as she waved mechanically at Thaddy, playing with Jebby Dusky in the twilight of the schoolyard. The boys came over and Jebby showed her his hand. Half her mind was on Chalk and the woman inside. The other half tried to pay close attention to Jebby in front of her. The stubs of his missing fingers were still pink, but healing nicely. She clasped them in her own hands a moment, though it was hard to think, hard to talk. "How's your mother?" she managed finally.

"Fine. She's over to the store gettin' supplies. And the blacksmith is shoein' our team while we're in town. Bill and Bess neither one got shoes in a long time. Ma let me and my brother and sister come over here for the free grub and to play."

She nodded. "Have you thought any more about school, Jebby?"

"I think about it all the time. Mama says if you, Miss Amity, gets to be the — the person who tells the schools what to do, I can go. If you don't get to be the — the —"

"County school superintendent," Thaddy helped him out, his expression serious.

Jebby nodded.

This was what she was here for, what she needed to keep her mind to. She smiled quietly. "Well, then, Jebby, if that's the basis that says whether or not *you* go to school, I'll see to it that I win."

The boys ran off, whooping, to play tag with others in the far corner of the schoolyard. Amity sighed. The impossibility of being with Chalk for her own good reasons was bad enough. But another woman in his life, one he obviously cared a lot about, hurt incredibly. She ought not to expect anything else, after keeping him at arm's length, rejecting his every overture. He'd wanted to marry her even after hearing about her past, but she'd insisted they wait.

"Nice day, isn't it, Miss Whitford?" an amiable male voice interrupted her thought. "Ah! Ah, oh, um, yes!"

Amity hid the turmoil in her heart with effort and smiled at Henry Strout, the owlish little banker. "Yes, it's a beautiful evening." Out here. Inside, where Chalk made a fool of himself over another woman was a different matter. She focused desperately on the banker, so that she wouldn't hurtle back inside and do something rash. Actually, she liked Mr. Strout, a self-possessed, well-dressed man whom she'd always found to be fair in their dealings. He rocked back on his heels, drawing on his freshly lit pipe. They stood in companionable silence for a minute, their eyes on the children at play while Amity struggled with her emotions.

"I don't believe your wife's here tonight, is she? How is Mrs. Strout?" It wasn't like Thisba to miss the affair; she'd want to be here, doing all she could for Seymour's campaign. From behind them, through the open door, came the hum

231

of voices, small explosions of hearty laughter.

"My sweet wife had to take to her bed. Woman's complaint." His voice lowered with embarrassment. "She nearly worked herself to death getting things ready for this party — the decorations, food. The council ladies couldn't've put a better person in charge. My Thisba does give her all, ah, um, yes! But then she suffers, yes."

Evidently the councilwomen hadn't mentioned that tonight's affair was Amity Whitford's suggestion, or Thisba would surely have given less than her *all*.

"Going to win the county superintendent's job, Miss Whitford?" he asked casually, sending a puff of smoke into the air. His expression turned on her was gentle, kindly.

"I hope to — expect to," she answered honestly. "It's my intention to be the best superintendent this county's ever seen."

"Good, good." He rocked back and forth. "Good, ah, yes, um, ahm, hum. Yes."

"I suppose you'll keep it in the family and vote for Mr. Purdue?"

He removed his pipe and whispered slyly, "Not on your life! No. No. I'm still trying to make up my mind between you and Amos Taylor. Wouldn't vote Seymour for dogcatcher. To tell you the truth, I can hardly wait to see the freeloader lose. At which time, I expect him to take off for distant parts. He's more than worn out his welcome at my house. Nearly eats us out of house and home. House and home, yes! Ah! Um hum. Yes!"

Although his odd speech habit made her want to giggle, Amity wouldn't have laughed at Henry Strout for the world; he was simply too nice a gentleman. It was amazing that he'd married Thisba, and she wondered how it had happened. Wondered, too, how Thisba would react if she knew her husband's voting preferences.

The banker seemed to read her mind. "Don't need to let my wife hear it, but I'll likely vote for you, Miss Whitford. I've gotten to know you pretty well the past three years and for my money you're the best one to help our children get their educations. Amos's highly qualified, too, but he's done enough for this county and deserves his rest. A rest. Yes! Ah, oh, um, yes!"

Henry shook his head. "My wife gets the oddest ideas, sometimes. Pure craziness even I can't understand," he mused.

Amity felt strong enough, she guessed, to put on a good face and go back inside. To try to act normal. To deal with Chalk and the other woman, and not carry on like a disappointed schoolgirl. Taking a deep breath, she offered the banker her hand, "I've enjoyed talking with you, Mr. Strout, very much. And if your vote does go to me, please accept my deepest thanks now."

Strout could give her a lot more than just his vote. His opinion was respected, and counted with folks in all walks of life in this part of the country. She knew, of course, if he chose to speak of his

233

endorsement of her to others, it would have to be privately, to escape his wife's wrath.

After assuring herself that Thaddy was still safely playing with friends, Amity grabbed a fistful of cobalt blue skirt in either hand, and returned through the open schoolhouse door into the milling, chattering crowd. She couldn't see Chalk and the woman, but they could be at the food table still. Closer at hand, she nodded and smiled at the familiar face of a wrinkled little woman from one of the outlying districts. Mrs. Waldo was speaking to her and somehow, she was answering back. "Yes, my campaign goes well, thank you. Making an impact? I believe so, yes. But I don't fool myself. Many voters would find it hard to choose a woman, regardless of qualifications. I know, normally it just isn't done, not normally. Is being a woman the only major hurdle in my campaign to overcome? Possibly so." If you didn't count the fact that at any point someone might decide to dig deeper into her private life, her background. . . .

"Hello, Amity. I've been looking for you —"

"H-hello, Chalk." She felt short of breath. "I was outside visiting with Henry Strout," she managed to say in a steady voice. "Quite an evening this has turned out to be."

"Lord, you can say that again." He chuckled deeply. "I want you to meet a very special lady, honey." His eyes sparkled. He whispered seductively, taking her arm, "You're more beautiful than ever in that dress and the way you've fixed

234

your hair. You have no idea what you do to me."

She drew away from him, thoroughly confused, though he didn't seem to notice as he placed her hand in the crook of his arm, taking her with him. He whispered again, "Look, I know folks aren't supposed to guess how we feel about each other. I'll behave, even though I'd like to scoop you up in my arms and run off with you this minute. I just don't see a whole lot of danger in taking you over to meet my sister and her kids."

"Your —" The sudden tumult of joy Amity felt buoyed her along to where Chalk's sister was tidying her children after their meal, wiping their faces, brushing their clothes. A beautiful family.

"Amity, this is my sister, Estelle Scarret. Sis, this is Amity Whitford."

His sister offered her hand to Amity with a warm smile, "Please call me Stella. It's nice to meet my brother's friends. My children, here, are Jenny and James."

"How do you do Stella, Jenny, James — it's very nice to meet you. Chalk has spoken of you." Dear Lord, thank you, *thank you* that it isn't Lilly!

"I'm afraid I took my dear brother by surprise." Stella made a face, her eyes on him filled with affection. "It's a long story, but we just got in an hour or so ago on the train and we were told we'd find Chalk here. We could hardly wait to see him. We left our bags at the hotel and rushed right over."

"Welcome to Syracuse! If there's anything I can do for you and the children, do let me know. I live out a ways, but I come to town now and then."

"Thank you so much. I'm afraid we're going to be a burden on my brother. We have hardly a kettle or dish to our name. As soon as possible, I'd like to have a place of my own, some kind of income. Perhaps you'll be able to make some suggestions?"

"There's no rush, Stell," Chalk growled protectively. "You've got a home with me and you know it. There's not a lot for women out here; Amity can tell you that. Although she's finding a niche for herself. She's got her own homestead and she's running for public office."

Stella looked shocked, doubtful, then intrigued. "Really? I hope you'll tell me about it sometime!"

Amity laughed. "I'd love to. Let's get together; I do want us to be friends. My boy, Thaddeus, would enjoy playing with Jenny and James." She looked toward the door. "Speaking of Thaddy, it's time I got him into our wagon and we started for home. It'll be well past his bedtime before we get there. It was very nice meeting you, Stella."

"Amity, let me walk with you. Be right back, Stell."

Chalk was careful not to touch her as they headed for the door. He didn't even take her arm this time. She looked up at him. "Is there some kind of trouble going on? You were late tonight."

"A couple of Kendall men were on their way to Syracuse to break up this party. A few of us got wind of it and went to meet them. We were too late. We found them badly beaten on the road just east of town."

"Someone from Syracuse did that?"

"Practically beat them to death, then left them there. Doc Gourley's taking care of them."

"Do you know who did the beating?"

He shook his head. "Not a clue. And the prevailing attitude is that the Kendall men had it coming and no punishment is called for."

"Which won't make the Kendall community happy."

"No, it won't." He swore softly under his breath. "It looks like this county seat fuss isn't going to go away easy. And if it gets worse, honey, if you win that office of superintendent, you'll be right in the eye of the storm as a county official from over here."

It was hard to take a personal threat seriously; at the moment she was too giddily happy for other reasons. She answered in a soft voice, "I'll take care, Chalk. Please, you be careful, too." It was more likely something would happen to him, as involved as he was. As they said their goodbyes, it was all she could do not to reach up and take his face in her hands. But she called for Thad instead.

Chapter Fourteen

"Missy, help!" It was John Clyde! Amity heard his desperate cry through the open door of her kitchen.

"Dear God, what — ?" She caught her skirts and raced out barefoot across the dusty backyard, zipping around the crude outbuildings.

The silage pit! She spotted wisps of John Clyde's hair above the stone curbing of the six-foot-deep cavern. No sign of Thaddeus! "No!" Sick with panic, she flew to the pit and fell to her knees, reaching down to help John as he hung on and pulled at the small limp figure half buried in the slippery green mass. "C'mon, son!" John Clyde pulled, then gently slapped the unconscious boy's cheeks with his other hand.

It might have been a minute or two, but to Amity it seemed like hours as they fought to free Thaddy, to pull him from the quicksand-like morass, clawing the silage away from him. The sweet smell of the silage nauseated her. Perspiration broke out on her forehead. She began to sob in relief when they finally drew him up and out. Thaddeus could have been a rag doll as John Clyde laid him gently on the ground. Amity gathered the boy, slime and all, into her arms, stroking his pale, dirty face.

"Honey? Thaddy! Thaddeus, love — !" She shook him, patted his face. "Oh, darling, please wake up!" Her hand shook as she laid it on his scrawny little chest, but she could feel a quiet, reassuring *thump, thump* of his heart. Yet he was so silent, so still. It was hard to be calm. Her lungs seemed to explode with fear. *Dear Lord, please don't let it happen again, please.* "Do something, John, please, I beg you. Thaddy can't — Chloe trusted me —"

"Missy, you got to calm yourself, it ain't as bad as it looks." John Clyde sounded less than convincing, though, as he knelt in front of them, rubbing the boy's arms. "C'mon, son, c'mon son. Wake up, now."

Zip crouched, whining, scooting closer and closer, until he licked the boy's face with his tongue. He laid his head on the boy's green-slimed leg and looked up at Amity with solemn eyes.

John Clyde met Amity's fearful, pleading gaze with a stiff, artificial smile. "Shoot, Missy, I've seed cowboys throwed from a horse be knocked out for half an hour and come out of it just fine. Let's give him a minute or two, he'll come 'round."

She asked in a stark whisper, "What on earth happened?"

He shook his grizzled head, eyes filled with regret, as he explained. "The lad was tramping the silage down at the edges. It was a slippery mess in there." His sinewy hand curled the boy's jaw and he wagged the small head back and forth, then he dropped his hand to rest on Thad's arm. "I was unhitching Ben and Max from the wagon so we could come in to supper when I realized the boy weren't nowhere around. Looked in here and found him unconscious, the roof closed down tight on the pit."

"Closed?" her voice was tight with shock.

He nodded gravely as he shook the youngster's limp arm. "The way I figure it, Thaddeus was jumping up and down on the silage to pack it in tight, slipped off his feet, and cracked his head on the stones lining it."

How could she have allowed this to happen? The boy did almost a man's work. Amity lifted Thad's head to examine it and found a huge lump rising. Her fingers came away bloody. She bit back a cry, looking at John Clyde in deepened alarm. "He could have a concussion from this! We've got to get him to Doc Gourley right away."

John Clyde stood up. "Poor little tyke. I figure he felt himself fallin', reached for something to grab onto, and hit the roof prop instead, bringing it down to close him in. They ain't a lot of air in there —"

Tears trailed down Amity's cheeks. If anything happened to her beloved boy she'd *never* forgive herself, never. Chloe had entrusted Thaddy's very *life* to her, and now — Her arms tightened and she rocked him. "Wake up, darling, oh, please, Thad, wake up. John, bring the wagon."

Instead, he turned back. "Missy," he said, his voice gentle but urgent, "you're holdin' the boy too tight. He needs air and you're smothering him all over again. Lay him out flat on the ground, now. Let's kind of raise his feet, put them in your lap. Maybe if they're higher the blood will go to his brain and help him come 'round."

"Of course, oh, God, I'm sorry." Amity forced herself to release the boy and they stretched him out flat. She held his bare feet in her lap as she leaned toward him, patting his face, giving him a shake. Seconds ticked by, a lifetime. When his first small faint whimper came, she thought it was from the dog. Then she saw Thaddeus's eyelids flutter as he tried to raise his head. Joy flooded through her. She was instantly calm and lay her hand on his shoulder. "Lie still, Thaddy, just rest. You're fine." Her breath released in one big *whoosh*.

With loving hands, Amity bathed the boy, applied ointment to the small break in the skin on his head, crowned him with bandage. Thaddeus resisted her coddling in a strong voice, but Amity remained firm. For two days she made him stay in the house and rest. She read stories to him, they drew pictures together, she played songs for him on the melodeon, and she kept an eagle eye on him for signs of downward change. The only signs apparent were that he was a healthy, rambunctious boy with an appetite, fully recovered from the ordeal within forty-eight hours. She had to let him go.

Though she could see with her own eyes that he was all right, and she knew that the accident could have happened to any farm child, Amity was scared. If Thaddeus hadn't survived, she couldn't have borne it; it would have been the end. He was her blessing. She ought not to think of, nor ask for, anything more. Nothing must take him from her. She was so worried that she even began to have second thoughts about the school superintendent job.

Family was more important. Chalk had his sister and her children with him now. She had Thaddeus and John Clyde; more than some had, the most that *she'd* had, since Mama and Papa died. The sensible part of her mind said that she should be content. Her heart reminded her that she'd never be totally content with life without Chalk. But for now, she had to try.

Amity scrounged in her garden patch for the few vegetables that had come up since harvest. She stood holding a small pumpkin on one hip and watching the rider etched against the autumn sky advance up the road at a slow canter. As he drew nearer, a dot of scarlet marked the horseman's tie. Her heart picked up a hammer beat; she felt a consuming joy. An involuntary hand went up to tuck stray curls in place; she brushed at her bodice, straightened her soiled apron, foolishly wished she was wearing her new dress and not this ragged yellow muslin shift.

It must be business to do with her campaign bringing Chalk to Dove's Nest. He'd spotted her watching, and he waved. She lifted a hand slowly and waved back.

She said something inane as he rode up and dismounted, she had no idea what even seconds later. She must have invited him to the house but couldn't remember actually voicing the words. He put up his horse and then fell in beside her as she made her way to the house, her arms still hugging the pumpkin.

She put the pumpkin on the kitchen table and poured them coffee, feeling a warm rush of color to her cheeks as Chalk's hand brushed hers when she passed him his cup. Their eyes met and a heat seemed to shimmer between them. She plopped down in a chair, her eyes sliding away from his as she tried to control her feelings. Her hand shook as she lifted her own cup.

At that moment, her black speckled hen, Agatha, mate of her Rhode Island Red rooster, peeked out from under the blanket that curtained off the bedroom and they watched, wide-eyed and silent, as the proud hen tiptoed to the open door and outside. An embarrassed blush crept into Amity's face. Chalk's puzzled expression made her laugh. Then his roar of laughter filled the room, too, and he slapped his leg. "My God —" he turned to her "— what was that hen doing in your bedroom?"

"She — she —" Amity ground her lips together to halt the giggles. "Agatha, m-my hen, does that when she finds I've left the door open. She must have come in earlier, while I was out plowing. Then I stopped at the vegetable patch. I don't know why, but she loves to slip in and lay her egg under my bed, before she tiptoes out again." Outdoors, Agatha commenced to cackle noisily, letting one and all know her job for the day, and possibly the season, was done.

Amity smothered a hiccup, took a deep breath. "I'm very, very sorry. You didn't come all this way to learn my hen's odd nesting habits. Is anything wrong? Trouble in town?"

Chalk ignored her question for a second, looking at her with a loving expression. "You're a sight for a man's eyes anytime, Amity, but you ought to laugh more."

She shook her head. "Please — ?"

He nodded at her impatience, and finally drawled, his eyes still drinking in her face, "All right, I came out to ask if you intend to come into town for election night. Normally, there's wild partying at elections, but with the competition goin' on between Kendall and Syracuse for the county seat vote, this one could be a real dangerous dogfight. Sometimes I think the fuss will never end. Anyhow, I want to come get you and bring you into town, if you want to be there." He held up his hand when she started to protest. "I know you don't want us to be seen together so much that we start talk, and I'd asked Sheriff Bell to escort you, but he'll be keeping the peace."

She sighed, and said so quietly he had to lean

forward to hear her, "Maybe I should just drop out of the race altogether. The closer we get to election day, the more I feel like a fraud, keeping my past secret from people I've come to care very much about. I'm glad I told you, but —"

"You can't quit! Purdue would win, for God's sake! Amos Taylor is out of the race as of yesterday. Doc Gourley found something wrong with Amos's heart. Amos is building Syracuse a new courthouse as his contribution. He hopes doing that will get Syracuse the county-seat vote."

"It's worry enough that someone may show up who knows what happened in Beaconsfield even before I get a reply to my letters. Chalk, if it's true, I won't be allowed to hold office; I could have Thaddeus taken away from me. I'm not sure why I ever believed I could do this."

"It's my fault. I should never have gotten you into this," he said huskily, getting to his feet and pulling her into his arms.

"Chalk, I wanted this job badly. And I don't want to let you down, or the others, but . . ."

"Then stay in, honey, though you'd never disappoint me, no matter what you do." He whispered against her hair, "Amity, oh, God, Amity."

When he said her name like that . . . She tilted her face to look up at him. They regarded one another in tender loving desperation and then Chalk slowly released her with a tortured sigh of regret. He turned to pick up his hat from his chair. "Got to get the hell out of here, *now*," he emphasized in a thick voice, "or all rules are off. But remember — I want you safe on election night."

"I will be. I'll ride into town with the Bergens, if I come."

He turned at the door and nodded, "Everything's going to be all right," he said hoarsely. "You. Me. The elections. Don't keep tearing yourself apart on the 'what if I'm guilty — what if I'm innocent' issue. Honey, I understand, but it isn't the real concern of the office. What's important is that you can do the job, and that you want it. That's what counts."

Her heart soared. "Oh, Chalk!" She raced to him and threw herself in his arms. With her face buried against his chest, her arms wrapped about his waist, she cried, "Thank you. Thank you for believing in me when it's so hard to believe in myself."

He held her tenderly for a brief moment, pecked a kiss on her mouth, clapped on his hat, and rushed out. She laughed that he considered himself a danger to her. Someday, she meant to sample more than his kiss. Embarrassed by the turn her thoughts had taken, she giggled, and then danced across the kitchen floor.

After Chalk's warning, Amity wasn't surprised to find Syracuse a combination gala picnic and armed camp on election night. Fearing harm to Thaddy, she'd insisted that he remain at the ranch. John Clyde argued to accompany her, until she told him Mr. Bergen would take her to town.

Looking around as they drove along the main street, Amity realized that no woman in her right mind would want to be out alone tonight. The doors of the saloons were wide open. Drunken cowboys stumbled in and out, firing pistols into the air, even though the street was crowded with townspeople, farmers, ranchers, a few children. Raucous piano music blasted from open saloons, adding to the noise outside. At the end of the street, a horse race was being organized, and closer at hand, on the sidewalk in front of the bank, bets were being taken for both the horse race and the election. There were men she didn't know, but she couldn't be positive they were from Kendall, come to stir up trouble.

She ran into the sheriff by the general store. Things would be different when the courthouse was finished, he told her, but for now the ballot box, an old sugar box tied together with string and with a hole cut in the top, was located in the back corner of the general store to be overseen by Buford Barker, the county clerk, and himself. Both were running for reelection. Amity thought wryly that perhaps the pair were selected to keep an eye on each other against stuffing ballots for themselves and their favorite candidates. Anything could happen in a cowtown election, though, she'd been told.

Chalk was nowhere to be seen, but she knew he would be out mingling in the crowds, trying to keep the peace, asking for a fair and honest election. She was familiar with his editorials arguing against irregular and informal county business, the carrying of records back and forth, and conducting business hither and thither, a benefit to none of them, really. Over and over, he'd begged for it to stop, for the dispute to be settled without bloodshed by the ballot box. He was personally in favor of Syracuse because of its central location in the county, the presence of the railroad, the proximity of the river, and as he jokingly declared, the presence of the county's "most popular newspaper."

She browsed in the store along with other women waiting for the voting to end and the count to be completed. She could scarcely believe the absolute chaos surrounding the voting. The room was crowded; the air was blue with cigar smoke, vulgar language, and loud talk. Some of the farmers and ranchers came in, cast their votes quietly, then led their wives outside to patiently wait for the count. On the whole, though, there seemed to be little or no regard for honesty, or the propriety of the occasion. Men, stumbling with drink, slyly accepted money, then went to vote the choice of the buyer; repeaters cast second and third votes, and weren't always caught in time by a watchful Wilf Bell. She overheard the sheriff threatening to arrest one man for trying to vote names he'd taken from the local graveyard. If they weren't careful, Syracuse's vote would be thrown out again for fraud, allowing Kendall to win.

It riled her anew that the women present weren't allowed to vote, as if they were second-class citizens without good sense! Good Lord, look at the way the legal voters behaved! She almost wished she'd stayed home, but there was to be a supper and dance after the polls closed. She ought to be there, since she was one of the official candidates.

Finally, Buford Barker, puffed up with importance, announced the polls officially closed. Everyone was ordered to repair to the Dunnington hotel for the supper and dance, while the votes were counted. Sheriff Bell urged Amity to go along with the other women. The probate judge had come in from his ranch and with help from his appointees would do the count. He would be over later to announce the winners in all the county races, including county clerk, coroner, school superintendent, the three commissioner seats, and choice for county seat.

Amity left the store gladly.

The large dining hall of the Dunnington was set for supper, candles lit on each table. A sideboard was laden with pre-dinner treats: candies, dried peaches and raisins, nuts, claret, blackberry brandy. A double door opened into a second room where an orchestra made up of men playing fiddle, Jew's harp, zither, and mandolin was in full swing. A few well-dressed couples from town and some rough-hewn ranchers and their calicoed wives were dancing. Recognizing the tune, "Golden Slippers," Amity could hardly keep her feet still. She hummed softly under her breath; it was hard not to feel excited. She remembered the day she met Chalk, and how he had talked her into coming here for pie while they discussed the possibility of her running for superintendent. It seemed ages ago. She'd been intensely drawn to him from that very day, she could admit it now. Tonight they might dance — they might even sit together at supper, with others. But they'd have to be very careful.

Seymour Purdue was there in a new suit of clothes, shaking every hand he could grab as folks came in. From his jovial laugh and the few words she overheard, accentuated by waves of his cane, he was celebrating as though victory were already his.

Thisba, her arm tucked through her cousin's, wore a breathtaking gown of striped taffeta in coral, salmon, cream, peach, and pink. Her hair was coiffed like a queen's. As she visited around, her manner proclaimed the evening was all hers.

Pride wouldn't allow Amity to react, as insignificant as she was beginning to feel. She smiled warmly at Thisba, when the woman finally pretended to notice her presence for the first time. Thisba left Seymour and swept her way. "Good evening, Amity, dear, how are you?" She offered her soft white hand.

"I'm fine, Mrs. Strout. May I compliment you on your beautiful dress?"

"You may! I just noticed you standing over here in the corner, dear. Feeling a little blue, I suppose? Tell me now, what will you do after tonight? What are your plans?"

Amity kept calm, refusing to acknowledge the insult. "You mean, what will I do *if* I don't win the superintendency? The same as I'm doing now, Mrs. Strout: I'll run my ranch. I'm really a tenacious person, you know, and quite resourceful." She smiled sweetly. "I beg you not to worry about me. Besides, I may win!"

Thisba squeezed Amity's arm before she turned away, giving her a look of pity.

Amity was visiting quietly with Mrs. Roy, president of the city council, when the church bells suddenly rang out, chiming loud and long. From the blacksmith's shop, anvils loaded with powder boomed like cannonfire.

"That's it, the counting's done," Mrs. Roy announced. "Now we'll see."

There'd been the snapping and popping of celebratory gunfire all evening, like food spattering in a hot skillet. But it had suddenly picked up in volume down the street, it seemed to Amity, and she felt a bit unnerved and frightened.

Moments later, a small balding man in brown flannel shirt and worn leather chaps staggered into the dining room, waving his hat in drunken excitement. "S-s-s—'s been a gunfight!" He weaved, eyes closing for a second. "Chalk Holden, the newspaper feller's been sh-shot. Can one of you wimmen come help the Doc s-see to him?"

Amity went totally cold. *Chalk.* She ran, calling to the man staggering back out, "Wait! Show me where he is!"

Mrs. Roy tried to stop her. "Miss Whitford, don't you go out there. Someone else can go, but you should stay here!"

Amity waved her off. "No, I have to go!" She yanked away, running pell-mell for the door, paying no heed as the whole room stared. Gripped with panic, she prayed to be in time.

Chapter Fifteen

Amity lost the drunken cowboy as soon as she gained the dark, noisy street. Two men stood talking in lamplight spilling from the hotel window. She clutched the burly arm of the nearest. "I understand Chalk Holden's been shot? Did they take him to Doc Gourley's? I'm to — to help." At the man's nod, she picked up her skirts and ran. Doc treated patients from his home, which was clear at the other end of town and in the residential district up the hill. She ran as hard as she could, considering the boisterous crowds.

"What's the hurry, miss?" The hand of a bystander reached out and snagged her arm as she passed the saloon. Amity struggled ferociously to be free. He held her in an iron grip; his breath was foul as he tried to kiss her.

"Let me go!" She pounded his chest. She stomped on his instep, leaving him howling, and raced along the shadowy streets lit only by coal-oil lamps spilling light from an occasional window.

Worry, as much as anything, had left her breathless by the time she reached Doc's door. No one answered her knock. She twisted the knob and stepped into a dimly lit foyer, rushing down the hall to a lamp-lit room with the door open. Doc Gourley looked up and nodded in recognition from where he worked over Chalk, who was stretched out on the table. Chalk's hair was mussed, his eyes closed, and she couldn't tell a thing. She could see a bare muscled shoulder; Doc seemed to be working on the other one. Someone had brought Stella Scarret, Chalk's sister, and she was setting aside a pan of bloody water and handing Doc a fat roll of white bandage. She looked scared but she, too, nodded at Amity. "Hello, Miss Whitford."

"H-how is Ch— Mr. Holden?" She clenched her hands to keep from wringing them. "Is he — will he be all right?"

"Took a bullet in the shoulder, but we got it out and cleaned him up. He'll be fine," Doc said, folding a thick pad of gauze to place on the wound. "Kendall men were trying to steal the tally sheet tonight. Guess they intended to either destroy it or fix it in their favor, since Syracuse won, seven hundred and sixty-two votes to their five hundred forty. Holden, here, took a bullet meant for Buford, the clerk."

Amity felt weak with relief as she stepped forward. "I was told you needed help, Dr. Gourley. I see Mrs. Scarret is here, but if there's anything I can do?"

"Just about finished. Sit up, son, so I can bind you up proper."

As Chalk slowly sat up to be bandaged, his voice sounded weak, tired. "I have to talk to

254

you, Amity, so stick around. When you're finished, Doc, sis, could you give us a minute alone?"

Though neither of the other two raised an eyebrow, Amity felt her cheeks color. The minute the door closed behind them, Chalk scolded, "You shouldn't have come by yourself, Amity! All hell's breakin' loose out there!" He glared, his face pale underneath his tan. He held his bound arm gingerly with the other hand, his teeth tight against the pain.

"I'm not the one who went and got shot!"

He grinned. "I was on my way to the hotel to dance your victory dance with you, darlin', when it happened. Buford, bless his cowardly hide, shivering in his boots, was no match for the hard cases from Kendall. Don't know where the sheriff got to. So I had to stop and help Buford."

And she'd hoped to dance one innocent dance with him. Slowly, what he'd said about a *victory* dance sank in. "I won? Oh, dear God, I won!"

"Yep, fair an' square. By only seven votes, but a miracle at that, since Mrs. Strout bought enough votes for Seymour to choke a hog. Yes," he said gently, smiling, pale, "you won. Good for the county, but scary as hell for you, the way things are going. It's going to take a Kansas Supreme Court order to settle the seat fuss and till then any officeholder needs to keep an eye on his — or her — back. Kendall's not giving up the part of old court records they hold. Though they didn't have an official nominee for county

255

school superintendent, they may or may not contest your election. You saw how things went tonight; you can bet your bottom dollar that Kendallites will claim fraud as soon as district court opens in the morning."

"What a mess! You mean they'll still try to keep part of the government running over there? But *I* don't have a direct rival?"

He nodded. "That's how it stands for now. In the meantime, you'll be careful, but go on about your official duties."

"Yes, I will." She caught the back of a chair and grasped it tightly, feeling indecently happy. Chalk was wounded, but he'd recover. She had the post. Some danger, maybe. A lot of work, certainly. And *one thousand dollars,* five hundred dollars per year for her two year term. What a godsend for Dove's Nest Ranch. Income that didn't depend on the vagaries of weather and the elements, whether seed came up and flourished or not, didn't depend on the increase of her cattle herd. Money earned, not borrowed.

"Amity." Chalk broke her spell. "I thought you came to nurse me? Come here, Miss Superintendent. A wounded man needs a kiss to get well."

"Oh, Chalk, you know what we said —"

"You made those rules about how we should act, not me. I didn't like it then, and I don't like it now. C'mere."

"All right," she whispered, darting a look over her shoulder to make sure Doc and Stella remained in the other room, "one kiss to get well on." She went to stand between his legs where he sat on the table. He pulled her close. She put her arms around him with great care, drew a long, sharp breath as her body touched his. "Doesn't it hurt? Really, you look awful — you should lie down."

"The only thing that hurts worse than I can stand —" hazel eyes looked deep into hers "— is that I can't do this morning, noon, and night." And his warm, firm lips locked with hers.

THE NEW HAMILTON COUNTY SUPERINTENDENT

November, 1887

Chapter Sixteen

Amity ducked to keep from striking her head on the faded wooden sign, MINNIE'S HATS, that dangled by a rusted wire over the doorway, and entered what was designated her *office* until Amos Taylor's promised courthouse could be built. The small front room smelled musty from mice and was so dirty she cringed. A broken packing box for a desk, a homemade chair with a broad board nailed on crookedly for a back, and a small, rusted Topsy stove cold as ice, were its meager furnishings. A few shelves had been nailed to the wall. Spider webs above, mice droppings below, dust everywhere, and cold — very cold this November day.

Because she wasn't replacing a predecessor, Amity had been asked to take over immediately and was quickly recognized by state education officials. A rumble arose from Kendall, but came to little. She doubted a single officeholder like herself, a woman particularly, had cause to fear for her life. She could carry on her business as necessary. But she knew that Chalk, and others, wouldn't rest until Syracuse was named the one and only seat of government in Hamilton County.

She turned her attention back to the cold, dirty room. She sighed, upset and miserable at having been given such a filthy place to work in.

Waiting at the door, was the high-collared county clerk, Buford Barker, his arms wrapped around a basket of papers, his smile indicating how much he enjoyed her show of distaste.

She shivered, drawing her coat tighter. What a welcome to her new job. Surely there'd been a mistake? She stepped around her trunk holding her bedding, clothing, and other personal items and laid a gloved hand flat on the cold stove. "Who's responsible for this? Why wasn't I consulted about choosing a place for my office? Surely there are better accommodations?"

"Mrs. Strout and I were put in charge. There was hardly room for you in my office. We went to some trouble securing this building for you." Buford smirked, an I-told-you-so look in his eyes.

"Really?" She gave him a flinty smile, thinking maybe he didn't deserve Chalk saving his life. As she'd suspected, she had more to be concerned about from her own locals, like Thisba and this man, than from Kendall malcontents.

Buford waved a free hand. "This place is plenty good enough. Anyhow, Mrs. Strout says you're not like other women, you don't mind roughing it — that you're used to it, as a matter of fact."

Amity shook her head. "I'll freeze to death in this — this filthy crackerbox. Why, you can see sky right through the cracks in the walls!" She turned slowly, hesitating as she faced the small front window. From the moment Buford had brought her there, she'd been more than aware that the *Banner* office was directly across the street. She turned her back to the window and faced Buford, red-nosed now from the cold. She glared at him, hating his self-satisfaction. Hating, but not surprised, that Thisba had had a hand in things even after Seymour failed to win.

"Maybe you don't want this job after all? We're doing the best we can for you, but you don't seem to appreciate it, Miss Whitford."

"Of course I intend to keep the job." Out of pride, she didn't reveal that she'd heard a suite of rooms had been set aside early on at the Dunnington for Seymour Purdue, in the event he won. But here she was. If this was all they would offer, she'd grit her teeth and bear it. The truth was, she could deal with the drabness, the close confines, even the freezing draft — providing she didn't die of pneumonia. What concerned her most was the building's close proximity to Chalk Holden. She needed to concentrate on her own affairs. Did an overflowing river need more rain?

Buford plopped the basket of papers onto the packing box, and went back to where a second basket waited by the door. "This building was good enough for Minnie; it was her home and her business." Amity's lack of response as she fingered the records didn't keep him from going on, "Six or seven years ago Syracuse wasn't much more than a watering place for ranchers and drift-

263

ers in miles of rangeland. Minnie couldn't make it selling women's hats since there wasn't hardly any other women here." His lecherous laugh caused Amity to turn, and he openly looked her over, up and down. "So she took to selling what else she had . . . to the men."

"I'm really not interested," Amity snapped.

"Wenching Minnie was brought before the judge and then run out of town when good women came, with families. We'll see how you do here in your — occupation."

She stared at him; finally found her voice. "Get out! Put those things down and get out of here!"

"Build your own fire, then." He smiled, rubbing cold-stiffened hands together. He tipped his hat to her. "There's a lean-to bedroom and a shed in back. Coal's in the shed for the stove. Cot's in the lean-to, for you to sleep on. Minnie's business bed."

Trembling with rage, Amity dropped into the lone chair as soon as he'd gone. This was where she was to spend most of her time now? Away from her cozy home, away from Thaddy and John Clyde? Here? A plague on Thisba and Buford. They were in this together to shame and humiliate her, to make her life miserable. Well, she wouldn't let them. She jumped to her feet, tightened her bonnet strings, and marched out the door and across the street to the newspaper office where she didn't bother to knock.

Chalk, whose arm was in a sling, looked up from where he was writing at his desk. Concern flashed across his face. "What's wrong?"

"The fools of this town have put me in that hellhole over there across the street, th-that old bordello, but I'll turn it into a confounded castle before I let it give me another moment's bother."

"Amity, I'm sorry. The building isn't fit for pigs. I tried to tell them that, but Thisba can sway folks to her thinking even when she's dead wrong."

"I don't care about that." Her hands flew into the air. "It doesn't matter a hill of beans. What I want is a broom. May I borrow yours? And a bucket and a rag?"

"I'll come help. I'll build you a fire."

"Don't." She shook a finger at him. "Really! I can see to the cleaning by myself, and I'm perfectly capable of building a fire. You're wounded, anyway."

"Amity, what'd I do — ?"

She met his eyes and shrugged, admitting, "Nothing, really. And I apologize for carrying on so. But that Buford and Thisba just — oh, never mind. Please, bring me the things I need?"

He started back toward his living quarters, turning when she called out, "Soap, bring soap, too." He nodded and dazzled her with a smile.

She took the things from him, careful not to let their hands touch. He made a soft sound in his throat as he let her out the door, and called after her, "I won't come over, myself, but my sister Stella can help you clean that pig-sty. She's at the store with the kids now. Soon as she gets back, she'll be right over."

Amity agreed with a lift of her shoulder and kept going across the street.

Two days later, her transformed office offered reasonable comfort and efficiency. A fire crackled in the small, newly blacked and polished stove; its sides were red from the heat. Walls and floors had been cleaned, airholes patched with lath, and the whole inside whitewashed. A decorative cloth from the department store covered her desk; Stella had insisted on buying her a small potted ivy. Now Amity sat at her makeshift desk, sorting the papers Buford Barker had left behind.

In going through the records she had found that the previous county school superintendent, who'd quit midterm to go back to farming in the Kendall area, was content to let things be and had made few improvements. Reports were few, incomplete, and in many cases nonexistent. That would change, in her hands. She would have teachers send her regular reports from their schools, so that she in turn could report to the state superintendent. She frowned as she read the financial ledger. Expenditures were minimal, which might be seen as admirable by some, but there was so much need out there in those small rural schools, and the funds provided for such had been used up, anyway, somewhere, somehow, though not recorded.

As she perused the mess, she thought with rising anger of schools like Meda Ginsbach's. The woman had been teaching in her kitchen from the time her own children were old enough to learn to read. The country was growing up; it was time Meda had a real school and the necessary supplies to teach the youngsters who came to her. Amity sighed. The school up north near the Greeley County line, in the Hudson District, was a dugout, a hole in the ground, where children were expected to learn and to better themselves. There were children like Jebby Dusky in other areas, particularly south of the Arkansas River in the sandhills, who had no school at all to attend. She'd already decided to take books and other supplies to the Dusky family so that they could learn at home. This past fall, a penniless young Easterner had been turned out by his rancher uncle near Coolidge for the crimes of being lame, an educated booklover, and a poor cowboy to boot. Will Quick was his name, and Liddy Dusky had found him wandering the sandhills, half-starved. Liddy and her children gave Will a home; he was able to do enough work on her place to earn his keep. Amity meant to pay him to teach the children to read. When she got a real school established down there, she hoped Will Quick would accept the job as teacher. If Liddy Dusky felt any last resistance, Amity would win her over. Those children needed a proper education.

Amity got up and began to pace, going to the window to look outside. Already she missed Dove's Nest and Thaddy. How proud Thad had been to enter school. The sod schoolhouse at Sand Creek was closest to Dove's Nest; Tannis Beneke would be a good teacher. Amity sighed. She could go home to the ranch some weekends, and possibly at other times, too. Come spring, she could return to the ranch for the season. Suddenly feeling self-conscious, as though she were being watched, she darted a glance across at the *Banner* office. Chalk stood at his own window looking across at her. She lifted her hand in a fluttering wave, before retreating to the safety of her desk.

She went back to writing down the goals she meant to accomplish while in office: Some kind of school at Sand Creek, more uniform texts and supplies, retesting for teachers. Then she took a large piece of brown wrapping paper and, with a dark pencil, proceeded to draw a map of rectangular Hamilton County. She drew a dark, slanted line representing the Santa Fe tracks down across the middle of the sheet, and alongside the tracks in a wavier line, the Arkansas River that the tracks followed. She marked off the five school districts in blocks and began to fill in the location of her schools.

Up on the northern line, in the center, was the dugout school in the Hudson District. A congenial but busy housewife and mother of seven, Eliza "La" Ellsworth, her own education dishearteningly scant, taught there. Married women were rarely given teaching positions, but sometimes there was no alternative. Nine miles southwest at the head of Bridge Creek, was Bridge School. Last year, Clarina Franklin had outfitted an abandoned shack, which had only one small window, and commenced teaching there. Amity worried about Clarina, too. In spite of good intentions, the girl with angelic looks, fluffy gold hair, and sea blue eyes seemed out of her depth teaching, which wasn't good for her students, who needed a confident leader.

Almost directly west near the Kearny County line, at Federal City, was Miss Corinne Wagner's school — a soddy in fair condition. Corinne was an older bookish spinster who refused to be a burden on her sister and brother-in-law and their large family. She was a fine teacher; Amity liked her and foresaw few problems in that district.

She would arrange it so that the attractive Richards twins could teach in two rooms at the hotel at Coolidge on the Colorado border. As long as they weren't separated again, they'd be wonderful teachers. Her one male teacher, Horace Simpson, a jolly, middle-aged bachelor rancher, taught at Lee School, a cottonwood log structure six miles southwest of Dove's Nest Ranch, near the river. Thaddy's school, Sand Creek, was four miles east of her homestead. His teacher, Tannis Beneke, was somewhat shy, but she was a determined, venturesome teacher with a future, in Amity's opinion. Meda Ginsbach, of course, taught in her farmhouse kitchen eight miles west of there on Shirley Creek. Amity filled it in with her pencil.

She sat back and chewed the tip of the pencil thoughtfully. There was the fine frame school here in Syracuse, taught by three teachers, reasonably well educated. Five miles south and east of Syracuse, Rochelle Harvey, an eager tomboy not yet sixteen, was in charge of Carlisle School students.

Chatty Lecky Lloyd, a country Venus, taught at the only school now located in the sandhills south of the Arkansas River; Amity remembered with fondness the night she'd spent there with the Lloyd family, and the way they'd backed her at the Fourth of July celebration. Little Bear School was small, and too far to go to, for some of the children located down there, like Jebby Dusky. She must get at least one other school in that district *this year*. Fortunately, she was able to realign districts and to create schools where needed.

When her map was finished, Amity unlaced and removed her shoe for something to hammer with, drew her chair over to the wall, and climbed up. She had a few nails she'd worked out of the walls before Stella helped her whitewash. Holding the nails between her teeth, she maneuvered the map into place and began to pound. Driving nails even with the hard heel of her shoe was slow going. Hearing a sound behind her, she started to turn, and struck her thumb smartly. Spitting out the nails, she shrieked with pain. She moved her stockinged foot ever so slightly but it was enough to put the chair off balance and it started to tip. "Ohhh, nooo!" The chair went over and she landed in a painful heap on the floor, her skirts flying. She whacked petticoat and dress down into place as she sat up.

"How about a hammer?" a husky voice asked.

Amity's head jerked around. Due to the racket with the chair, she hadn't heard the door open, or his footsteps.

Amity jumped to her feet, and tried to look as dignified as possible. "What are you doing here, Chalk Holden?" Good Lord, had he been watching the whole thing?

He held the hammer aloft by way of answer. He grinned at her, his thick brown eyebrows raised.

"Thank you." She took the hammer and stepped back, trying not to look helpless. Her pulse picked up a rapid beat; she felt shaky with excitement. Chalk's eyes glowed. He whispered, his voice deep and intense, "Amity . . . ?"

She looked away, and down, watched his booted feet move across the floor toward her, positive he was going to take her in his one good arm, wanting him to, desperately. But if he touched her — anything could happen.

"Chalk, I've been thinking about my job, and other things, and I don't think we should —"

He stopped. "I came over to help. Can't I even drive a nail for you?"

She laughed and tried to make a joke. "But I'm the one with two good arms, not you. Just go on back to work and don't worry about me."

He just stood there, his charming smile fading. His long ragged stare spoke of confusion, desire, anger. "All right," he finally agreed in a flat voice. He pointed at the hammer she held. "You don't have to come over with it when you're done —

271

just yell and throw it across the street."

"Chalk, that's ridiculous."

"Sorry," he said softly, "I thought ridiculous was allowed."

He turned and went out, leaving her itching to throw his hammer after him, walk away from this place, go to the other end of the earth, and never see him or it again.

She took the hammer and banged away, hanging her map. Surely the man understood why they had to be circumspect. *Why* her behavior must at all times be above reproach. The income she'd desperately needed was now assured. She absolutely wouldn't lose this position she'd fought so hard to gain. *Wham.* It wasn't only that she had the homestead to keep up, and must not lose it. *Thwack, thwack, thwack.* She now had young Thaddeus in her care. He was as dear to her as if he were her own flesh and blood, and she wanted to provide the best she was able for him. Besides, their chances of marrying soon looked even more unlikely now that Chalk had his sister's family to support. Surely, he could see all that, and she didn't have to keep explaining? Calmer as she climbed down from the chair, she lifted his hammer, the rough warm handle where his hands had touched, to her cheek.

Still, how could she expect Chalk to wait when she had so little control over her own feelings?

With her school map hung, Amity sat at her desk rereading as a sort of self-punishment the agreement she'd signed. It wasn't fair, but she had agreed to abide by the teachers' own regulations as laid out uniformly by the schools' educational boards, setting herself as a model.

Women teachers who marry or engage in unseemly conduct will be dismissed. It was all right for a woman to teach if she was already married when she began, though married women were seldom offered teaching positions. Possibly because she was the first female superintendent in the area, there was no legal ruling yet about her position and marriage, but she had little doubt the matter would be frowned upon and then some. When the time came and she and Chalk — she'd fight for the rule she wanted! But she'd only just got the job, and she wanted everyone to know how good she was at it before she started asking special favors. As her thoughts started to stray, Amity shook her head and turned her eyes back to the page. *Men teachers may take one evening each week for courting purposes, or two evenings a week if they go to church regularly.* No courting whatsoever mentioned for female teachers. *Every teacher should lay aside from each pay a goodly sum of his earnings for his benefit during his declining years so that he will not become a burden on society.* Well, few jobs offered pensions anyway. *Any teacher who smokes, uses liquor in any form, frequents pool or public halls, or gets shaved in a barbershop will give good reason to suspect his worth, intention, integrity, and honesty.* She must remember to stay out of barbershops!

There were other rules for her teachers, having

to do with filling lamps and cleaning chimneys, bringing in a scuttle of coal and bucket of water for each day's session, whittling nibs for the pupils' pens, and the like. Finally, she went to a shelf and buried the paper under a stack of books, sighing heavily for all she was giving up. Her glance slid toward the front window and across the way to the *Banner* office and Chalk's figure moving inside. He turned and looked at her.

Well, she didn't have to stand there and be gawked at by a hot-blooded, one-armed *male*. If he thought she'd weaken and run panting to him, he had another thought coming!

Chapter Seventeen

Once she was settled in and organized in her office, Amity decided there was no time like the present to get out and visit her schools. Also she would not have to put up with another visit from Seymour Purdue. Almost from the moment she'd won, he'd taken to dropping in unannounced. He pretended that he wanted to help; she was sure he hoped to see her fail.

Forget Purdue. She spent the early morning planning her first trip, and that accomplished, she packed her small satchel with papers, books, hairbrush, nightgown, and spare undergarments. Although she'd likely be invited to share meals with her teachers' families, she packed her own food to be on the safe side: hardtack, cheese, coffee, a tin of tomatoes. Coffeepot, can opener, spoon. Plenty of matches. She'd decided on a three-to-four-day tour of her schools in the northeast quarter of the county.

A cold silver dawn barely streaked the November sky when she walked to the livery next morning, carrying her bag. Her expense allowance provided for a light, horse-drawn buggy and she had only to ask for the rig. Mica, the older hostler, a bewhiskered, gnome-like man, grinned at her in surprise, a note of caution in his voice, "You ain't plannin' to go nowhere far, are ya? We might be fixin' for some real weatherin' today."

"I'll be fine, Mica, thank you. I need to make this trip, and now seems the best time. The weather can only get worse the next several months." She decided against telling him how far she intended to go, or how long she might be gone. Though she made no objection to the wrapped, heated bricks he brought from the livery stove to keep her feet warm.

The wind, blowing at an unworrisome velocity when she left Syracuse, rose to a low whine by the time she was five miles on the trail. The ashen sky began spitting snowflakes that settled on her brows and lashes, stinging her eyes and making them water. Her face ached from the bitter-cold wind. She could still turn back, but saw little need as long as she could see the trail. She was happy to be out and tending her job, making her first school inspection. It was only coincidental, she told herself, that Thaddy's school, Sand Creek, being about four miles to the north now, was the first in line on her tour. But she couldn't lie to herself about her eagerness to see him. She sank into her wrappings to endure the final distance.

West of Sand Creek, she passed her own Dove's Nest Ranch. It'd been only a few days since she'd left home and there was no need to stop. She'd be seeing her dear little Thaddeus at his school very soon, anyway.

Snow was blowing hard and Amity was chilled to the bone when she finally pulled into the open-front shed that sheltered the ponies of children who rode to Sand Creek School. She climbed down stiffly, hitched the horse to a post, and stumbled against the wind to the schoolhouse door.

Tannis Beneke, wearing a heavy knit shawl over her faded gingham, her mousy light brown hair escaping the bun at the back of her head, stared at her visitor in open shock.

"M-may I-I c-come in?" Amity asked through chattering teeth. She brushed snow from her coat sleeves and stamped loose snow from her boots.

"Oh, do!" Tannis exclaimed suddenly, stepping back to allow her entrance. "Amity, Miss Whitford, what're you doing — Oh, excuse me, you must be frozen half to death. Come over by stove. The children and I had hot cocoa with our lunches. There's some left, come now —"

Amity was shaking with cold as she removed her coat and mittens, allowing Tannis to take them and drape them on a bench by the stove. Her heart filled with pride as her eyes found Thaddeus, seated on a bench with another youngster. His own eyes lit up when he saw who their visitor was. She smiled at him. Even though she was his guardian, she felt she couldn't show him preferential treatment when she was on duty. But she could hardly take her eyes from him, and wanted nothing so much as to wrap him in a huge hug, kiss that handsome little face looking so adoringly, so pridefully at her. He'd started from his seat when he saw her, but the way he settled back now, his head dipped in a sweet smile, she knew he realized she was here not just for him, but for the whole school.

She took the reheated cocoa and settled in the teacher's chair that Tannis brought close to the stove. It was hard to keep her teeth from chattering, and her insides felt turned to ice. She waved away the young girl's apology when Tannis told her, "We were just havin' art, is that all right? Sometimes the children's minds seem to just wear out, practicin' nothing but readin', writin', and arithmetic. I told them they could make Santa Clauses and Christmas trees and we'd put them up around the room." She lowered her voice and confided, "It's really special for the children who don't have much Christmas at home."

"I think it's wonderful," Amity said, taking in the teacher's desk cluttered with scraps of saved paper, pots of paste, bits of cotton, and fabric scraps. "Please go ahead with what you were doing, I'd like to sit back and observe. And if you don't mind, I'll have the lunch I brought along, with this delicious chocolate."

When she was finally warmed through and her stomach content, the children and teacher absorbed in their art, Amity got up and walked around, quietly, to examine the shelf of books, the school's library in back of the teacher's desk.

Obviously these odds and ends were also Tannis's teaching tools: a tattered Bible, a *Poor Richard's Almanac,* two *McGuffey's Readers* and one falling-apart *Webster's Speller.* Such a mixed assortment made group readings or class assignments difficult if not impossible. She took out her notebook. She must stress the importance of books to her superiors, must find a way to provide texts and supplies uniformly throughout the districts.

She was examining some worn copies of the *Youth's Home Companion,* deep in thought, when Tannis came to stand at her shoulder. "I use the magazines a lot," Tannis whispered, with a look over her shoulder to see that the children were all still industriously occupied.

"Good! I enjoyed these myself as a child in Cairo, Illinois. Such wonderful stories and articles, the puzzles — I'm happy you have these, and if possible, I'll see that you get some newer issues."

Tannis nodded her thanks.

"I have one suggestion. Something our schools did back home," Amity said softly. "It's nice to read the stories aloud, but it's even better if the pupils assume the different characters and play them out. I'd like to see that made a weekly part of your school's program. As you said, the three R's, important as they are, need enhancement with other activities. We want to implant in these youngsters a deep and abiding love of reading along with their more practical studies."

Tannis nodded. "Your Thad is an excellent

student, Miss Whitford, a very bright boy."

Amity refrained from gushing like a proud mother hen as she actually wanted to do, "He knew his ABC's and could read some when he came to live with me. I started him on his times tables and simple addition this summer and he seemed to catch on very fast."

It wasn't until Amity was preparing to be on her way again to the next school, that she and Tannis realized how much the storm had built up outside. "My goodness!" Amity exclaimed, stepping back inside, closing the door against the blowing snow. "Tannis, I think you should dismiss school. Let the children go home while they can still find their way."

Tannis, who'd looked outside over Amity's shoulder, was already pulling down coats from the pegs on the wall. "Children, school is excused for the day. Leave things as they are and we'll finish tomorrow — if the weather is such that we can get to school in the morning. Come on now, collect your coats and lunch buckets."

Thaddeus had come up to clasp Amity's hand and she gave him a tight hug. "How many of the children have ponies?" she asked Tannis. "About four or five?"

"Five. They're not really that far from their homes and the ponies will light out fast for their own barns and feed-boxes on a day like this. The parents of the others won't know to come get them this early. Amity, Miss Whitford, if you see that Thaddeus gets home, and take the Bergen children to their house, I can see to the others."

"Of course. I meant to make the nine miles on to Hudson School before dark today, but to try would be foolhardy. I'll stay tonight at Dove's Nest and continue on in the morning." Amity helped Tannis see the riders off toward their homes and lock up the school. They loaded the youngsters into Amity's buggy and the teacher's old farm wagon. "Are you sure you'll be all right?" Amity asked Tannis.

"Yes, I'm sure. But I'm glad we're goin' now and not in another hour and a half. It won't be that far to Mother's and my place after I'm finished deliverin' these children. Will you be all right?"

"Of course. It's only four miles west from here to my farm, and I only have to circle out of my way a bit to see the Bergens home. Tannis, you keep a very nice school," she complimented her, above the whine of the wind, then climbed into the buggy and took up the reins.

When Amity saw the Bergen youngsters into their house, she and Thaddeus accepted warm, fragrant slices of fresh bread and jam before continuing on to Dove's Nest. On their way again, Amity drove with her arm about Thad's shoulder, her heart happy in spite of the frigid cold, and the difficulty of following the road in the blinding storm.

John Clyde stomped out of the barn when they

arrived. He'd saddled Texas Max and was about to ride to the schoolhouse to pick Thaddeus up early, before the storm worsened. He took charge of Amity's horse and buggy and ordered her and the boy into the house.

The soddy was deliciously warm, and good smells came from a stew that John Clyde had simmering at the back of the stove. Amity removed her outer garments and hung them to dry in back of the stove, along with Thaddeus's on a lower peg. She was filled with emotion as she shivered by the stove, feeling guilty for such adoration for her home, for the sheer joy of being here with her own things, her own four walls about her. And the boy; in just a few days, she had missed him so —

"Did you like my teacher?" Thaddeus asked as he pulled off his boots, wet through to his stockings. "Miss Beneke is going to let us have a Christmas tree at school, a party for our parents —" he stopped short "— and everything. Will you be able to come, Ammy? You and John Clyde?" Recently, Thad had taken to calling her *Ammy,* a sort of combined "Mommy/Amity," which she loved.

"I think you have a really fine teacher. I like her very much, and wild horses couldn't keep us from your Christmas party." She knelt before him, taking first one small cold foot in her hands, then the other, rubbing warmth into them. "Right now, I'm just so glad to be here at home with you and John Clyde . . . but you understand

282

that I can't stay very long, that I'll have to leave in the morning to visit other school children up north?"

"It's all right. I'm glad you're here, too," he said with a shy grin. "John Clyde said this morning that we could have popcorn and apples tonight, after I do my homework. He's going to tell me some stories about when he was a boy my size, down in Texas. You want to hear the stories, too, don't ya, and have popcorn?"

"Absolutely, dear. I can't imagine a nicer homecoming party."

The snow fell all that night and by morning it was piled to the eaves. John Clyde tied a rope from the house to the barn in order to find his way back and forth through the blizzard. He went out several times to break the ice on the watering troughs, and to see that the animals were fed. Amity cooked all day; potato soup, beans, another stew, homemade bread, biscuits, cornbread, and stewed apricots, so that Thad and John Clyde would have plenty to eat after she left. The food could be stored outside to prevent spoilage.

By the third day at Dove's Nest, she was consumed with guilt for not tending to her superintendent duties. Then by midmorning a warm wind arose and the snow began to melt.

"It'll start snowin' agin before you can say scat, wait an' see," John Clyde argued with her when she began preparations to leave in the morning. "I wisht you'd either stay here at home or let

283

me drive you back to that office in town."

"I have to go on to Hudson School," she insisted. "It's my job. I began the circuit and I'll finish it."

He gave in, but he didn't hide his disapproval. To appease him, she let him press on her almost enough supplies for a hundred-mile journey. Biscuits and bread, a lard can of her soup, matches and twists of straw should she need a fire. An extra amount of grain for her horse. "If it gets to blizzardin' agin an' you get stopped som'eres without shelter, just dig in and stay warm but on no account do you go to sleep. That's a sleep few folks wakes up from. Jest wait out the storm; I done it myself many's the time." He brought her his smelly old buffalo robe to keep warm under. "Got enough matches?" he asked for the umpteenth time. She assured him that she had. They'd heated the bricks in the stove and when she went out to her buggy, a well-bundled Thaddy placed the foot-warmer under her feet, and climbed up to kiss her cheek.

Her throat filled at the unexpected gesture. She reached out and touched the cold little lip with the thick scar. "Be a good son. I'll see you soon."

The plains were a broad, flat expanse beginning to show dark patches in the white, the sky was a dome of incredible blue. Amity sat and drove, wrapped almost to her eyes in coats and hide, reins in her gloved fingers. The horse's breath made white clouds of steam in the frigid air as they moved along. For hours she and the horse seemed the only living things on earth. Later, she saw a herd of cattle, bunched against the wind. Later still, a prairie wolf crossed the trail ahead, and looked her way. It sniffed the wind, then kept going, loping off into the distance until she couldn't make it out at all.

The sun was bright, the air brittle cold as she reached the side road to Hudson School. For some miles she experienced growing alarm; she should be seeing smoke from the school's chimney. Finally, she reminded herself that possibly Eliza Ellsworth just hadn't gotten around to reopening school after the storm, although most roads, and even blind lanes, were passable now. Or maybe Eliza had closed the school for a few days, absenteeism being high from colds and such.

When she reached the desolate dugout, however, it was obvious that it had not been used for some time. There were no tracks, no piles of shoveled snow, no coal supply in the shed. Amity climbed down, stiff and cold, and tried the door, not surprised to find it locked. She would have liked to go inside, build a fire to thaw herself out, and eat a bite before going on. But her fingers were too stiff with cold to get the single window open and the door was impassibly locked. She wiped at the dirty window and looked inside. Dust was so thick on the benches and tables it was obvious that school hadn't been opened that fall, that no one had been inside in months. Feeling numb and unbelievably tired, she got back into the buggy and urged the horse back onto the road in the direction of the Ellsworth soddy located a mile to the northwest. There were other homesteads scattered up here on the plains, but Eliza Ellsworth's was the closest. The snow began to fall, gently at first, then swirling in the wind.

Amity's eyelids drooped, her head bobbed drowsily, and time and again she shook herself to stay wake. It would do no good to fall asleep now and lose her way. She thought of Chalk. If he knew she was here, how numb and miserable with cold she was, the danger she was in of freezing to death, he would want to protect her, take care of her. She thought of how warm and strong his arms would feel holding her close, and though it was only a dream, she felt warmed as long as the image lasted.

When she finally reached it, the Ellsworths' soddy was a dim shadow in the blowing white. Amity sat in her wagon staring at it, her mind denying what she knew, even in her bone-chilling numbness. There was no one there, either. No smoke from the chimney, no animals in the shed or corral. There were no washtubs or benches on the porch, no curtains at the two windows reflecting the setting sun blankly back at her.

Her rented horse stood with head down against the blowing snow. He needed shelter as much as she. He needed grain; she needed something hot in her stomach and a warm bed. The Simpsons' homestead was four or five miles further west. She hated going still further in the opposite direction from Syracuse and her own ranch, but it was too far to go back; she'd never make it, particularly if the storm were to turn into a real blizzard. She urged the horse onto the road and headed west.

She was beyond feeling, her whole body numb. It was difficult to think as they plodded the dim trail. She lost track of time. The miles seemed to stretch longer than usual. Did it normally take this long to cover a distance of four miles or five? She peered into the blinding white. Had she passed the Simpsons' without seeing their place at all, any sign? No, it still had to be ahead of her, somewhere. *Ahead, ahead . . .*

She awoke to see Mrs. Simpson's smiling, moonlike face just inches above her own. Amity was in bed, piles of warm quilts pinning her to a corn-shuck mattress that rustled with her movement. She remembered, now, driving into the Simpsons' yard, feeling frozen to the buggy seat, unable to move. Someone had lifted her down. Her hands, face, feet and legs were bathed gently from a steaming basin. The woman had poured a hot broth between her lips, put her in this heavenly bed. "Th-thank you, Mrs. Simpson. How long have I been here?"

"Just the night, darlin'. You got here last night after dark. Like an icicle, you was, when we pried the reins from ya and took ya out of your buggy. Put your horse up, too. He's all right."

Amity ran her tongue over her chapped, cracked lips. "I went to visit the Hudson school. No one there. The Ellsworths gone, too?"

Mrs. Simpson's smile faded, and a frown creased her broad forehead. "Eliza, La, miscarried her eighth. She near bled to death before they come for me to see to her. La's man said enough was enough. Sold their stock to neighbors for money to travel on, packed up the rest, and lit out for their folks's back east."

"Poor Eliza. I wish I'd known."

"Sorry, Miss Whitford. It's been nip and tuck around here, just no time or way to get word to ya. But we been meanin' to, any day now. They tuck off in September. No schoolin' for the youngsters in these parts yet this year. You'll get us another teacher?"

"Of course, as soon as possible. I understand about poor Eliza and her family, but the children up here need to be in a classroom, learning." She reached for her clothes folded across the foot of the bed. "How's the weather?"

"Pretty as a new baby's smile. Storm's over, sun's out, snow's a'meltin'."

"Good. I must be getting back, then. I appreciate your taking me in, Mrs. Simpson. You likely saved my life."

The plump shoulders shrugged. "You woulda done the same for me." She winked. "You ain't in such a hurry you ain't got time for a big hot breakfast, now are ya?"

"No, I'm not in that much of a rush. Just wait till I get my clothes on. I'm starved!"

Chapter Eighteen

A week later, Amity sat at her office desk, her head in her hands, trying to think who might replace Eliza Ellsworth at Hudson School.

A tap at her door brought her head up; she tucked a dark tendril of hair behind her ear and smiled, standing up as Chalk's sister entered on a wave of outdoor chill. Behind her, drifts of snow glittered like diamonds in the sun. "Stella, come get warm! What brings you out on a day like this?"

"Would you believe I had to get away from my darling youngsters for a little while?" Stella rushed to where a fire glowed in the small stove, yanked off her mittens, and held out her hands. She unwound her blue knitted scarf from her head. "Go ahead and smile. You can't possibly understand, having a place of your own over here. Now, if you were cooped up in Chalk's small back-room quarters for days on end, with two bored scamps — well! Of course, he suffers, too. We're fortunate that Chalk doesn't throw us out into the street."

Amity looked toward the newspaper office. Cooped up with Chalk, with or without mischievous youngsters, was something she'd die for and couldn't have.

"Not that I don't love my babies dearly," Stella was saying, "but I sometimes wish I'd listened to my parents when they warned me about life should I marry Lorenzo Scarret." Stella shrugged wearily and drew the only other chair nearer the stove, shivering.

"You must have been married young to have children the ages of Jenny and James?" Amity filled a china teacup from a pot on the back of the stove and handed it over. From Stella's expression, she was obviously desperate for talk with another woman. Amity welcomed the opportunity to get to know her better. Besides, she had a headache from thinking about the Hudson School problem; she deserved a break.

Stella took a sip from her cup. "I was sixteen — hardly knew Lorenzo any time at all. The way to school passes the warehouse where he worked as a customs officer. He was a charmer, coming out of his office to stop me on the path, talk a while." Tilting her head, she looked at Amity with an expression asking for her folly to be understood. "He was a little on the stout side, but to me was the handsomest young man in the whole of Baltimore. He had the warmest black eyes and dark curly hair, like my youngsters', and a way with words that beat all. To a young schoolgirl, every word the man uttered was poetry." She made a face.

"And your parents didn't approve of him?"

"No." She sighed. "And with good reason, though it took me years to see it. I really loved him, but they saw that weak, irresponsible scalawag for what he was. If you must know, Amity —" her eyes twinkled and her jaw jutted obstinately "— I was a rather daring girl. No one could tell me anything. I met Lorenzo on the sly down by the harbor at every opportunity. My parents planned to disown me when I finally married him. Chalk supported my wishes, even though he didn't care any more for Lorenzo Scarret than my parents did. He finally talked them into at least being civil to my new husband and me."

Amity wasn't surprised that Chalk would defend his sister. Even if he didn't approve, he wasn't the sort to cut ties and abandon a person he loved.

Stella made a wry face. "We all made the best of it whenever we were together. Surface politeness, you know. One hundred percent dislike for Lorenzo underneath. Then our parents died. Not long after, Lorenzo took a tobacco boat to Europe, paying his passage from my inheritance, and that's the last I heard from him. Our account was under his name, since he was the husband, head of the house. When I checked the bank, the account was empty. And you know, I still loved him, even knowing that he'd stolen from me. For a long time I was sure he'd have a change of heart and come back. It's a hard stubborn head I have, Chalk always did say so." She shrugged. "Ah, well, no use to carry on so, 'the milk plumb spilt' as the saying out here goes."

"You don't seem overly bitter. Certainly a healthier attitude for you and the children. I commend you."

"Fiddle-dee-dee, how else to feel? What else can I do? He's dead, you know. He was run down by a carriage on the back streets of London. He was on his way to a — a house of ill repute. I got word just before I came here. He died as penniless as he left me." She shook her head. "Nothing to do except make myself a burden to my poor brother. Chalk doesn't complain, bless his soul, but I'm not fooled for a moment — he'd much prefer his bachelor holdings restored to the way they were before we came."

"I'm sure he doesn't mind, not really. From what I've seen, Chalk adores Jenny and James. I'm sure it's a pleasure to have all three of you with him."

"You're kind." In a moment, Stella took a sip of tea, eyeing Amity over the rim of her cup with a knowing shine in her eyes. "And you're in love with my brother, aren't you, Amity?"

Amity's jaw dropped; her face heated. "What? I beg your pardon?" She looked at the papers on her desk, smoothed a sheet with her fingertips. It took incredible control to lift her gaze to Stella's with any sort of calm. Her heart beat crazily. Could she lie and say that she didn't care for him? "Your brother is a fine person with many admirable qualities. He's done a great deal for this community in the short time he's been here. I mean — practically laying down his life at the recent election and all. And he's working as hard to organize our ridiculous county government as I am trying to organize county education. I probably would not have gained this office without his assistance — certainly he was the one to bring it to my attention. But — but —"

"Just as I thought." Stella laughed, clapping her hands in delight. "You're as much in love with him as *he* is with *you!* What a perfect pair you'd make. So what's stopping you two? I may be prejudiced, but my brother seems quite the catch to me. I wouldn't mind marrying again, if I could find someone like him."

"You'll find someone," Amity assured her, still not answering Stella's question about her feelings for Chalk. "There are rules of my office. Rules against seeing someone. I have to set an example for my teachers, the unmarried ones. No romantic entanglements." Until she had a chance to set up new rules.

"How awful!" Stella made a face. "I don't think I'd let anything stop me from latching on to someone like my brother, if I were in love. Now tell me what was bothering you when I came in. Maybe I can help? It would take my mind off my own woes for a while."

Amity shook her head. "I don't think you can help in this case." She went on to explain the problems with Hudson School — that a replacement was needed and at the moment she couldn't think of a soul to ask.

Stella had begun to smile as she listened, hand on her collarbone, fingers idly playing with the ruffle there, her eyes wide and shining with interest. Guessing her train of thought, Amity shook her head. "No, it's not a place for you, Stella. The school is a dugout. A cave in the ground. Like nothing you were used to in Baltimore. Chalk told me a few things about your family. You lived very well. Your father was a respected attorney, a good man, though incredibly busy. Your mother —"

"A too-strict, religious woman up to her eyebrows in temperance," Stella submitted with a touch of rancor. "Yes, Chalk and I grew up in a large, red-brick house with white marble steps," she added mockingly, fluttering her hand, "on the right side of town — a very good life. But that has blessed little to do with my present circumstances! I don't have a nickel to my name. After Lorenzo took off with the money that belonged to me, I had to sell our home, our furniture, everything except the clothes on our backs almost, just to put food in the mouths of my children. I sold the last of my mother's jewelry to make the trip west."

"Stella, if you don't want to tell me this —"

"I'm not complaining, understand. A lot that happened to me was my own fault, because I was blind and hardheaded. I came to Chalk because I had no choice left. But *I want to make my own way from here on out*. You know how it is, Amity. Chalk's told me about you, too. How well-to-do your parents were in Cairo. But still you built your own soddy and worked your own homestead. I want a place of my own. I beg you. How can you deny me this opportunity?"

"I do understand. But Stella, unless there's some way we can get the Ellsworths' place for you, there'd be nothing for you but the two-room school. No place to live."

"Big enough. I'd live and teach in the same rooms. I've taught my own children. I'd not be the first to live at the schoolhouse."

"Chalk would pitch a fit if he knew we were even discussing this. He wouldn't want you clear up there in the north part of the county, so far from him. I'm positive he wouldn't agree to it. He expects to look out for you. He cares deeply about you, Stella, you and the children."

"God love his heart, yes, he does. But that doesn't mean my dear brother *owns* me. I do as I please. If you recall, I already told you that I can be hardheaded and stubborn. And, Amity, I want this teaching job, I truly do."

A lengthy silence followed while Stella waited and Amity considered. It would be a godsend for her, no question about that. Stella would need a teaching certificate, but there was little doubt she'd pass the tests. Finally, Amity placed both palms flat on her desk, looked at Stella, and took a deep breath. She smiled. "All right, the plan is agreeable with me if the rest can be worked out. Like a decent place for you and the children to live."

"Thank you, Amity, from the bottom of my heart!"

"Don't thank me yet. You haven't seen Hudson School."

"As long as I can be in control of my life and earn my own money, everything else will be fine, I swear it."

Neither woman realized the door had opened until Chalk sang out, "Stella! Listen, sis! You better come home and see to your youngsters."

"But I left them napping — ?"

"They woke up. James inked Jenny's pigtails; she clobbered him with the mallet I use to tap type into a chase. Both of 'em are crying."

"Oh, my goodness." Frowning, she pulled on her heavy coat and hurried to the door. "Wouldn't you know!" Over her shoulder Stella said, "We'll continue this conversation, Amity. Don't forget."

"I'll be right along," Chalk called after her. "I want to talk to Amity about the Hudson situation, get a few lines for the *Banner*." They stood looking at one another, an undercurrent quivering between them. The door closed. "I heard you nearly died making that trip up there. If anything had happened to you —" His height and broad shoulders seemed to fill the tiny room. "I lied to Stella about the kids," he said, husky-voiced. "They're both sound asleep. Sis will know as soon as she sees them that I just wanted to be over here with you, alone."

"It's lovely to see you, but you shouldn't be here."

"I'm here for a story, perfectly legal. Tell me about your trip up north." He took out a pad and pencil with his good hand and went to sit at her desk. His eyes were kindled with desire, and a sinful grin shaped his mouth. "C'mon, Amity, I need a story. But God help you if you ever endanger yourself like that again!" He gave a warning shake of his head.

She looked out the window, willing her racing pulse to slow down. She still worried that someone might see him here and get the wrong impression. How could any one with half a brain see them together and not know the truth of their feelings for each other? It relieved her that the cold, snowy street was empty except for one rider passing by, head bowed against the wind. She nevertheless kept the stove between them, pacing back and forth, hands held tight in front of her, as she told him briefly about her trip to Hudson School. She detailed the unfortunate situation there for students since the Ellsworths' departure. She thought of mentioning that Stella had asked for the Hudson teaching position, but decided that his sister might prefer to give him the news herself.

It was wonderful watching his big, tan-knuckled hand form the neat script, as he wrote. When she stopped talking and he stopped writing, the silence in the room was intense with feeling. Amity looked at him and excitement pounded in her veins. Both of them had begun to breathe erratically as he circled the stove toward her. Passion glowed in his eyes, mirroring her own fierce yearning, a fire that could only be quenched by his touch, his kiss. It wasn't mere attraction; he reached something deep inside her, so right.

"We shouldn't — you can't — we're supposed to wait." Stella had said, *I don't think there's anything that could stop me from latching onto someone like my brother if I was in love with him.* One kiss, one brief heavenly moment being held — what could it hurt? Besides, she'd finally received an address for the Fairleighs; her letter was on its way to England, so part of their muddled path to marriage was on the way to being cleared.

"To hell with waiting." He reached for her and, mesmerized, she went to him, felt the ripple of his muscles as she planted her hands on his chest, the lines of his hard body against hers as he pulled her to him. In the circle of his arm as he kissed her closed eyes, her cheeks, sweeping to her lips with hunger, she felt dizzy with emotion. She returned the kisses, greedy for the touch of his lips on hers, the soft, tickling brush of his moustache. "Chalk, I —"

A hunger to see his face, each handsome feature, brought her eyes open. For a few seconds she ignored the sense of movement in the periphery of her vision, beyond his shoulder. Suddenly, she knew *who* it was outside the window. She let out a small cry. "Oh, no!" She planted her palms against him and shoved back, causing him to yelp in pain as she struck his sore shoulder. "My God, Amity, what — ?"

"Chalk, I'm sorry, but stop! Oh, dear heaven! She must have been watching us!" Amity motioned outward toward the woman, brown and walrusy in fur, stiffly erect, charging across the street toward them.

Cursing under his breath, Chalk exclaimed, "What the hell, Amity? It's just Mrs. Strout."

"I'm positive she saw us! She saw us —"

"Damn it, Amity, we weren't doing anything wrong! We were kissing, that's all. There's nothing wrong with feeling the way we do about each other. Neither of us is attached to anyone else."

"I agree, Chalk. But that woman could cause a scandal that would lose me everything I have! Since I've moved into town, I've managed for the most part to avoid her. I mean, I've always found her attitude toward me unsettling, to say the least, and now that I'm in the office she didn't want me to have — well, I don't expect her to accept it with good grace." She took a deep breath. "I have Thaddy to think of, and John Clyde. Chalk, I-I'm s-sorry. As much for them as for myself — I can't risk losing my place." She was babbling but couldn't stop. "I haven't received my first paycheck and already Thisba could have me out of office." She whispered, "Help me, Chalk, please, please help me."

A curse died half-uttered on his lips. "All right, here she comes." He turned to Thisba with a broad smile as she walked in without knocking. "Hello, Mrs. Strout, is there something we can do for you?"

"I wish," Thisba said, her face almost blue from the cold, "that the whole county could have observed what I just saw. Miss Whitford, you're not being paid to — to dally on the job with — men."

Before Amity could say a word, Chalk was explaining, with a dangerous glint in his eye. "We understand what you *think* was happening here. I came over to speak with Miss Whitford about writing a column for the paper, about activities involving the superintendency. Am— Miss Whitford tripped on a chair and I stopped her from falling."

"You expect me to believe such nonsense? I'm not a fool, Mr. Holden, as you and Miss Whitford will find out. Your days in office are numbered, Amity Whitford, mark my words!" With that, she flounced out, saying over her shoulder, eyes narrowed at Amity, "I should think someone with the reputation you have would be more careful."

"What the hell is that supposed to mean?" Chalk asked when the door had closed. "*Reputation,* for God's sake?"

Amity sighed. "I don't know why, but she hates me, Chalk, pure and simple. There's never been any love lost between us, and as much as I dislike giving her credit, Thisba is right about my reputation — it's flimsy at best and I'm a fool to take risks."

"Honey, I'm sorry," he said. "But remember that we may be the most *right* thing on God's green earth and nobody can change that." Chalk waited another minute before he kissed Amity's palm so fiercely she wanted to throw her arms around him and declare that nothing mattered but the two of them. If only it were so.

"Chalk —" she reached out to him as he closed the door and bounded across the street.

A while later, she sat writing in her journal with such a heavy hand it almost tore the page: *A plague on being a model for my teachers, a plague on Thisba and her favored cousin, a plague on Beaconsfield. Everything! Real prison can be no worse than this, forcing one's heart to take back what it feels!*

Chapter Nineteen

Thaddy's Christmas party turned out to be Amity's last outing from town for several weeks. Heavy blizzards covered the area right after it. The hardest part of being snowbound in Syracuse was the misery of not knowing how John Clyde and Thaddeus fared at home. She missed them dreadfully, and memories of the past two winters, when some of her animals froze and her own bones jutted out from lack of nourishment, haunted her.

Only twice in two and a half months was she able to make her way to the ranch and see for herself what good care John Clyde took of Thaddy. But she knew the boy missed having her around as much as she missed him. Fortunately, winter chores were few and Thaddy and John Clyde managed, though John's strength and stamina seemed less than it was before the summer's bout of food poisoning. When she was home she took over as much as possible.

In town, she waited for an answer to her letter to England, wondering if her letter had gotten lost, wondering if she would ever hear from the Fairleighs. Surely, they didn't hate her so much that they couldn't at least write and tell her what happened that day?

She attended ice-skating parties, dances, and hayrides, glad for the opportunities to see Chalk. As much as she tried, Thisba could hardly fault them: Amity and Chalk were leaders in the community and their attendance at such functions was almost mandatory. But putting on a facade of casual acquaintanceship was a struggle for both of them.

Luckily, he was as busy as she. He had several new law cases, and there was always his paper to get out. She knew he was doing what he could to get Syracuse made the permanent seat of Hamilton County once and for all. He was seeking agreement from citizens both of Kendall and Syracuse to cooperate and keep cool heads until the election records could be investigated and the court came to a decision they could all abide by. She doubted even he could count the number of meetings where he acted as arbitrator and prevented violent disagreement from leading to lost lives.

Chalk's sister Stella was eager for the weather to break so she could take over her school. Despite the fact she still hadn't set eyes on it, Stella had so many plans for Hudson School — equipping it properly, ideas to raise money to acquire the needed cash — that Amity had to laugh in amazement.

One day, after lunch with Stella, Amity walked back to her office as fast as the drifted, slippery streets would allow, anxious to get inside out of the cold. She bolted through the door, started to strip off her gloves, and then saw the fat man seated behind her desk. Anger overcame surprise and she was blunt. "What are you doing here again, Mr. Purdue? You lost the chance — the right — to sit in that chair, remember?" There seemed to be no escaping the loser in the superintendent's race.

"My," he drawled, taking his time about getting up, "you seem terribly upset today. The burdens of the office have finally got to be too much, I gather? If I recall, you were cautioned not to try for a man's job." He looked down at the paperwork on her desk, piled high and askew.

"Don't be absurd. I love my work." She yanked off her snow-wet scarf and gloves and tossed them on a chair.

Breathing heavily from the effort of standing, Purdue shuffled his way around the desk. He came to stand so close in front of her that she could smell his bad breath; he had the audacity to take her hand in his. "Don't deny it, dear. Overseeing the schools of this godforsaken, deficient area is a lot of work. There's still time to get out, you know. You don't have to do this; you could give it up. I can make it easy for you. Just say the word and I'll take over, remove the burden from your pretty shoulders —"

She yanked her hand free. "Perhaps you didn't hear me, Mr. Purdue," she said in such a fury she wanted to slap him. "My work suits me perfectly. I haven't had a problem to date that I've not been able to handle as well, possibly better, than any man could." He stood shaking his head, his expression bland and unyielding.

She pointed to the door. "I don't know what brought you here, *once again,* or why you would possibly think I might give up this office to you, but you're wrong." Thisba was sending him, of course. "Tell Mrs. Strout that I'm in this job for the full term of two years, tell her that I intend to run for a second term when this one's over, tell her that I intend to make a career out of being county school superintendent. Tell her —" she ran out of breath she was so inflamed, and she took a long, shuddering gulp of air, "— tell her that I'll still be here in this valley when she and I are both old and gray! You'll get this job over my dead body!"

He mumbled something like *"That may be sooner than you think."*

An icicle traveled her spine. She regarded him coldly. "I beg your pardon? What did you say? Are you threatening me?"

He smiled calmly. "My cousin and I are afraid that you've taken on more than you can handle, dear, and you're working yourself to death. Really, we want to help you."

She'd believe that when hell froze over. "I would like you to leave, please." Again she pointed at the door. "I have work to do and you're taking up valuable time."

He nodded, his whole countenance one of good

cheer and benevolence. "Watch out for yourself, dear lady, that's all I suggest. You and that editor — Well, just let me know when you change your mind." He lumbered slowly to the door, where he bowed before going out.

The man gave her a terrible headache. After hanging her coat on the hook by her office door and peeking across the street to see that Chalk was still away from his office, she went in the back room to lie down on her cot. What did Seymour mean about *sooner than you think?* A bit of vindictive nonsense, meant to frighten her, of course. She sat up and turned to the pitcher and bowl on the packing box that served as bedside table, poured a bit of water, took up a cloth and wrung it out, and lay back with it on her forehead. In a few minutes, she was fast asleep.

The room was pitch-dark when she awoke to a sound from outside. Recalling Purdue's implied threat, she sat up slowly, her skin prickling with goosebumps. As she listened intently, she thought about the gun John Clyde had given her, which was out in her desk drawer. She got up slowly from the bed. And then a cat meowed plaintively. She went weak with relief, guessing it was the alley cat that had visited her on a couple occasions before. She got a dish, broke a small amount of bread into it, and poured milk over it from the crock she kept in a box nailed outside the back door. "Here kitty, kitty, here kitty, kitty." He came, curling his scrawny yellow body against her skirts as she knelt to place the dish on the muddy snow. As he began to lap, she tentatively brushed a hand down his back and thought how much she missed her creatures at home at Dove's Nest. Missed the invigorating, if hard, outdoor way of life there.

After taking a light supper at the restaurant, Amity went back to work at her desk by lamplight, feeling defiant. Her resentment began building anew, because of Seymour's insinuation that she wasn't up to doing a good job. Finally, she had to smile at herself, sure that she'd been making mountains out of molehills — he was trying to get her goat, and she'd let him do it.

Sorting the papers on her desk and stacking them in order of importance, she relaxed and sighed, admitting that the demands of her job were by no means small. First, she filled out a form supplied her to apply for a state grant for funds to hold a two-day normal school for her teachers later in the spring. She thought they might borrow the school building here in Syracuse for the classes. Of course, all her county schools would be dismissed those two days, so the teachers could attend. She wrote an accompanying letter to the state superintendent, giving a report of the district changes she'd made thus far, among them the plan to install Stella Scarret at Hudson School. At the same time, she asked for a standardized test she might give for countywide eighth grade examinations.

It was well after midnight and she was bone-weary when she finally blew out the lamp and prepared for bed. She fell asleep, exhausted, only to wake a short while later to dwell on Seymour Purdue's annoying comments. What was he trying to tell her? Was it a real threat? Why was he continuing to come around when she showed him no welcome and did everything to discourage his visits? Was she supposed to back off, pick up her marbles, and go home? And if she didn't, what was supposed to happen?

Lying there, her breathing shallow, she tried to empty her mind, sure that her fears were in the long run uncalled for. Every sound from outside, though, seemed magnified, unusual, filled with danger. Yet, by listening carefully, she could identify each rustle and thump and she had to laugh at herself. *There.* That was the big yellow cat prowling about, moving its dish. *That* was the wind ruffling the shingles on the roof. Those other noises were perfectly normal night sounds even if she couldn't name them. She closed her eyes, tried to drift off, but still her heart palpitated. She wished she was not so alone. At home at Dove's Nest she'd be with Thaddy and John Clyde, among her own beloved, *safe,* things.

It was pure stupidity on her part to take the big man's idle chitchat for something drastic and evil, though. He'd simply meant what he said, that she'd taken on a lot for any mortal to handle: running the county schools in addition to her homestead, and raising another woman's child. All simply the truth.

Seymour Purdue stopped in again a few days later with a plate of cookies. "Made them myself," he boasted, putting them down on her desk while she sat there speechless. "Raisin. Lots of applesauce in them, too. Go ahead, try them, they're delicious." He nudged the plate of cookies toward her. "Dear, I realize now that you've misunderstood my visits. I want us to be friends." His voice softened. "You're one of the most beautiful women I've ever seen, Miss Whitford. I don't believe I could stand having you think ill of me." His doleful, puppy-dog expression, almost sincere, did little to dispel her mistrust.

"I don't dislike you," she lied, shaking her head. "But I am very busy. I have all these district reports to go over." She pointed at the papers on the desk. "Leave the cookies if you like. I'll have them later — with a fresh pot of coffee. No time to make a pot now."

He bustled toward the stove. "I'll make it for you."

"No!" She jumped to her feet. "That's not necessary, and I don't have time for it now, anyway. I apologize if I seem rude, but I really must get down to business. Thank you, Mr. Purdue. Good day —"

"Seymour," he corrected with a bow. "It would give me a great deal pleasure if you'd call me Seymour. Good day, dear, and I urge you again to take care of your health. Don't work so hard." His fat forehead creased in a frown, although his

310

eyes still smiled as he twirled his cane in a beefy hand.

When he was gone, she pushed the cookies away as if they were poison, and then, ashamed of herself, ate four of them as fast as she could stuff them down. They were quite good. But become that man's close friend? *God forbid!*

When she found time to turn to her mail, there was a copy of the rather shocking *Lucifer*. Why did this paper continue to come to her when she hadn't ordered it? The publisher, Moses Harman, saw his paper as ushering in a new day, but Amity doubted Kansas was ready for his reform efforts.

He was a strong believer in natural rights and insisted all laws passed by legislature were in violation or invasion of those rights. Farmers and laborers ought to organize their own credit, according to him, and "free themselves from this vulture, 'usury' that now fed and fattened upon their vitals." Religion, he felt, was dangerous, because "fear begets hate, and hate results in oppression, war, and bloodshed." Problems of life should be investigated from the standpoint of *nature* rather than theology.

As if that weren't enough to set the status quo on its ear, he considered marriage to be an unequal yoke, that marital rights limited rights to the man, the wife but a slave to her master, the husband. Marriage should be abolished, he believed, claiming that the best sexual union for human beings would be resolved only after polygamy, monog-

311

amy, polyandry, and absolute freedom were all given a fair trial.

Amity sighed. Her own views of marriage had developed from first-hand viewing of her parents' happy, loving union. If she could only have that . . .

There was one thing in the *Lucifer* writings she agreed with. According to Harman, women would never have political independence until they earned enough money to command respect. In that she found more than a kernel of truth. If by some miracle she should someday marry Chalk, she couldn't imagine being happy unless she was her husband's equal.

Unfortunately, that *if* was very big. She put down the paper, her eyes smarting, her heart heavy, as she looked across at Chalk's office.

Chapter Twenty

Amity sat at her desk with chin in hand, glowering. Was she going to have to order a span of mules to remove Seymour Purdue once and for all from her office? After the cookies, he'd brought candy. Finally it was clear that he had it in his head that he was courting her. An unattractive prospect at best, almost worse than the fear she'd felt the first few times he'd visited and she thought he wanted her dead. She damned herself for accepting his infernal cookies.

Today, he'd brought a square, flat box tied up with mauve ribbon which he opened and put on the desk in front of her. "For you." Moist lips the same shade as the ribbon formed a smile. His eyes, the color of wet clay, were speculative, hungering. Amity looked away as his sausage-sized fingers lifted one lace-trimmed hankie to show the others beneath. As though he were luring an ignorant peasant girl who'd welcome his attentions!

He had walked in without knocking, without invitation, and she was boiling with annoyance. This was, after all, her private office. She got to her feet and swept back a strand of hair. The pulse at her temple thumped erratically. She didn't like him and whatever his designs, evil or otherwise, bestowing gifts upon her was out of place. "Mr. Purdue, I cannot and will not accept gifts from you."

He leaned across the desk, breathing heavily as he surveyed her. His hand came to rest near hers on a stack of papers, his thumb seeming to accidently caress her little finger. She moved her hand away as if his were a snake, and his hand quickly came back to cover her much smaller one and press it down. Her stomach churned from the hot, sweaty feel of his flesh. She tugged, but was powerless.

"I find you most attractive, Miss Whitford," he said in his velvety, almost childish drawl. "But —" he laughed and raised his hand from hers "— a gentleman knows when to bide his time." He started to move away.

"Take the handkerchiefs, please. I cannot accept them."

He laughed again. "No, dear. They are yours." With that, still chuckling, he headed for the door with his wide rear swinging from side to side, cane tapping.

She was still on her feet, frozen to the spot, trying to decide what on earth she could do about Purdue, when Chalk burst through the door. He was hatless, his hair tousled. A frown creased his handsome forehead above the spectacles he still wore from work. "What the devil was Purdue doing here again?" There was worry in his voice for her. Behind the spectacles his eyes flashed. "Is he bothering you, Amity? You'd never know he lost the post the way he's always over here."

Trying to remain calm and self-assured, she said, "He's a pest, but I can handle him." She was intensely aware of Chalk's lean, hard-muscled physique as he came around the desk. The noises he was making in his throat reminded her of the prairie grouse crooning to its mate. There was no way she could ignore his arms reaching for her.

"My God, Amity," he whispered, kissing her hair, "you're shaking like a leaf. What the hell's he doing to you?" He held her away, his eyes staring into hers. "Did he hurt you? If he ever so much as touches you, I'll send the big bastard butt over teakettle. I'll go after him right now if he's —"

"No." She summoned a soft laugh. "Calm yourself." She liked being where she was so much she didn't move. Besides, over his shoulder, she could see the street outside was empty. She stood thigh to thigh with him, her breasts brushing his chest. "I can take care of it. It's nothing, really. He brought those handkerchiefs." She nodded toward her desk. "It seems he — he 'finds me attractive.' " At Chalk's angry hiss of breath, she said, "He's just a huge blowfly. The right swat will get rid of him. Let me take care of it, please. It's not necessary for you to get involved, Chalk." Reluctantly, she tried to move away. Someone could pass by any moment.

He refused to release her, and instead pulled her closer. "Are you sure you're all right?" His expression was anxious. She was well aware that he hadn't promised to stay out of her affairs.

"Y-yes. I'm j-just cold; I need to stir up the fire." She looked out the window again; the coast was clear. "But, Chalk, for just a minute, would you hold me really tight, please?" Her face flooded with color that she'd audaciously requested out loud what her whole being craved.

A smile quirked the corners of his mouth, and his eyes shone with delight. He answered in a gravelly, emotion-filled whisper, "There's nothing I'd rather do and no one in the world I'd rather oblige." He drew her close, closer, until her breathing almost stopped. Roughly, he caressed her arms and back, and, finally, searched for her lips with his own. She melded tightly to his thumping heart, her mouth clung hungrily to his, her craving answered for the moment.

Driving toward Dove's Nest ranch the following weekend, Amity's spirits rose in direct proportion to the rise of the tableland north of town. It was a bright, sunshiny day; the snow was all but melted and soon the plains would be sprouting a new green. She was going home for a few days and just the thought made her heart light and happy. *Home.* Her home that she'd established with her own hands and hard work, that nobody ever could take from her, especially now that she was earning enough money to support it.

Not that she wasn't happy with her superintendent's job, too. Satisfactions in her office were stacking up. Stella Scarret's move to Hudson School had gone nicely, and she was already planning a St. Paddy's Day pie social to raise funds to fill out the school's scant supplies. Amity had little doubt that before Stella was through, Hudson School would be one of the best seated in the county, and a real school building would be next. Chalk's sister had great determination.

Yet another school was still desperately needed, Amity thought, a real one, not just a provision of books and materials, down in the sandhills close to the Dusky children. Somehow, she'd get it for them; it was only a matter of time and strategy.

The state superintendent of education, a kindly, older gentleman, Mr. Lawhead, had paid a call on her from Fort Scott, and, pronouncing her work exemplary, had raised her annual salary by forty dollars more than promised. He wanted to know if she'd run for the office again, but she hadn't given him a definite answer. Although he'd looked disturbed when she brought it up, he indicated that he'd have no objection to her marrying while in office; he'd like to keep her where she was, and happy, as long as possible. He had asked her to please fulfill one year of service first, if possible. That was only through the next November, and by then she would surely have word from England, too. She'd been especially gratified at Mr. Lawhead's promise of support if local leaders gave her a problem. She wanted the superintendency long enough to see some changes put into effect, but at the same time, if she could make a decent living off the ranch for herself and Thaddy and John Clyde, she felt that that was where she should be. The next several months would reveal if she would run for a second two-year term, even though she had told Seymour Purdue to tell Thisba that she meant to make the superintendency a career! She hadn't cared a snap what she said at the time, but she might have to eat those angry words.

Seymour hadn't bothered her of late and she'd relaxed, sure that she'd been making too much out of his attentions. Through the worst winter months, she'd rarely seen Thisba, had for the most part escaped that look of Thisba's that, particularly since the election, willed her off the face of the earth.

As she neared her own land, Amity dismissed her thoughts of Thisba Strout and began to smile, anticipation making her heart pound. How she missed it all: the boy, her ranch, her own things, John Clyde. She hoped to find him in much better health this time.

At first, from a distance, it didn't register what the odd lumps were lying queerly on the ground surrounding her back-field haystacks; when it did, she whipped the rented rig into a ground-eating run. Those were her cattle, and they weren't just lying down resting! Something was terribly wrong! The air was putrid as she came to the first felled cow. Flies hung over the carcass. Amity drew back on the reins, leaping down to the ground while the wheels still turned. Had the poor critters been shot? She raced forward and fell down by the cow that lay stiff in death on its side, its body full with its unborn calf. Last year's horrible winter had left her cows skeleton-thin in the spring, but all of them had fattened nicely in the summer on pasture, and this fall on corn silage. She ran her fingers over the bristly hide, searching for bullet holes, blood. She found neither. There was a dried white substance on the muzzle and cheek. *Poison?* A tight knot of pain and anger formed in her throat as she moved among the fallen cattle. *Poisoned?* With a hand to her mouth in horror, tears swimming in her eyes, she studied each carcass, twisted and stiff in a paralysis that betrayed the agony of its dying. My God, what'd happened? Had someone done this intentionally?

Eight dead cows, six dead calves, including Thaddy's nearly-grown pet calf Buttermilk. In the distance, she could see Flora grazing near the soddy. Only pregnant Flora, her black-faced jersey cow, had survived, being fed mostly grain and staked to graze near the house. *Her entire beef herd had been poisoned.*

She climbed back into the buggy and drove on into the yard. How had anything so fiendish occurred? It wasn't the corn silage; John Clyde had finished feeding from the pit a good month ago. Suddenly, she considered John Clyde, remembered how sick he'd been since last summer, and wondered if there were a connection. He'd dismissed his own situation as food poisoning at his own hands, but what if — what if someone were trying to destroy her and all that she loved? *Thaddy?* Her mind screamed his name as she tumbled out of the buggy, nearly falling, running to the soddy and shoving against the door. "Thaddy? John Clyde?"

There was no sign of either of them in the house. The room was cold, cluttered. She'd had John Clyde move into the house when she was not there, but he usually preferred his own quarters in the barn. Thaddy often slept there, too, on a makeshift cot near John Clyde's potbellied stove. Terror squeezed her heart as she left the house and raced for the barn, skirts clutched in her hands, afraid of what she'd find.

They were both in their beds, wrapped in quilts, and for a moment she thought they were dead, too. Then Thaddy, awakened by the noises she made, sat up, rubbing his eyes sleepily. "John Clyde's been sick, an-an' I guess I fell asleep." The youngster rolled off the cot, fully dressed. "I made him some cornmeal gruel, an' broth like you made for 'im the other time. He quit takin' it yesterday." Amity hugged the boy tightly, speechless with joy that he was alive and well.

She hurried to John Clyde and fell to her knees by his bed, reaching out to touch his face. "Oh, God! Oh, dear God!" He was burning with fever. But alive. She made a strong effort to calm herself and not to scare the boy. But her beloved handyman's breathing was labored, his skin an awful yellow. She'd seen something much like this before, when as a small child she'd gone out with her mother in Cairo to care for a sick neighbor. What'd they called it — *bilious fever?* Some derangement of the digestive system from poor eating habits, in the case of Mama's patients. *Poison* in John Clyde's case? He smelled *sick.* In the back of her mind was still the image of her dead cattle, scattered about the haystacks.

Last time, she'd treated John with spring tonic — sulphur and molasses — and he'd gotten better. But obviously, this was more serious. He needed a doctor, and even then she might be too late. He moaned, his face twisted in pain; his hands crept up to his stomach.

Thaddeus whispered anxiously, moving close to Amity's shoulder as she knelt by the bed, "Should I go to the house and warm the broth again? Or get him a dipper of water?"

She'd all but forgotten he was there as she tried to think. "No, son, I'm afraid we need more than that. Would you bring your sled, dear? We're going to put John Clyde on it and pull him to the house. I want him inside, in my bed, where I can look after him properly. After we've done that, I want you to saddle Ben and ride into Syracuse. You know the way. I want you to find Dr. Gourley and bring him here as quickly as you can. Tell him about John Clyde. Make sure he knows that it's an emergency. Hurry, now, get the sled!"

She rolled John's limp form tightly into his quilt. She didn't want him catching a worse chill on the way to the house. As always, it was really quite snug and cozy in his room. But she wanted him where she could see to him every moment.

As soon as they got John Clyde into the house, Amity forced him to drink a glass of mustard water, then held the pail to catch the vomit. She might be too late, but she wanted his stomach empty of any poisons that might still be there. She was preparing the whites of eggs for him, which she'd follow with strong tea, when Thaddy returned from saddling Ben, his face pale with shock. "Am-Am-Ammy, d-did you see? The cattle are all dead. Every one of 'em is just layin' out there. Buttermilk's dead!" Tears rolled down his cheek.

She took him by the shoulder, pushed back his hair from his eyes. "I know, son," she said gravely. "I saw them when I came in. Later on, we're going to find out what happened. Right now, we have to think about John Clyde. He needs Doc Gourley as quickly as we can get him. Scoot now, ride to town fast as you can. Be careful, and you come back with the doctor, hear?"

Thad nodded, wiped his nose on his sleeve, and turned to run out the door.

Some three or four hours later Amity heard hoofbeats approaching the house outside, followed by Dr. Gourley's and Thaddeus's voices as they dismounted. It'd taken them so long . . . But

322

it couldn't be helped; it had probably taken Thaddeus a long time to find the doctor. During the wait, she'd continually bathed John Clyde's face, chest, and arms, desperate to reduce the fever that just seemed to keep climbing. She'd talked to him most of the time, anxious, scolding, loving words that she wasn't sure he heard, but it didn't matter if he did. She stood up now, as the doctor came hurrying into the house, Thaddy on his heels. Trying to keep her calm, she told Doc his symptoms: "He's been bilious since last summer when we thought he had food poisoning. He had stomach pain, lost weight when he was already thin as a rail. He was often sick to his stomach, vomiting. Other times it was hard for him to eat. Now he's got fever and chills, and as you can see, his color is off. It's — it has a pale yellowish cast."

"Go on in the other room and let me have a look at him." He waved her and the anxious boy out of the way.

From the kitchen side of the quilt curtaining off her bedroom, Amity flinched each time John Clyde groaned in pain. Without actually observing, she could tell that Doc Gourley was pressing strategic spots on John's body in a search for the main site of his illness. It seemed a long time before the doctor came out from the bedroom area. She stopped pacing. Thaddy, in his chair, swiped at a tear on his smudged cheek and sat up straighter.

The doctor scratched his gray head, and motioned for her to sit in her rocking chair. She'd put coffee on the stove, and it was percolating. Hearing it bubbling away, the doctor found a cup and poured himself some half-made before he sat down at her table. At her look of desperation, he told her before taking a drink, "Now, Missy, don't worry."

That was exactly what John himself called her, *Missy*. Tears prickled her eyes. "What's wrong with him, exactly? What can we do for him? He is going to get well?"

"Don't you let John die!" Thaddy said furiously, coming off the chair, his young eyes hot with warning. It was always a shock when he showed anything other than his usual gentle, sweet nature. She looked at him, aghast, then at Dr. Gourley. She tried to explain, "Thaddy thinks of John Clyde as a grandfather. Is he going to be all right?"

Doc nodded, his own expression asking for their patience. "At first I thought Mr. Rossback — John Clyde might have liver disease, maybe even cancer, in which case his chances would be very poor indeed. I'm now of a mind, from probing and from the history you gave me, that he's plagued with chronic gastritis. His stomach lining is burned away from some kind of irritant, maybe partially from eating something turned bad. Whatever it was, something made the situation flare up and get worse."

"But he won't — he won't — ?" Amity's voice trailed off. Thaddeus said nothing but his eyes still held terror, along with a belligerent threat for the doctor. His calf was dead; he could remember how his mother died. Amity's heart went out to him. She got up and went to stand by his chair, putting her hand on his shoulder.

The doctor sighed and he took a long draft of coffee. "The man's condition is very serious, but that's not to say he's at heaven's gate, yet, or perdition's gate, either one. He's going to have to stay in bed." Amity nodded. Thaddy's shoulders slumped in relief. He looked less angry at the doctor, who was saying, "Right now we aren't going to even try to get him to eat. That stomach needs to settle, start to heal. Moderate liquids will be enough — water, a little milk, broth. Bland foods when he's ready to eat again. Does he smoke?" Amity nodded. "He ought to quit." He got up slowly and went to the satchel that he'd placed by the door after he came out of the bedroom. He put it on the table and flipped the latch, spreading the case open. He took out a dark amber bottle with a label that read, "Hostetter's Stomach Bitters" and handed it to Amity. "Six spoonsful every day. I don't think he's true jaundiced from liver involvement; I do, however, believe he's anemic. So give him this Johnson's Pure Herb Tonic, too. One big spoonful every day."

At her anguished expression, he added gently, "It may take a while, Missy, but he'll come around. You can't keep an old hoss like him down, I can tell you that. Just follow the directions I've given you, and I'll be back in a few days to see how y'all are doing."

Only then did he bring up the subject of her dead cattle. "Boy told me about your herd. Let's have a look."

Amity pulled on Papa's slouch hat and drew a shawl over her shoulders and the three of them went outside. She lifted the shawl over her nose; the critters on the ground smelled worse by the hour. Thaddeus was trying not to gag. Doc Gourley looked at the dead cattle carefully, rubbing some of the dried foam from one animal's muzzle between his fingers, then he checked the ground. He walked over to a haystack next, and began jabbing at it with a hayfork, drawing out strands, poking and pulling.

"Here it is," the doctor said finally, "some still here in the heart of the stack." He held a two-foot stalk, thinly leaved, drooping at the top with withered creamy-white flowers with purplish hearts. "Here's more, heavy with seed." He pulled it out of the stack. "Larkspur. This plant contains an odorless, crystalline substance, alkaloid. One of the strongest poisons known. Plains larkspur. *Delphinium virescens* — deadly to cattle. Doesn't seem to bother horses or other animals as much. Deadly to cattle — seeds, roots, any part of it," he repeated.

"I know about larkspur." Amity strode forward, yanking the stalks from him and throwing them aside in outrage. "We don't have it on our range. There was some when I first came but

326

I cleared it out, and John and I always keep watch when we cut hay or herd the cattle any distance from home."

The look he gave her seemed to say, *But it's there in your stacks, so someone wasn't as careful as they thought.* "You said your hired man hasn't been himself since way last summer. Maybe he cut and stacked it without noticing?"

There was that time when she was at Beaconsfield and he was alone, working, and sick. She shook her head. "I just don't believe it. Our neighbors helped with the haying this summer, too. There's no way they would've allowed larkspur in the hay they cut. I was there *myself* for a lot of the cutting and putting up." Chalk Holden, too. A sudden thought came to her. "I sold some to Obedience Moffatt. She would've come to me in town and told me if she'd lost her cow."

"You're not saying someone did this deliberately?"

"I don't know," she cried. "I don't know what I'm saying except I just don't believe John Clyde would make a mistake like this." Knowing how ridiculous, how farfetched it would sound, she still had to ask: "Doc, if someone wanted badly enough to ruin me, could they somehow — ? John — my cows — ?"

He ruminated on that and then shook his grizzled head. "No need to even think it for a minute. There's no connection between your herd dying from feeding on larkspur and your sick hired man in there. None," he said emphatically. "From his age, I'd say your helper is a veteran of the war. He wouldn't be the first to come home with a ruined stomach — a lot of them did. Now that's *his* problem. This larkspur in your hay is another matter entirely. Likely one of those things that just happen, an accident, so don't let your imagination start running wild, my dear. If I were you, I'd burn the hay immediately to make sure you get rid of all the larkspur. It isn't any use to these dead cows. There'll be forage enough for your horse with spring comin' on, if you got some grain in the barn." He started for his mount, a big gray tethered at the back of her soddy. "I'll send somebody out from town to help you dispose of the dead cows. Bad as they smell, there's no use to try and salvage the meat, but you can keep the hides."

"Doctor, wait." He turned and she caught up with him, her jaw set. "It isn't necessary to send help for the cows." Someone was always trying to shove into her privacy when she could manage without them. "I've seen John Clyde dress antelope, and helped him with some. I know how to hide an animal."

He looked puzzled, then shook his head sadly at her stubbornness.

"Thaddeus can help. We'll use a team — my horse, Ben, and John's Texas Max — to drag the skinned carcasses into a pile and I'll burn them with the hay, keep a fire for a week if we have to." She gnawed at her lip for a moment, and thinking out loud, she said, "I'll need someone in my office, to check the mail, and to let me know if any special needs or emergencies come up."

"My sister, Marajean, can do that for you. I'll send her to talk to you about what exactly needs to be done. She'll be in her glory."

She nodded in relief. "Thanks, Doc. Marajean will be perfect." Dr. Gourley's spinster sister filled her time by loaning books from her home, and was the closest Syracuse had to a real librarian. "I'm going to stay here and take care of John Clyde until he's on his feet again." Seymour Purdue would love to get his fat hands on her work, take it over from her entirely, but she didn't want him around. "Tell Marajean that she'll be paid." She felt a flush creep up her throat into her face. She'd forgotten to mention paying the doctor's fee for coming all the way out here to see to John Clyde. "How much do I owe you for this visit, Doc?"

"I don't figure you owe me anything, the way you jumped in and helped do my job last summer, sewing that boy's fingers up the way you did." He read the question in her eyes. "No, his mama didn't pay me for your doctoring on his hand. But I felt paid, just the same, seeing that those children were all right, didn't you? Sometimes that kind of pay is all we want or need."

"Thank you, but I am going to pay you for this, Doc Gourley, in cash money. I'll keep track of today and each time you come to see John. If you don't bill me, I'll see that you get paid, anyway."

The smoke and awful stench from burning rotted flesh drifted on the wind and brought her neighbor, Mr. Bergen. Overriding her objections, he went back home and sent his oldest son to help her and Thaddeus, and his wife to help in the house. When Amity protested, pretty, blue-eyed Marta Bergen pooh-poohed her into silence. "Is why we have friends and neighbors, for goodness' sake. You do for our children, make them so smart, we do for you now you need us. No argument!" She clambered out of the wagon and bustled to the house like a war general with a job to be done.

Amity, realizing how much she needed their help, how dead tired she was after long, messy hours skinning the cattle, ceased to argue and went back to keep the fire going and see that it didn't skip the firebreak she'd plowed around it. Smoke billowed into the sky for a day and a half.

Other neighbors came and with few words jumped in to help. That, and the gifts they brought, dispelled any last resistance and made her want to cry. Buckets filled with grain from their own supply, three wagonloads of precious hay — free of larkspur. Two baby calves whose owners insisted they were runts they didn't want to bother with. An endless line of food to feed the helpers. Wives came to do the serving and cleaned up after. She thanked them all, over and over, so touched she was constantly on the verge of tears.

That none of them had lost cattle to larkspur poisoning made her all the more certain that her own case happened by somebody's evil design. But no one she spoke to could believe anyone in these parts would do anything so despicable, especially to her. It was much easier for others to believe the bad hay was an accident caused by John Clyde when he was too ill to pay attention to what he was doing. He believed it himself.

Everyone had gone home to their own families and chores, and Amity had seen to John Clyde and fed Thaddy his supper. But she couldn't swallow a bite of food herself. So she went outside to the back field, finding it hard to leave the site of the calamity, still furious that it had ever happened in the first place. Earlier, when the last sparks of the fire had gone cold, she'd hitched Ben and plowed and plowed. Now, the only sign of the atrocity was the patch, almost a half acre, of turned ground, earth as dark and cold as her feelings.

The sound of someone approaching on horseback brought her head up and she saw Chalk Holden sitting high in the saddle, riding into her yard at a fast trot.

Chapter Twenty-one

According to Doc Gourley, Chalk had been out of his newspaper office the past few days, having some kind of business to tend to in Wichita. He'd likely just heard of her loss.

He rode to where she stood before swinging his lean, muscular frame down from his horse. In the shadow of his hat, his features seemed more serious than usual. Then, even, white teeth framed by the thick, butternut brown moustache flashed her a tender smile.

She was glad to see him, but too tired, too filled with despair, to show it, though she let him take her in his arms. For a long time he held her close against him, murmuring soft words of affection against her ear, while she tried to respond, and failed. He kissed her forehead and stroked her hair. "I'm sorry as hell that I was away when this happened. The publisher of the *Wichita Eagle* has a new web-perfecting press I wanted to see. A few more law cases and I may be able to get one. Sorry I wasn't here to help you."

"It doesn't matter, it's over." She wanted to tell him what she believed happened: that she was sure her cattle were intentionally poisoned in an effort to get to her, to destroy her. That possibly there was a connection to John Clyde's illness in spite of Doc's firm opinion otherwise. But, afraid she'd sound to him like a silly, irrational woman, as she must've to the others, she held her silence. She'd get to the bottom of the matter somehow. He held her so gently and his touch was so soothing that she might have given over to tears, but she had none. At her core, she felt cold and calcified, and she responded almost mechanically to his kisses, his endearments.

"You're tired," he said finally, scooping her into his arms and carrying her toward the house. "Take my advice, darlin', and go to bed and don't get up again till you feel like it. Doc told me what happened — about the larkspur in your feed. Poor old John, he must have been pretty mixed up last summer. But Doc says he was out to see him just yesterday and the old codger is getting better every day. Don't worry about him, sweetheart. Don't worry about anything." She bit her tongue and nodded. She was exhausted. Her head drooped onto his shoulder and she left it there. A tired hand went up thankfully to graze Chalk's whiskery cheek, his strong face.

Thanks to Doc's medicine, and also to the women who'd come to help care for John Clyde during the crisis, he was back on his feet in a little under three weeks — peaked, scrawny, but unstoppable. There was probably not a home medical remedy, or a dish for the nervous stomach that had not been tried on John — with the desired results. Although *he* claimed he'd never take milk again, in any form, and that custard was for the feeble in mind as well as body. Unfortunately for him, Flora's fresh milk was the one abundance they could count on.

Thaddeus, who mimicked John too much already, was ready to give up milk, and custard, too, until Amity put her foot down, pointing out that he was still a growing boy. She loved them both dearly, and it was with a not quite easy mind that she was able to return to her work in Syracuse, while the two of them began the spring plowing.

Spring normal school was practically upon her, with many tasks to see to besides catching up with the work that had gone undone in her absence. From all indications, Marajean Gourley had done a good job, and Amity had been able to pay her from the few dollars earned from sale of the cowhides. Everything was neat and orderly when Amity settled in again, plowing into a tidy stack of letters and notes that Marajean had left for her. A quick perusal showed that there was no mail from England.

A letter postmarked Valley Falls and addressed to her office turned out to be from Moses Harman, publisher of the *Lucifer*, recommending that she introduce sex education to the children of Hamilton County. How on earth had he heard of her?

Had he taken her name from a list of all county superintendents? Children's natural questions should be answered, he said, by blackboard illustrations of the reproductive system. Problems of sex would be more apt to be solved, and knowledge was a child's birthright. She agreed, but she also knew the rural people of her area well enough to realize that if she so much as breathed the proposal, she'd be fired on the spot. She committed the letter to the trash basket.

As much as she tried to turn her mind to further business, going through the tasks at hand was all mechanical. At the back of her mind always was her dead cattle. Cruelty to helpless creatures was always terrible, never mind the serious loss of income to her and Dove's Nest ranch. She and John Clyde had had a dreadful row as he got stronger and they got around to discussing the matter. He insisted it was his fault and he readily accepted the blame. The larkspur in the hay was not much different from his foolishness in eating rotten beans when he ought to've known better. Sometimes she wondered if he wasn't taking the blame to protect her in some way. From whom, though, from what? Likely, he had no idea himself, but every time she considered the question, the image of *Thisba Marcellus Strout* loomed in her mind. The woman hated her and was likely deranged on top of that — if she'd done something so despicable.

One bright spring day when Amity could stand it no longer, she got her shawl, tugged it over her shoulders, and hurried out into the street. She would get right to the point and tell Thisba that this silly feud between them had gone too far and had to end.

On the way across town, Amity relaxed somewhat, taking note of her surroundings, the white puffy clouds floating in the blue sky, the sweet smell of spring in the air. There was more hustle and bustle along the main street than usual. Farmers and ranchers were in town to look longingly at new equipment, buy seed, have a drink with friends at the saloon, and talk politics again. The state supreme court, as a result of investigation of last November's elections, had scheduled a special election for permanent county seat on June twentieth and the whole county was abuzz. More women than usual were about, wives come to town with their men to shop perhaps for the first time in months. A boy rode a bicycle wobblingly along the muddy thoroughfare.

At the Strouts' two-story frame house a few blocks northwest of the town center, Amity knocked on the door several times. She'd hoped for a confrontation to end their friction, but hope was deflated when no one came to the door. She could be wrong about Thisba having something to do with killing her cattle, but she doubted it. After being a maid at Beaconsfield, Thisba had enjoyed the prominent status of banker's wife until Amity came along again to upset things. As an elected official, Amity had eclipsed that some; she was more recognized in Syracuse, the whole county, than Thisba was in her social position in town. The woman was a jealous fool and, Amity was beginning to suspect, a potentially dangerous one.

Disappointed that Thisba wasn't at home to thrash it out, Amity made her way back to her office, trying to stir her mind to other things, tasks that needed seeing to for spring normal.

She'd been back at her desk for only a few moments when she heard a tap and the sound of her door opening. She looked up with a scowl, expecting Seymour, but it was Chalk.

"Hello. Come in, I'm pretty busy, but . . ."

He simply stood there, leaning against the door frame. His expression was serious, his eyes clouded, as though he were trying to come to a decision, and his lean hand kept dragging at his thick moustache.

An inexplicable chill caught at her. She stood up slowly. "What is it?"

He came on into the room. "I have news, kind of."

Her throat dried. She waited for him to go on, thinking it had to do with her work, or the county dispute, but it didn't.

"I've been doing some digging, Amity, into old newspapers, other records, about Beaconsfield."

She felt struck dumb, followed by an agony of panic. "Me? You found out about me?" She felt her whole existence begin to crumble, her life-blood begin to flow away. "What did you learn?

Oh, God — ! Why did you have to . . . ?"

"That's just it, honey. I couldn't find a thing about *you*."

Her breath caught, her heart seemed to still. "What are you saying?" She leaned against the desk edge for support, her palms pressed flat on the surface as though to hold down her world and keep it in place.

"Take it easy, honey," he said softly. "There are newspaper accounts of the child's, little Nora Fairleigh's, death. Not a single write-up mentions the cause. There was no autopsy, no coroner's report. Published accounts consist of her parents' names, and where they lived, Nora's age, and the date, July 1884. There was a little memorial verse. Not one word about you. In fact, in all the accounts I read about Beaconsfield, from the time it was organized, through all the social doings, to the end, your name didn't appear once. Like you never lived there at all."

"B-but I did!" she protested. "And I wouldn't have been mentioned in the society columns; I was an employee." Though a favored one, for a time.

"If you were really responsible for the little girl's death, I think a great deal would have been written about it. If I were you, I'd put all this behind me, Amity." He wore a gentle half smile.

"No. No. Something happened. I was accused. Chester Fairleigh did take me to Great Bend and abandon me there with only a ticket to Kansas City." She hated remembering, but she told him, "It was an unimaginably terrible time, Chalk. For

338

days I wandered around Kansas City, starving. I had no place to go. I-I ate garbage. I slept in places so horrible I can't talk about them. Twice I was almost raped —"

"Oh, Christ, darling —"

She moved back, wouldn't allow him to comfort her until she was finished. "That section of town was called the Bottoms, down along the river, and it was a cesspool of vice. Ironically, not far away, up on the bluffs, was Quality Hill where Kansas City's richest families resided."

"Couldn't you have gone up there to them, asked for help, for work?"

"I asked. I might as well have tried the moon. They could barely tolerate me on the premises long enough to offer me a handout of food and toss me an old dress as if I were a ragpicker, let alone give me work in their fine homes." She sighed. "I couldn't have presented an encouraging picture. I looked terrible from the way I had to live, and the first weeks I hated myself. Remember, I'd been accused of a child's death and the burden was fresh — raw."

"It's hard to picture you — under those conditions."

She motioned him to a chair, and brought them coffee. "I — I finally found work as a laundress, in a horrible neighborhood. The owner attacked me. He owned the brothel nearby. He intended for me to — to take work there." She licked her dry lips. She looked at him, stricken.

"Amity —"

"Let me finish, please. I couldn't stay, keep fighting him. I ran away, willing to die of starvation on the streets rather than give in to him. Then —" she swallowed, "then, I found out I could file on a piece of land all my own, in western Kansas. That I could live free. I'd never have to depend on anyone else again, for anything. Chalk, I *walked* across most of Kansas. *Fought* my way across might be a better word." She took a long draft of coffee to steady herself.

"Good Lord, darling, you're a woman! You never should have —"

She shushed him, and in the next hour or two, told him the whole story, every last detail. She finished, "I did all kinds of work in exchange for bed and board, and a few dollars here and there. For my stake, I made rugs the whole winter through. But I never sold myself. Sometimes, I think I was watched by a guardian angel. It's a wonder I made it, and I don't think I was supposed to."

There was admiration in his face as he listened, but really all she wanted was for him to know, and understand. She smiled at him. "When I saw my land that first time, in the spring of '85, the wind blowing free, I knew I'd come home and nothing could uproot me, or hurt me as much, ever again. And more than anything, I knew I could do for myself. And the naive, innocent young girl from Cairo was no more."

"Jesus! I hardly know what to say —" He ran a hand along his jaw, his sigh tortured. "I'm sorry

340

I made you explain all this. I just wanted to help us, clear the way for us, give you a gift of the peace of mind you deserve, because I know you're innocent."

"Don't you see? Loving me makes it easier to believe in my innocence but it doesn't make it fact. God in heaven, I wish it were true!" she told him. "But *something happened*. I was accused. I'm sorry you went to so much trouble. What you've learned is meaningless. When I was able to, I scrounged through trash to read the Kansas City newspapers, trying to find out what really took place that day in Beaconsfield. I read the same pieces you've read, I'm sure. Nothing's changed, nothing's been solved, until I get that letter. I don't like the wait either."

The shadows in the room had lengthened with evening. "When I first came here," Amity told Chalk after a long silence, "I just wanted to be left alone. I was sure I couldn't trust anyone ever again. And then there was John Clyde, and Thaddeus, and — you." She cleared her throat. "I'll light the lamp. It's getting dark."

"No, don't light the lamp yet," his voice rumbled softly across the room. And then she was in his arms, holding on tightly.

Chapter Twenty-two

Syracuse baked in June sunshine. It was only slightly less hot, and nearly airless, in the frame school building where Amity sat at the desk in the front hall. She ached in every limb; her mind was numb with fatigue. Endless duties connected with running her first teacher's institute had kept her constantly on the go, and it was one of the few times she could sit down.

The task before her was simple enough. She was to sign certificates for her teachers who at the moment were attending their last session, a lecture on bookkeeping. She took a long, deep breath and tried again. Moving the pen in the requisite fine penmanship was turning out to be almost as difficult as budging a bear from a bog, she thought with a tired shake of her head. She wasn't sure how much longer she could keep her eyes open.

She stirred and tried to sit up straighter, listening for a moment to the soft, industrious hum from the classroom down the hall. For the most part, the workshop for teachers had gone well. The art teacher she'd engaged had sent his regrets at the last moment, but Levant Lancaster, as it turned out, was well qualified to teach penmanship *and* drawing. She nipped at the top of the penholder, smiling to herself. The first school year was coming to an end. Summer meant fewer duties here, and much more time at home. She dipped her pen and slowly scratched her name on a certificate.

Only a few days ago, she had returned from another round of visits to her schools, making inspections and suggestions, handing out praise where deserved, urging teachers to attend the normal school. Some school boards were asked to pay their teachers' expenses to come; she'd had to find ways to help others, but most were there. She'd handed out eighth grade diplomas in schools where students had completed the proper courses, and made nearly a dozen commencement speeches as the visiting dignitary. She'd even supplied a broom to Bridge School on east Bridge Creek where Clarina Franklin heretofore had used a turkey wing to sweep the floor of her one-room-shack school!

It had been a taxing journey around the county, made more so by lack of sleep. She had tossed and turned in a different, strange bed each night, arising to take to the road again to inspect yet another school. How long had it been since she'd sat down to a proper, restful meal? It would be the most wonderful, wonderful thing in the world to get back to Dove's Nest for the summer, and her Thaddy-Son.

On that score, she could count her blessings.

Sighing, she laid down the pen for a moment to contemplate. She rotated her aching shoulders. Each visit home revealed how content Thaddeus was at Dove's Nest. He loved the two calves that had been given to them, and he took pride in their care. John Clyde, whose health continued to improve, was like a doting grandpa to Thaddy. And although there were signs that Thaddeus still missed Chloe, he seemed more sound with each passing day. His pure affection toward Amity indicated that his child's heart had room for her as a second mother. She could hardly ask for more.

Although it would take a few years to recover from the loss of her cattle, new seed crops were in the ground, on time, and with the proper amount of sunshine and rain — Ah, well, that was the farmer's lot — to wait and see, to gamble, year after year.

Amity's fury at the loss of her cattle had faded somewhat over the following weeks, but she was sure Thisba and Purdue were at the bottom of it. If she was right — then in all likelihood there would be another 'happenstance' designed to put her down, because she was still here and very much hanging on.

She'd hoped to purchase machinery this third year on her claim, but due to her cattle and crop losses, they would continue to broadcast by hand and harvest by scythe. The three of them had become forced vegetarians, eating no meat except for occasional game they could trap or shoot; rabbits, sagehens. She sold most of the eggs her chickens laid, and most of Flora's cream was religiously made into butter to sell. Thaddy could go barefoot this summer but would need shoes by next school season. The poor youngster was used to going without, as he had with Chloe, but still, Amity wanted to give him more than she was able. The only gift she'd been able to buy him so far was a two-cent bag of marbles. By next year, they should be doing much better, but for now every penny earned must go to her debts, with a little put by for seed and the most necessary food supplies. Sometimes, worrying, she forgot to eat; many a night it was impossible to sleep. She felt the wear and tear of it all as surely as would an ant caught in the paddles of a butter churn.

Suddenly, there was an explosion of laughter and clapping from the classroom, and a burst of chattering voices, as the door opened and women spilled into the hall, milling, talking, moving slowly her way. Amity scolded herself for allowing her mind to stray from the task at hand. Quickly, she signed the last three certificates, her hand rising with each fanciful flourish on the scrolls. She looked up, a smile on her face, ready. Whether garbed in thready dark taffeta or bright calico starched with potato-water, each lady wore her best; and fanned the heat with study papers. From their shining eyes and animated expressions, Amity knew just how successful the sessions had been. Chalk's sister, Stella, hadn't moved out of the doorway, and was deep in conversation with the didactics instructor, Professor Brohlin, a tall, darkly bearded man with intelligent blue eyes. He'd had no objection to finding a substitute for his post at the University of Kansas in Lawrence while he came here to teach for two days. Amity considered herself very fortunate to have snagged him.

"Oh, Miss Whitford, this has been the grandest experience of my whole life!" Clarina Franklin's sea blue eyes, usually full of uncertainty, glowed with new confidence. Fluffy gold wisps had escaped her coronet of braids, framing her excited, flushed face. "I've learned so much." She giggled softly, adding to her comment, "I didn't know there was so much to learn!" Two little lines creased her smooth white forehead then. "I only wish school would continue right on, and not break for the summer — I'm so anxious to put my new knowledge into practice."

Amity laughed. "I'm pleased that you feel that way, Clarina, and I'm sure you'll be even more eager when school reopens in the fall." In the beginning, Amity had feared that seventeen-year-old Clarina wasn't up to the rigors of the schoolroom, but she was going to work out quite well, given sufficient encouragement and guidance. "Are you still having discipline problems with the bigger boys in your school?" Two older boys at her school were almost twice the size of Clarina and rarely took her scoldings to heart. Neither was truly mean, as bullies were; they were just disrespectful scamps who needed to be taught their place.

Clarina patted her notebook, and her pretty little chin jutted out. "I have all of Professor Brohlin's secrets," she smiled in the direction of the handsome professor. "I can handle those boys!" She waved her hand and turned away, moving back toward the group of chatting, fanning, teachers. Amity sighed. It would be her misfortune that one of those older boys would ask for Clarina's hand in marriage about the time she made a really good teacher of her. "Clarina, we'll be giving out the certificates in ten minutes — don't forget."

Tannis Beneke, Thaddy's teacher, smiled at Amity and she waved in return. Clarina hurtled herself at Tannis, face exuberant. The two girls soon had their heads together in conversation. Pretty girls, Clarina in rose-print cotton, Tannis in blue gingham. Good teachers.

Meda Ginsbach and Corinne Wagner were next to stop at Amity's desk. She wanted to stand, but was afraid she'd fall if she tried. Was it only her imagination or had the smell that permeated the school, of homemade library paste scented with cloves, grown stronger? She managed to smile at least. "Meda, Corinne, did you enjoy the institute? Do you feel you benefited?"

"Makes me want a real school to teach, *ya!*" Meda beamed. "But I make out at my kitchen table, you don't worry, Miss Whitford. I know you get me school when you can. Is something to look forward to."

Corinne, her square-shouldered stance as starched as her dark gray broadcloth dress, but with warmth in her brown eyes, clasped one of Amity's hands in both of her own. "It was a fortunate day when you became our leader, Miss Whitford. These two days have been very fruitful, very, and we thank you so much."

Not wanting to appear ungrateful, Amity got to her feet hurriedly to take their hands — too hurriedly. The room swirled, and she sat back down with a plop. "Amity?" Corinne asked. "Are you all right?"

The woman's voice seemed to come from a distance. Amity shook her head to clear it. Through a kind of haze she saw lines of concern creasing Meda's round face. "Is something wrong, Miss Whitford?"

She felt terribly embarrassed as she got to her feet again, shaking her head and bracing her hands on the edge of the desk for support. "My, how silly of me. Just a touch of dizziness. Now that I think about it, I do believe I've forgotten to eat today, with so much to do and so much on my mind. What a goose I am. I apologize. Now, where were we?" She went around the desk and hugged each of them in turn. "I'm happy you got so much from our institute."

Meda still looked worried. "You work too hard is what. You don't rest after hard trip visiting around the county, I think." She shook her head in reprimand. "You eat better, you rest, Miss Whitford." She fanned Amity with her own paper,

348

saying, "Is hot enough to fry egg on bald man's head, ya!"

"Come with us, later," Corinne said suddenly, her hand grasping Amity's arm, "for supper at the Blue Door café." Her plain angular face was lit by a kindly smile.

Meda nodded at her friend's suggestion. "*Ya,* cook make *kraut fleckerl* tonight. Good noodles and cabbage give you strength, I betcha! Apple dumplings with cream he promise, too."

Amity laughed. "Mmm. Your suggestion sounds positively marvelous. But I'm afraid that I can't. I must see our visiting professors off on the train, and there are a few matters to clear up here at the school before I can leave tonight. I tell you what — don't wait for me, but if I can make it, I'll come along later. How's that? I'll take the risk that there'll be an apple dumpling left for me."

"Good." Meda leaned to kiss her cheek.

"We'll bring some of the other teachers. We'll make it a party for you, Miss Whitford. A thank-you party." Corinne Wagner squared her shoulders, obviously pleased she'd thought of it.

"Oh, please, don't go to any trouble. I —" What she wanted more than anything was to return to her quarters in the old millinery shop, crawl into bed, and sleep forever.

Corinne and Meda didn't hear her objection as they moved on, smiling and joining in on a nearby group conversation. Bits and pieces came to Amity's ears. ". . . want my pupils to believe

349

in themselves as much as I believe in them."
Corinne spoke resolutely and Amity smiled to herself in tired satisfaction.

A few minutes later, the teachers filed back
into the room where the certificates were to be
given out; the instructors and Amity followed.
Professor Brohlin towered over Amity, telling the
top of her head, "Finest institute where I've had
the pleasure to teach, Miss Whitford." The short,
balding, U. S. history instructor, Mr. Kaylor, not
to be outdone, pushed up to say, "Very well organized; you did a superb job, Miss Whitford."
Two steps behind, the remaining instructors, Kate
Bristow, Levant Lancaster, Mr. Dayton Berry,
and Mr. Jameson, added their own compliments.
Amity smiled graciously around at them all, glad
for their comments but feeling guiltily thankful
that in a very short while they would be on the
train, returning to their respective homes and col-
leges. The spring institute, her biggest chore in
office, would be behind her.

Amity took her place at the head of the room.
For the remaining hour, she pulled strength from
she knew not where, reviving enough to do and
say the proper things. She was so grateful for
the flutter of fans moving the air. Even so, closing
activities and final goodbyes passed in a kind of
blur.

Finally, it was over, and she could escort her
visiting educators to the train.

Amity's eyes burned as she watched the train

slowly move away, belching smoke, pistons driving harder as it picked up speed, *clackety-clack*ing eastward along the track, shaking the very earth where she stood. Like many a Kansas June day, the temperature refused to go down even a few degrees with the passing hours and it felt like torches were pressed against her; there was hardly a breath of air. She turned away, hot cinders burned through the soles of her shoes. Gritting her teeth from the pain in her head, she laughed dryly at the irony of it: She was stronger, tougher, since she had come to the plains and had endured so much. But once in a while the elements chose to remind her that she was but a speck on earth, not impervious to a stiff wind that could blow her off her feet, or heat that could sap her to the marrow, like now. She hoped Meda and Corinne would understand when she didn't meet them for supper, but she just couldn't do it.

Amity started the mile walk back to town and her office on uncertain legs, eager to get to her back room and her bed. Her head hurt so much it was difficult to focus her eyes, and the heat robbed her of breath. She continued on rubbery legs, a slow, zigzagging path, hoping to reach her office before she *had* to sit down. But damned if she'd faint — she wouldn't!

She had left the residential area and passed the livery. The new pine boardwalk ordered by the ladies of the council ribboned ahead into the main part of town. Not much further. All at once, out of nowhere, two figures loomed before her. They blocked her way like an impenetrable wall. She tried to ask them to move, but her tongue was a ball of cotton. Her stomach felt queasy; the world began to tilt. She felt herself begin to slide to the ground. The blurry figures — one hourglass-shaped, the other a gigantic ball — made sounds of exclamation, but she couldn't reply as she felt herself pulled down, suffocating, into nothingness.

Amity stirred, heard herself moan, opened her eyes slowly. A female face, distorted monstrously by the afternoon sun and shadow, leaned down close to her own, leering, threatening. Amity sat up, screaming. The sound reverberated in her ears, shrill, terrible, animalistic. Sickened with fear, she recoiled, scooting backward along the plank sidewalk on her elbows and rear. It was *her!*

"Wait!" the woman said. "Wait a moment. Stop!"

Amity screamed again, the sound rending the air. She tried to rid herself of the honeysuckle scent filling her nostrils, closing her throat. She closed her eyes to blot out the face that filled her with such dread she thought she'd die of it. A voice droned, "Come now . . . I won't hurt you. . . ." It was so hot, so white hot. Vague, shrouded outlines of buildings loomed, faded, loomed again. "You'll feel better. . . . Come with me for some water."

The words brought with them a crushing sadness, a terrible memory. Amity tried to get away, clawing and scratching at the hands that grappled to catch hold of her arms, her shoulders, her waist. "Don't touch me! No, no, leave me alone!" Her senses reeled. The boardwalk was blistering hot when she put her hand down, but inside she was as cold as the child when she touched her . . . ice . . . still as the child — dead. "No, no, no!" *Nora, come back, don't die.*

"Poor thing." She recognized the voice. *Seymour Purdue.* Through a dazed blur she saw his round face, big as a pumpkin and nose to nose with her own, his weak mouth curved into a nasty smile.

"Leave me alone! Leave me alone!"

"I do believe her mind is totally gone!" *Thisba Strout.* Her pleased laughter had a sound like a rusty doorhinge. "The girl is headed for the Topeka lunatic asylum, don't you think?"

The words were like cold water to Amity's senses. The fog in her mind began to clear. "No, no, I'm all right. Don't touch me, though, please." Amity pulled away, becoming aware of where she was, of the buggy waiting at the curb, door open. "I-I fainted, that's all," she whispered, fighting returning terror. "I thought I was somewhere else." They leaned closer to hear, shaking their heads *no* as though she couldn't know what she was saying. "I haven't eaten or had any water all day — the heat is so intense." Amity covered her face with her hands, drew in long, shuddering breaths of the hot, still air. She fought the clutches of despair that threatened again to claim her, struggled to keep her whirling brain clear. Trying to stand was like pushing up through a ton of suffocating muck, but she pushed aside their helping hands and made it to her feet.

"I'm sorry," she said to Thisba Strout and her cousin Seymour. They looked very ordinary now. Mrs. Strout wore a frilly baby blue gown, Mr. Purdue a light suit, the coat straining at the buttons. "Sorry if I troubled you." Amity pushed his hands away, feeling frantic. "I don't need help, now. I can manage to get home by myself." With strength born of determination, she tore out of the grasp meant to restrain her and broke into a run.

By the time Amity reached the millinery shop, she was covered with cold perspiration. She locked the door behind her and ran on wobbly legs to the back room, pulling the slop jar out from under her bed just in time.

Chapter Twenty-three

Over and over Amity tried to convince herself that Thisba Strout and her cousin had simply happened by that last day of her teacher's institute, seen her staggering back from the train depot in the terrible heat, and stopped to help. That was all. No evil intent behind their behavior.

The more she tried to accept that concept as fact, the more her subconscious mind had questions of its own: What did they intend to do with her once she was in their buggy? If they'd meant to take her somewhere she didn't want to go, what would've happened if she hadn't run away? Would she have ended up dead, like her cattle, in an *accident?*

She had no desire to discuss the strange episode with anyone. Anyway, who would believe her odd fears, her suspicion that Thisba would stoop to anything to make Amity vanish from the sphere Thisba wanted to rule? But why? And why had the whole incident called up that final day with Nora Ann?

She waited for word of her "fit" to get around. When not a single soul mentioned it in the next few days, she wondered if she'd imagined the whole episode. Her sanity definitely seemed to have left her for a few very frightening minutes that day. And no wonder — what else could she expect? She'd truthfully been over-taxed; she hadn't eaten a bite the day of the institute — and the heat was intense enough to fry a person's brain. Regardless of what had happened, she was fine now. She had to put the whole matter out of her mind. And she'd make a point of taking better care of herself in the future.

Too many others depended on her.

She ate more regularly, drank plenty of water, and began to take a short nap following her noon meal, habits that gave her renewed vitality.

One day, she was just arising from her nap, when in the other room, the floor creaked under someone's heavy tread.

"Afternoon, Miss Whitford. Are you here, dear?"

She froze at Seymour Purdue's high-pitched voice. All the terror she'd felt at their last meeting flooded back. Her gun was in her desk in the other room. She had to get to it. She swallowed her fear and strode out to the main room to face him. "What are you doing here?" She went to stand behind her desk, her hand inches from the drawer.

Without answering her question, he asked his own: "What's the matter, dear? Gracious, you're so pale. What's happened now?" His moon face was clean-shaven and shiny, and he reeked of hair-tonic. He'd been holding his hat against his huge, apron-like stomach, but now he moved it to show a clutch of daisies in his beefy fist.

"Mr. Purdue, I believe I told you not to bring gifts."

He shrugged as though he couldn't help himself, and held out the flowers. "You know how desirable I find you. You've been on my mind constantly since I watched your sweet little body collapse on the street."

He was a harmless fool with a handful of flowers. She had to get control of herself. Her ears felt warm; she couldn't look directly at him. She mumbled that she was fine, but made no move to take the bouquet. "I was a bit drained from the heat and I had a headache that day, that's all. I wish you'd go, Mr. Purdue. I have a lot to do."

"No, dearest little doll." He smiled. "I can't leave just yet." He leaned over the desk toward her. The smell of his slicked-down hair made her stomach turn. Her jaw set in defiance as she tried to stare him down. The lustful heat in his gaze added to her fright in another way, and chills traveled her spine. He came around the desk, took her hand, and planted his wet lips on the backs of her fingers. She pulled free, anger, greater than her fear of him, igniting inside her.

"How dare you? I've told you before, Mr. Purdue, that I have no interest in you."

He nodded. "Yes you did, but I beg you to change your mind. When you passed out right on the street from overwork, it nearly broke my

357

heart. It doesn't have to be this way for you. I will shelter you, take you out of your sorry life." He mumbled on about a plantation and servants in Virginia that she richly deserved, but the blood in her ears was roaring so from anger, she hardly heard him. Until his final remark, "You must give up that miserable piece of dirt you call a farm, love. A pretty name doesn't make it more than it is. *Dove's Nest,*" he said with a snide smile, a light chuckle.

Belittling the fruits of her hard labors, her land, her dreams! She slapped him hard, her fingers left white marks across his fat red cheek. He caught her raised hand, looking surprised for only a second. His eyes gleamed. "Fine! I like a little action with my kisses. Go ahead and fight, my sweet Venus!" His superior strength yanked her to him; he planted his sloppy mouth on hers while she wrestled with all her might to be free. He croaked hoarsely, "Let me —" and pushed his belly against her, shoving her backward. She tried to move aside, and cracked her lower back sharply against the edge of her desk. Her cry of pain went unnoticed in the heat of his intentions. "Marry me, and I'll show you how you really feel. You'll swear that I'm the embodiment of Eros, Miss Whitford." He was breathing heavily, leaning into her, slowly grinding his hips. His hand came up to catch her chin and pull her mouth to his again, and that was when she bit him, her teeth sinking deep into the side of his hand. He howled and jerked back, releasing her, his hand raised to strike.

She was much faster. She jerked open the desk drawer and took out her gun, leveling it at the spot where his furry brows came together on the fat bridge of his nose. His face was a moon of surprise.

"I'll pull this trigger," she warned in a flat tone, "if you so much as look cross-eyed at me again, let alone lift a hand to me. I swear I will. Now get out, and don't ever come back."

"I'm not finished," he huffed. "This isn't over."

"Yes, it is! I know who sent you and I know why. Take me away from all this? *You?* I'd rather live in the gutter with rats than be married to you. And tell your dear cousin Thisba she can stop trying to get me out of Kansas." Her lip curled at him. "She should have better sense than to send you to propose marriage. Take me away? Tell her that I turned you down. No, I'd love to tell her myself."

"You're going to be damned sorry for this! You had your chance." His face, swollen with rage, reminded her of an adder. The veins in his temples stood out. His eyes glittered. He looked at his hand where blood had started to ooze from her teethmarks through the skin. "Damnable bitch. I could've kept you from being a cold-assed old maid, or worse."

She gasped at his vile words. "You're an awful man, do you know that, Purdue? A filthy-minded, weak-spined *nothing*. Get out!" She pointed the

359

gun, her finger just itching at the trigger. She held her hand steady, though she quivered sickeningly inside.

He stood planted, staring at her for an eternity. Finally, he smiled and shook his cane at her. "You've bought your ticket, wait and see!"

She waved the gun. "Out!"

He shuffled to the door, and was about to make a last remark when something he saw on the street stilled his tongue. He went out, slamming the door behind him. His huge bulk moved past the window and on down the street.

Amity felt weak with relief. Across the street, she could see Chalk was just riding up to the *Banner.* She whispered his name aloud.

As if he heard her, he looked toward her office for a few seconds, then his gaze turned slowly in the direction Purdue had taken. He tied his horse at the hitching rail, and started across the street toward her office. She opened the desk drawer and quickly shook the gun loose from her trembling fingers, closed the drawer, smoothed her hair and skirts. Spotting the flowers scattered on the floor, she scooped them up, ran to the back door, and flung them into the alley.

When she returned, she saw that Noah Porter had intercepted Chalk. They'd moved back to the sidewalk in front of the newspaper to talk. She had a chance to pull herself together. Because right now, if Chalk stepped in, if he looked at her in that certain way, eyes lit with warm fire, if he asked her a single soft-voiced question, she'd pour out everything to him, even though she felt it was wrong to look on him as her savior. She'd sworn to herself a long time ago that she'd look out for herself, and she must.

She went back to her desk and shuffled papers without seeing them, or caring. When she looked up again, Chalk and Noah had disappeared, likely had gone to the saloon to finish their conversation. She put her head down on her arms then, and began to cry soft, quiet tears of frustration.

A week later, Henry Strout came to see her. Amity was surprised when she opened the door to find him, then somehow knew in the back of her mind that his wife was behind the visit, Seymour having failed to spirit Amity away. "How can I help you, Mr. Strout?" Henry had been good to her; he didn't fill her with the uneasiness and fear she experienced in Seymour or Thisba's presence these days. She gave him a chair. When he started to tamp out his pipe, she put up a hand to stop him. "I like the smell of a pipe, please don't put it out on my account."

He looked relieved. "Thisba, dear woman, can't stand it, ah, um, no. I must say it's one of the few things we disagree on, mmm."

I'm a big one of those few, I'll wager, Amity thought.

He sucked on the pipe, his thoughtful gaze fixed on the pretty young woman. "We're at the beginning of a new season," he began. "Seems hotter to me than this time last year. Only the

Lord knows what the elements have in store for us in the coming months. Ah."

"I doubt if *He* knows, at this point. It could be a very good year for ranchers in western Kansas, given fair prices, a decent chance. We had a couple good rains after the planting. I'm optimistic, Mr. Strout."

"I've been thinking your situation over very seriously, Miss Whitford, since you were in the bank making a payment the other day. We both know how hard that payment was to come by, um hum. Perhaps I've been doing you an injustice, stringing you along, um, with the small loans I've made you from time to time. Oh ah." He shook his head. "Even with your little job here, you're barely keeping pace, barely surviving, but you know that, ah yes."

She leaned forward, interrupting before he could go on with his estimation of her situation, her worth. "Mr. Strout, have I missed a payment yet? I've been late a few times, but that's all. I *am* keeping up!"

He fidgeted and brushed at his impeccable vest-front. He sucked at his pipe, took it from his mouth, and eyed the ceiling as though searching for words on the plastered adobe. She wanted to pat him as she would a child to make it easier for him, but at the same time she didn't want to hear what he was going to put to her. She chewed the inside of her cheek and waited politely.

"You don't deserve such a hard life as you've

got, Miss Whitford," he said, squaring to face her. "It's going to make you old before your time, break a pretty young woman like you, ah!" He shook his head sadly. "You've had my admiration the whole while I've known you and watched you struggle, um, yes." A brief spark showed for an instant in his eyes, then vanished as if he must stay with his mission. "Thisba, dear woman, told me herself that if I really wanted to help you, I'd find a buyer for your investment in your claim, or buy it myself, and allow you to clear your debt."

Thisba, naturally. "Oh, she feels that way, does she?" First the woman was ready to cart her off to the insane asylum, or worse. And now that Amity had turned Seymour down, she had persuaded her husband to buy her out. "Please tell your wife she needn't concern herself about me."

Henry missed the rancor in her voice. "With your debt cleared and a little surplus, you could set yourself up somewhere else more civilized, ah, um, yes!" Behind his owlish glasses his gaze was sincere, warm with the affection he plainly felt for her. He took his glasses off and wiped them on a snowy handkerchief. "Here's what I can do — in exchange for your ranch, I'll cancel your interest, cancel your mortgage, and give you a thousand dollars besides. That's a fair deal, and a lot better, ah, um, yes, than losing your health, *and* the land, eventually, anyway. Um ahh."

She came back at him swiftly, unable to stay

calm, her voice strident. "Fair? My place is worth more than that, Mr. Strout, to anyone. Especially to me. Anyway, it's not for sale at any price! Dove's Nest is my whole future!"

She wanted to be civil with him, because he really did care what happened to her. That Thisba had slyly instigated today's offer, for reasons of her own, was probably beyond his ken.

She laughed in soft irony, and shook her head. "Seems everyone wants to come to my aid these days. Did you know that your wife's cousin also offered to help me out of my 'predicament'?"

"Oh?"

"Yes, Mr. Purdue asked for my hand in marriage." She kept her voice casual, her smile sweet while her anger climbed again, remembering.

Henry looked scandalized. He sat forward, teeth clenching on his pipe, a hand on either knee. "Hump, humph, what?" She was not really surprised that Henry hadn't known that she'd been approached by a member of his own household. Dear Thisba did keep her secrets well.

"The fool! My God, you could have any man you want. Lord! Ahhh, umm, oh. You did put him in his place? You're much too good for him, dear, much too good, ah, yes!" He slid to the edge of his chair, waving his pipe. "Like a leech, he is. Sometimes I don't think I'll ever shake him loose, get him to go back where he came from. I've let him stay on this long only to humor the missus. Ah, oh."

She sat back and let Henry Strout vent his

spleen, feeling in a small way vivified, restored. She answered his question. "Yes, I did reject Mr. Purdue's proposal. And I must turn down your kind offer. You see, Mr. Strout, I don't mind the hard work, the sacrifices I'm making toward owning my own ranch. I'm as happy here as I've ever been anywhere. Though times are hard, there've been periods in my life when I was much worse off. I don't intend to make any more debt until I've cleared that already against me. You've no worry on that score. May I say that here in town you aren't able to see how we're making strides in the right direction out at Dove's Nest?" Her voice revealed her excitement. "Come see us this summer, Mr. Strout. Let me show you — tell you the plans I envision. I think you'll be surprised. But my last word is this — I love my place, and I won't lose it, nor will I leave it." She took a deep breath. "Don't you feel that anyone who survived the past two years out here would likely stay on for good?"

He'd listened carefully, frowning at first and then with a slow smile building on his owlish face, finally creasing it in a rainbow of lines. "Good!" he exclaimed, jabbing his pipe into his mouth and giving her desk a hearty thump with his knuckles. "By heaven, ah um, yes! I knew you had it in you. I told the little woman you'd likely not agree to my offer, but she said to do my best. Twist your arm, she said. She worries what you're doing to yourself, but maybe she just doesn't really understand the strong stuff you're made of, um, no, being delicate herself."

Thisba delicate? Amity hardly thought so. In her estimation, under that elegant, proper exterior was flint and steel, and more than a little pestilence and mystery.

He stood up. "Miss Whitford, you're a lovely woman and a wonder to boot. You have my support." He frowned severely.

"Is anything wrong?"

"Oh, no, not really. But my darling wife is going to be very angry with me. She'll consider that I failed today, but she doesn't know my business as I do. Anything I can do to help you, Miss Whitford — short of loaning you more money for the time being — do ask, ah, um, yes! I consider you a valued customer of my bank."

"I don't intend to ask for anything." *Now more than ever.* If he believed she couldn't make it without being constantly propped up by his bank, she'd have to somehow show him that wasn't true.

She saw him to the door moments later, and shook his hand congenially in thanks. She'd like to keep Henry Strout on her side as a friend, but it would be a cold day in hell before she'd ask him for money again, giving his wife a tool to use against her, to pry her loose from the community. It made things more difficult that he was blind to his wife's nasty side. But it was understandable that Thisba's true nature would be kept hidden from her husband. Above all else,

Thisba demanded the better things in life, and Henry could provide them. And there was, Amity felt, an element of luck in that, because Thisba would stop short of anything that would diminish herself in Henry's eyes. At least Amity hoped that was the case.

The confidence with which she'd spoken to Henry began to evaporate almost as soon as the door closed behind him. She tidied her desk and thought about the work she should be doing, but couldn't put her mind on it. She was not fooling herself, nor him. She had a hard row to hoe and most of it lay ahead of her. She sighed, feeling suddenly lonely, wanting to run to something, or away from something; it was hard to say which.

Thoughts of Chalk drifted across her mind. She wondered if he might like company, for just a little while. He was alone over there, since his sister Stella and the children had moved north to Hudson School. Her cheeks were hot, her heart racing, when she finally stepped outside and locked her office door, feeling like a brazen hussy. She looked up and down the street, her own furtive behavior embarrassing her. But she'd never crossed the street to Chalk with quite the motives she was feeling today, either. She ached for the sound of his voice, the touch of his hand, his kiss. Controlling herself, she walked across sedately, though her feet wanted to run to him.

Chapter Twenty-four

On the way over, Amity considered a reason to explain her visit to the *Banner* office and decided she needed to borrow ink. She stepped through the door. The surprise in Chalk's eyes meeting hers, from where he cranked his press, turned knowing. Her excuse flew out the window. "Chalk —" she began.

"Afternoon, Amity." He wiped his hands on a rag. He beckoned, holding out his hand. "Come here." Outside at the far end of town the shrill whistle and rumble of the four o'clock train sounded, matching her racing pulse. She went to him, put her hand tentatively in his strong grasp.

They both spoke:

"I shouldn't have come —"

"I'm glad you came."

Their hands remained clasped as he drew her back into the shop, away from the windows.

"We don't want the whole town watchin' me kiss you."

"A plague on the town. I'm really pretty sick of it."

"Would you like to come back to my room?"

She took a deep breath. "We'd better not."

"What's bothering you, darlin'? Come here in my arms and tell me."

Talk could wait. She moved to him slowly, buried her face against his chest, and took a long draft of the spicy smell of him. Her fingertips glided along the muscled planes of his shoulders, his arms. Flinging propriety to the wind, she tucked herself tight against him and raised her lips to meet his. The kiss made her whole body quiver. Talk could wait — a long time.

Leaving the *Banner* office one day, after a particularly passionate session in Chalk's arms, Amity felt euphoric, happy at least with this single moment in time. Then, on the street, coming back to earth, cheeks flaming, she stopped to smooth her hair and skirts and, looking down, rebuttoned her bodice. She hastened across the street to her office and had just stepped onto the walk in front of her building when she felt someone watching her. She turned slowly. Up the street, three figures stood under the wooden awning of the Primrose Tea Garden. It was clear they'd been waiting for her to leave Chalk's place. Amity's heart began to thump in alarm. The trio consisted of Sadie Branch, meek, palsied wife of the Methodist preacher; Abigail Limbaugh, black-haired, shrewish wife of the wagonworks and livery's owner, and, last but not least, Thisba Strout decked out in her usual finery, so out of place in Syracuse. The women's heads bent together in a sudden buzz of conversation. Amity stood rooted, feeling as though her life's blood flowed from her body and into the street.

Even from a distance of several yards, she could detect Thisba's smirk, her triumph at having trapped her. And suddenly, she couldn't stand it; she would have it out with the woman once and for all. Head high, heels smacking the planks sharply, she marched back across the street and along the walk, to halt in front of them. "Is there a problem, ladies?" she asked flatly. "You seem to be watching me?" *How long has it been going on, from the first day I ran to Chalk's arms because you were making my life miserable, Thisba Strout?*

"You seem affronted, Miss Whitford?" Thisba mocked, gloved hands fluttering. "Are we the ones neglecting our duties in an elected office to dally with the newspaper publisher? Behaving like a slattern under the noses of the whole community?"

Her cheeks heated and she couldn't meet their eyes. "I didn't — I'm not — What do you plan to do about it?"

"Tar and feathers come to mind. At the very least, I believe a petition for recall is in order." Thisba's voice was stern and her expression outraged, but her green eyes gloated.

"You can't do that! I've done nothing wrong! I'm entitled to a personal life the same as anyone!" There were rules, and she'd broken them, but at the moment she didn't regret it one bit.

370

"What's the real reason you're out to get rid of me, Mrs. Strout?" The woman's eyes narrowed as Amity plunged on, "Are you jealous that your husband Henry helps me, likes me? Did I take an office you secretly covet? Or perhaps your daughter, Doridee, is doing poorly in school? What is it, exactly? I demand to know, and I demand a halt to this ridiculous push of yours to see me off the face of the earth." Her mouth was dry when she finished, but she felt purged, too, of something she'd held back too long.

Thisba gave her a haughty glare. "A strumpet has no right to lead our children and our teachers, as I've stated from the first."

Abigail Limbaugh, her cheeks points of color in her sharp features, accused Amity, "You say that if you do your job well that's all that matters, but it isn't. We can't have a harlot in an office of authority over our children and teachers. You refuse to answer our questions about your past. You're hiding something!"

Thisba, even more than Amity, gave the woman a sharp look. Though momentarily thrown off, Thisba turned back to her victim. "But that's not the half of it. What you're brazenly up to right before our eyes is enough to have you on the next train out of town!" Her nose wrinkled in distaste. "Coming from the newspaper office *half-dressed*. I've not trusted you for one minute. You should've been routed from Hamilton County long before this. Now look at the mess we have on our hands. It doesn't surprise me that you're a 'free love' follower of Moses Harman." She turned to her friends, explaining, "He's that awful Valley Falls man who puts out obscene papers."

"What? *Free love?* You're being ridiculous!" Amity's face grew heated. Things sometimes got a bit out of control when she and Chalk were together but she certainly didn't subscribe to Harman's preachings, let alone his paper. "I've gotten some mail I didn't send for," she said icily, "but that hardly makes me guilty of what you're accusing me of!" Harman's papers continued to fill her mailbox and now she had a very good idea who'd had the subscription sent to her.

The three women's expressions all but called her a liar. Sadie Branch's head bobbed like a pale tulip in a brisk breeze, while her blue eyes heaped scorn on the nasty, unredeemable, Miss Whitford. She said in a soft childish voice, "I doubt it'd do any good to have my husband speak with you. You've gone too indecently far."

Abigail Limbaugh had also bitten like a carp for rotted bait. "Free love?" she cried, looking as if she might faint, but enjoying the juicy tidbit too much to do so, "our *county school superintendent* with him at the *Banner?*" She looked at Amity and back down the street toward the newspaper office.

Amity, so furious she couldn't speak, was about to bite her tongue in two.

"Him, and who knows who else!" Thisba replied, shrugging her elegant shoulders in ladylike embarrassment. She gave Amity a smug look. She had plowed and planted the ugly seeds; the other women could take them from there.

Spittle glistened on Abigail's lips. "Dear God! With others, too." She had a faraway look, titillated by whatever image her brain had conjured up.

"You see the point, Abigail," Thisba sniffed. "Next thing you know, this *person* here will be teaching her sinful ways to our children. We have no choice but to be rid of her as soon as possible. You'll hear from the proper officials on this, Miss Whitford."

"You can't do this — it's wrong!" Amity cried at their backs as they turned and swept inside the tearoom, hissing with gossip. She wouldn't go after them, wouldn't beg. Her spine was stiff all the way back to her office, but every step seemed like a mile. Though she loved Chalk with all her heart, look where it had gotten her. She'd lost this round to Thisba, had likely lost everything. Lord, but she hated the woman. She'd felt very strange in Thisba's presence today, a feeling apart from what was being said, something that had been at the back of her mind since her collapse on the street. There was something locked in her head, and she had no key. What? Something — answers, maybe, that she couldn't grasp.

More than once lately, she had considered that Thisba had lied about not being at Beaconsfield at the time of Nora Ann's death.

Amity sighed, feeling a twinge of guilt. What did it really matter? This latest damage was her fault and no one else's. She'd have to deal with it the best she could. But she wasn't finished. She couldn't be.

Amity was packing the last of her things for the trip home to Dove's Nest for the summer. She folded garments mechanically, depression threatening to swallow her, except for the one bright thought that soon she'd be gone from this terrible place for a while, living on her own land with her dear ones. She was in the outer room, packing the last of her papers to take with her, when the door burst open and Chalk charged in.

"Have you seen this?" he bellowed, waving a copy of the petition now being circulated all over the county by Thisba Strout and her friends.

"Fifteen minutes ago, Buford Barker brought one by to wave in my face. Three other people have stopped since to tell me about the petition. One of them was even sympathetic, if you can believe it."

"I'd like to kill the woman!" He paced back and forth, wadding the paper in his two fists.

"If you want my permission, you have it. God knows, I don't know what I could have ever done to Thisba Strout. Perhaps her life of idleness as a lady of society isn't enough to fill her time. Making my life intolerable seems to be her hobby."

"Good God, Amity, how can you make jokes? Have you read the petition — the garbage she's accusing you of?"

"Yes, I have." She put a top on the wood crate she'd been packing, took up a hammer, and nailed the lid down. "I know full well her accusations. That I'm a follower of Moses Harman, a fallen woman — nay, a whore, wallowing in 'free love' with — you, and countless others."

"Honey, your reputation?"

"Not much of it left, is there?"

"You've got a case for slander, Amity. Sue the damn woman. Let me have the case!" She'd never seen Chalk so incensed. "I could prove her wrong, repair the damage to your reputation, and get you a five thousand dollar settlement to boot. Please agree!"

She should. Her financial troubles would be over. But what if Thisba, crossed, would throw open the doors to the Beaconsfield business? Amity couldn't take the chance. "No." She shook her head. "I don't want to go through anything like that."

Chalk swore. In three long strides he crossed the room and pulled her into his arms. "Then let's get married, right now, as soon as we can get to a minister. That'll halt the lies before they get worse."

She only allowed herself the luxury of staying in his arms for a few seconds before she pushed away. She felt a strong, stubborn pride, a wish to fight this her own way. "If we married now it would make truth of the lies. We didn't —"

"Didn't we, almost?" he questioned gently.

"Thisba Strout and her ilk are treating me like a clod of dirt, like filth, Chalk! And I'm not like that! I won't have it, do you understand? Let them circulate their petition, let them do anything they want, but they better understand that they have a fight on their hands! I won't lie down at their feet like a damnable dirty carpet. And I don't have to marry you to prove I'm decent, because I am decent, Chalk — I am. If there are any good people left in these parts, they already know that, and they'll support me."

"Oh, sweetheart, of course you're a fine, clean, wonderful woman. And you do have friends, a lot of them. I've already talked to Amos Taylor 'n Noah 'n Beady Moffat. They're mad as hell and doing all they can to squelch this nonsense with a petition of their own to keep you. They know you and they'll back you up. But it's a big gamble, don't you see? And if we let it ride — if we don't get married — do you know how it's going to be for us from now on? After this?"

"Yes, I do. If I invite you out to my place, if we attend a dance together, or simply talk on the street, it will become fodder for Thisba's gossip mill. I'd like us to get married, too, but when the time is right. I'm not going to marry you just to kill talk!"

He looked at her for a long moment. Pain, confusion, anger, all blazed in his eyes. "Damn it all, Amity, why do you have to be so stubborn, so independent? It doesn't have to be this way! Lord, I need a drink." He strode to the door and almost yanked it from its hinges going out. The small building rocked for a full half minute after he slammed the door. And he didn't look back.

When Thaddy and John Clyde came for her in the wagon less than an hour later, Amity had washed her face and fixed her hair. She made every effort to smile when she hugged Thaddeus and caught John's hand in a tight grasp, grateful beyond measure to be with those she loved, who loved her. "Thaddy, oh, Thaddy, I'm so glad to see you. John Clyde, it's so wonderful to be going home!" And it was. These two were stable, rooted, real — her family.

They finished stowing her things in the wagon and started out. John Clyde drove, Thaddy sat in the middle with Amity's arm about his small shoulders. She looked ahead, knowing that being at home on her ranch was the salve needed to heal her heart, the mess of her life.

She would miss being right across the street from Chalk, miss seeing him coming and going from the newspaper on his many business errands. She'd miss the sparkle in his eye, the touch of his hand on hers, being in his arms when he crossed that street to see her, or she crossed to see him. But it would be so much better if she could just forget him. . . .

"What's that?" Thaddy asked, when they were

almost to the end of main street, heading west.

At the sound of shouting behind them, Amity looked back. The doors of the saloon swung open and two figures spilled into the street. Recognizing Chalk Holden's lanky frame and Seymour Purdue's huge bulk, she gasped, "Oh, dear God, no!" Her hand flew to her mouth, then she reached across John Clyde to yank the hickory-handled, braided leather whip from its socket on the driver's side of the wagon. Chalk and Seymour were squared off in the middle of the street, hammering one another with their fists. From the look of them, dirty, staggering, they'd been at it for some time inside the saloon. "Turn the wagon around, John," she said tightly, "and let's stop that nonsense before he kills him." She considered her holstered revolver under the wagon seat but its aim was so unreliable she could wind up hitting Chalk by mistake.

"Stop the fat man from killing Holden, or t'other way?" John Clyde asked, looking over his shoulder then turning around to saw at the reins.

She threw him a dark look, half frustration, half fear for Chalk's life. "Do I know? The fools just have to be stopped!" Without waiting for John Clyde to turn the wagon clear around, she leaped down, gathered her skirts in one hand, gripped the whip in the other, and raced back to where the two bloodied men continued to bash one another blow for blow. "Will you stop?" she screamed. "Stop, now!"

Chalk threw her a burning look. "You handle

things your way, I'll handle 'em mine." Seymour Purdue, tottering on his feet, took that opportunity to land a huge fist on Chalk's temple, a stone-hard blow that rocked the slighter man back on his heels. Chalk had a dumbfounded look; his eyes rolled back into his head, and he dropped to his knees. Before Amity could reach him, he staggered up again, motioning her out of the way. He drew back and swung a right from the ground up, sending Seymour crumpling to the street, breathing heavily, blood pouring down his face.

Seeing Seymour grope at his vest, Amity cried, "Chalk, watch out!" The big man pointed the derringer at Chalk's head but the newspaperman's booted foot flashed out and kicked the gun, sending it skittering several feet up the dusty street. Amity ran and snatched it up, brought it back, and handed it to Chalk, who held it on Purdue. "All right," the huge man puffed, "stop." He sat there, head between his legs like a huge bear.

"Damn — damn right, stop!" Chalk panted with whistling breaths, standing back, holding his ribs with one arm.

"What did he do? What did Seymour do? You had no right to take out your frustration on him, Chalk Holden."

"He was laughin', watching you leave. Boasted of his hand in your ruination. Referring to you in uncalled-for ways, in front of God and everybody. The Strout woman isn't just jealous of you, Amity. It's a whole hell of a lot more than that." He wobbled over to Purdue. "Get up, damn you. You're coming back to the *Banner* office with me and you're going to do some talking about that wire-brained lady cousin of yours. We're going to get to the bottom of this muck, or else." He turned to Amity. "You're invited, sweetheart, if you want to come."

Amity hesitated, thinking him a wonderful, lovable fool. "I'll come." John Clyde had pulled up in their wagon. Thaddy, on the high seat beside him, craned his neck for a good look at the goings on, eyes lit with excitement at the blood and gore. She'd keep him from this ugliness if she could. "John, will you and Thaddeus wait for me over at the café for a while? There's a few coins in my handbag. Get yourselves some pie and something to drink. Dinner if I take too long." She handed him the whip she hadn't needed.

She ran to catch up with Chalk's tall form. The butternut brown hair stood on end, making her smile even as her throat caught at the rest of his appearance. His clothing was rumpled, dirty, and splotched with blood. In front of the Blue Door Café, he stopped to flip a coin to a towheaded boy of about eleven watching from the boardwalk. "You know banker Strout? You tell him to bring his wife and come right away to the *Banner* office. There's an urgent meeting and they'll both want to be there." Then he weaved on down the street, gun in hand, herding a stumbling Seymour Purdue toward the *Banner* office. Seymour was like a huge, bloodied bull, cowed for the moment, but Amity knew that only a bullet would stop him if he should suddenly turn on Chalk. Possibly it would take more than one. But if their luck lasted, maybe they *would* get to the bottom of this muck. It was worth the world to try.

Chapter Twenty-five

Almost on their heels, Henry Strout came huffing into the *Banner* office, pipe in hand alone.

"Where's your wife?" Chalk asked.

"Ah-she refused to come because —" As his eyes adjusted to the dim interior following the sunny street, the little banker's eyes widened in shock. Chalk straddled a chair backward, derringer in the hand resting on his thigh, his chair blocking Seymour Purdue who was backed against the wall, his knees about to buckle. Strout removed his homburg for Amity, standing in the shadows nearby, and finished his explanation. "Said there could be nothing — no reason, for her to meet with the two of you." He looked from Amity to Chalk. "Ah, um, no. What's this all about, hmm?" He sucked nervously on his pipe.

Chalk filled him in, adding, "It's too bad your wife didn't come, Henry. We either have a private discussion here and now, or we take her and her cousin here to court on charges of harassment and slander." He shot Amity a look that said not to dispute him. "That could be very expensive for you, and it'd be detrimental to everybody concerned. It is not too late to save Miss Whitford's reputation and her work, and we have to try. If we had some idea of your wife's true motives in all this, it would be a beginning."

Henry nodded. "I want both of you to know I didn't know about the petition until it was too late. I don't agree with a word in it. I'm not sure what's eating my wife. In every way but her dealings with Miss Whitford, she's a good woman. Truly, she is. And — I love my wife."

"Maybe Seymour can help us?" Chalk barely moved the small gun resting on his thigh, but the muzzle pointed more directly at Purdue.

Seymour regarded Chalk with pure hatred. His voice came high and strained. "She had a bee in her bonnet over Miss Whitford and the campaign, that's all I know." He spluttered at the newspaperman, "Why should any of this be important to *you?* It's none of your business. Maybe Thisba is right, and it's true you and the school superintendent are up to hanky-panky?" His bruised and bloody lip curled.

From her spot, Amity held her breath for Chalk's reply, her face heating up.

"Miss Whitford was my candidate in the election," Chalk replied calmly. "Now there's this attempt to recall her with damned insufficient cause. If Thisba Strout was my candidate and was being wronged, I'd be standing up for her. I'm a gentleman. What else would you expect me to do?" He actually smiled at Seymour, but there was a glint in his eyes that didn't fit with the smile.

Thisba herself ought to be here, Amity thought. She was the one they ought to wring the truth from. She watched Seymour's eyes darting from time to time to the gun in Chalk's fist, as the discussion continued.

Chalk was saying, "There's something going on that's as smelly as old fish, and I think it has little or nothing to do with Amity's holding public office." Gun in hand, he gingerly rubbed the back of his knuckles across his cheek where the broken skin had started to sting. "There has to be a better reason than we've heard for Mrs. Strout to be so all-fired set against Miss Whitford."

Seymour fidgeted, plainly discomfited to be discussing his cousin. Amity thought Seymour really cared about Thisba, or was scared of revealing something he didn't want known, or both. "It's just Thisba's way," he whined, "to want things just so and proper. She was born with a silver spoon in her mouth — but she never got the taste of it, of the fine life she felt she had coming, not for years. Not till she married Henry here. Though it's nobody's business," he maintained stoutly, glaring at all of them.

"She made herself our business with that vile petition," Chalk growled. "Keep talkin'."

Seymour's fat shoulders slumped, his demeanor indicating he only wanted to get this over with and nurse the wounds Chalk had inflicted on him. Without looking at Amity, he said, "Aunt Kreta, Thisba's mother, was a flighty, unstable woman.

384

Right after she gave birth to Thisba, my aunt went totally mad. She tried to kill the newly born babe." He ignored Amity's sharp intake of breath and went on in high, icy tones, "But Thisba was only unconscious under the pillow her mother tried to smother her with when she was found. Aunt Kreta then slashed her own wrists. She bled to death. Thisba was brought up motherless, she and her brother. And their miserly father worked them like dogs in his mill."

Henry looked upset, but he motioned to Seymour to go on, humming and mumbling that he'd known little of this.

Seymour wagged his head, then grasped it between both hands to still the pain. He glowered at Chalk through bloodshot eyes.

"Get on with it!" Chalk, enduring pain of his own, was without mercy.

In a thin, tired voice, Seymour continued, "Thisba's weak, ne'er-do-well brother, Tom, was always the favored one with their pa. Aunt Kreta, when she was alive, doted on him, too. Thisba was a young girl, thirteen years old, when their father took sick. For almost two hellish years, she took care of that cruel old man night and day —"

"She was looking ahead to having the old man's fortune?" Chalk interrupted, "and all it would buy?"

"Anyone would've, in her place!" Seymour defended her.

"Chalk, please — !" Amity protested softly.

"She was penniless when we met, ahh, um, yes," Henry interjected. "What happened? Her father surely left her something. Mmm?"

"Why, naturally, *no*. The male child, her brother, inherited it all, by law." Purdue shrugged, grimaced. "In one weekend of drunken gaming, her brother lost the whole shebang — mills, money, their home. She came to me. My own family had lost everything to the Yankees in the war. From then on, I was the one to take her side and try to help the poor thing. I helped her as much as I could."

Chalk nudged his boot toe into Seymour's fat leg to hurry him up. The man winced, and went on, "Tommy Marcellus committed suicide not long after the gambling incident. He fell — leaped — off a fast moving train. There was an investigation, and they ruled it accidental. But it was suicide. He jumped."

"Where were you when it happened? Where was your cousin Thisba?" Chalk asked bluntly.

Seymour looked daggers at him. "We were all three there on the train at the time. We were going to my folks for Christmas. We couldn't stop him! Tommy was depressed, half-crazy like his mother, I guess."

"After the old man died, and the son lost the fortune and then killed himself, where did Thisba go? What'd she do then?" Chalk asked.

"Chalk, this is going nowhere," Amity put in. She felt it was of small use to bring up Beaconsfield with Thisba not present, but Amity took the plunge. "Did you know that for a brief time Thisba and I were employed by the same couple, at an English colony in central Kansas?"

Both Seymour and Henry looked surprised. Thisba wouldn't have mentioned to Henry ever having held a position she felt was so much beneath her, Amity thought, so it didn't mean very much that he hadn't known. Seymour leaned forward, blustering, "If you were there, why are you asking me about it?"

"Never mind, just forget it —" Amity began, but Seymour was really angry now.

"I don't want to gossip about the poor woman any longer!" He tried to move aside to leave. "Enough's enough."

"Hold it," Chalk growled, throwing out a long leg to bar the man's way and waving the derringer. "You're not finished till we find a connection in all this to Amity."

In the end, there was not a shred of anything Seymour could tell them that had to do with Amity. Maybe there was no hidden secret and Thisba simply fought her from an inexplicably jealous and hating heart.

As kind to Thisba as Seymour tried to be in the telling, as he went on, a sordid picture of the woman began to form. Thisba at fifteen, a conniver from necessity practically from the cradle, seduced an older man. Her plan for matrimony backfired when she, pregnant with the man's child, learned that he was already married. For the next few years, she and the baby, Doridee, lived hand to mouth. Thisba supported them with odd jobs, making artificial flowers from the hovel in which they lived, and working as a shop girl — a life she despised, feeling she was owed so much more by birthright.

"Does anybody know how she came to be here in Kansas?" Chalk asked, looking around at the other three. "It's a ways from Virginia."

Seymour shrugged. "She moved around, looking for something better for herself and little Doridee. I think she traveled in the company of a gambler when she came here, but parted from him as soon as she could. I don't know what that has to do with anything."

"It probably doesn't." Chalk turned to the banker. "Henry, you look like you were about to say something?"

Henry took a long pull on his pipe, smoke wreathed upward. His owlish face was haggard, sorrowful. "Thisba hasn't talked a lot about her past. I never cared to hear, ah, um, no. Didn't matter. I met her in the Junction City train station, umm." His voice softened, some of the distress left his face. "There she was, so lovely and helpless, fighting to carry a satchel, mind a trunk, and hang onto her little girl. Well, the satchel fell open and spilled their clothes all over the depot floor. Ah, umm, yes. Thisba started to cry. The whole scene just grabbed my heart." He studied the others' faces, to see if they understood why and how strongly Thisba affected him. "I went over to offer my assistance and ended up inviting the two of them to share supper with me." He sighed.

"I was just coming home from a profitable, but very lonely business trip. Ah, ah. I didn't need a picture drawn to tell me fate had been unkind to the pair, no, no, umm. Well, in the course of the evening, I offered them a home, offered Thisba a position as my housekeeper. I understood when she suggested marriage. It wouldn't have looked right, otherwise. Ah, um, no, no. Pretty woman like she is." The owlish eyes shone with sincerity. "And folks, I want you all to know that ours has been a good union these past two-and-a-half years, very good in some ways. My wife, Thisba, takes excellent care of me; we're devoted to one another. I enjoy having her and the girl in the house. The place used to be like a funeral home before they came. Um, um, yes."

A lengthy silence followed. "I don't know that we solved anything here," Chalk finally spoke up, "but there sure is a snake in the woodpile somewhere, and I'd give my life to find it."

Amity nodded. In the back of her mind was the thought that Thisba probably appeared in Syracuse only months before she did. No doubt Thisba had hoped never to see anyone from Beaconsfield — the same hope Amity'd had when she arrived — but fate deemed otherwise. It was pretty obvious that Thisba would want no reminders of a time in her life she'd hated. Reminders that could interfere with the new life she had constructed.

"I can go?" Seymour scowled at Chalk, shoving against the leg that barred him from moving. Chalk pulled his leg back and waved to Seymour that he was free.

Henry caught the man's beefy shoulder. "I don't want anything that passed between us here to go beyond these doors, do you understand, ah um? Not a word, Seymour! It'd only hurt my wife, um, yes. I intend to see that she toes the line. I won't have her hurting innocent people like Miss Whitford out of some old bothersome hates from a bad childhood. Ah, no, no. I'm going to see you to the train, Seymour, this very day. Ah, yes! You won't be helping my wife, then, with your nasty bits, ah, no, no. I can handle the dear girl, but you have to go! Absolutely, yes, yes, ummm!"

Seymour, walking away, looked at Henry, his eyes blazing in fury at the humiliation. He suddenly hesitated in half stride and his outrage was replaced by a look of cunning. His puffy lips formed a sly smile, as though he saw an advantage in all this for himself, after all. "I like it here, Henry. Thisba is my family. In any event, I can't do what you ask without funds." Seymour's hands spread out to each side as he waddled painfully toward the door. Then he stopped, rubbing at the street-dirt on his sleeves.

Henry sucked hard on his pipe, eyes on Purdue's back. "I'll give you the money you need, and more, if you'll guarantee to never come back this way. We'll think of something to explain your abrupt departure to my wife, ah, umm, umm."

Amity realized all at once that she had a monstrous headache. The street fight and the discussion about Thisba had given her a bad taste in her mouth. Even though Chalk had tried to get to the bottom of her problems in his own way, nothing had really been resolved. She had an overwhelming wish to get away to Dove's Nest, away from everything in this town, even Chalk.

Instead, as soon as the door closed after Henry and Seymour, she jumped up and headed for the blanket-covered door to Chalk's private quarters.

"What're you doing?" He caught her just as she pulled the blanket aside.

"I'm going to boil some water and take care of those cuts on your face."

"That's not necessary, they aren't that bad. I can do it myself." A tired grin lit his battered face. "Aren't you worried what folks will think, you staying on alone here with me?" He held the back of her hand to his mouth but she took it away.

"It'll take a mere five minutes or so. And there's nothing wrong with seeing to a man's wounds. Any woman would do that."

"Yet — you don't really want to be here?" he commented, getting to his feet, studying her face, puzzled. "You were on your way out to the ranch, weren't you, when the fuss started?"

She nodded. "I'm going home for the summer,

and yes, I'm quite anxious to be there again. If you're sure you can treat those cuts yourself, I'd better go. John Clyde and Thaddeus are waiting for me."

He sighed heavily. He seemed to have a problem where to put his hands and he finally clasped them behind his back. "Please be careful, darling. Way things add up, Henry's wife could be crazier than a bedbug. Henry thinks he can put a lid on her, but I'm not so sure. You watch out for yourself."

"I'll be fine on the ranch. Perfectly safe."

He shrugged. "Not if she wants to really harm you. I'll be coming out to check how you're doing as often as I can."

The look in his eyes told her that she'd be seeing him as soon, and as often, as he thought best and let the devil take the hindmost. Stubborn wonderful fool, he'd be the end of her yet.

Chapter Twenty-six

Whether it was the pressure from Henry, the threat of Chalk's lawsuit, or her cousin Seymour being banished, or all of them together, Thisba withdrew the petition for recall. Amity felt an immense relief. The damage to her reputation was slight, something she'd fight to overcome, and she had kept her office. She could continue with important projects; she still had her sorely needed source of income.

Deliriously happy to be home, Amity dug into work at Dove's Nest with relish. For long, long hours, she weeded the vegetables and corn that she'd helped plant on earlier weekends. She prayed for ample rain with nearly every other stroke of her hoe. She redded up the house, pulling down the muslin ceiling, washing and drying it and tacking it back up. Today, she whitewashed the interior walls, after pulling the furniture out into the sunny yard. When she finished, on impulse, she sat down at her organ in the yard and began to pump and sing until the ranchyard filled with music. John Clyde and Thaddy came grinning from the barnyard where they'd been trying to wean Flora's calf to drinking from a bucket. Zip slunk to the far side of the house, disliking the noise.

Lowering her voice and chin for the male's line, Amity sang, "I'll give to you a paper of pins, for that's the way true love begins, if you will mar-ry me, miss, if you will mar-ry me." In her own voice, she sang back, fingers on the keys, feet pumping hard, "I'll not accept your paper of pins, if that's the way true love begins, for I'll not mar-ry you, sir, for I'll not mar-ry you."

Thaddy knew the song "Paper Of Pins" from singing it with her. While John Clyde squatted on his haunches, taking the time to roll and smoke a cigarette, Thad stood by the melodeon and sang the rest of the male lines, offering the maiden in turn a little brown dog, a dress of red, a coach and six, a key to his chest of gold, only to be turned down in song each time by Amity. Their voices raised for the last stanzas: Thad, hand on his chest, sang out, "I'll give you my hand and heart that we may love and never part, if you will marry me, miss, if you will marry me."

Amity answered, smiling broadly, "I will accept your hand and heart that we may love and never part, and I will marry you, sir, and I will mar-ry you!"

John Clyde clapped for them, sending ashes scattering from his cigarette. He ground it out with his boot, and motioned to Thaddeus. "C'mon, boy, we got work."

"As soon as I get this furniture back in the

house, I'm starting a very special supper!" Amity called after them, grabbing up a chair. "So don't plan to spend all night with that stubborn calf. I'll need help to get the organ back inside." She liked this time of year especially for the food that was available. New potatoes and a pot of fresh greens from her garden, catfish rolled in cornmeal and fried crisp and brown in bacon fat. John Clyde and Thaddy's catch from the river was a nice change. For dessert, maybe she'd splurge and expend five eggs and her time to make Mama's vanilla pudding and meringue recipe she called Floating Island. She didn't fool herself; she knew it was guilt for being away so much at her other work that made her want to cook endlessly for these two, and fatten their skinny bones.

The very next day she went to work making hand cheese, which Thad especially liked. She had allowed milk to curdle for days in a pan on the back of her stove to make cottage cheese. Now she formed the cottage cheese into balls the size of a child's fist, squeezing out the excess liquid. She placed the balls in the empty pan at the back of her stove. The cheese balls would gradually turn yellow with aging, and the taste would become sharper. When ripened all the way through, the hand cheese would be ready to eat.

As she went about her work in the yard and fields several days after her return to Dove's Nest, Amity began to feel that she was being watched.

Sometimes, she would jerk about suddenly, to stare at the empty horizon, and make a slow circle with her eyes. Usually, a cold perspiration would break out on her skin, her heart palpitating fiercely. Below a huge dome of blue sky, the broad, green plain would be empty, marked only by the fringe of brush and trees along Plumb Creek. Arguing with herself next that it might be Chalk watching over her, she'd wrinkle her nose in a scolding smile and get back to business. It was likely only her imagination, anyway. If Chalk were around, he'd ride in to see her.

Sometimes she put the feelings of being watched down to a residue of fright left over from her set-tos with Thisba Strout, nerves she hadn't quite conquered. To be on the safe side, she began to wear her holstered gun about her waist. Twice on her walk from the house to the cornfield, she'd seen rattlesnakes, and that was an easy excuse to give John Clyde and Thaddeus for wearing the gun. One day, coming from the outhouse, she killed a four-foot-long rattler.

"Over there, Ammy, look over there! Can we swim there?" Thaddeus hugged the picnic blanket he carried and pointed with his other hand in the direction of the water-filled depression in the sandhills to their right. For some time they'd been following skimpy Plumb Creek southward from home, looking for a spot in the water wide and deep enough for swimming. They'd had a good rain a few days previous but the sun was out again, scorching hot; a perfect day for swimming and a picnic. His steps slowed. "Can we? I'm gettin' hot an' tired, Ammy, aren't you?"

"Yes, dove, I'm hot and tired of walking, too, but we can't swim over there because that water's very muddy and not as deep as it looks. There's not a lick of shade. We can find a very nice place to swim, and a shade tree to picnic under if we just keep going. The creek widens and gets deeper when it starts to spill into the Arkansas River."

His gaze was still glued to the wide dip in the sandy landscape. "That's a buffalo wallow, ain't it?"

"*Isn't* it," she repeated, "and, yes, it's a buffalo wallow." Some things that Thaddeus picked up from John Clyde, like poor grammar, didn't please her. She meant to spend as much time as possible alone with the boy while she could. "There are hundreds of such depressions all over the high plains. I gather that the buffalo enjoyed a good wallow in mud, and any sinkhole where a little water gathered was an invitation. But," she said, "not to us, Thaddy dear, not to us."

"We've come pretty far." Thaddeus sounded wistful, his patience about gone, a show of temper on the verge. "We've come a hundred miles, I betcha."

She laughed at him. "More like three or four, dear. Soon we'll find a good pool." If her words cheered him, it didn't show. She lamented, "But I honestly don't know what possessed me to feel walking was a good idea, except that it's just such a beautiful day and Ben deserved a rest from all the work we've put the poor animal to lately." She switched their picnic basket to the other hand, and sang out, quoting:

"Then let us, one and all, be contented with
  our lot;
The June is here this morning, and the sun
  is shining hot;
Oh! let us fill our hearts up with the glory
  of the day,
And banish ev'ry doubt and care and sorrow
  far away."

Thaddy grinned at her as he walked along, his displeasure vanquished for the moment. "You can say poems pretty good, Ammy. I like to hear you."

She curtsied as well as the picnic basket and her pistol belt would allow. "Thank you, son. That bit of verse is from the Hoosier poet, James Whitcomb Riley." Guessing the question he was about to ask, she told him, "*Hoosier* means someone from the state of Indiana. Riley got to know the country folk of Indiana very well, their dialect and ways, when he traveled with a medicine show as an actor. He wrote songs, poems, and plays for the show company."

They walked in perspiring silence for perhaps another fifteen minutes. Thaddeus had begun to scowl again and complained, "I don't think the shade is going to get any shadier, or the creek any deeper, Ammy. D'ya want me to run ahead and look?"

She tossed her head and laughed, wanting to hug him. Sometimes, especially those times when he opposed her, the youngster reminded her of Chalk Holden. "All right, run ahead and pick us a spot." He bolted like a stone released from a taut slingshot, zipped maybe two dozen yards along the creek before he shouted back, "Here, Ammy. Here's perfect!"

He skinned out of his trousers and shirt and was down to his underwear by the time she reached him. Young grasshoppers hit the air when she put her basket down in the grass under a warty hackberry tree. Above, the leafy trees made an umbrella against the sun. Around them, painted lady butterflies flitted in yellowspine thistle. It was indeed perfect. Amity spread the quilt Thaddy'd dropped and placed the picnic basket in the center. She sat down on the edge of the quilt and removed her moccasins and gun belt.

Standing up, she caught the hem of her cotton shift in both hands and pulled it over her head. Underneath she wore a navy blue flannel bathing suit from her Cairo days, that luckily still fit her. A few feet away, Thaddeus giggled, startled more than shocked at sight of her legs, which were bare from the knees down. Then he shouted, "C'mon, Ammy, c'mon!" as he ran down into the water, splashing and laughing as he bobbed up and down. She joined him in play, her slicing hands sending silver sheets of water into the air until she felt wonderfully cool and clean. She swam for a while with smooth, even strokes, back and forth the several yards depth would allow. Later, lying in a shallower part of the creek, she let the water ripple over her body while her mind emptied, letting care float away. She closed her eyes, listening to the song of birds in the thicket. At a particularly musical *sweet, sweet, sweetie-o-sweet,* she looked up to see a yellow warbler singing from a crotch in the hackberry.

Closer to hand, Thaddeus talked to himself as he launched a boat formed from twigs and leaves from the hackberry tree.

They ate lunch on the quilt, laughing and talking as they devoured delicious corn dodgers — cornmeal and bacon drippings mixed and baked in lumps — boiled eggs, hand cheese, baby raw carrots, and the plum tarts Amity'd made from the last of the previous year's preserves. "My, I've eaten far too much," she said later, rubbing her middle, "but the swim made me ravenous." Her appetite was likely helped by the fact that for another wonderful day, she wasn't beset with worry, but felt relaxed and carefree.

Out of the blue, Thad asked, "Ammy, are you going to marry Mr. Holden, the newspaperman?"

Tarnation, did this child, along with everyone else, know of her bond with Chalk? "Uh," she stalled, totally discomfited by the question, "why — why do you ask, Thad-Son?"

The smoke-dark eyes twinkled at her. "Oh,

'cause I think he likes you. He comes to see us lots, but — he looks at you all the time." He snickered, "With eyes like this —" He made a wide-eyed, open-mouthed face to show her. "I think he wants to marry you. I thought —" suddenly serious, he took a bite of plum tart, chewed, swallowed, his expression pure innocence "— that if you married him, he might be — kind of my father."

She choked on a bit of her own tart, and made an effort at composure. "Oh, Thad, I just don't know if that will happen, or not. I am fond of Mr. Holden. But there are . . . difficulties. Is it important to you, having a father?"

"If you didn't marry Chalk, Ammy, I'd still have you and old John."

"Yes," she said, "forever and always." She reached out a finger and wiped some of the purple jam from his scarred little mouth. "We'll have to see what happens, honey."

Thaddeus had gone back to play in the water several yards downstream where a fallen hackberry shrub formed a shady canopy. Looking in his direction every now and then, thinking what a solidly happy dimension he added to her life and hoping she did the same for him, Amity lazily gathered their picnic things and leftover food to put in the basket. The first *crack* she heard sent birds fluttering from the brush into the air. She decided Thaddy had snapped a branch to build another boat, and she ignored the sound. But a second sharp report followed fast on the first and

401

a bullet opened a furrow in the quilt right by her knee. Frozen for only a second, she cried out, "Thaddy, down, son! Down in the water! Hide! Someone's shooting at us!" Her own gun lay with her moccasins some feet away. Amity dove for it, rolled down over the creek bank with the gun in her hand, drawing back the hammer with her thumb and rotating the cylinder with the other hand. She usually kept five chambers loaded, the hammer on an empty one.

Her mind spun while she lay panting. Who on earth could be shooting at them and for God's sake, *why?* A quick peek showed Thaddeus crouched in the tangled branches of the fallen hackberry shrub. His wet hair, eyes, and nose were showing just above the water, beaverlike. She uttered a silent prayer of thanks for his safety, and begged for nothing to happen to him. Slithering on her stomach, she backed into the water, gun hand aloft, keeping low but moving fast in the opposite direction of the boy. He might feel better if she joined him but she couldn't chance drawing rifle fire his way. She moved fast, expecting a bullet to split her brain any second. She found her own sandy overhang and clung there to an underwater root.

A third shot struck the bank just above her head and sprayed sandy soil down into her hair. Amity's whimper turned into an angry curse. Did they mean to torment her to death, or did her attacker have the poorest aim west of the Mississippi? She felt like a sitting duck, but rose just enough to try and glimpse the sniper. She saw movement behind the hackberry they'd picnicked under. She'd be lucky to hit anything beyond twenty-five feet. She was taking careful aim at the shadow on horseback behind the tangled hackberry trees when the ambusher's rifle cracked again and something *zinged* right next to her ear. She realized she'd been grazed. The whole side of her face felt instantly numb, then burned like fire. Stunned with shock, desperate for her life, Amity gulped for air and sank down into the water with only her hand with the gun exposed. *Who? Why?* If they killed her would Thaddy be next? She couldn't let them do this, not this time, no, God no! She came up for air.

"Who are you? What do you want?" she shouted suddenly. There was no answer. The hair on the back of her neck stood on end. "I've no money if robbery is your aim! No horse or wagon." She heard a sound, a snide chuckle, from behind the hackberry tree up the bank. Nearly petrified with fear, gritting her teeth, she aimed the gun in the direction of the sound, closed her eyes, and squeezed the trigger. A sharp cry intermingled with a soft thud and rattle of gear. A terrible moment of silence followed. Then she heard pounding hoofbeats.

Amity listened as the drumming of the earth, heavy at first, grew fainter. After an interminable, deafening silence, she heard a soft whisper. "Ammy? Ammy?" Dear Lord, the boy mustn't show himself.

"Don't move, son!" she whispered frantically. "Stay where you are!" *They must make sure the attacker had gone.* She crouched in the water until her whole body felt as if it had turned to rubber. Her wrist ached from holding the gun aloft, poised to fire if their attacker suddenly reappeared. Was the shooter alone, or were there others?

A lifetime passed while she waited. Every few minutes she ventured a peek to make sure that Thaddeus remained in his hidey-hole, safe. Her ears finally picked up a sound and she strained to make it out. Hoofbeats, she was sure. Their attacker returning? Cold fear washed over her. It was hard to breathe. The sound faded, then came louder, more definite. "Son," she hissed, "don't move. Stay out of sight!"

Panic tightened her throat. Her heart seemed to stop. She gripped the gun tighter. The hoofbeats slowed to a walk right above her. "Missy?" John Clyde called out. "Boy? Where you be?"

Amity went weak, tears of relief welled in her eyes. She guessed he had found them by coming upon their things on the creek bank. She took several deep breaths to rid herself of the feeling of faintness. "W-we're here, John Clyde!" she gasped. "Here in the creek. Down here." An icy residue of fear remained at her core. "Someone tried to kill us! Are they gone? Is it safe to come out?" She peeked out, saw John Clyde climbing down off his long-legged, reddish brown horse, Texas Max. It was a most welcome sight.

He didn't reply for a few seconds, and then

he told her, "You don't got to worry none, Missy. Looks like you done took care of things. But I come quick when I heard gunfire."

She waded out of the creek, following John Clyde's gaze as he stared off in the opposite direction, toward her ranch. He shook his head, muttering, "Lordalmighty!"

"*Who* is it?" she asked. "Did I — ?" In the hot, hazy distance an unfamiliar horse lifted its head to look their way. Close by on the ground lay a dark mound, the body of the person she'd shot. "Who?" she questioned again with a shuddering breath. She stumbled into a run toward the body on the ground. She stopped in amazement when she saw who it was: Seymour Purdue.

Chapter Twenty-seven

Amity was nervous, almost to the point of illness, as she drove along Syracuse's main street with Seymour Purdue's blanket-covered body filling the back of her squeaky wagon. She would have liked nothing so much as to complete this terrible task unnoticed, which was impossible, of course.

Gape-mouthed loiterers came off their benches to stare. They fell to and followed her lumbering wagon down the middle of the street. Their tromping feet stirred further dust, and their voices punctured the air with exclamations. Merchants burst from their stores, joining the group, asking questions — whose head and feet were showing from under the shroud? Ignoring them all, she drove, white faced and silent, toward the small sod house of the undertaker. Chalk Holden saw the commotion through the window as he worked on his newspaper. He charged out, giving a horrified glance at the blanket-covered heap in back, to join Amity. He leaped onto the rolling wagon to sit beside her. "It's Purdue," she said softly.

"I figured that out. What the hell happened?" he whispered, his look grim with shock. "I was with Henry Strout when he put Purdue on the train out of town. How come the big bugger's here in your wagon?"

In spite of trying to be calm and in control, her chin quivered. "I didn't kill him." A tear crept down her cheek. "Although he tried to kill me." She swiped the tear away and stared straight ahead. Drawing a deep breath, she said in a tight voice, "I'm going to tell my story only once, to the undertaker and sheriff. I suppose Thisba and Henry should be there, too. If you need the details for your paper, you can get them then."

Chalk cursed under his breath. "My interest here is in a lot more than that, Amity, and you know it! It's you I care about." He reached over and tried to take the reins but she held them in a death-tight grip. Chalk growled, "He tried to *kill* you?" As he looked back over his shoulder at the huge corpse, he wrinkled his nose. Seymour had begun to smell and flies droned at the edges of the blanket. "Couldn't John have brought the body in after he killed him, for God's sake?"

"John Clyde didn't kill him either. I had to have his help getting Seymour's body into the wagon, but that's all I let John do. This whole thing is my responsibility."

"You're talking in goddamned riddles, Amity." He snorted in annoyance, his facial muscles taut with worry, when he got no response.

She hid her own feelings of sadness, confusion, *fear*. She wasn't about to let him see an ounce of weakness or he'd insist on taking over when this was *her* job, alone.

At the sheriff's office, Wilf Bell, the wiry, mustachioed sheriff; Geoffrey Melton, the blonde, smooth-faced undertaker; and Henry Strout, as well as numerous on-lookers, listened to Amity's story. Thisba Strout had been given the news, but had chosen not to come. And, it was said, had taken to her bed in a screaming fit. Amity spoke quietly, trying not to show that she was a bundle of nerves herself. "Though I couldn't catch him at it, someone watched my place for days. Evidently, it was Seymour, come back to do me in. My boy, Thaddeus, and I were on a picnic on Plumb Creek, not far from my place. We'd gone in swimming when Seymour fired on us. I returned fire, but struck Purdue only once, a simple bullet wound in the shoulder." The undertaker nodded sober agreement. Amity went on, "It seems that Seymour fell from his saddle, maybe struck his head, and his foot got caught in a stirrup. His horse, trying to be shed of the — the enormous burden, kicked and stomped Seymour to death."

There was a shocked silence. Melton agreed that her explanation fit his examination of the corpse.

"Why would the fella want to kill you, Miss Whitford?" Wilf Bell stroked his lengthy moustache, eyes squinting as he leaned forward to catch her answer.

"I — I'm not sure, exactly. I did defeat him in the election, if you remember. Later, he asked me to marry him and I refused. He was humiliated, furious, when his own cousin's husband ordered him out of town — because of me." She sighed. "Also, he might've been trying to frighten me into giving in to him. He was obsessed with the idea of me going away with him, to be his wife. Of course — I wouldn't." She looked at Chalk, and her glance flew away. She added firmly after a moment, "But neither did I want to see Mr. Purdue dead. In spite of the fact that he threatened me, even — manhandled me in the past. I — I'd never fire on another human being except in self-defense, or to save someone I love. I was afraid my boy was in danger, there at the creek."

"Seems clear-cut to me," Sheriff Bell drawled, after consulting with Melton again. "You're free to go, Miss Whitford. If there's anything else we need, I'll let you know."

Relief filled her eyes, and she felt near collapse. "Th-thank you."

The sheriff barked, with a wave of his arms, "Rest of you folks clear out of here! Ain't any of this your business, nohow! G'wan!"

Amity could scarcely wait to get out of the room, but walked slowly past the people standing aside to let her by. Many stared. But they seemed to have accepted her statement as truth, at least for the present.

"What're you going to do now?" Chalk Holden asked, catching up with her on the sidewalk. "You can't just walk off from this *alone* without talking to me. Damn it, Amity, I'm worried as hell about you!"

She squared to face him. "I don't mean to be rude. It's just that I'm not used to killing people. I hope I never have to again." She wanted him to take her in his arms, but of course he couldn't in the middle of main street with everyone watching. "I really must go," she said, studying her feet, then looking up at him again. "I've got weeds trying to take over my crops, and —"

"I wish to hell I'd had an inkling of what was going on. I wish I'd been there so you wouldn't have had to do this. But I'd driven up to bring Stella and the kids back to Syracuse for the summer."

She sighed. "What happened couldn't be helped, but thank you. Anyway, it's over. Seymour is gone, Thaddy is safe, and so am I."

"We can't be sure that you're safe. When I think that *anyone* would want to see you dead —" He took his hat off and pushed long fingers through his hair, then shook his head. "*Damn!* I wish you lived here in town where I could keep an eye on things till we're sure there's nothin' more to worry about — If you have any long trips to make, to see your teachers this summer or visit your schools, maybe I can drive you —"

Amity shook her head. She didn't want to hurt his feelings, but as long as she was forced to remain single, she had to take care of herself and Thaddeus. "I promise not to take any chances. How's that?" she said quietly, as Chalk took her arm and they headed for her wagon. "But don't you concern yourself unnecessarily about me, either. You have work of your own, and you can't be everywhere at once." Her voice warmed with pride for him as she went on, "I understand that since the supreme court handed down their decision a week ago making Syracuse the permanent county seat, you may be the most highly regarded and busiest man in the county." She'd read of the ruling in his paper. It was easy to guess how folks felt about him, considering his peaceable contribution to the cause. She'd heard from his sister, Stella, that there were plans afoot to run him for county attorney or better in the next election.

Chalk lifted her into her wagon, and for a long moment they looked at one another. He caught her hand and squeezed it tightly. He turned her palm up and looked at the calluses. "Take care, darling."

She smiled at him. "Of course!" But there was tension in the air, and she knew he wasn't happy to see her drive off, alone.

A few weeks later, Amity delivered some books she had finally received to the Dusky family, staying over to give Will Quick instruction for using the texts. She went away with a feeling of tremendous satisfaction. The young man was going to make a fine teacher, and she was able to give him work he was far more suited to than being a cowpoke.

On more than one occasion, traveling the dusty wagon roads and blind lanes delivering the rest of the books, Amity would see a lone rider in the distance and would know it was Chalk, checking on her, keeping watch. One time, she rode hard to catch up with him, and told him he needn't do it. But he simply insisted that he was out on errands for his newspaper. On that occasion, sure there were only the two of them on the wide plains, they'd kissed for a long time, both hating the hands-off policy they'd had to adopt for the public eye.

One silvery, midsummer dawn, as Amity stepped from the sod barn after milking Flora, a movement to the southeast caught her attention. The rider, loping in a direct line for her soddy, was not Chalk Holden, whom she could always recognize easily and from a distance. This stranger on a big black horse was out early if he was coming from Syracuse. What could he want of her? He looked to be well dressed, no rough and tumble dusty cowboy.

The man, riding in close, tipped his black hat to her in greeting; his fine gray suit showed hardly a speck of dust, and she felt like a grubby peasant by comparison. Lifting her free hand in a wave, she set her bucket of milk down and waited. "What can I do for you, sir?" she called out. He didn't look dangerous, but one could never tell. Thaddeus was still in his bed, and John Clyde had already gone in from choring to eat his breakfast.

"Morning!" The man took off his hat as he climbed down, showing raven black hair salted with gray, worn neat and long behind his ears. He was slim, lithe, not quite as tall as Chalk. His trim beard broke to reveal an engaging smile. Nice crinkly eyes, she thought, but those were surface things; he could be the devil himself. "You're Miss Whitford — Miss Amity Whitford?"

She nodded. "I am." Something about his finely etched features, the intense gray-blue of his eyes, seemed slightly familiar. "Do I know *you*?"

"I don't believe so. My name is Peter Shields." He had a mellow voice, very self-assured. "I've come a long way, looking for you. Looking for my son."

"Looking for . . . ?" Her heart began to pound, and her hand crept up to cover her mouth. Her mind refused to believe what her eyes were telling her: this man was an older version of her very own Thad! "I don't know what you're talking about!" she said, bristling.

His manner was serious, but kind. "I'm sorry. But I have it on good authority that my son lives here with you. The woman you knew as Chloe Brady was my lawful wife. She had a little boy, Thaddeus."

"No, there's no boy here." She was breathing hard, feeling near to fainting. "You might as well

413

get back on your horse and leave. I don't know what you're talking about, but you're on private land, my land. And I don't welcome strangers."

"Miss Whitford. I have a legal right to my son. I want to see him, talk to him. If you'll give me a chance —" He broke off as the back door opened and Thaddy stepped out, hair uncombed, rubbing his eyes sleepily, only one suspender fastened. He stopped in his tracks, seeing the stranger with Amity. He shaded his eyes against the morning sun, watching them for a moment. Then, when neither of the adults said anything, the boy ran forward to stand protectively close to Amity.

Shields stepped forward almost involuntarily. His eyes on Thaddeus sparkled with fascination, giving further rise to Amity's alarm. The man could be lying; just because he had the same coloring and similar features meant nothing, really. Chloe had given Thaddy to her to raise and no one could ride in and claim him.

"Go inside. Go on, son," she told Thaddy, pushing him away. Her heart was so gripped with fear she was barely able to maintain any semblance of calm. She snapped, "Go in, right now, I said!" She'd never spoken so sharply to Thaddeus before. He stared at her for a moment, confusion and hurt in his young face, then he turned obediently and headed for the house, looking back over his shoulder twice. Her heart went out to him, but she couldn't call him back to apologize. She wanted him inside, safe.

"Now —" Amity faced the man who called himself Peter Shields "— I want you to clear out of here. I know enough of Chloe's story — I saw enough of how she lived — to know that it's not possible she was married to anyone like you. You with your fine clothes, and expensive horse. You obviously live a good life. But Chloe and Thaddy were in desperate straits when I found them! You have no claim on that boy in there!" *And if you did have any sort of claim at all, it would be nothing to what Thaddeus is to me.* "Do I have to get a gun, or will you go while you're still healthy and all of a piece?"

Chapter Twenty-eight

The dark, handsome stranger held his ground, as solid as a block of granite, increasing Amity's apprehension. He spoke softly, with control. "I could leave and come back with legal papers or the sheriff, but I don't think you want that, Amity Whitford. I think you'd prefer to hear me out first." He smiled, sincerity in his eyes. "You don't look like the kind who'd kill in cold blood, anyway. Why not invite me in to talk this over? I believe I smelled fresh coffee boiling when the boy came out? I'd appreciate a cup, very much."

Nothing he could say or do would convince her to give up Thaddeus, and she intended to make that very clear. She invited him in with ice in her tone. "All right, I agree to hear you out, and you're welcome to coffee. Please come in."

John Clyde was about to strap on his gun when they walked through the door. Thad must have told him about the stranger who'd brought such a change in his Ammy. "It's all right, John Clyde. This is Mr. Shields. We'd like to talk privately. If you and Thad have eaten, would you please see to Mr. Shields's horse? Then go ahead and hitch our horses to bring in the new hay from the west field. I'll join you soon." Her eyes said *Guard the boy with your life.* John Clyde seemed to catch her meaning, and sized up the stranger with a keen eye. He nodded, and with his hand on Thaddy's shoulder, they left.

Peter Shields's inquisitive glance was glued to the door the boy had passed through for a full minute. Finally, he sat down and took the cup of coffee she held out to him. She remained standing, hands on her hips, defying him to say one word that would alter her thinking. Her mind was made up, regardless of anything he might tell her. "Mr. Shields, if you were married to Chloe, as you say, why did she use the name Brady?"

He stroked his salt-and-pepper beard, a look of sad self-recrimination clouded his gray eyes. He was silent so long, she thought he might not answer, but then he told her, "Chloe was afraid of me. She was hiding from me — rather, from the wild hellion I used to be."

His honesty surprised her. Her mouth dried. Whatever could he have done to make Chloe so afraid of him, fine-looking gentleman that he was, that she would run away, change her name, live as she did — hand-to-mouth? "What did you do to her? Why was she afraid of you?" *Should I be?*

"Allow me to begin at the beginning, please?"

"You've got about two minutes." She used a harsh tone. Although she didn't feel in physical danger from him, she felt inestimably threatened in other ways. "That's all the time I can give you." Despairing and shaky on her feet, she took a chair and plunked into it. What a turn of events! She motioned for him to go ahead.

He laughed softly. "You don't give a man much leeway, do you?"

She pressed her tongue between her lips and waited, arms folded.

He shrugged and spoke. "When I met Chloe, I was a carefree, aimless, spoiled young man, studying medicine at the University of Kansas in Lawrence. The truth is, I was there simply to be with my best friend. He was the one really serious about the future — I had no real goals of my own. Except one — I didn't want to follow in my father's footsteps as the 'cornstarch king' of Iowa. I didn't care to inherit management of the family mills in Des Moines." A dark expression filled his face, he spoke quietly, "My hard-working, hard-studying, undernourished buddy died of consumption. It should've been me. I was the useless one.

"Losing him," he went on, "was the worst thing that had ever happened to me. Right after he died, I tried to take up his dreams, but as hard as I tried to apply myself, it didn't work. I wasn't Todd. I started drinking heavily, carousing, taking life as it came without giving a damn about anything.

"That's when I met Chloe. Beautiful Chloe. I was passing a market one day on the way to yet another saloon. She'd come to market in a wagon filled with bushels of red apples to sell. I couldn't take my eyes off her. She was so fresh faced, her cheeks as rosy as those apples. Her smile was like sunshine. I was staggering drunk — she had to know it — but when I stumbled and fell she came to help me up."

Amity held her breath while Peter Shields struggled to maintain his composure, to do battle with his feelings of guilt. He finally went on, "After that, I passed that market a dozen times a day, hoping to see her again. I even cleaned up a little, left the bottle alone for a while."

"Go on." Amity cleared her throat. "You must have finally found her again?"

He nodded. "Just when I thought I'd never lay eyes on her again, I was directed to where she lived, on an old farm that she ran with her mother's help. Chloe's father was shiftless and mean. We fell in love, Chloe and I, but I couldn't leave demon rum alone for long." He sighed. "I resented her insisting that I change. I accused her of not liking men in general, which, because of her father's treatment of her, wasn't far off the truth. We talked of marriage, but she kept putting it off because of my carousing. When Chloe," he said softly, "became pregnant, she was disowned. Her pa threw her out. She agreed to marry me since she had no other choice. We fought some. One night, I drank too much, and we argued about another woman I'd dallied with . . . I . . . I struck Chloe. Lovely Chloe, and

419

my child —" A terrible anguish filled Shields's face. "She fell with our baby in her arms. His mouth was cut on the iron fender around our stove. That's all she needed. To protect the baby, Chloe ran away. Vanished. With my child, our son."

"I don't blame her for leaving," Amity said acidly. "I would've done the same. She had to protect her child, and herself as well. Chloe was a wonderful woman, a fine mother. That strength is there in her son. He got only his looks from you, and a scar on his mouth."

Shields spoke in a low, tormented voice. "I hated what I did to Chloe and the baby. I tried in every way to find her, make it up to them, show her how sorry I was. But it was as if she'd disappeared off the face of the earth. She'd always been independent and clever."

"And afraid of you," Amity reminded him tartly, "for sufficient reason."

"Yes," he agreed, sighing, "she — was afraid of me. Her leaving knocked the sense into me I'd been badly needing, but by then it was too late. She was gone. I loved her," he said simply, "with all my heart. I wanted her and the infant back so badly. I stopped drinking; just the sight of a bottle reminded me of what I'd done. I went home and ran my father's mill for a while. In time, when I couldn't find her, I wondered if Chloe had found someone else. I used to dream that she had, and I prayed she was happy, had someone to take care of her. I came close to marrying twice, but I couldn't forget Chloe."

"My," Amity said with a disdainful sniff, giving him no quarter. His claim to be a different person now was obviously his bid for sympathy — a way to soften her to get what he wanted. It wouldn't work. With that past, he seemed poor goods for a father. She felt relief about that. She'd fight him with everything she had, but he wouldn't get *her* boy.

His dark eyes showed no rebuttal, no anger. He smiled complacently, as though he welcomed her chastising look for the costly mistakes he'd made in life. "I returned to Kansas to search for her many times," he went on. "A few times I believed I'd found her but they were false leads. When my parents died, I decided I didn't want to continue producing cornstarch. I sold my holdings and moved to the Flint Hills of eastern Kansas. The closest I'd ever felt to finding Chloe was in that area, though I couldn't locate her."

Amity shrugged off a momentary feeling of sympathy. With resumed stiffness, she asked him, "What do you do, Mr. Shields?"

"I'm a rancher; I raise cattle. I live alone with a cook and housekeeper, my ranch hands. Except when I'm in Topeka at the statehouse. A few years ago I got into politics —"

Her breath nearly left her, and she asked quietly, "You're State Representative Shields?"

His face crinkled in a devilish grin. "Last time I looked in the mirror, I was."

She wanted to strike him, both for the grin

421

and his superior position.

He didn't seem to notice. "I try to do what I can for people, remembering Todd, my college friend, remembering what I did to Chloe." He shook his head, and his jaw set. "I couldn't believe it, when I saw her homestead, and her grave. People who lived the way she did are difficult to trace."

"Likely, that was her reason. How did you find her?"

"She'd taken a different name, not even her maiden name, which was Jenkins. Eastern Kansas newspapers carried the story when she died — an odd woman who had struggled for years to homestead out from Great Bend. Chloe's an unusual enough name — and since her boy was the right age, I began checking it out. I've always followed anything that seemed like a lead. I was shocked that she'd raised our son in such crude surroundings, so minimal an existence." He looked grim. "I could have given her so much — everything. I wanted to. But of course, she didn't know that I'd changed; she would only have remembered the unfaithful, drunken lout who struck her."

"Unfortunately," Amity sniped unkindly, but he didn't seem to mind. Her chin jutted up. "How did you find me?"

"You'd reported Chloe's death to the Great Bend authorities. They remembered you. When you sold Chloe's stock to a trader in Great Bend, you talked about your own place. After that it was a matter of getting on the train to Syracuse, hiring a horse, and riding out here."

"That's too bad, because you cannot have Thaddeus."

"More than anything else in life," Peter Shields said, "I want to do right by my son. I want him with me. I want to raise him, give him what I should have given his mother. Make up to her memory for what I did."

Amity bridled, her heart filled with apprehension that the greatest loss of all her living life could be even remotely possible. It must never happen! "I'd say you're much too late to help Chloe, and the boy doesn't need you. He's very happy with me. I'm sorry, Mr. Shields, but for all your claim that you're his natural father, the boy doesn't know you. You and his mother weren't even together beyond his baby days. You're a perfect stranger to him — and to me. It's preposterous of you to expect me to accept your story and just hand over the boy. In all ways except blood, he is my son, my own son."

Shields studied her face for a very long moment, his eyes shrewd but revealing little of what he was thinking. "May I have more coffee?" He held up his cup and she went to the kitchen stove and brought back the pot to pour for him. Her hand shook and she spilled a scalding splash onto her thumb. She wiped it on her apron.

Inside she was trembling like a leaf and she had to sit down after filling her own cup. She fought the further realization that, if this man

423

was telling her the truth, he could give Thaddeus everything she could not — now, at least. Someday, things would be better here at Dove's Nest, for all of them. For now, she could give the boy a decently good life, a whole lot of loving. And when she and Chalk could marry, she'd give him a father, too. She was confident that Thaddeus would never leave her for this stranger. Thaddy loved her. He loved his "old John" like a grandfather. Loved the ranch almost as much as the home he'd shared with his true mother. No, he wouldn't go.

She'd been so deep in thought, it was a moment before she saw that Peter Shields had taken a photograph from his hidden pocket and put it on the table in front of her.

Dismay wracked her, and her heart went very still. There was no denying what her eyes could clearly see.

Amity gazed down at a young and beautiful Chloe, a wealth of wavy hair falling to her shoulders, the curve of her cheek fresh and innocent. She was wrapped in the arms of a younger Peter Shields. They were both smiling, the most handsome couple she'd ever laid eyes on. And they looked like Thaddeus, both of them. For a long time, she couldn't speak. When she finally found her voice, she told Shields, "What you're showing me indicates you did know Chloe, but that's all. Thaddeus's mother gave him to me. I gave her my solemn vow that I'd always take care of him, raise him as my own. He's all I have." *In all*

424

likelihood, all I will ever have. "He is very, very happy here. You can't uproot him, take him off to a strange place. It would be terribly unfair."

Peter Shields stood up, and going to the west window, pulled back the lace curtain to watch Thaddy driving off for the hay field with John Clyde. "I would never force him. But I do want to get to know my son, Miss Whitford, and I want him to get to know me. For now, that's all I ask. And I beg you to remember, he *is* my son."

You once hurt him, and you wronged his mother, her heart argued. Yet she was well aware that this man had money, power, and all manner of means to take Thaddy from her if he so chose. Better to let him visit the boy now and then, while she searched for a way to prevent this terrible thing. There might be a chance, if Peter Shields was truly the decent sort he appeared, that he would let the boy stay with her for good when he saw how content Thaddeus was — saw how much she'd taught him and how much more she could teach him. It would be tragic to fight over him like dogs for a bone. An intelligent man like Shields would see that.

As though he'd detected from her manner that she'd come to a decision, Peter Shields turned, his thick dark brows raised in question.

"You may visit the boy here on the ranch. As long as your visits don't interfere, don't disrupt his life here, or make him unhappy in any way. I must have your solemn promise that you'll not reveal to anyone, Thaddy especially, that — that you believe you're his father, without discussing it with me before you do."

Shields reached out and took her hand. "Thank you." She thought she detected tears shining in the blue-gray eyes. She'd often seen Thaddy's glimmer just so.

At the window, she watched Peter Shields mount his horse and lope out to the field where John Clyde and Thaddeus raked and pitched hay, side by side. Shields got down and stood talking to the pair for some time. Once he reached out a hand as though to touch Thaddy's head, then he let the hand drop. It was all she could do not to run screaming for Thaddy not to let Shields near him. Instead she stood stock-still, her feelings taut, ready to explode. She had never wished real ill on another human being, but at the moment she was close. "Go away!" she whispered, her voice cracking. "Go away and never come back! Oh, God, never!"

When Thaddy came to the house later for a piece of cornbread and jam to hold him till supper, he questioned her about the stranger. Hiding her tension under a facade of calm, Amity explained simply that Mr. Shields was an acquaintance who might be coming to visit them now and then. Impulsively, she pulled the boy to her from behind, arms crossed tightly in front of him, her cheek lowered to press hard against his. "You do like it here at Dove's Nest with John Clyde and me? You're happy, aren't you, son?"

At the desperation in her voice, he turned in her arms and cocked a glance at her as though she were daft. He licked at the jam in the corner of his mouth. "Sure, Ammy. Gotta go." He pulled away. "John's waitin' for me to bring him a jar of buttermilk and some corn bread."

She smiled, patted him, and let him go. But the fear in her heart that she might lose him stayed.

John Clyde, of course, would mind his own business, would never question her about her personal life unless he felt she was in danger of some kind. If he'd seen something he didn't like in Peter Shields, he'd never have gone to the hay field, in spite of her orders.

In the weeks of summer that followed, the blistering heat sapped Amity's energy, but she couldn't allow that to make a difference with the monumental chores facing her; they had to be done. Cultivating her row crops, haying, picking and preserving wild plums, gathering medicinal roots and herbs to dry. Searching out edible plants to fill out the endless, necessary meals from her pantry. Coming out of bed each morning she was more tired than the day before.

Peter Shields's intrusion on her life put her constantly on edge, although she had to admit in many ways he was the perfect guest. Twice he'd returned to Dove's Nest. Leaving his well-made coat in the house, he'd rolled up his shirtsleeves and pitched right in, helping John Clyde and Thaddeus cut and haul hay, telling them jokes, laughing at theirs. Nor was he above filling the water bucket for her kitchen, or bringing in a basket of fuel when she needed to cook. At mealtimes, like today, Peter regaled them with stories of life at the capitol, or at his ranch.

He knew Teddy Roosevelt, and had been a guest at Roosevelt's ranch on the Missouri in North Dakota where they hunted buffalo and talked politics. Teddy, or "Teedie" as he was better known, had visited Shields in the Flint Hills to buy cattle.

"Finest meal I've had this week," Shields took a moment to compliment her, dark brow lifted, smiling. He refilled his plate with fried potatoes, boiled beans with ham, and fresh cooked greens. Between bites, he told them about another fellow they might have heard of named Frederic Remington. He worked as a cowhand on a neighboring ranch in Butler County. Peter and Remington often hunted and worked cattle together.

Unable to contain her interest, Amity blurted, "You mean the artist who sends sketches of the west to *Harper's*. You know him?"

Shield told her with a smile, "He came out here to Kansas a few years ago for his health, you know, after he finished at Yale Art School. He's no great shakes as a cowhand, but he does fine artwork."

"I understand that Easterners want to think we're a great deal more violent and trigger-happy than we really are out here. So that's how Remington paints us," Amity said, mostly for Thaddeus's benefit. He was so agog at Shields's stories, he gulped his food and forgot to swallow. It would have given Amity a host of pleasure to find the man a liar. Unfortunately, she believed he told the truth, mostly.

It was impossible to keep Thaddy away from him, or vice versa.

That evening out in the backyard, with chores done and a few hours of daylight left, Shields taught Thaddeus how to build a box-trap to capture prairie chickens, then helped him make a slingshot worthy of the one David used to kill Goliath. Amity had brought her rocker just outside the back door to watch them, and there she rocked and worried. Shields had brought presents for Thaddeus, too: a three-volume set of books in the Sailor Boys series, jack-straws, a stereoscope, a handsome bicycle — better suited to the city. These gifts she couldn't give Thaddy had sent the youngster into spasms of delight, and made her so jealous she could hardly see straight. It wasn't fair.

At the moment, the boy and the man were silhouetted against the darkening sky as Peter showed Thaddy how to hold the slingshot and aim. Thad said something and Shields's laughing reply sounded of fatherly pride and affection. In their coop, her chickens clucked quietly as they settled for the night. Down by the creek, the mourning doves cooed their sad refrain.

"I'll be taking that slingshot away," Amity suddenly called to Thaddeus and Shields in a sharp tone, "the minute I see it aimed at my chickens. There will be no firing of stones at doves just because they're wild, either!" No one had to tell her how ridiculous she sounded. Amity felt ugly and mean, and she hated herself. At the very least, she ought to be happy for Thaddeus that he'd found his father after losing his mother when he was just a tad. But it was hard, so hard, knowing she was probably losing him that there was little she could do to stop herself.

If only Peter Shields had never found Chloe's homestead; if only he'd never traced the boy to her, here at Dove's Nest. Thaddeus would've been just as happy. He didn't need the expensive toys Shields gave him. Shields could never love him any more than she did, even if he was the boy's father.

Shields departed for Syracuse early the next morning to catch his train back to the Flint Hills. Amity was glad to see him go. She wished the earth would just open up and swallow him for good. A few more visits, and Thaddeus would be so attached to him, Shields would be begging to tell Thad their true relationship.

The possibility nagged at her daily, creating an anger inside her that threatened to explode. During a slack summer afternoon, she decided to use the time to put new shoes on the horses, a process her old Ben had never particularly cared for, though he was docile in ordinary circumstances. In the barnyard, Amity stood at Ben's head to keep him calm, while John Clyde, his back to Amity, held the horse's left front hoof in his leather-aproned lap, paring away at it with a chisel. After a while, she released Ben's halter to wipe her perspiring brow with her apron. The flutter of white in the horse's face startled him and he reared sideways, sending John Clyde sprawling to the ground. "What the goddamned hell!" John Clyde exploded, rolling out of the way of the shying horse. Ben whinnied shrilly.

"I'm sorry," Amity said, wiping her face and smoothing the apron down. She felt weighted from the heat, from stress. "But I couldn't help it. It won't happen again."

John Clyde dusted himself off. "I can do this by myself. Go on to the house and get some rest, Missy." He didn't really show anger, but he said, catching Ben's halter, "Your fidgetin' is makin' this horse nervous an' it ain't doin' me no good, neither." He stroked the long neck. "There old hoss, there now. Calm down, ain't nothin' hurtin' ya."

Amity's mind snapped. "I said I was sorry. And I'll thank you to remember that I'm the boss here, Mr. Rossback! Ben is my horse. This is my ranch. No one tells me what to do, till I'm ready." She bit the inside of her cheek. "If I could keep that boy off that infernal bicycle, he'd be here helping you and I wouldn't have to."

"An' mebbe he'd get kicked in the head, the

way you got this animal riled up!" John Clyde looked at her sternly. "Now, Missy, please, go on to the house and let me do my work."

"Ohhh, fudge!" She snatched up her skirts and stomped away. Out in the stubbled west field, Thaddeus wobbled a fast path on his bike, Zip racing along with him, barking. A brown cottontail rabbit sailed along ahead of them, out of reach. Amity went the other direction toward the creek where it was cooler, to try and get herself together. It was as though she couldn't do anything right anymore. She felt weepy at the least cause; she snapped unjustly at those she loved. It had been a while since Chalk had come by. Compounding that heartache was Shields's determined drive to know his son and win him away from her. Lord, sometimes it was just too much.

After a bit, the turmoil of her feelings eased and she heaved a heavy sigh. She was thinking of getting to her feet and going back to the house when Chalk rode up. She turned to watch his approach, her heart pounding with excitement. He dismounted and sauntered over to where she sat. His hat was tilted forward, shading his face against the bright sunlight. Fighting for composure, she suppressed an urge to jump up and throw herself into his arms, let him kiss her until she was mindless.

Just the sight of him, though, was a touch of heaven.

"Hello, Amity."

"Chalk," she replied quietly, getting to her feet. "What's brought you to Dove's Nest? Not an emergency, I hope?"

He shook his head and removed his hat taking a moment to study her without seeming to. "Joe Samuels happened to mention that you've been entertaining an important visitor pretty regularly this summer. I thought you might have a story for my paper."

So that was it. The important Mr. Shields. She caught a strand of hair that blew into her eyes and tucked it behind her ear. Was that a note of jealousy she detected in his voice? "Not really," she said huskily. "Mr. Shields is an old family friend, and he enjoys visiting the ranch." The lie came easily; it was the answer she'd given to the few who had asked. Peter Shields did remind her of the old days in Cairo. He was very much like the people in her parents' social circle: moneyed, cultured, interesting. She was not about to reveal to anyone, even Chalk, that the man was her Thaddy's father and that he meant to take her boy from her. Because it wouldn't happen — if she could stop it. And that was the main thing she had to deal with *now*. *She* was gambling, risking everything, but she saw no other way to try and keep her Thaddy than to allow Shields's visits.

Amity sighed heavily. "Would you like to stay for supper?" Inviting Chalk was the civil thing to do. But later, at the table, it was hard to keep her hungry eyes from his face; she had to keep her hands busy so as not to reach out and touch him. She must look haggard and awful to him. He'd taken her aside for a brief moment to ask if she was feeling all right.

Throughout the meal, Chalk talked animatedly about Peter Shields. He seemed to know all about him as a statesman from the papers he received gratis from fellow publishers, particularly those in the eastern part of the state. "He's a good, straight-thinking gent, for a politician. I'll bet he's got some thoughts how Kansans might depend less on the government and help themselves in these times of boom and bust."

"Possibly," Amity murmured. Peter spent so much time with Thaddeus when he was there, she'd never gotten around to talking issues with him, but she couldn't explain that to Chalk. "Is there something you want, Chalk? I've a feeling you're asking a favor of me, in a roundabout way." She'd rarely seen him as galvanized as he was this evening talking about Shields, and she felt almost hurt. In a way, he seemed hardly aware of *her*. He probably didn't notice that Thaddeus and John Clyde had left the table to go outside.

Chalk sat back in his chair. "I'd give anything to meet the man, spend a little time discussing with him some problems we have here in our part of the state. If he comes again, could I get an invite?"

Amity wished that he'd forget about Shields and everything else but themselves. Her voice, when she responded, was flat. "If you like, next time Mr. Shields visits, I'll send you word and you can join us for supper."

Chalk's head came up quickly, he looked at her shrewdly. "You don't like Shields? I thought he was your invited guest. What do you find wrong with him?"

"I don't remember saying I didn't like him. Mr. Shields is an intelligent gentleman, yet very down to earth. There's nothing wrong with him, basically. There's certainly more interesting things he could be doing, so his visiting us is a surprise — and an honor. That's all I was thinking."

Chalk growled, "You're enough to bring him here. A man doesn't need any other reason."

Amity's spirits lifted at once. All evening Chalk had been distant, and now — His flattering comment was like an arrow placing a direct hit. "Would you like more lemonade?" She pushed back from the table so hard she almost tipped her chair over. After refilling their glasses, she determined to change the subject. "It's been ages since any of us have been to town. What's new in Syracuse? I understand from neighbors that the new courthouse is all but finished, three stories, limestone and brick? It must be quite imposing." Before he could reply, she asked what she really wanted to know. "How — how is Mrs. Strout taking her cousin's — death?" On top of everything else, Amity had worried about Thisba getting wind of *Shields's visits* and using it against her.

With his thumb, Chalk pushed his spectacles higher onto the bridge of his nose, his eyes thoughtful. "The Taylor building is about finished. You're going to have a really decent office to move into this fall. Thisba's got herself busy of late, planning all kinds of ways to raise money to buy furniture and supplies for the new courthouse."

When Thaddeus and John Clyde came back in, Amity did her best to behave normally as the four of them played a few hands of Old Maid, with cards that were a gift from Shields. She was so aware of Chalk's proximity, though, it was hard to concentrate even on the simple game. When it came time for him to leave, she walked with him along the moonlit path to the barn where his horse was tethered.

They stood in the shadows, facing each other without touching. He spoke quietly, "Amity, Shields wasn't my only reason for riding out here tonight."

She waited, wondering if he wanted to talk about them; their future, their relationship. Because if he did, she had something to say that was going to surprise him.

"I came to warn you." His voice deepened. "I did some digging about Thisba's past in old records and newspapers. That 'accident' of her brother's was damned suspicious. Hardly suicide as Seymour called it. There's nothing to fear from Purdue anymore, but in my estimation, Thisba's capable of anything — and for her own insane reasons, she's got it in for you. For God's sake, Amity, keep an eye out. Take care of yourself."

She nodded in the dark and waited for Chalk to beg her to marry him, as he often did. She was ready to tell him *yes*. Not so he could take care of her or keep her safe from Thisba — she hardly cared about that; she could take care of herself. But they loved one another and they'd make wonderful parents; and maybe if they were married, were a true family, Peter Shields would let her keep Thaddeus. Even if she and Chalk didn't marry immediately, they could set a date; she could begin proceedings to clear the matter with the county board, and she would inform Mr. Lawhead, the state superintendent, and . . . She waited, and waited, and waited. But this time Chalk didn't ask.

Chapter Twenty-nine

Misgivings ate at Amity's heart as Peter Shields continued to be a frequent visitor during the long, hot weeks of summer. Thaddy clearly was starting to worship the man. Peter, just as obviously, adored his son. Perhaps she had been wrong to allow Peter even one visit. But if she'd denied him, he could've brought his legal papers, and the authorities might have let him take Thaddeus from her before now. This way, at least, Thaddy was still with her, and a miracle granted by God might prevent his being taken. Of all these things, Amity wrote in her journal nightly, when she couldn't sleep.

The moment she had been prepared to tell Chalk she'd marry him had come and gone. If he should ever ask again, she wasn't sure what her answer would be. She was so in love with him it was like a disease. To the point she could even believe that the power of their love might overcome the misfortunes of her past. But he behaved differently toward her, as if he had something on his mind he couldn't share with her. He was civil, kindly, even affectionate in a friendly way, but it wasn't enough; she craved more. It truly plagued her that he might have finally given up on *them,* perhaps even found someone else.

To compound matters, after his first meeting with Peter Shields, Chalk managed to show up at Dove's Nest as often and at the same time as Peter did. The men would ride out together after Peter's train got in. Usually, Chalk would take over her part of the chores, helping John Clyde while Peter played with Thad. At dinner and after Thaddy's bedtime, the two men never seemed to run out of subjects for heated, but friendly, discussion. Whether the chief topic of the evening was better integration of new immigrants to help settle and civilize the plains; a more dependable tax base to support a steady, permanent population; the civilizing influences of schools, churches, literary societies; or the growth possibilities of the small towns, the conversations fell under one heading, *What's Good For Kansas,* the plains in particular.

Amity joined the discussions and both men seemed to welcome her opinions. She had to admit she enjoyed the stimulating evenings.

"Water is a big answer to many western Kansas problems. Irrigation," Chalk was saying one evening as the three of them sat outside in the yard talking. Down by the creek, the mourning doves cooed. From the general direction of the barnyard could be heard the faint coaxing laughter of Thaddeus, and the sharp, joyful barking of the dog. "The Arkansas River should be utilized here in

Hamilton County more than it is. We could have canals from the river, like they have around Garden City. We could be an Eden, too. Raise sorghum for sugar, put through some bonds to pay for sugar mills —"

"No," Amity shook her head emphatically. "That's prairie over there, and best suited to production of vegetables and fruit. The plains should be left alone for raising stock. And maybe wheat. One way to provide water for our cattle is to dam the draws so they create reservoirs in times of decent rainfall. But this is cattle country; I'm finding that out more every day. And raising stock is what I intend to get into, in a big way, eventually."

"I agree about the plains." Peter nodded, leaning forward to prop his elbows on his knees, dark bearded chin in his hands. "When Coloradans take their share of the Arkansas River for irrigation, it could get down to a trickle in these parts. The expense of those canals would be for nought. This is cow country." He sat back, hands behind his head, grinning at Amity. "If you're getting into the cattle business on a serious basis, Miss Whitford, I could sell you a seed herd, maybe thirty head, of purebred Hereford calves. That'd start you off."

She stood up, smiling down at him. "Mr. Shields, when I have the money, you just might have a deal." Hearing a commotion down at the barn, she asked, "What is that boy up to with that racket?"

Chalk started to say something, but Shields cut him off, telling her, "He and that dog of his, old Zip, are trying to dig a ground squirrel from its burrow out back of the barn. I think the varmint probably dug his way into Colorado to outrun them, but a boy and a dog have to do these things," he said tolerantly.

"Well, I hope they don't disturb John Clyde. He's resting in his quarters in the barn. Thaddy and Zip can get pretty noisy." She didn't mean to stop them, though. It gave her a great deal of satisfaction when Thaddy abandoned his fancy new toys to find his fun right here on the ranch.

Chalk interjected quietly, "You both sound like you have a claim on the boy, like an old married couple."

Amity gasped. Though Peter had the audacity to laugh, she darted a look of astonishment at Chalk. She was glad she had, because if that wasn't jealousy in his eyes, she'd never seen it anywhere. "Excuse me," she said primly. "I'll be right back with some gingerbread and coffee." She swept to the back door, smiling to herself.

She returned with the cumbersome tray and both men started to their feet, but Shields was faster. Chalk glared, his jaw hardening as Shields motioned for Amity to sit down while he held the tray, waiting for her to help herself.

"Thank you, Peter."

"You'd look right nice in an apron, Shields," Chalk growled as he balanced his saucer of gingerbread on one big knee, and took a steaming

441

cup of coffee. It was supposed to be a joke, but the smile wasn't there.

They ate quietly, Chalk's brows knit in a scowl, Peter placidly enjoying the refreshments. Amity's thoughts raced. *Jealous*. Here she'd believed Chalk was only coming out to Dove's Nest because he so admired Peter Shields and wanted to share ideas with him, as well as to get stories for his paper. But it was more than that, and it had to do with her. Chalk came because he didn't want her alone with Peter any more than was necessary!

She knew she was right a while later when Peter went to fetch Thaddeus to tell him it was time to turn in, and she and Chalk were alone for a minute in the yard.

"Where does Shields sleep?" Chalk asked bluntly.

"I beg your pardon!"

"Shields doesn't sleep in the house, does he?"

"Of course he doesn't. Peter's a gentleman. He sleeps in the barn. But I don't know that it's your affair where my guests sleep!" Or *anyone else's*. Dear God, if the gossips didn't leave her alone . . .

An angry snort of dismissal and a chopping motion of his arm was Chalk's reply as he stalked off in the direction of the barn where his horse was tied. He had never stayed the night, always having too much work awaiting him in town, and more, importantly wanting to preserve her good reputation.

Amity watched his tall, shadowy figure move

into the night. Her feeling of joy that he cared so much returned. She covered her mouth with both hands to smother a giggle, and then fairly danced her way along the path to the house.

After settling Thad into his bed, she got into her nightgown and scribbled a few happy notes in her journal. Then, she went to lean just inside her back door, waiting for the men to vanish from her yard so she could go to the outhouse. Male voices rumbled enticingly loud and she cracked the door just a bit, surprised Chalk hadn't yet ridden out.

"You're in love with her, you know goddamned well you are!" Chalk was insisting. "You came here to find her. There was something between the two of you in the old days, right? Now you want her back, you're trying to win her, and damn it, man, she's in love with me. Or she was till you came!"

Oh, Chalk, you fool, hush!

"Hell, yes, I'm attracted to her. She's beautiful — a spunky woman any man would claim if he could. But that isn't what I'm here for."

Amity's breath caught, her nails biting into her palms as she clenched her fists. *No, no —*

But Peter was saying smoothly, "It's none of your business, Holden, why I'm here, but it's not what you think, and I have no wish to hurt anybody. If you want your woman, hell, man, marry her. If you don't, I make no promises."

Amity crossed her legs tightly and waited for them to finish their stupid discussion. A short

443

while later, they seemed to come to some kind of understanding. She could even picture them shaking hands before Chalk rode out on his horse and Peter went to the barn.

A few days later, Chalk returned alone and Amity wasn't surprised. His manner was agitated, his face set in a dogged, worried frown. He looked tired, despondent, at the end of his tether.

He was a tall shadow tailing her as she moved about the backyard, doing laundry. They exchanged a few polite, meaningless words. She could almost feel sorry for him in his misery. He helped her carry the tub of hot water from her open fire to the laundry bench closer to the house, stood by as she shaved soap into the steaming water from a yellow bar. Watched as she scrubbed garment after garment on a washboard, then dipped them in a second tub of cold water before wringing them out and dropping them into a basket. She let him stew in his own juices, perfectly aware of what was on his mind, but not about to aid him in his foolishness. *Jealous.* As if she could ever care for another man, as in love with this one as she was!

"Shields comes here a hell of a lot, doesn't he?" Chalk finally came out with it as he dogged her tracks to the clothesline.

"Quite often." She chose a pair of Thaddy's overalls to pin on the line.

"Why?"

"We're old friends, I told you."

"You've told me nothing! Aren't you worried

444

about scandal? I'm supposed to keep *my* distance. Now he keeps coming out here and you act like it's just fine."

"Chalk Holden, don't use that tone with me." She pinned John Clyde's shirt to the line, and then a pair of his trousers.

"He's in love with you, Amity. At first I was kind of glad to see him here, a good strong, decent fella. I felt you were safer with him *and* John around. But I don't want Shields here anymore, 'cause he's in love with you."

She felt her face heat up, but she tried to breathe naturally. "I don't know what you're talking about."

"Shields. I'm talkin' about Shields. A man knows when another man wants his woman. Is that what you want? Do you want him?" he asked belligerently. "Sure you do. He's well known in high places, he's rich, he's got the kind of looks females fall all over themselves for, and he's crazy about you."

"Chalk Holden," she said through clenched teeth, "you're talking the most outright nonsense that's ever come to my ears."

"Oh, yeah, really? Then what's he doing, coming here all the time? And if you're not in love with him, why do you let him stay? Why is he welcome here at all? Surely a man like him's got better things to do than travel clear out here all the time to the end of goddamned nowhere!"

"Nowhere, is it? My place is *nowhere?* And I'll thank you not to swear, please."

"Goddamn it all to hell!" he stormed. "If you don't have designs on Shields, and he sure can give you a world more than I can at the moment, I want you to tell me what's going on!"

"You're being childish, Chalk Holden. Your jealousy is totally unnecessary." Oh, Lord, it was, it was so unnecessary. Tears welled now in her eyes. "You're the only man I could ever love, but maybe it's a good thing circumstances have kept us from marrying. I don't want to quarrel. That's not how I want to live, and —"

"Then tell me why that man keeps coming here. Tell me that."

A few minutes ago she'd been going to tell him the truth. She'd delayed because they'd had so few opportunities to talk when Thad wasn't around, and she certainly didn't want to discuss the situation in front of Peter. At the same time, she admitted that acknowledging Peter and Thad's relationship in words wasn't going to be easy for her. She wanted to tell Chalk. But he had made her so confounded angry, there was no way she'd tell him now. He had to learn to trust her love for him. "He has his reasons that have nothing to do with me!"

"Maybe that was true when he started coming here, but the man is in love with you now. And I don't want him here!"

"*You* don't want him here?" Amity began, but Chalk stormed off, got on his horse, and rode away before she could go on. Well, he'd just have to wait a while to get his explanation if this was

446

the way he was going to behave.

"Stella!" Amity exclaimed a few days later after opening her door to a soft knock. "Do come in!" Although Amity was sure Chalk had sent his sister, she was more than glad for another woman to talk to. "Please excuse the mess. As you can see, I'm up to my elbows in syrup making."

"It smells delicious in here, and what a cozy place!" Stella said, looking around before taking a chair.

"Thank you. The reason for the good smell, I suppose, is all that." She waved her hand at the herbs hanging in bunches from her ceiling: sage, licorice, soapweed, goldenrod. Seasoning herbs, soapweed for cleaning, goldenrod for tea. "And this is prickly pear syrup I'm boiling down today. Thaddy gets so tired of sorghum on his flapjacks and he purely loves this." She scooped some in a teaspoon, blew on it, and handed it to Stella.

"Mmm, very good." Stella smacked her lips. "Prickly pear, you say? Now that's one thing we didn't have in Baltimore." Her eyes danced with good humor.

"Well, we have it in abundance in the sandhills and my boy and I gather all we can. Peeled, the pulp is delicious as a fresh fruit. It also makes a fine poultice for wounds and bruises — a versatile plant, to say the least. But you didn't come here today to hear about my gathering and preserving . . . ?"

Stella shook her head. "I heard a rumor from the other teachers that you've come by some extra books, readers. Will I get some for Hudson School?"

"Oh, Stella, I apologize for not getting up north or into Syracuse to see you before now." With hot pads, she pulled the pot of syrup off the burner to the edge of the stove. "So many things to do here at the ranch, so much going on — But I did save a couple *McGuffeys* for you; I know how badly you need them." She got up and rummaged in the trunk behind her bedroom curtain, wondering if Stella could smell the old rose and lilac fragrance of the sachets that lifted from the trunk when she opened it. She put the books on the kitchen table and Stella immediately picked them up, an appreciative gleam in her hazel eyes that were so like Chalk's.

"If children can read well, they can do anything," she said, smoothing the covers. "I'm so pleased to have these."

Amity asked after Stella's children, Jenny and James, who were in Syracuse with Chalk. A few minutes later, sitting down with their tea, they proceeded to discuss school matters. "When we last talked, you were working on reorganizing your school day to get the most benefit for each child," Amity said. "Tell me about it. I may want to suggest your plan to the other schools this fall."

Stella spoke up proudly. "I've set up a schedule so that I'll be able to devote forty-five minutes apiece to the first and second grades in recitation time each day, forty minutes to the combined third and fourth grades, sixty to the fifth and sixth combined, and fifty-five to the combined seventh and eighth."

Amity leaned back and clapped her hands. "You're a marvel!"

"It will work. Each student will know what they're to be doing when they're not reciting, believe me." She elaborated, at Amity's nod to go on, and went through each segment of the day.

"Whew," Amity said, "it makes my head spin. But organization is the key. I'm very proud of you, Stella."

"I can't take the credit for what I learned at the institute, though I will implement the plan." She rolled her eyes. "I wouldn't mind a few more lessons at the feet of that handsome didactics instructor, Professor Brohlin, the tall, dark one? I do hope you'll engage him for normal school come next spring, Amity."

Amity sighed, then laughed dryly. "For a while I doubted I'd be returning for another year as superintendent. Those free love accusations Thisba Strout was spreading, the recall petition —" She shook her head, chewed her lip. "But let's not talk about that."

Stella sipped her tea, seemed to make up her mind about something, and set the teacup down. "All right, let's talk about you and Chalk. What's happened between you two? He's next to impossible to get along with these days. I thought you might be able to enlighten me — if it's not too personal?"

Amity shrugged. "There are all kinds of complications I won't go into. But — part of our troubles stem from Chalk's overprotectiveness. He — *hovers*, wanting to see to my welfare. Which is a threat to my job, since the rules of my office are against our being together so much, and courting is out of the question for this first year. No matter how much I protest, he is here, there, everywhere, following me —"

"Chalk isn't stupid, Amity." Stella flatly defended her brother. "If he thinks you're in danger, you likely are."

"But I must look out for myself, don't you see? And I *can* take care of myself. A few times in the past that was doubtful — I made some stupid mistakes — but I've managed pretty well since then and I'm blessed proud of it!"

Stella smiled, somewhat sadly, and nodded. "Of course, honey, you should be proud. It's just that you and my brother are so right for each other, and it seems a terrible shame that you can't be together. You do love him?"

There was only one answer, but Amity took a moment to give it. "Yes," she said in a soft, firm voice, "I do. And it seems a terrible shame to me, too, that life must be this way. But it is for now, and that's that."

Stella looked as helpless as Amity felt. A glimmer of sympathy showed in her eyes. "I love you both, you know, so much. Sometimes I could just tear the Strout woman's hair out, for her part in this! Even though we're supposedly 'friends.' "

Amity was taken aback. "*Friends?* You and Thisba Strout? The cream and flower of Syracuse?"

"Thisba has welcomed me wholeheartedly into Syracuse's social circle this summer while I'm staying with Chalk. She has her reasons, I guess, for cultivating me. Maybe she thinks I have some influence over Chalk at the *Banner*. She likes to keep a finger in everything in town, if she can."

Amity took a breath, asked quietly, "Stella, has she ever said anything about me? Anything that would indicate why she's made such an effort to get rid of me?"

A frown creased Stella's brow. She nodded. "She's let things slip now and then, you know — she's made snide little comments. That you're not fit for the position you hold in the county, that sort of thing. She seems to think you're too independent, a smite on proper womanhood or something. I doubt that she likes it that her husband, Henry, usually comes to your defense."

"It's hard to understand why she hates me so much!"

"If there's anything else, it's likely just the poisoned imaginings from some evil little soft spot in her brain."

A poisonous flower. "I suppose. Well, all that's over and done as far as I'm concerned. Would you like more tea?"

"There *is* something I'm not supposed to tell." Stella got a mischievous sparkle in her eye. "Something my dear brother's been up to, for you."

"What on earth?"

"It's supposed to be, supposed to've been — I guess the matter's on indefinite hold — a *big* surprise."

"For heaven's sake, Stella, will you either tell me, or not?"

"I'll tell!" She scooted forward on her chair, her eyes gleaming, her pretty mouth tilted in a smile. "Chalk found a small shack, which he bought and refurbished for a schoolhouse for you."

"He what — ?"

"A school building. He wants to move it south to the sandhill country —"

"He does? Oh, I need one there desperately!"

"I know. So does he. He did the carpentry and plastering. He let me help fix it up with curtains. It's darling, Amity, you should see —"

"I want to see it as soon as possible." Her heart warmed with pure love for Chalk that he would do this for her. The precious Dusky children, including Thaddy's little friend, Jebby, were to have a *real* school. She reached out and caught both of Stella's arms. "I'm so excited! This is truly wonderful. I had no idea that Chalk — that he —"

Stella's mouth and lightly freckled nose puckered in a frown. "I'm sure I'm not supposed to say anything about it, since Chalk's changed his mind and says he's not giving you the building for a school after all, since —"

"He won't let me have it?"

Stella blew out a light breath. "He's been so angry and envious of this man Shields. Peter Shields? The one who spends so much time at your place?"

"What are they saying in town about Peter Shields . . . and me?" Amity interrupted. She'd expected a ranting visit from Thisba before now.

"You wouldn't believe the wild speculation — !"

"Oh, yes, I would."

"Most folks argue that you wouldn't risk having the man around your place on the heels of Thisba's petition unless the two of you were related."

"And . . . ?"

"Well, the consensus is that Shields is really your brother or your stepbrother. It's been generally agreed that you have connections in high places and have kept it a secret for some reason. Maybe you're the black sheep of the family. . . . They're still debating that."

"Good Lord, what fertile minds!"

"Chalk doesn't seem to agree with the brother-sister theory, though. In fact, Chalk's gotten so frustrated — you know, romantically — and furious with you that he — he —"

"What?"

"He's been charging around like a mad bull, and threatening to turn the remodeled building into a bordello! He's a man, you know, tired of waiting —"

"A bordello?" After a moment, Amity started to laugh. She covered her mouth but couldn't smother the giggles. Finally, between chuckles, she said, "He needs a bordello, does he? I'll take care of that!"

Stella looked shocked. "Amity — ?"

She felt the color flood her face. "Good heavens, Stella, I meant that I'll have to talk with him. I'll convince him I need a school much worse than he needs — than he needs — a *bordello!*" she said, laughing until she got a stitch in her side.

Stella joined in the merriment. "Men!" she gasped, "are such foolish creatures, and the thing is, they don't know it. They think *we* are!" Both women nearly fell from their chairs in laughter at that.

When they both had sobered to a state of hiccups and a need for more tea, Stella wanted to know the truth about Shields. "I've seen him around Syracuse a few times, getting off the train. He's godawful handsome, isn't he? Chalk introduced us without really saying what your relationship to the man is. I was impressed, very impressed, though. *Is* he my brother's competition?"

Amity shook her head. For the first time, she wanted to tell the truth about Shields, why he was coming to Dove's Nest so often. Stella would keep the story to herself. So she told her about Chloe, how she'd met her near the old site of Beaconsfield, how Chloe had died in her arms after making Amity promise to take her son and raise him. Then she told her about Peter Shields's tumultuous life, that he had once been in love with Chloe Brady, and fathered her son. "He wants to take my boy away from me," Amity finished, anguish tearing her apart. "I could lose Thaddy, Stella, and if that happened, I'd die. Sometimes, the way things are, he's the only chance I see for a child of my own — he's mine!" Suddenly, she was sobbing like her heart would break, crying as hard as she'd been laughing earlier.

Stella came over and knelt by her chair, pulling her into her arms. "There, honey, there, there. No such thing's going to happen. You deserve better than that. The boy loves you, honey; you're his second mother. Nobody can take him from you. They can't." She stroked her back for several minutes while Amity cried harsh tears. "There, there." She pushed her wet hair back from her face. "Chalk knows, doesn't he?"

Amity shook her head, pulling away to look at Stella. "I haven't told him. I haven't told anyone but you."

Stella stood up, pulling Amity up with her. She reached for a dish towel hanging by the work table under the window. "Here, dry your face, honey." She waited, then shook her finger. "If you don't tell Chalk, I will. Are you going to tell him?"

"I . . . I'll think about it. I've wanted to tell him, but I've been so angry with him lately, and he's been so upset with me. . . . So much confusion. It's hard to please everyone. To always do the *right* thing." She bunched the towel in her hands and then tossed it aside into a chair. "Chalk should see that I'm trying; he shouldn't doubt me about Peter Shields . . . about anything."

"A man can get a little jealous, especially when he doesn't know the whole story. You two need to have a talk and not keep any secrets. Don't hurt one another over this."

"I don't want to hurt him. Things are bad enough as it is. I love him so much. I'll love him all of my life. The question is, can he put up with waiting for me? The one thing I *can* do is tell him the truth about Shields — why I could never be attracted to the man. And —" Amity saw her reflection in the mirror hanging by the door, saw how unhappy and haggard she looked. She smoothed her hair, managing to smile at her foolish reflection. "We'll see what he says about this *bordello* nonsense!" She could speak lightly, but deep down she worried about their chances; it was a frightening thought that, what with one thing and another, they might *not* marry.

Two days later, when Amity rode into Syracuse,

she found Chalk at his desk in the *Banner* office. Her heart thudded furiously when he looked up, surprise and more in his eyes. She told him, "I understand you have something for me."

One eyebrow rose; he tapped his pencil on his desk. She found the noise very irritating as he sat back, still tapping, and stared at the wall. "Well, here she is." His delicious mouth pursed thoughtfully. "How about that."

"The gift!" she repeated. "I want my present!"

He cocked his head in a shrewd, unsmiling study of her and then got up slowly. "My sister has a big mouth."

When his long legs headed for the door, Amity scrambled to keep up. She asked the broad-shouldered back, "If it's here in town, how will we ever move it down south?"

"I haven't given it to you yet," he muttered from the corner of his mouth. At the door, he turned and yanked her roughly into his arms, kissing her mouth until it felt bruised; her whole being pulsed with wanting him, and she panted for breath. "Now," he said, "I'll think about it."

Chapter Thirty

Chalk's weeks of pent-up frustration gave way in a single moment as he observed Amity looking at the tiny peak-roofed building he'd painted bright red. She stood with clasped hands, her beautiful heart-shaped face radiating delight. He mumbled, "If you still want it, the — *schoolhouse* is yours."

Amity looked up at him, more in love with him than ever. He couldn't hide his joy at pleasing her; in spite of his diffident stance, his eyes showed an almost boyish pride. She could still feel the burning impression of his mouth on hers, and she knew he'd kissed her because he was nearing the end of his rope with her, his tolerance for their situation all but spent. She cleared her throat. "Where on earth did you find it?" It was adorable, perfect in every way, the most wonderful gift she'd ever gotten from anyone.

He drawled, shrugging, "Old town site on Duncan Wagner's land that never came to anything had a couple shacks still standing. He took the only other building to his homeplace for a henhouse."

"He donated this one for the sandhill children's

schoolhouse?" The building was perhaps ten by twelve feet, big enough. There were two windows on each side. She dared a closer look at Chalk while he formed his answer. He looked rugged and endearing at the same time, standing with one hip jutting out, his hat held against his thigh, the wind riffling his butternut brown hair.

"That penny-pinchin' skinflint? Nah —" he waved the hat "— I traded him an ad to sell his newly broken horses for this shanty. Dunc got the better end of the deal even so. Your little schoolhouse wasn't much for the eyes when I brought it to town, dismantled, in a borrowed farm wagon." He rubbed his jaw. "Wind blew the roof out of the wagon, twice. Chased over hell's half acre after it."

She ducked her head and smiled. "It's the prettiest little school I ever saw." Her glance skidded toward him again. "I'll pay you back as soon as I can get an increase in my operating funds."

"Don't bother; it's my gift. But delivering it down to where you need it may pose a bit of a problem." He stroked his moustache, his eyes expressing more interest in her than in their discussion.

She shook her head. "My neighbor, Able Bergen, has a big sledge and a strong team of black Belgians. I'm sure he'll take on the task for me. And, unlike Duncan Wagner, he'll be glad to do it for the children down there who need this school so badly." She knew that well enough, from the needful times the Bergen family had come to help her.

With that sparsity of polite words, the school was given and accepted.

Moving at a snail's pace for a whole day, looking like a bright red flag passing among the sandsage- and bluestem-covered hills, the school, roped to the sledge, was delivered late that week. The location Chalk had picked on land donated by Liddy Dusky was a sandy knoll covered with pretty pink morning glory bush and prairie sunflowers. A small creek trickled along at the foot of it. Amity accompanied the school, driving a wagon load of desks and other supplies, including a basket containing the crisp, blue gingham curtains that Stella had made to hang at the windows. Amos Taylor, good-hearted as usual, had donated slates, chalk and maps.

Chalk rode along on horseback, to help in case of emergency and to assist getting the school set properly. Catching sight of the strange apparition, the Duskys and Will Quick, one or two of the far-flung neighboring families, and a lone cowboy scouting cattle range rode out to meet the party.

Amity named the place the Dusky School, and thus eliminated Mrs. Dusky's remaining resistance to having her children educated. She'd been weakening on the subject, anyway, since Will Quick had come — reading to the family in the evenings and teaching her children the words in the books. The proud little family strutted around and around the school named for them, exclaiming, examining every inch of it. Will Quick, a slender young man in brown, hobbled about with a look of eager satisfaction on his face as he explained to the little Dusky girl where the books would go, where they might hang art, where they could set up the desks. When he ran a hand over the smooth surface of a small desk, she did likewise. Jebby's face held a constant grin as he sauntered back and forth through the open door, thumbs hooked in his suspenders, announcing to his brother that the only bad part was that Thaddeus wouldn't be attending this school with them. Liddy herself christened the little red building with a quart jar of spring water leftover from an impromptu picnic of fried sage hen and cold morning biscuits.

Most of the day Amity was relaxed, enjoying herself to the hilt, hanging curtains and placing desks, but now that the others were gone and she was left alone with Chalk, she began to feel oddly formal again in his presence. They stood side by side a few feet outside the little red building. She glanced at him discreetly, watching him roll a cigarette, his face thoughtful in the shadow of his hat. Although Chalk had given her the school, he hadn't apologized for his ridiculous behavior over Peter Shields. There'd been that furious kiss back at his office. Of course, she'd done nothing to mend the broken fences between them either, believing it best to leave things as they were. All day they'd kept their distance from each other, hiding their feelings.

461

"I really should go." She broke the silence. "Liddy and the children are expecting me to share supper with them and spend the night." Her wagon and Ben waited in the meager shade of the building, along with Chalk's saddle horse.

"Umm," Chalk answered, running his tongue along the tobacco paper to moisten the edges and fasten it.

Amity tore her eyes from his mouth. "I'm so pleased with Liddy Dusky's change of heart," she blurted, "but I doubt the woman knows the full importance of today in her children's lives, their educations." She sighed. "There's a lot of work yet to be done in my school districts. But even little Dusky School could produce a future president. Maybe even Jebby himself will become an important leader in our state. Wouldn't that be something for Liddy? One never knows —"

Chalk nodded, agreeing with her line of thinking. "We're still a land apart out here, rough and in need of taming. We have to learn to use what we have to the best advantage for everybody." He grinned, drew on the cigarette and exhaled, wispy curls of smoke circling the lean planes of his face, his strong brows. "And cattle and wheat may be the best, but I still plan to look into sugar manufacturing. Folks out here are starving for real sugar and nobody has the money to pay Southern prices. I think sorghum cane raising and sugar mills would be a big boost, too, to our economy, may make the difference whether this part of the country flourishes or not. Though Pete Shields insists, and he's probably correct, that any progress out here will be slow as molasses till we're better represented in state government." He seemed to have further thoughts on the subject, but he didn't voice them.

"I suppose I should've told you before now —" Amity looked at the ground "— about Peter Shields — the truth of why he's spending so much time at Dove's Nest."

Chalk's head jerked to look at her, and she could feel his eyes on her face, searching, wondering, worried. Suddenly, it hurt to breathe and her legs felt weak as water. "Can we go inside to talk? I'd like to sit down."

She squeezed into one of the six small desks, and Chalk knelt on his haunches close by. "It — it's Thaddeus, my Thaddy." And she told him all of it. "I'm afraid," she said around the pain in her throat, "that Peter Shields will eventually take Thaddeus from me."

Chalk swore under his breath, his expression thunderstruck. "The hell he will!"

She reached out and grasped his arm. "There is nothing you or I can do within the bounds of law, I'm afraid. And the worst of it, in a way, is that Thaddeus has gotten to be very fond of Peter. They've grown very close this summer. I — I believe that Thaddy would be delighted to know that he — that he's Peter's own son."

"He doesn't know yet?"

"No. But Peter's anxious. He's giving me the chance to tell him myself. So far . . . I just can't."

Chalk reached gentle fingers to brush away the tears that rolled down her cheeks.

"A hell of a note," he exclaimed, "showing up like that out of the blue, to say the boy belongs to him. Can't he see he's torturing you?"

"He loves his son." A sigh tore raggedly from her throat. "And I'm afraid Peter has the money and power to do pretty much what he pleases. He's asking now that Thaddy visit him at his ranch across the state —"

"You'll let the boy go?"

"How can I prevent it?" She shook her head. "Though I can't bear the thought. I may have to, for Thaddy's sake. It's not fair to think of — to think only of myself." Chalk pulled her up and held her against his chest.

"I could kill him for this," he muttered, pushing her hair back from her face and placing his lips tenderly on hers for a moment. "Damn Shields to hell!"

"No," she argued, "he has a right to his son, and Thaddy has a right to know his father. It's just that sometimes life is so unfair. Chalk —" she met his eyes, blinking away tears "— if Thaddy is taken from me, if he's where I can't see him, touch him, help him grow up, I think I'll die!"

Chalk kissed her eyes, her cheeks, her mouth. He stroked her hair. "Oh, my darlin', I can't stand to see you hurting this way. I can't —" His mouth met hers once again, this time pouring his love into her, trying to take away the pain.

"I love you, Amity," he whispered against her mouth. "Oh, Lord, so much. Do you know how much? My green-eyed jealousy could only have made things harder for you. I'm so sorry for the fussing and fighting we've been into lately, when you had all this other on your mind. Can you forgive me?"

"I'm sorry, too." She kissed him back. "And I love you, Chalk, with all my heart and soul." She wrapped her arms around his neck.

He continued to kiss her tenderly, then eagerly, then with hungry passion. She swirled in a lovely whirlpool from his touch, aware as she responded that they were cozily alone in the schoolroom filled with twilight shadows. Alone. Together. Her body, her soul, ached for him. It was always this way, always. Would always be. Her hand caressed his jaw, his throat, dipped down into the front of his shirt to feel the curling hair of his chest. He gasped with delight, tipped her slowly down onto her back on the floor. His hand brushed the side of her breast, slid down to her waist, cupped the curve of her hip. Involuntarily, her lower body half lifted toward him. She'd begun to tremble all over, her body quivering for want of him. "Please, Chalk, make love to me."

"You're sure?" he whispered huskily, his mouth close to her own, his sweet breath joining hers. He hesitated, his hands stilled on her sides.

"Yes, I'm sure. I love you. Show me — Help me —" She half rose to a sitting position to snatch at the buttons of her dress. He took her hand, kissed her fingertips. Then he took over the unbuttoning of her bodice. The backs of his knuckles brushed against her, arousing such feeling that it was all she could do not to grab his hands and cup them over the throbbing fullness of her breasts. Unable to wait for his big, deliberate hands at the buttons, she snatched them away and tore her dress open, pulled the top of her chemise down to bare her shoulder, the top of her breast.

With a low moan of delight and want, he lowered himself over her, his lips coming to rest on the milk white curve of her shoulder, the swell of creamy breast below. She gasped sharply at the touch of his mouth on her skin, the hardness of his body fitting to the length of her. Her hands grasped the back of his head, his hair crisp under her fingers as she pulled the warmth of his mouth against her flesh. "Chalk," she half sang his name in a fevered whisper, silent love music playing in her mind, "oh, my love, Chalk."

"Darling —" he whispered back against her skin. "Love."

She moved beneath him, overcome by a delicious, insane desire, feeling the fit of his wonderful body to hers, feeling more alive than she could've ever dreamed with his hands on her body. *So this is how it is? This heady closeness that makes one feel quite mad.* Why had they waited? For a single moment, why?

Suddenly, as from some far distant world, she realized that Chalk was no longer with her in feeling, though he held her as close as ever, tenderly, his mouth against her ear as he groaned. He kissed her brow and spoke. "Honey, maybe we shouldn't —"

Don't stop. "Chalk, what is it? It's all right, really," she whispered urgently, all at once afraid. *You do love me?*

"I love you, Amity, darling, so much," he whispered hoarsely, in perfect answer to the question in her mind, "but — I can't do this, because — what if you became pregnant?"

She lay still in his arms, the moment suspended, her senses reeling. As though adding to his warning, there came the far-off ringing of a bell, a true sound this time and not the music of her heart. Gradually desire ebbed away. She opened her eyes. Cold reality returned, though her disappointment weighed heavily. She felt suddenly overcome by embarrassment and humiliation. Good Lord, she and Chalk were lying on the floor of the schoolroom half-dressed! And it was he, not she, who'd called a halt to their love making. He must think she was brazen, much too forward, *asking him to do this.* Maybe that was part of why he didn't want her. She struggled from beneath him, pushing him aside even as he was already lifting himself away from her.

"Oh, God, Amity, I'm so sorry." He cupped a hand behind her head and tried to pull her against his chest.

"It doesn't matter. The bell!" she cried. "The bell! Can't you hear it?" Coming to her knees, she clutched at her open bodice, fingers shaking as she tried frantically to button herself up. "It's the Dusky family, ringing for supper. Will you move, Chalk Holden, and set yourself to rights, please? Jebby, or — or Will could come through that door any moment; we mustn't be found like this." If Chalk hadn't stopped them — but he had. For the moment, she was grateful.

Her glance darted to the windows to make sure no one looked in. Outside, the plains were purpling as the sun set. It was darker inside the schoolhouse, the corners inky with shadow. From the gloomy front of the room, the faces of George Washington and Abraham Lincoln watched from their frames as she and Chalk hurriedly made right their clothing. She redid her hair with speedy fingers.

Amity practically ran for the door, Chalk close behind. He caught her when, in the dark, she struck her knee on the wooden wash bench just inside the entry. Jarred, the tin dipper rattled in the empty bucket. She shook loose from his grasp.

Outside, Amity noted that the bell had stopped ringing. The lamplit window of the Dusky soddy could just barely be made out to the west. They headed toward the meager beacon in silence, Amity sitting straight in her rattling wagon, Ben snuffling, Chalk riding his horse alongside.

"Don't be angry with me," he stated finally. "You know that I had to stop what we were doing, for your sake, darling? Otherwise —"

468

"Please, it's all right. I don't want to talk about it."

"Honey, you're not ashamed about tonight? There's nothing wrong with what we were doing. It's only that if we start a baby when we're not married —"

If the truth be known, she only felt bad that they'd stopped when they had. Although they were very fortunate to hear the bell before someone came looking for them. Did he expect her to feel ashamed, regret what brief intimacy they'd shared? Because she didn't, not one whit, although she wouldn't want to have been caught in such an intimate moment.

"Someday, honey, it'll be right for us. I'll wait for you forever, Amity, if I have to."

"Chalk, please, we're here," she said as she drove into the Dusky yard.

The door opened and lamplight spilled out. "Where y'all been? I vow we almost give up on ya," Liddy Dusky declared.

"You're sure you'll be all right getting back home tomorrow?" Chalk asked later as he was saying goodbye to Amity, following supper with the Dusky family and Will. "It wouldn't be any trouble for me to stay over, sleep in the barn, and see you home safe."

"No! I'll be fine. There's no need for you to stay." *Safe* with him? Traveling miles and miles alone together? After tonight in the little school? Amity's face heated, recalling how far they'd

469

gone, there on the floor. "If you don't mind traveling after dark yourself, I certainly won't keep you here."

She sensed, there in the shadows, that he wanted to reach out and hold her before he left. But if he so much as touched her, she knew she'd want him to stay, or she'd want to go off with him tonight. She backed through the doorway into the full light of the Dusky front room. A glance over her shoulder showed the youngsters saying their goodnights to their mother before climbing into their beds. She turned back, her heart in her throat. "Goodnight, Chalk. Thank you very much for the school, for — everything." She closed the door gently, feeling instant relief that she'd managed to deport herself properly in contrast to her heated, churning emotions.

When she turned, there wasn't a Dusky who wasn't watching. Will Quick wore a big grin. *Lord,* was it written on her forehead that she was in love with the man? She sat down and folded her hands in her lap, trying to look very ordinary. "It's been a fine day, hasn't it? And now we have our school. Thanks to Mr. Holden, of course."

In the days following delivery of the school, the image of herself and Chalk building a life together became so real in Amity's heart and mind that she could almost touch it, move in it, revel in every pleasure it would bring. Having come so close to joining in the act of love that beautiful

470

twilight night in the schoolhouse wasn't wrong. What was wrong was denying their love and life together. Shouldn't she accept the miracle of his feelings for her and set aside all else for the most important thing that'd ever happened to her, or ever would?

With the decision made, she had the feeling of being catapulted to the top of the rainbow, weightless, reassured, filled with joy. Chalk was away, looking into prospects for sugar in western Kansas. She was anxious to tell him. There were so many things to discuss with him. Deciding where they would live would be a problem. But she wouldn't give up Dove's Nest. Her homestead, this place she'd built up with her own hands, would be her true home till her dying day. She felt sure Chalk would agree, and together they could implement her plans to expand the ranch to a full stock-raising operation. She'd like a small wedding; the lovely dress Beady Moffat made for her would be perfect to wear. And if they possibly could manage it, a wedding trip, possibly to Wichita or as far as Topeka, would be divine.

As she and Thaddeus went about their August chores together, once again harvesting the garden, shucking corn, and shocking wheat, she would often stop and hug him out of love and the feeling of overwhelming joy that filled her soul. She and Chalk would have a whole slew of children like this fine boy, and, God willing, Thad would always be with them as their older brother.

Waiting for Chalk to return to tell him the good news seemed like the longest three weeks of her life. She was feeding cracked corn to her chickens in their pen the morning she looked up to see him on his horse, coming toward Dove's Nest in a steady canter, trailing a dust cloud. Amity tossed her pan of corn into the air, scattering her squawking flock every which way. She gripped her skirts in tight fists, and ran to meet him. "Chalk! Oh, Chalk — !"

He whipped his horse to a gallop, and she could see his grin as he raced toward her. Coming abreast in a cloud of dust, he reached down and with one arm snagged her up off the ground into his arms, where he settled her close in front of him in the saddle. He nipped her ear. "Oh, Lord, have I missed you! Now, seein' you run to meet me like that, hell, it's a wonder my heart doesn't burst wide open! Tell me, now, darlin', what's got you so excited? Can it be that you missed me the same?"

"I did, Chalk, I've missed you terribly. But there's more! I have something to tell you!"

"You do? Then clearly it's a day for celebration because I've got big news for you, too, angel-sweet."

They turned his horse over to John Clyde. "You first," she said as they walked toward the house with their arms around each other. "What do you have to tell me that's such big news?"

Chapter Thirty-one

"I'm thinkin' of getting into state government as representative for our district here in west Kansas," Chalk told Amity as he sat at her kitchen table with a cup of coffee in front of him, a glimmer of thoughtful, forward-looking excitement in his eyes. "Peter Shields claims that I can make a difference out here. Maybe I can. I'd like to give it a try, anyhow."

Her surprise lasted but a second as she considered that every moment she'd known Chalk had been leading to something like this. "Of course! My, yes! These rugged, independent souls out here still need help, and someone to speak up for their rights."

"Yeah, they do need somebody. Folks out here and that includes you and me, deserve a hell of a lot better than we're getting. Naturally, our region being sparsely settled has a lot to do with our being underrepresented in state matters. Right now, honey, can you believe it? The Kansas house of representatives has one hundred thirty-three members — and only twenty are from western counties. That has to be changed."

"You'd be marvelous — we couldn't find a

better man to speak for us. You were instrumental in getting us the county seat, and —"

He looked embarrassed as he laughed. "Yeah, well, I first got into that damnable squabble to keep hotheaded fools from killing one another over the issue. Wanted them to use their heads to settle the fight. For a while I thought we might see Syracuse slide into oblivion like butter off a hot knife."

"We're fortunate there," she agreed.

"Funny, isn't it?" he laughed softly, stroking his moustache, eyes twinkling at her. "I came to Syracuse, Hamilton County, to live a good life in a free land. Indulge in a little Western adventure, maybe. I had no idea nor plan of gettin' involved. I just suddenly *was*." His voice grew huskier. "I think it started about the time I persuaded you to run for county school superintendent. That opened my eyes to how little folks have out here, how much they deserve to have. On the other hand, for some reason hard to figure —" he grinned "— some of the most destitute folks seem to be by nature too proud and stubborn to ask for help. I won't name names."

Amity shrugged, but failed to hide her smile. An ache had settled in her throat; it was hard to breathe. Had he ever been as excited about *them* as he was this moment about *western Kansas?*

Chalk went on, sitting forward eagerly, "I've come to the point I'd really like to see my part of the country not just survive, but prosper. Securing the county seat is only the beginning of the good things that could happen, and I'd like to have a hand in it." He sat back, his expression thoughtful. "We've some ways to go to reach real prosperity, I'm afraid. But I'm convinced irrigation is the answer. Then everything else should fall into place."

"If you'll lead us, I'm sure it'll happen." Amity's hand rested just below her collarbone. She sincerely meant every word of encouragement and praise she uttered, but at the same time, she was trying to see how her decision finally to marry him might mesh with this desire of his to take on a government role. If a man wanted a wife in his brand new venture, it was up to him to say so. "It sounds as though you have everything all set," she said softly.

"Not at all! It's not definite that I'll run. I have the *Banner* and my law practice, small as it is, to think about. I want to get the considered opinions of a lot of people. You happen to be the first I've discussed this with, because —" He waved away whatever he was about to say. "I want to be certain I'm right for this as I look into all the needs of western Kansas. There's people I should get to know, whose help I'll need if I do run. It's going to be a very busy fall and winter, before April filing time." He hesitated, then asked, "Is something wrong?"

Amity tried to make light of what she was about to say, although in all this, he hadn't mentioned *them*. "My news doesn't exactly jibe with yours or . . . maybe it does." Her smile was wry. "I was going to suggest that we forget the past, and go ahead and set a wedding date. Since I haven't heard from the Fairleighs by now, it doesn't seem as if I ever will. Also, the state superintendent said there were no regulations against my marrying while in office, though he'd hoped I'd wait since the district board might need convincing. Stella seems to be doing better and better on her own and I thought, finally —"

"Honey, we don't have to wait because of me!" Chalk protested. "I've only been waiting for you to say the word! Don't you know that you're more important to me than anything else in the world?"

She felt better, and it was easier to tell him, "Waiting a little longer won't change things very much. I'd like a proper wedding, and that takes planning. I'll be as busy as you, too, you know. I've been making plans to build up Dove's Nest. A large portion of my superintendent's salary is going to go for seed cattle. I've decided to buy a purebred Hereford bull." She laughed, not without a touch of inner pain. "Goodness! I hardly sound like a bride, do I?"

"Amity, are you sure about this? I'll be busy, but we —"

"I'm sure."

Once again she must break with propriety, Amity thought, and decided to accompany Thaddeus on a visit to Peter Shields's eastern Kansas ranch. She couldn't let Thad go alone, and she had to see that he would be all right there. She was risking her job, her reputation, but her boy's welfare was far more important.

Besides, the journey would be a diversion from matters that, for the time being, she could do nothing about. And it was an opportunity to see a large ranch in operation. She just hoped that the common belief that Shields was her relative still held.

"This is incredible; it surely reminds me of the bonanza farms that I've heard are being developed in North Dakota and Minnesota. Except you're more into cattle than grain." Amity sat erect on the buggy seat and spoke over Thaddeus's head to Peter Shields about his Flint Hills spread. They traveled along a long dusty lane lined with a carefully tended osage-orange hedge. As far as the eye could see in three directions, cattle dotted the rolling green hills. The other way lay far reaches of gold-stubbled wheat fields, already cut and threshed. The air was fragrant, summery. In the past few minutes, she'd learned his spread contained some twenty thousand acres in bluestem pasture and wheatland. He presently ran thirty-five hundred head of cattle, and raised quarter horses and a few Arabians.

Shields had met them at the train station in a spanking black buggy with fringe on top and yellow wheels, drawn by a sleek pair of bays. They'd been greatly stared at in town, and Amity had been annoyed as well as embarrassed. She hadn't wanted the boy to travel alone on the train, and she'd wanted to see for herself what Thaddy would be subjected to on his visits with his father.

She hadn't expected to enjoy herself, nor to feel such excitement that wouldn't be quelled even at sight of Shields's immense holdings.

Peter was smiling at her. His driving was very relaxed. His free arm rested along the back of the buggy seat, his hand drooped close to her shoulder. His intense, kindly blue-gray eyes sparkled. "I'm pretty small potatoes compared to the cattle barons of Wyoming and Texas."

"This would be big enough for me," she breathed. She could feel the rapid beat of her heart in her throat. As big as her plans were for Dove's Nest Ranch, she hadn't dreamed on this scale.

"Wow-gosh, is that the house?" Thaddeus piped up suddenly between them, almost falling forward off the seat in awe while Amity pulled him back. "It's like in a storybook!" The boy stared at a brick mansion in a setting of trees that had come into view.

Peter looked pleased. "That's it, son. What do you think?"

Thaddy stared in wide-eyed wonder. "Does it have secret doors and passageways? Do lots of people live with you? Servants and stuff?"

"Not so many questions, Thaddeus," Amity chided. "It's not polite." She ought *not* to've read so many fairy tales about castles and such to him. Naive, innocent, he was far too impressed with

Peter's home, when, guiltily, she'd hoped he'd not care for it at all.

"He's all right." Peter patted Thad's knee affectionately. Thad looked up and smiled, a mirror of his father's face looking down. Amity's heart squeezed with the fear of loss. A feeling of being on the outside. "Actually," Peter said, "I live in the house with my foreman, Bill Whipple, and Mrs. Craig, my housekeeper."

From the house's size, one would certainly think it could hold an army, Amity thought, piqued and embarrassed, considering that she'd entertained Peter in her humble soddy, put him up in her *barn*.

The house admittedly was a garnet jewel in a setting of large old elm trees. It had numerous windows, a mansard roof, and a balconied tower high above the front entry. Amity was curious, herself, to see inside, as they came to a halt in the circular drive. She was only half-aware when Shields introduced her to his foreman, Bill Whipple, a courteous, weathered man who'd come from behind the house to take the horse and buggy. With a squeal of delight, Thaddeus scrambled down to run to a double swing built on a tented frame that sat in the shade of the elms. A hammock was tied between two other trees. It all looked very serene, comfortable, elegant.

Thaddeus was less interested in going inside, though Amity felt fascinated by everything that met her eyes. She wandered slowly across the porch at Peter's heels, taking it all in. It seemed centuries since she'd been in such a house. Both front and side porches were furnished with wicker furniture and potted flowers. They entered the cool vestibule and Carolina Craig, the cheery little house-keeper, took their gloves and hats. To the right off the main hall Peter showed them the parlor, and to the left, his study. Sturdy but finely crafted country furniture was casually arranged on carpeted floors; tapestry drapes and lace panels adorned the windows of the high-ceilinged rooms. The fireplaces were so huge, Amity could have walked into them by only bending a little. Surely they were just for looks; there couldn't be logs big enough to burn in them, not in Kansas.

They came to a central stairway that divided the front rooms of the house from the dining room, kitchen, pantry, and washroom in back. Peter led the way to the upstairs bedrooms, all eight of which were furnished in simple Shera-ton-Hepplewhite furniture that Amity guessed had been inherited. There was a separate boudoir, or woman's dressing room, if Amity cared to make use of it. "I'll have your things brought up here," Peter said, showing her the bedroom nearest the boudoir. "And Carolina is just down the hall if you need anything."

"Choose any room you like," he told Thaddeus with his hand on the boy's shoulder, "unless you'd rather sleep in the bunkhouse with my hands, be like one of the cowboys?"

"In — in the bunkhouse," Thaddy nodded, nearly speechless with joy. "Can I, Ammy?"

480

"*May* I," she corrected. "We'll see. I suppose it's up to you and —" She caught herself just short of unthinkingly saying *your father*. "You and Peter," she emphasized, exasperated with herself.

"Maybe you'd like to rest awhile before dinner?" Peter asked, taking in Amity's stricken face.

"No," she said sharply, "I'm fine." *Don't treat me like a lily-white city girl, which I'm definitely not, not anymore. Or like whomever that pretty little boudoir was designed for.* "I'd like to see the rest of your ranch, the cattle in particular. I'll be wanting to make my selection."

"There's plenty of time for that —"

She shook her head. "We may not be staying beyond tomorrow morning, so there isn't 'plenty of time.' "

Thaddy looked at her like she'd announced the end of the world. Peter's eyes told her that this was not their arrangement.

"All — all right," she stammered. "Perhaps we can stay — a few days." Thaddeus immediately brightened; Peter simply nodded, arching a dark brow at her in silent question of what she was up to.

Which only served to rankle her further. How did he think she'd feel in this place, with what was happening?

Amity hardly spoke at all over the sumptuous dinner served in the dining room later. She was far less interested in the house than earlier, but

481

she admitted to herself as she ate, half listening to Thaddy's chatter about the cowboys he'd met outside, that this room with dark harvest-red-and-green decor was about perfect. Porches and windows lined either side, on the east to face the rising sun, on the west to catch the sunset. The real house she'd build some day would have just such a rich, pleasant room, she decided.

That night, Amity fell asleep immediately in the billowy featherbed. She didn't wake until Carolina brought her a pitcher of steaming water for her basin next morning. When she went down for breakfast, Carolina told her that Peter and Thaddeus were already out giving orders for the day to the hands.

That first day spent at the ranch, Amity was treated to a thorough tour of Shields's operation. He told her how he'd bought up several smaller farms to build this ranch. Thaddy bounded along with her and Peter. He found things of delight everywhere they went: a wood carving of a bucking horse on a shelf in the chuckhouse, an apple from the more than ample storeroom of provisions. He ran his fingers adoringly over the shiny silver conches adorning saddles in the shed attached to the blacksmith shop, he admired the tools of the forge. The happy youngster raced up and down the rows of Carolina's kitchen garden, which was lush compared to their own poor dry patches at home. He loved the barns, corrals, and horse pasture. In one of the corrals, a young quarter horse was being trained, and they couldn't have pried Thaddeus away with a crowbar.

This was what she wanted, but would she ever see the day? It was hard not to feel green-eyed envy. Amity selected her thirty young critters from Peter's prize herd and knew she'd made a good bargain. In four or five years on the shortgrass plains, the same animals would be worth ten to twelve times what she was paying, maybe more. She wished she had the money for a thousand head. But the cows would produce and her herd would increase accordingly.

The following day, Peter insisted on treating them to a visit to Emporia, a pretty town on a low ridge between the Cottonwood and Neosho rivers. At the railroad depot, Amity made arrangements for her new cow herd to be shipped to Syracuse. There would be too many fences blocking it to make a drive across Kansas. She disliked accepting charity from Peter, but he claimed from the beginning he'd included shipping costs in the price given her because he expected to pay the freight bill. Naturally she didn't believe him, but he would brook no argument.

From there they went to the barbershop for Thaddy's first haircut from a regular barber, an act which he seemed to think made him a king. Amity waited on a bench outside next to the candy-striped barber pole. She sneaked a peek through the window and saw Peter and Thad getting their shoes shined at the same time. Wearing an enormous grin, Thaddeus was studying

483

his slicked-up reflection in the barbershop's mirror. Amity felt a stab of anxiety, wondering if Thaddeus had noticed the incredible resemblance between himself and Peter. Even a youngster would have to be blind not to see it.

"You're spoiling the boy dreadfully," she snapped at Shields that afternoon. Following their noon meal at an expensive café, he suggested a soda, a treat Thaddy'd never had. Peter led them to a drugstore where they sat at the soda fountain faced with many flavors to choose from: orange, banana, ginger, wild cherry, raspberry, lemon, vanilla, pineapple, root beer. To her dismay, Peter allowed Thaddeus to have a soda they named Don't Care, a combination of all of them. "He's going to be sick tonight, wait and see."

Peter lowered his voice so Thaddeus wouldn't hear. "I don't think so. I think Thad has an iron stomach like his pa. And anyhow, nothing would give me more pleasure than to spoil both of you every day for the rest of your lives."

Amity gave a start, but didn't look at him, deciding not to waste a moment exploring his meaning. Peter Shields was the enemy, and he ought to know it. Perversely, she ignored him, going back to her raspberry soda. Changing her mind, she announced, "If you want to 'spoil' me, grant me Thaddy's total guardianship. And then please leave us alone!"

He seemed to be weighing if she really meant what she was saying as he sized her up, stroking his neat, salt-and-pepper beard. He said nothing, but shook his head, the gray-blue eyes looking stormy.

She might seem unreasonable from his point of view but she was being honest, Amity thought.

She ought not to be here with him at all! She felt more helpless than ever when Peter insisted they remain in town for an evening concert. As they walked to the park toward twilight, her anger had cooled somewhat, as curiosity about all she saw took its place. For one thing, it was hard not to notice how much fashions had changed without her being aware. The women of Emporia all seemed dressed in their finest and though she'd worn her second-best dress, the pewter taffeta, Amity felt hopelessly out of step. Skirts, she saw, were being worn much fuller; not only were bustles exaggerated in back, but there was fullness over each hip, too. With the fullness of the skirts, bodices had become simpler. Striking her as new and strange were dress sleeves quite puffed up at the shoulders. For her own active life, she'd long since done away with trappings of beading, fringe, and braid, which only added to the cost and weight of a dress, anyhow. This lack of adornment was the only bit of fashion she shared with the other women present tonight.

From time to time, Amity felt, but refused to acknowledge, Peter's eyes on her as they sat on the grass in the park and listened to the concert band playing waltzes. She recognized the lilting refrains of some of them: Kiss Waltz, "Pretty Pond Lillies," the Cornflower Waltz. In the back

485

of her throat she hummed along. A few young couples had gotten up to dance, and they swayed and swirled on their toes about the park. She prayed that Peter wouldn't ask her, even though her feet fairly itched to be up and dancing. With anyone else, she would, but not with this man she was trying to dislike with all her soul. Thaddy was leaning against her, about to fall asleep in her arms. He'd had quite a day, and she couldn't deny that he'd enjoyed every moment. She snuggled him closer, loving the feel of him in her arms, ignoring the feeling at the back of her mind that it couldn't last.

It was late when they returned to Shields's mansion. Amity tucked Thaddy into bed, kissed him. "Goodnight, Thaddy," she whispered, but the boy was already asleep. She yawned, weary in every limb herself from the strain of the day. As she left his room, she saw Peter waiting at the head of the stairs. "Please join me below in my study. We have to talk about the boy."

Though she'd been anxious to turn in, she nodded, suddenly wide awake, apprehension heavy in her breast, making breathing all at once difficult. Downstairs, she took the chair Peter offered.

"The boy knows."

"I beg your pardon?" She leaned forward.

"Thaddeus knows that I'm his father."

"You told him? But you promised me that I would be the one to tell him, when the time was right. How could you?" She threw him a furious look, though her anger was for everything — the whole situation moving out of her control.

"Hold on," he cautioned with a frown, "it occurred by accident. Yesterday morning Thad came looking for me in my bedroom. There's a picture of Chloe on my bedside table —"

"You put it there on purpose!" She half rose from her chair, then sagged back.

"No, it's always been there; I just forgot to take it away before you came. Listen to me, Amity — the boy feels the tie between him and me the same as I do. After he saw the picture and asked if I was his papa, he told me he'd thought so for a long time. Honestly, the boy told me that himself. He's an intelligent youngster. I think they often know a lot more than we realize. Anyway, he knew without either of us telling him."

With a hurt inside like none she'd ever felt before, Amity put her head in her hands and began to cry. How could she give him up? How?

"I'm sorry about this, I truly am," Peter said, coming to kneel by her chair. "Please don't cry, dear, listen to me. There is a way for you to have the boy, you know. You must've guessed by now that I care for you — very much. I believe in time you'll come to care for me. Amity, please marry me."

Amity's hands came down and she stared at him.

He went right on, taking her silence as agreement. "I was so happy when you came along with Thad and I could show you what I have to offer. You'll never have another worry the rest of your life. We'll be fine parents, we can raise the boy together." When she started to reply he told her quickly, "I could've taken him away with me that first day I went to your place. But one look at you, Amity, and I knew how much I wanted you both."

Rage against him — that he forced her to choose between her own life at home and having her boy — showed in her face.

Peter looked at her in alarm and growing concern. "Great God, darling, understand, he's my son."

The problem was, he spoke the truth. A big, big truth.

Chapter Thirty-two

If she hadn't been so wrapped up in her own problems and hard work, maybe Amity would have seen Peter's marriage proposal coming. He'd threatened to court her when he'd argued with Chalk. What she'd simply written off as his charm at times could have been deemed romantic overtures, she supposed, but he'd definitely taken her by surprise now. She swallowed her anger at his idea of a solution to keeping Thaddeus. "Please understand, Peter, I'm flattered by your proposal." She even managed a smile, a soft tone. "But I'm in love with someone else. When I marry, it will be Chalk."

"Holden's a damned fortunate man," he said quietly.

She didn't reply. Thaddeus would be taken away from her and there was nothing she could do to stop it, short of marrying Peter. Which was impossible because her heart belonged to Chalk.

"If you'd just give me a chance —" Peter said huskily and before she realized what was happening, he'd taken her into his arms, his mouth finding hers. She pushed out of his arms and,

ith one furious look at his red face, turned and
led from the room.

Breakfast was a polite affair except for
Thaddy's chatter. As soon as he went outside
to play, Peter turned to her, contrite. "I'm sorry
about last night, Amity, but I had to ask. As
long as you're not married to someone else, or
spoken for, I can't give up."

"How foolish of you!" she said frostily.

"I'll take you to the train whenever you wish.
I can see how unhappy I've made you, but I
want Thaddeus to stay on, and get used to the
place and being with me —"

She made a face, looked away.

"I'm not the beast you're making me out to
be, Amity! Look at me!" Unwillingly, she faced
him. "I want you to know," he went on, "that
Thad and I will be coming to see you as often
as you'll have us. I doubt the boy can tolerate
total separation from you, ever, and I can appreciate that. You've been a mother to him and
more. You're always welcome here to see him,
for extended stays, if that's what you want. God
knows, it would please the hell out of me." His
voice grew solemn. "If Thad isn't happy here
with me, then I'll bring him back to live with
you, if that's what he chooses. But hear me: Thaddeus Shields is, and always will be, my son."

Amity could hardly wait to return to Dove's
Nest, wanting to go home more than ever after
Shields's proposal, his attempt to kiss and woo

her. She endured the rest of the visit for Thaddy's sake. For the youngster, she also buried her devastation at their parting. She knelt at his level on the train station platform and forced a cheery smile. Behind them, the waiting train hissed steam. People rushed to get aboard, called their goodbyes. "You'll be a good boy?" she asked around the pain in her throat. *Are you sure you want to stay, are you absolutely positive?* Her heart pleaded to know, though it was unfair to ask now that decisions were made. Thaddy had told her himself that he wanted to be with his father for now.

"I'll be good, Ammy. I — I wish you would stay here with Papa and me."

"I know you do, darling. But — but I can't. I'm needed at home. We'll see one another often though, so there's no need to worry. Your — your papa says he'll bring you to Dove's Nest soon. And I — will come see you every chance I get." And every visit would be torture when it came time to give him up all over again. "Oh, Thaddeus, Thaddeus —" She pulled him to her in a tight hug. "You're such a good boy, in every imaginable way. I'll always be so proud of you. I — I love you more than anything else in the world."

"More than Dove's Nest, more than the children in your schools, more than Jebby Dusky?"

"Yes! More than anyone or anything else in this whole wide world, I do love you!" She kissed him, wanted to leave her mouth against his smooth young cheek forever. She felt a hand on her shoulder and looked up to see in Peter's face that it was time. "Well, Mr. Thaddeus," she said through a tight throat, "I'd better go or the train is going to leave without me."

He burst into tears, giving impetus to her own tears she'd tried hard to hold back. She ran a gloved finger under each eye, then staggered as the boy threw himself against her skirts, clinging tightly for a moment before letting go to take his father's hand.

All the way home she remembered those last moments, Thaddy's tears and her own. But the fact remained that he'd stepped back from her in the end and had reached for his father's hand. It was what he wanted, and something she could give. She was glad he'd found his father, more relieved that, as long as Peter was going to take the boy from her, Thaddeus loved him. But it hurt, oh, it hurt.

The next time Chalk came to see her at Dove's Nest, Amity told Chalk the conditions Peter Shields had set for her to keep Thad. "You tried to tell me how Peter felt, Chalk, but I just didn't see it. I could have headed off his proposal. Still, it seems so unfair that he would ask me to make a choice like that."

Chalk's expression was as dark as a thundercloud. "I suppose he kissed you?"

She shrugged.

"He makes me as mad as hell, but . . . ,"

Chalk admitted, "in his place, I'd have done the same thing. Do you want me to call him out, have a word or two?"

"Of course not, he understands about us — that eventually we plan to marry. There's nothing more to be said to him on that score." She changed the subject. "Tell me, how is the campaign going? I want to hear everything about the trips you have made to the capital." She smiled at him. "I suppose all the women in Topeka are beautiful, very fashionable and cultured, and fall over themselves inviting you to parties?"

He grinned back. "That's about the size of it. But nary a one of those ladies could take my mind off of you." His voice deepened. "How soon did you say we could get married? I'd give my all to show you off in Topeka."

"I didn't say, but, God willing, it will be soon. I have some work and a few business matters to take care of first. And I don't want to distract you, for now, from what you have to do."

He reached for her, pulled her close in his arms. Just before his lips touched hers, he said huskily, "You are a distraction, and that's God's own truth."

Amity's cattle arrived in Syracuse, and she and John Clyde drove them home. Two long, hot days of branding followed as she marked ownership of the cows with her Dove's Nest brand.

For the first time since she'd staked her claim, Dove's Nest showed a profit from sale of her wheat and broomcorn brush, a difference she could actually see. Not much, but with her new cattle herd and the superintendent's salary for the next year and later — should she run for another two-year term — her financial situation could only get better.

Amity made her payment at the bank and put the rest in a savings account. After the bank, she went to the general store for a few supplies, but also to put off returning home where it was quiet and lonely. Stella, shopping with her children, Jenny and James, spotted Amity and threw her arms about her in a hug. "Why the long face, Amity, hon? Has something happened?"

Amity smiled with effort, took a deep breath. "Thaddeus — has gone to — live with his father. Seeing Jenny and James just now — I miss him so much!" She gave Stella the details. "I'm happy for Thaddy, I truly am, but I'd give anything if he were still with me . . ."

"Would you like to talk about it?" Stella asked gently, studying Amity's face. "It's been too long since we have had a good long chat — let's go to the tearoom for lemonade and cake." Her children bobbed up and down, eyeing one another in excitement.

Amity's tension released in a soft laugh. "Yes, let's! Wait while I get my mail, then we can go."

At the tearoom, Stella gently scolded James for tipping over a chair in his eagerness. At a table across the way, Thisba Strout frowned at the disturbance, then went back to visiting with her lady friends. While Stella settled the children, Amity shuffled through her letters. At her gasp, Stella asked, "What is it?"

"It's come, it's finally come — I can't believe it — the letter from England!"

"The one you've been waiting for?" Stella asked in excitement.

She nodded, and tore the letter open. Her breathing seemed to stop as her glance swept the page. "How odd," she whispered. "My goodness!" Stella leaned forward eagerly and Amity told her, "This letter is from a man who used to be Chester Fairleigh's solicitor. He says that Chester Fairleigh no longer lives in England, and — that my letter was passed from hand to hand until it was given to him, Mr. Severn, the solicitor." She took a deep breath. "Mr. Severn writes that Chester Fairleigh has returned to Kansas to reestablish the colony and make it work this time!"

Stella reached out and clasped Amity's hands. "He's back at Beaconsfield? Then that means you can go to him, wretched man that he is, and get the truth!"

Amity nodded, momentarily speechless.

"Are you frightened . . . of what the truth might be?" Stella asked. "I'm very happy for you, Amity, but what if — ?"

"I *have* to go," Amity maintained staunchly. "I want to know."

There was a sound at the next table and Amity looked up. She'd forgotten all about Thisba. The woman was rising from her chair to leave. Her glance skimmed over Amity like ice, and she said something that made her friends laugh. With her usual hauteur, Thisba swept past Amity's table and out of the restaurant.

Watching her go, Amity thought that Thisba might have picked up part of their conversation. A little shiver traveled her spine. But, she told herself, she was ready to deal with the truth, however it might come out, so it mattered little what Thisba might do about Fairleigh's return.

A while later, Amity left the tearoom with Stella and the children. She walked back to the *Banner* office with them to tell Chalk the news, and let him know that she would be away for a few days.

Chapter Thirty-three

Between the next day's morning and evening chores, Amity filled the hours doing the washing and cooking extra meals for John Clyde to have during her absence. All the while, her mind was as busy as her hands. John Clyde was off exchanging a few days' work with Able Bergen, but there was plenty to do while she waited for him to come home and take her place. This time, she was going to tell him where she was going and why. No one had been so unquestioningly devoted to her as John Clyde Rossback. Soon she would know how she might have caused little Nora's death; the confused images would be cleared. She wasn't a sick, bewildered young girl this time, accepting accusations at face value, agreeing to be punished for something she had little memory of, allowing herself to be banished. No, this time she had questions, many questions, and Chester Fairleigh would answer them! If she was guilty, at least she would know the truth of what happened.

Before bed, she packed her satchel with a muslin nightgown, a clean dress, underclothing, and stockings. She folded her shawl and laid it atop the satchel. She got money from the teapot on the top shelf of the cupboard, tied it up in a clean hanky, and put it in her reticule.

Finally, she sat down by lamplight to write the startling news she'd come by and the possible import for her future in her journal. But her thoughts were too jumbled for her pen to make sense of them. Finally she went to bed, but it was after midnight before she managed to drift off for a few hours of sleep.

Following morning chores the next day, she heated water for a bath, undressed in her sectioned-off bedroom, and sank into the tub. She washed her hair and combed it out. It was some time later and she was in her petticoat when, out in the new corrals, Ben whinnied sharply as though he knew they were going somewhere and couldn't wait to be on the road. In a moment, Flora, her milk cow, answered with a low bellow. Some of her other cows picked up the refrain, faint and distant. My, a regular chorus, Amity thought, grinning to herself as she wound her damp hair in a knot and pinned it behind her head. Then her hands dropped with the sudden realization that something could be stirring her stock up, bringing trouble. It was rare that a coyote strayed this close to a house, but a rabid one might do anything. She quickly pulled her dress over her head, planning to get her gun and check outside, when she noticed an odd scorched smell. She sniffed the air, rushed into the kitchen area to see if she'd left a skillet from breakfast on the stove. She hadn't. She went to the window and pulled aside the curtains to peer out. A pall of smoke that hadn't been there an hour before hung in the air over everything. Then she saw flames.

For a second or two she froze. "Dear God — !" She grabbed a blanket from her bed and raced for the well outside. She turned in a circle, her eyes following the line of prancing red flames that rimmed her property on three sides, eating the distance inward to her homestead. She'd plowed a fireguard herself; how had it skipped inside? Or was it only inside? *Intentionally set?*

Even as Amity watched, her heart in her throat, the only escape — to the southeast toward town — was eliminated by wind-whipped flames. She was caught in a circle of fire.

Frantically, she drew up a bucket of water, soaked the blanket, drew the bucket full again, and another bucket and another until the blanket was thoroughly wet, giving her time to gather her wits.

Wind-carried sparks were striking small fires all around her. Wearing the wet blanket over her head, she ran for the corral. On the way, she stopped for a moment to free her chickens from their coop. "Aggie, go, shoo!" She flapped the edge of the blanket at the hen who wanted to linger. The small flock fluttered and squawked before her as she ran them toward the creek. Hoping they'd continue to safety on their own, she whirled back and, moving fast, opened the pole gate and shooed a frenzied Ben and Flora from the corral. "Go, go!" she shouted and slapped Ben's back. "Run!" She followed them halfway to the creek, running, screaming, waving the heavy blanket at them. She hoped once they smelled water they'd keep going clear to the creek, have sense to stay there. She couldn't see her new stock, and she prayed they were safe on the other side of the fireguard.

The flames were advancing at an unbelievable rate. She could hear the roar of the fire now, a demon racing to swallow her up; the acrid smell filled her nostrils. Sparks set the grass afire in small patches everywhere as she turned back toward the soddy, her only hope. The earthen parts of her soddy wouldn't burn. She'd roll up in the wet blanket and wait out the fire. With a cry of fury, she beat out patches of fire as she went. Her whole ranch was framed by flames and black billowing smoke. She gagged on the acrid taste. Her eyes watered until she was nearly blinded. Her sense of direction became confused. Her breath came in sobs as she ran erratically, trying to find the path to the house, stomping and beating out flames that kept licking up in front of her, cutting her off, leaping and crackling as if with glee.

Closer and closer, edging in, the head fire grew — roaring, crackling, a scarlet, devouring demon below boiling black clouds of smoke. She tried in vain to see where she was. The heat was oppressive; it was all she could do to breathe. Perspiration ran in rivulets down her back, pooled under her breasts and at her waistline as she fought on. Suddenly, above the roar of the fire, she heard a human scream, the sharp whinnying of a horse, and knew she wasn't alone.

Amity whirled in the direction of the sound, and stared aghast as a black horse plunged through the wall of flames to the north. The animal reared up, pawing the air, only to drop and plunge in a frenzy of terror. The buggy it drew whipped wildly around. As the vehicle tipped, the figure of a woman in full skirts was ejected. The horse, still hitched to the swaying buggy, raced off, disappearing southward into clouds of smoke.

Holding the wet blanket over her head, Amity headed as fast as she could run over the fiery ground toward the form sprawled in the smoking grass. As she grew closer the woman got up and staggered in circles, emitting ear-piercing shrieks above the noise of the fire.

Thisba Strout. Amity called out to her to get her attention, but the sounds of the wind and fire ate her words. Finally, through the swirling black clouds of smoke, she reached the woman, aware that Thisba had meant her to die in this fire. Thisba was trying to kill her. When Amity reached her, Thisba had fallen again to her knees. Amity threw half her wet blanket around her and drew Thisba to her feet. Thisba's face twisted horribly, her eyes were red rimmed, her mouth gaped as she gagged on the smoke. "No," she finally managed, "you have to die, Amity

Whitford!" She shoved fists like rocks into Amity's chest.

She caught Thisba's wrists in an iron grip and held on as the woman tried to twist away. "Unless you want to fry to a crisp out here with the grasshoppers and rabbits, Thisba Strout," she gritted, "you'd better come with me. I'm your only chance." A very slim chance at that, but she didn't say it. If they did live she'd force Thisba to tell her why she wanted her dead.

The wind shifted slightly, and Amity got her bearings as well as she could through the momentarily thinned-out clouds of smoke. She headed at a run back toward the shadowy outlines of her ranch buildings she'd sighted, one hand gripping Thisba's arm. "Run," she cried, "we've got to hurry!" Thisba, coughing, barely able to maintain her feet, cried out, "I think my rib is broken." But she ceased to fight and allowed herself to be pulled along. Now and then she whimpered, "Henry. Henry."

"Hush. Save your breath, your strength, and run!" Stooped in a crouch, pulling Thisba along, Amity moved, as fast as she was able, away from the flames coming close on their heels. They'd never make the soddy, now, but if they could just reach the well before the fire met from all sides in the center of her place —

Suddenly, Thisba screamed sharply in Amity's ear and struggled in her grasp. Amity looked to see flames eating up Thisba's skirts from the grass. Amity threw her on the ground and rolled her in the blanket, then pulled Thisba to her feet and began to run again. Thisba followed, moaning in pain. Half her skirt was burned away and smoking bits of charred stocking clung to the red, burned flesh of her legs.

An eternity later, Amity groped through the smoke and found the low stone wall of the well. Coughing, gagging, half-blinded — the sockets of her eyes burning as if they were on fire — she slipped her arm around Thisba, who was sagging on her feet, near to fainting. "Thisba! We're at the well. Help me get you over the rock wall and down inside. Take this rope —" she shoved it into her fingers, "— and keep going down hand over hand. Give me room —" Thisba let go of the rope, started to slip to the ground. Amity hauled her up and slapped her sharply. She put the rope in Thisba's fingers again, half lifted the woman over the edge, and pushed her down inside. With a sharp cry that echoed off the walls, Thisba descended into the well, frantically moving down the rope hand over hand.

With blistered fingers, Amity grabbed the rope and followed, lowering herself into an even darker void than that above them. Forty feet down, Amity's scorched feet finally struck the cool, wet water and she slid into it, a half sob of relief escaping her lips. She sank into the water, holding the rope with one hand until she found she could touch bottom. It smelled dank and cool there and she drank it in. Standing in the mud, the cool water came just over her shoulders. She could hear nothing but the terrifying artillery-sound of the fire over them, no sound from the other woman. Then, as her stinging eyes became accustomed to the gloom in the well, she saw Thisba less than an arm's reach away, about to go under the glistening surface of the water.

For a flash of a second, she had the urge to look away and let it happen. Then she reached out and grabbed Thisba's yellow hair, which had come free from its haircombs and floated on the water.

She held the woman's head up until Thisba gasped for air, coming around; then she let her go. "I meant to get away," the woman rasped finally, "but my buggy mare just lost her mind."

"Maybe if you hadn't waited so long to see the fire do its damage, you could've escaped free and clear. But you stayed around to see me dead — so now we're both here together! It'll be a long time till we're found, *if* we're found." Amity's voice echoed off the stone casing of the well. She coughed, cleared her throat. Took a minute to splash water on her face and hair, and breathe deep. "What is it you have against me? What?" she swallowed hard. "I promise you, you'll never leave this well until you tell me."

Thisba laughed suddenly, a sound so eerie it sent shivers along Amity's spine. "If I could only see your face! So Chester Fairleigh has come back from England? I got that much from your carrying on in the tearoom. Of course, I couldn't let you go there if he is back. The two of you together

504

might figure out what happened to the little girl, and if you told my Henry —"

Amity stood rigid, her throat tight, staring at the other woman's vague shadow. "You were there. You were there all along, weren't you? You *know* about Nora Ann — !"

Thisba leaned back against the rock wall of the well. Her eyes glittered in the gloom. She couldn't resist telling Amity, "I was every bit as pretty as you! Fairleigh had an eye for me, too, you know. With you out of the way, and then Mrs. Fairleigh —" Her next words, "I'd — have — a chance —" were mangled by strangled coughs. She gasped with pain from her injured ribs.

Amity strained forward, her mind racing. She clutched Thisba's shoulders in the water. "I want to hear all of it, now."

Thisba shoved her hands away. Words dripped like acid from her tongue. "I shouldn't have been there. I had no choice, had to take menial work as the new maid to survive, to take care of my little Doridee. I hated you the first minute I saw you, the pretty governess. I saw you with the Fairleigh children, saw how the master treated you. I could see where that could take you. Where *I* deserved to be. His mistress, maybe even his wife, in that fine house." She rasped savagely, "When the opportunity came, I latched onto it. I meant for you to die with the child."

"My God, what did you do?" Amity's flesh had begun to chill from the cold water; her blood

505

ran even colder from what she was hearing. She coughed, clinging to the rough dank sides of the well with both hands for support.

"You don't remember, do you?" Thisba almost chortled, proud to tell her, possibly to prove how clever she was, how strong her need. "The Fairleighs and their two older children, in fact, nearly everyone in the colony went away to Kansas City for a week for the trotting races and fancy parties. I would've loved to go, too, but I was a lowly maid and wasn't wanted, though Fairleigh didn't mind coming after me when his wife wasn't looking."

"Oh, Thisba, you're such a fool!" Amity shook the woman. "What happened to little Nora Ann? How did she die?" She held her breath. The pain from burns on her feet and hands had set in, but she scarcely noticed.

"My little Doridee was just teasing when she coaxed Nora Ann to run and hide from you. Doridee came back but the toddler kept on wandering and got lost in the fields. It was very, very hot. Sunstroke —"

"Sunstroke?" Amity interrupted. Her mind struggled to remember. Suddenly, there was a noisy crackling from the fire above as the timbers holding the windlass caught. In another moment their rope, burned in two, came slithering down to fall between them in the water with a spray of hissing sparks. The wheel for the rope followed with a splash, causing both women to cry out and duck.

"Sunstroke?" Amity repeated. "What about it? What about the child?"

"You went looking for her and it took hours for you to find her. At first, I thought you'd die out there, both of you. It was one hundred and eleven degrees in the sun and you were gone a long time."

"But I did find her? I tried to save her?"

"Well, you brought her back. You reached the edge of the village with the baby in your arms before you passed out, too."

Amity made a small sound of relief. She had tried —

Thisba was still talking. "I'd hoped not to see you alive, again, but there you were, Miss Smarty Governess, bringing the baby home."

Amity choked, "Nora Ann was still alive? You did try to help us, didn't you? You couldn't be so cruel —"

"Oh, at first I tried to revive you both. There wasn't time to prepare ice-water baths, but you were both out there in the heat for a long time and the child, especially, was about dead. I put the two of you in the icehouse —"

"Icehouse?" Amity asked hoarsely, waiting as Thisba was overcome by a spasm of coughing, choking and crying out with pain.

"You kept fainting," Thisba rasped after a while, "so I still thought you might die. I hoped you would. It was stupid to drag you inside the icehouse. I shouldn't have. But I did, you and the child. I placed her on a shelf —"

Shelf in an icehouse. Intense heat, then bone-chilling cold. After all this time, the old nightmare images began to come clear.

Thisba declared in self-defense, "It was *cold* in the icehouse, especially after being out in the hot sun. There were still huge squares of ice packed in sawdust. So I went out and closed the door after me, for a minute or two." In the gloom, her hair fallen about her face, her eyes shining, she looked truly mad. "Then I thought about it, and I realized in order to have Chester for myself, all I had to do was leave you there to die." She laughed again and under the surface of the water, Amity felt goose bumps spring to life all over her cold, numb body. . . .

"But the child, little Nora Ann, you could have saved her —" The woman was a demon, a murderer. If the whole truth came out, Thisba would be found not just negligent, but a killer. She could be sent to prison. No wonder she was constantly afraid Amity Whitford might someday remember, and talk. . . . Thisba's life depended on her silence. Today, by setting the fire, she'd meant to silence her for good. Amity felt sick, her whole body was trembling hard. Knowing Thisba as she now did, she knew what the woman had been after at Beaconsfield. To someone like Thisba, any man of means would be considered fair game. Even after such a brief acquaintance, possibly from the moment she was hired, Thisba saw winning Chester Fairleigh as a chance at the elegant life she felt was her birthright, and that had been denied her by a cruel father and a weak brother. Amity could almost feel sorry for Thisba, and yet, the poor child, baby Nora —

"I had to do it," Thisba was saying in echo to Amity's thoughts. "I was cheated, cheated, every time, in my life," she sobbed brokenly, "always, always cheated. But never again, never. What's mine is mine. I have Henry now," she gasped, and fell silent.

When the Fairleighs returned home from their excursion, they'd found their small, thinly clad child, their precious baby — dead. Amity felt intense grief for the toddler and Chester and Leila Fairleigh. Nothing could've been simpler; Thisba just pointed the finger at the silly governess, who had been unconscious, who was ill from sunstroke and confused.

But she wasn't guilty. She wasn't. It wasn't she who'd done the child harm. Slowly, Amity began to feel a cleansing relief, there in the well. Felt the dark, confusing shadow on her soul that she'd lived with for so long begin to evaporate. She was free. Even if she never lived another day, she was free. Tears rolled down her face. Then she began to feel anger, and in minutes she was shaking with rage.

"You could've told me everything at any time!" she accused, glaring at Thisba's pale face in the shadows. "You've known all along that I am innocent, that I didn't hurt the Fairleigh child!"

Without the overlay of guilt, her life would have been so different these past four years. But

Thisba had accused her to their employer, and had been believed. The life she could've begun with Chalk — So much time had been wasted. For a moment, she hated Thisba enough to push her head under water and hold it there.

Then sanity and reason returned. The effects of the tragedy had brought her here to homestead on the high plains, to a life that for the most part she found very good. If she hadn't come, she wouldn't have met Chalk Holden. She hardly cared that Thisba was still talking, but then something the woman said made her pay attention. The other woman's voice was raw from coughing, and growing weaker.

Amity touched her painfully scorched cheeks and adjusted her uncomfortable position against the jutting stones of the wall; her lower body felt turned to chilled rubber. Speaking to Thisba's shadowy face Amity said, "After you found Henry and had what you wanted, it must've disturbed you a great deal to learn that I was here in Hamilton County, too."

"Yes." They could have been friends sharing confidences now, except for the coldly dispassionate words. "Seymour was supposed to help me get rid of you. I wanted that from the start, you know, and that's why I sent for him. But he was squeamish — never liked what we did to my brother. It was Seymour's idea to run against you. He was sure you'd lose, pick up, and leave the country. I never should've listened. He bungled everything. So when I heard you say that Chester Fairleigh was back, I had to take matters into my hands and burn you out. Make sure there was nothing left of you."

The woman spoke with such chilling finality that Amity cringed. At first when Thisba's hands came up out of the water with a soft splash, she thought the other woman was reaching out to her for forgiveness, or aid, or support. Watching, shrinking back tight against the cold stones, she saw the white fingers were trying to find Amity's throat. She grasped Thisba's wrists tight enough to break them, causing her to cry out. "It's too late, Thisba," Amity said quietly. "Don't you know that? We've lived very different lives. I'm a great deal stronger than you. If you gave me good cause, I'd have to fight you, hold you under the water till you couldn't hurt me. You don't want that; you know you don't."

Thisba turned away in a swish of water and began to sob, crumpled against the wall.

Amity's own head was spinning from inhaling so much smoke but she had to stay alert, keep them both sane and awake till help came. The fire would be seen for miles. Folks must be out there on the fringes, fighting it already, with wet blankets and hides and carpets. She looked up through seared eyes but dark smoke continued to blot out the sky — or was it night? She had no idea how much time had passed in the well. Possibly it was only a few minutes but it seemed like years. Was anything of hers still standing? She said a thankful prayer that Thaddy was with his father and not enduring this horrible night-mare. John Clyde would've seen the fire by now from the Bergen place, and he'd be one of those fighting the fire, trying to reach her. But they wouldn't know she was in the well.

"Thisba, you have to stay awake. I'm going to try to climb out of the well and get help. Do you hear me?"

The other woman moaned.

Amity turned to face the wall, reaching up to catch a handhold on a rock, her foot coming up to another. It was very slippery, the rocks could come loose. The rock casing covered only the lower part of the well; above, the sides were earthen. She could never climb that unless she dug handholds with her fingernails. She inched upward, weight on the foothold. She went a little further. Then her foot slipped on the slimy rock, her ankle turned, and she fell back into the water with a sharp cry.

Thisba laughed weakly. "It's no use," Thisba whispered, "no use without the rope. We'll rot here in this stinking well, together."

"That's what you say. I say otherwise." Amity rested a moment, then began to shout, "Help! We're here, help! In the well — !"

Once again Amity tried to climb up using the slimy footholds, only to slip back.

Except for deep wheezing from smoke-filled lungs, Thisba had been quiet for a long time, might be losing consciousness. Poor fool of an insane woman, Thisba.

Amity took a deep, restoring breath. Maybe after this things would be different. She knew they would be, for her.

Or would she be found here — in the well — with her longtime enemy — dead? She wanted to live. She wanted to tell Chalk how much she loved him, wanted him to know that she was not to blame for little Nora's death. That she was free, free to show him her love through all enduring time. If — "Help!" Amity gathered her strength to call again, louder, "God, help us, please!"

Minutes passed. Hours? She couldn't tell anymore.

"Amity? Amity — ?"

Was she dreaming Chalk's voice? Now the hoarse shout seemed to come from just above. "Amity!"

Chapter Thirty-four

One Month Later

"Hup, Ben, get on there!" With a gentle touch of leather to his singed hide, the cutting blade of her plow set deep, Amity followed in the opening groove of charred black earth curling back to rich shiny brown. She'd dressed warmly in her old barn coat, with Papa's hat pulled low, extra burlap wrapped around her moccasined feet, but still she was cold.

Overhead, the sky was a thick gray, telling of the coming winter. She wanted her wheat in the ground before the first real snows, before her Christmas wedding. Whatever the decorations for the ceremony, there would be no red. She wasn't sure she could tolerate black, either, and was going to ask Chalk to wear his gray suit.

She would be a long time forgetting either the lurid, scarlet glare of the fire Thisba'd set, or the black dust that covered everything afterward. For weeks now, it had been like living in a bucket of pitch, acres of blackness in every direction. Her sod house and sod barn had withstood the flames, and after cleaning and repairing them, she and John Clyde had whitewashed both as soon as possible. The new corrals he was working on today would also be white. She'd lost three head of her new cattle that had been on their way home ahead of the others, and all of her hens, though Ben and her Flora-cow survived the fury by standing in the creek. Perhaps she and Thisba would have been all right, if they could have found the creek and stayed with the animals, but she'd thought the deeper well was the better choice. Thisba's mare was found roasted with the harness still on; only the hubs of her buggy were found.

Amity trembled, remembering, and shouted again to Ben. She stumbled as he lurched forward, nearly yanking the plow out of the furrow. She leaned her whole weight on the plow handles to hold it steady.

The sliced earth made her think of Thisba's grave. She had been buried three days ago. Thisba might've survived her burns, her broken ribs, but she'd caught pneumonia from the smoke in her lungs and, after lingering a few weeks, slipped away. Henry Strout was heartbroken at her passing; he'd really loved her.

"I know it's a lot to ask of you, Miss Whitford, after what she did, but if we could just bury her terrible deeds with her, without anyone else knowing? Doridee was just a child at Beaconsfield; I don't think she ever really knew that her mother was responsible for what happened. Dori has come to be like my own daughter, um, yes, and she wants to stay with me. She'll be all right, I think."

Amity had granted Henry his wish. What was done, was done. Thisba Marcellus Strout's whole life had been a punishment, anyway. And now Amity turned the earth in furrow after furrow, turned over a new day while all around her grew quiet, hushed. In a while, tiny white flakes of snow began to drift down, flecking Ben's brown hide, the dark ground. The contrast, the cleansing purity of the snow, brought a surge of tears to her eyes. She lifted her face, letting the cold, clean flakes mingle with her warm tears. She released the plow handles and lifted both arms, feet spread, and let the snow fall on her.

After a minute, she pulled the plow from the ground. "It's only the first light snow," she told Ben. "When it's gone, we'll finish. Let's get you in the barn, old son."

They headed across the field toward the little white soddy, the white barn. Next spring her land would be green again, along with the six hundred forty acres Chalk was buying next to hers for their increasing cattle herd. He'd be here to help run the ranch most of the time, and if he won state office, she would manage the ranch whenever legislature was in session. She had granted him the promise that she would spend as much time in Topeka with him as possible, if he won. That was a way of life she wasn't sure she could pick up again, though for Chalk, she would try. She put Ben up in the barn, told John Clyde to quit the new corrals when he was ready.

Amity had changed into a clean dress and put a fresh pot of coffee on when Chalk rode in. He shook the snowflakes from his hat before he came in, grinning ear to ear. "I was afraid I'd find you out plowing today," he said.

She looked at him, faking surprise. "Who, me? Do I look like I've been plowing?"

"You look beautiful. The most beautiful woman God ever set on this earth."

She laughed softly. "That's what you said when you pulled me out of the well, and me with no eyebrows, my hair singed, fingernails broken, too hoarse to talk but babbling that I was free to marry you. What a wonderful liar you are, Mr. Holden."

He shook his head. "All I want is you."

"Oh?" With a blissful sigh she went into his outstretched arms. "And I want you. *And,*" she mumbled against his chest, "Our ranch. My work with the schools yet a while, and helping you at the statehouse . . . A whole raft of little Holdens."

He snuggled her closer, his lips lowering slowly toward hers, admitting with his heart in his voice, "A fair exchange, I'd say. Quite fair, if I have you."

The thing was, he really meant it. *A big white farmhouse to raise our children in* —the list went on in her head as he kissed her dizzyingly. But there was time to tell him. Sweet, sweet together time.